SOUL TETHER

B. JOYCE

For the ones who long to know themselves fully

MOON BEETLES SERIES

Book One: *Moon Beetles*
Book Two: *Soul Tether*
Book Three: *Mind Fracture*

Moon Beetles Companion Novel

Shadowless

Note: Shadowless can be read at any time. This novel takes place during the same time period as Moon Beetles. It is a stand-alone novel that provides more exploration of Illyson and the beloved characters within the Moon Beetles series.

CONTENT WARNING

This book contains instances of anxiety, depression, suicidal ideation, mentions of a parent who died by suicide, derealization, mental manipulation, blood, violence, death, mentions of sexual assault, discrimination, self harm, drug use, gun violence, and illness/vomiting. If these are sensitive topics for you, please only read if you are safe to do so.

The Province of Emberstead

KEY:

Ancestral Shrine

City

Capital

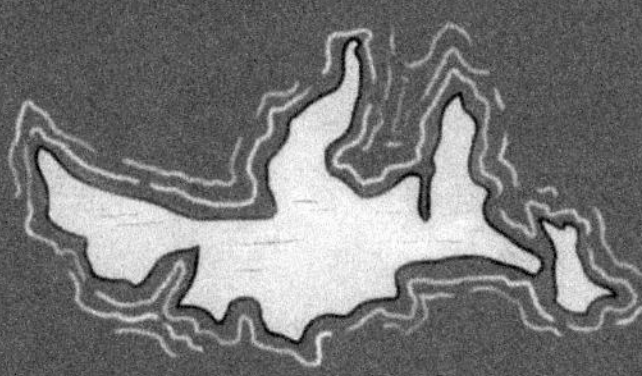

ILLYSON
Sea of the Lost
TORETH
ARIA
VALISOR
SARR
Lotis
Sea
EMBERSTEAD
EETH
YUGON
LAKAR
HALAAN
Atorian Ocean

THE LESSER WORLDS

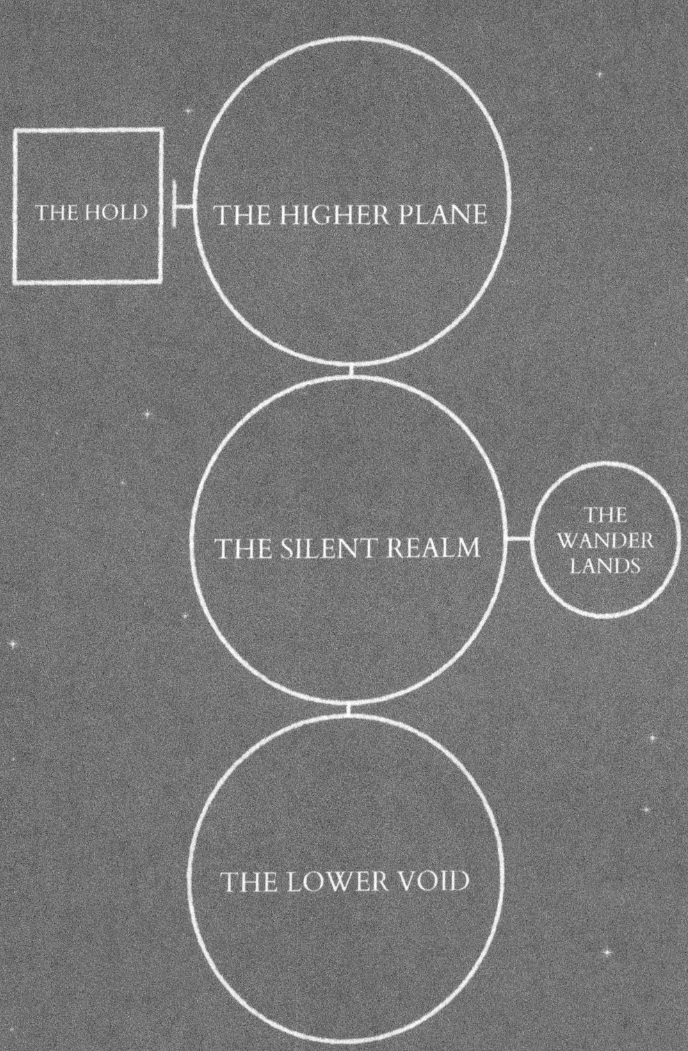

ENERGY ALIGNMENT

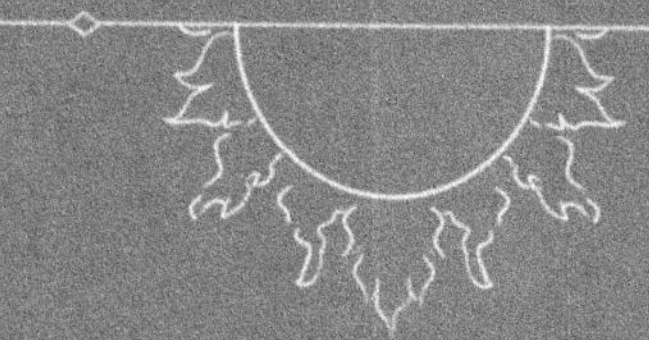

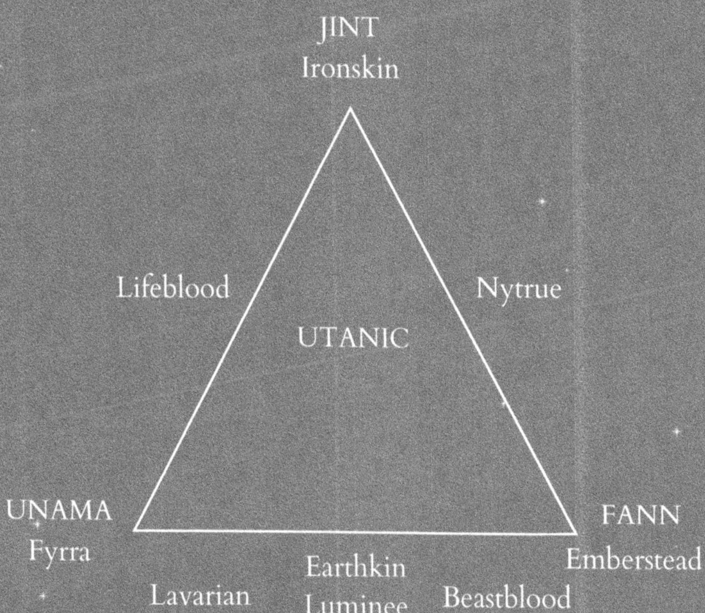

RIN

The pause between the ticks of a clock pulls at me. The pause is long and heavy; the ticks are rushed—close, maybe only a few metres away. But the clock in my apartment is electrotech. At the academy, Eliote's sweet scent fills our room, and her even breaths soothe me as she sleeps. Here, there is nothing.

I never wake up alone. Not even when my father passed or when my mother left us or when Stephen's presence faded. Liam and Eliote are always close by. But closeness doesn't feel real. Distance does.

A string of vibrations rakes through me from the ticking in my ears, down my body to wind my heart into heavy beats, and my muscles into knots. I draw a deep breath.

My eyelids heat and scrape my eyes as they open, unveiling windowless, concrete walls. I might as well be in some type of hell because everything is wrong, and everything burns. The walls are ghastly white, the ceiling too far away with a crack in the paint like a crooked smile. Lamp light flares in the corner of my vision. My red jacket hangs opposite a bookcase stuffed with titles I don't recognize. They would be comforts, but in the absence of company and explanation, they are cruel. There should be a blue jacket beside mine.

I never made it to Liam. They took him because I didn't see it. I didn't put the pieces of Liam's spirit sight together fast enough.

Drawing tight breaths through a dry and bitter throat, I clench my fingers around the smothering white sheet covering me and rip it off. I swing my legs off the bed, but my chest tightens, doubling me over as I cough with a rattle deep in my lungs.

The man I last saw had a mask, which means he tossed the gas. It knocked us all out, me and the Revival. So, who was he with? And his eyes. He looked right at me with my father's eyes. It's still impossible, just a trick of the gas.

Tears wash over my eyes. Good. Wipe out his face. I shake my head into my hands, pressing at the sting. I have to get out of here.

Standing with my hand on the small of my back, my body moves without pain. I let go of my breath, thankful my weak spot wasn't hit in the fight. Was Stephen with the attackers? A shudder jerks through my body. I need to find out what happened to Liam.

The face of the clock on the wall glares at me. Nine thirty. In the morning or evening? A raindrop slips down the arm of my jacket into a puddle on the floor. If it's still wet, then it couldn't have been too long since someone hung it there, intending me to stay awhile with the books. Malicious intent couldn't have set up this room, but there's still a possibility that it could be a bribe from the Revival to placate me into cooperating with them. Liam might be somewhere outside that door too. I have no idea.

Every beat of my heart sends a rush of blood and adrenaline to my tight muscles. I grab my jacket and throw it on, zipping it right to my chin, like somehow it can armour me or hide me. If anything, it's mine, and it smells like home and rain and even Eliote's perfume. My fingers wrap around the memory of my team in the pocket. I run my thumb over the glossy image, letting its damp, frayed edges ground me. But my breaths still rage.

Setting my hand on the doorknob, I wait for the crackle of my jacket to settle so the sounds beyond the door can meet my ears. A deep hum comes through like the vibration of a core-energy hub, but nothing else, not even voices. Holding my breath, I try turning the handle.

The door creaks open. I cringe. A cage shouldn't open so easily. Hot air creeps over me from the long hall with white walls and ceiling. A line of fluorescent lights sterilizes the atmosphere, contradicting the heat. The hum grows louder as I slip out of the room, my stomach churning with hunger, and my head spinning from the heat and not enough coherent thoughts.

Down the hall, to the right, there's a door with a small window in it. To my left, a light flickers over several doors, but they don't have any windows. I scurry over to the one with light spilling through the cut of glass, and a clanking sound fills my ears as I draw close. Voices echo down the hall from behind me. I press the handle down, my tongue going dry, my vision tunnelling on the door. I pull the door open, slip through, and draw it shut.

I step onto a grated walkway. Heavy machinery clunks and whirs in the centre of a wide factory hall below. Workers shout back and forth to each other. I duck and backtrack to the wall, hunching in on myself, regretting putting on my red jacket, hoping no one looks up. Heat and body odour radiate up to me with an earthy scent mixed in. Below the metal grate, there are bins filled to the brim with different coloured stones caked with dirt. On the far edge of the room are similar bins, but those hold neatly sorted, gleaming stones. A powerstone refinery.

"What the hell?" I whisper.

A burst of laughter comes from one side of the room. A blinking light accompanied by a screeching beep and a hiss of steam from a machine swirls around my head from the other side. My heart rate spikes as I try to get a glimpse of the workers' faces, trying to find those eyes. But I can't look for those eyes—they're not real. I need to find Liam, or Brand, and figure out how I got here.

I clench the cuffs of my sleeves, and the door opens behind me. Jolting, my heart leaps to my throat and I dash across the narrow walkway above the workroom, my knees unsteady with the vibration of metal under my feet. My skin tingles with cold energy. Blue sparks through my eyes and I throw my fists up in front of my face as I turn to the door, ready for round two with the Revivalists.

Brand stands across from me. She folds her hands in front of her, keeping her cold-grey eyes on me. Her curly hair is twisted into a bun with shorter strands tumbling around her light-brown face, and she wears her black leather jacket. Every muscle in my body tenses as she stands there.

Her eyes lock onto me. "I leave you for two minutes and—"

"Where is Liam, Brand?" I shout, arms falling like weights at my sides with the fading blue light.

Her lips part, giving me a glimpse of her teeth, almost bared as she avoids my eyes. "The Revival took him. We weren't able to catch up to them."

It's a slap in the face. But the sting is deeper than a slap, more permanent, and it aches through my whole being. After all these years of trying to keep him safe, I've lost him. I couldn't keep him out of the hands of people wanting to use him. I was supposed to protect him and love him, but all I did was leave him.

"Fuck!" I turn and slam my hands on the metal railing, sending tremors through the entire platform and a thrum through my bones.

Brand steps toward me and I step away from her.

"I have to go after him," I say.

"I have a team tailing the Revivalists to find Liam. Bringing him back to the Vein is their top priority."

The Vein.

The name sweeps through me, stirring my memories. It came up in heated arguments between my mother and father, hushed conversations about my grandparents. It was an organization that my parents were somehow involved in, not a Guardian organization, or at least I didn't think it was, but I never asked them about it—I wasn't supposed to know. My stomach sinks. If it caused so much tension in my family, then I don't want to be here.

"Is that supposed to make me feel better?" My face scrunches and my strength to stand is fading under the heavy air. The noise builds around me, too rhythmic and mocking.

Brand slips her hands into her pockets, eyes wandering away from me. She sighs, long and heavy. "Of course not. Please just come with me and I'll answer any question you have."

All I want is to get to Liam, and she might be the only person in the world with the answers. But she's the reason I'm here and not in Akinnera, so I can't help but wonder if this would have happened if she'd been honest with me from the start. She wasn't honest about being Ironskin, and I don't know what else she has kept from me.

The urge to scream tastes like metal and pinches my lungs like a vise. I press my lips together and swallow long and hard so I can nod. A scowl burns on my face as Brand motions toward a staircase down to the factory floor. I follow her, leaving lots of space between us. She must know how much this is killing me, but she takes her sweet time.

On the ground level, we pass two Fyrra. They stand at a workstation chiselling excess dirt off stones and sorting them before sending them through a machine. Behind them, the logo for the factory is painted on the wall. **East-side Refinery**. That's Senn's main refinery, just outside the city wall in the mountains. I'm still in Senn, but how does this factory connect to the Vein? Whatever the Vein is, it's been here my whole life, right under my nose.

We continue through the workroom, passing workers of every lineage. They share smiles freely between each other, making it hard to believe we are actually just outside Senn. At the far end of the room, before a wide door leading down another fluorescent hall, is a woman alongside a cart filled with gleaming curestones. She runs her pale hands along the smooth stone surfaces and uses a glass to inspect each one. Her long, white hair is braided loosely and hangs down her back. Black coveralls conceal her tall, thin frame. Looking over her shoulder, she captures me with storm-cloud eyes, light skin crinkling around them as she smiles.

My heart leaps inside me. The strange sense of familiarity washes over me, like it does every time I lay eyes on Brand. It prickles like being too close to core energy. *Ironskin.* It's so different to be in the presence of Ironskin women. Oron and Liam are around me all the time, but my mother was the only female Ironskin presence I've ever known before Brand.

A sharp pain spreads through me as my eyes itch. Blinking only chases the itch with a thrill of heat. Wrapping my arms tight around myself, I drop my eyes from the distractions in the room that are slowing my feet. The noise is fading to the back of my mind, the colours are draining to grey, but Brand's voice catches in my ears.

"Peter, hold on, give her a little space." She holds her hand up in front of a man, but he pushes around her.

His footsteps are heavy, and they slow as he gets closer. This man steals the rest of the noise away. Silence rings in my ears as an alternate reality forces itself on me. My heart fights against my brain. It's not real. This man in front of me isn't my father. My father is dead.

Breath catches in my throat. It forms a lump that refuses to dislodge and let me breathe. With my lungs shutting down, my heart races. I take a step back, but my foot is a cement block, too heavy, too dense, as it touches the floor, making a sound that clashes with the ringing in my head. My eyes widen as this man moves slowly toward me—his eyes sunken and grey, sparkling with tears.

"Rinny."

People fade to ghosts and light pulses around my vision as my eyes catch on the gas mask hooked onto his belt.

No. It can't be him. He looks like my father, with the long face and wide jaw. But this man has more wrinkles around the eyes. And my father is dead. I saw him in the casket. Fucking casket. His hair is the same dark brown as my father's with a slight curl, but it's greyer. Broad chest and shoulders—he's larger than life.

A shiver runs down my spine.

"I–I'm sorry about the gas," he says, lowering his head. He even sounds like my father. "I tried to call out to you, but you couldn't hear me over the life affinity."

The muscles in my face twitch. He takes a few steps forward, closing the gap between us to just a foot. A scent I thought my body had forgotten tangles around me—something like sawdust and pinichu berries and cold. Tears spill down my cheeks and the cold spreads through my muscles, drawing them tight. My vision sways and my body pitches off balance as his arms come up, bringing in his smell and strength and locking it around me.

"Rinny, I'm sorry it had to be this way but I'm really here. I'm real," he says, his voice muffled.

His shoulder stifles my breath and my tears seep into his jacket. My arms come up but stop, hands hovering in the air, like they'd get burned if they touched him. But I'm icy inside.

His death was real, it shaped my reality, a reality I wanted to run away from, and now he's here. He's in it again. Or has he been here the whole time? I'm not the girl he knows anymore, and there is no way he is the man she knew. The man she knew would have gone back to her. So why is he here now, when I'm a shadow of her, formed by shitty mistakes and dark corners and Ease and bloody knuckles and so many weeds?

I grit my teeth. My jaw is like rock but my head is like a balloon about to fly away.

I've wanted this for so long; this hug should be easy. It shouldn't make my stomach sick and my body squirm. I shouldn't want to pull away.

I squeeze my eyes shut and expel all my tears. My jaw unlocks. "Let go," I whisper.

His arms loosen, but they keep their hold. I flex my fingers. Energy builds inside me. It shrugs my shoulders and shakes my arms and hands in desperate jerks. They still can't touch him or even shove him off. They're not ready to feel his reality yet. I step away and his arms fall.

This man towers over me, face wet and drawn in a long frown. His lips part, close, then open again. Running his hands down the sides of his pants, he takes a step toward me. I step back. His eyes, deep pits of grey, used to be comforting, but now they pierce me like silver blades. I can't look anymore, so I turn my head to hide his face from my blurring eyes.

Will those blades cut through me and see it all? The long, dark nights I left Liam alone, the clank of saphrite in my pocket after a few hours of beating my opponents in illegal fights. The song that played at Ralin's party pricks my ears. I take a sharp breath, but my lungs fill with Ease, burning and chilling my body. I slip into the deep pit of darkness in my mind where I have no home and no purpose in this world. My fingers stretch and clench into fists at my sides.

Breath comes in short bursts. "We have to find Liam," I say.

I glance past the man to Brand. She plants her hands on her hips and says, "We need to wait for intel from our team in pursuit."

The clang of stone and machinery crashes in on me, and I turn away from them. Out. I need out. Where is out? My feet move me back. Through the workroom and to the stairs. The only way I know how to move forward is back.

Feet shuffle behind me. Within the time of a heartbeat, a hand clamps around my wrist, bringing along the rough and sweet scent. I rip his hand off me as a blinding flash of red explodes from my eyes. "Leave me the hell alone," I yell, and push him away from me. He stumbles and falls to the ground. Right in front of my burning ember eyes, his face contorts with horror.

My mind swims through a murky sludge. Energy surges through me and I slam my fist into one of the powerstone bins as pain compounds on my forehead. With the burst of energy, the lights above explode, and I fall to my knees as the glass tinkles to the ground around me.

"Peter," someone says, but I can't look up. The demon inside me wants nothing more than to curl into the darkness. I can't look at him. I clutch my head and my shaking hands find solid energy pulsing in the shape of two horns on my forehead.

Gasping for breath, I let go of my horns and dig my fingers into the cold cement. The slab cracks beneath me, and I clutch a handful of rubble, nerves firing with every crunch, and it crumbles to dust.

People rush to help my father off the floor. Someone pulls me away from him. He hasn't seen me for six-and-a-half years, and now all he sees is the demon.

Hot breaths rattle in and out. My body teems with energy.

I struggle against the hands that hold me, unable to resist the Ironskin grip. My eyes are burning, itching. I can't rub them.

Murmurs of workers throughout the refinery swell around me.

"Are you all right, Peter?"

"I'm fine."

"Is that your daughter? What happened?"

"Nothing. I just made a mistake."

Brand appears in front of me, her skin is pink under the glow of my death eyes. She grabs me by the shoulders with a firm grip. "Rin," she says. "You need to focus. Focus on your breath."

Air shudders inside me. My fingers unravel and dust spills between them. A line of mud remains on my hands where sweat and dust have mingled. The breath escapes and my body goes limp as the demon inside slithers free. I fall into Brand's arms, sweating and panting and squirming with spasming muscles and burning skin.

When I was young, the rain never kept me awake. Even when I'd moved into my apartment and the thin windowpanes rattled and the building shook in the wind, the steadiness of the rainfall was always soothing. It was consistent, a hush over the more menacing sounds of Senn.

But one night, I lay wide awake on my back staring at the cracks in my ceiling, the rush of rain the only sound, and knew something was happening inside me. My sheets, worn thin and soft, left my skin prickling with heat. Each frayed fibre of my quilt irritated the hairs on my arms. Even though I lay perfectly still, my hair was soaked with sweat at the crown of my head, and my t-shirt was damp, my mouth parched.

My eyelids were heavy, waiting for sleep, but my body said no. I threw off the blanket with a huff and padded over to the kitchen for a cup of water. I drained the cup and padded back to my bed.

Starlight filtered through the gritty city smog and spilled through my window like noxious gas. It swept over my bed. It swept over a rusty red stain in the middle of my white sheet. My brain pinged alarm signals through my skull and over my arms with a bitter shiver. I held my gasp inside so it wouldn't wake Liam.

My stomach dropped and my hand swung behind me to my weak spot, where blood had spilled with so much pain a few months before. And yet here was more blood, but no pain, no cut, no sharp edge. The nurse at school had encouraged girls in my class to carry hygiene products, even if our cycles hadn't started yet. With all the things I had to remember for school, for Liam, for our move, that was the one thing I forgot.

I stood still in the poisonous light, one hand on my scarred back, one hand on my lower belly, and blood trickled down my leg.

I knew what it meant. I knew what it was. I just didn't know what to do.

The rustling of sheets pricked my ears as Liam rolled over in bed. I glanced over my shoulder at him, heart pounding in my throat, but his eyes were closed, his chest rising and falling with easy breaths. My shaking, icy hands left my wounds to run over my sweaty face.

Swallowing hard, I stripped the sheet from my bed.

"Shit," I whispered, with the bloody sheet clenched to my chest.

The blood had soaked through to the mattress.

I flung my quilt over the stain, grabbed a clean pair of pants, underwear, and a sweater. In the bathroom, I dropped the soiled sheet in the tub and drew the curtain around it so I didn't have to look at it until I figured out how to clean it, and first clean up myself.

The strength in my knees faltered. The mess of blood in my shorts was more than I had imagined. The scent of iron wafted over me. I sat down on the toilet, the rust-red stains burning themselves like a brand on my memory. How long had I just been sitting in my blood, sweating in irritation?

I braced myself on my knees with the bloodied clothes pooled at my feet. What could I use to soak up the blood while I went to the store to get the products I needed? All my dishcloths were dirty. The cloth I used to clean the bathroom the day before sat crumpled in a bucket, mocking me. Toilet paper would have to do.

Oron was at work that evening, and I wouldn't have known how to ask him for help if he had been there. Maybe just for the money to go get the products, but at that hour? He wouldn't let me go by myself.

I stuffed as much paper into my underwear as I could and pulled on my clean jeans. My blood-soaked nightclothes got left behind in the bathtub. As I searched my apartment for stray saphrite coins and my keys, I attempted to get my sweater on. My head went into the armhole with the first attempt, and my hair sprawled over my face with the next. Heavy breaths bubbled in my chest and my eyes stung. I grabbed my coat, stepping out of the apartment before waking Liam.

A cloud of Ease floated up from the floor below. I tried not to breathe, but holding my breath put pressure on my heart, which pulsed blood too hard through my veins. My hand wavered over the first lock with each pulse of blood. The key in my trembling hand clicked against metal. I braced my hands against the door to steady them as much as possible while I guided the key into the lock with my fingers. A quick sip of poisoned air between locking each bolt left my vision spinning.

Leaving Liam alone set a fire in my legs, and I clambered down the stairs, each step echoing through the dingy stairwell to assault my ears. I flipped up my hood and sprinted down the street to the corner store. A few paces away, I pulled up short. The toilet paper bulged at my inner thigh. It was so easy to forget I had only just become a woman when I already had a child in my care. I tugged at the hem of my jacket and pushed into the store, my face melting with the wave of heat from inside.

I blinked away the glare of the fluorescent lights and scanned the aisles. The cashier and a group of men turned their heads to me. Invasive eyes and emotionless faces trailed me as I tracked rainwater into the hygiene product aisle.

The products blended together while the men's chuckles churned in my gut.

Nothing in the colourful packages was familiar. Was it the hygiene gauze packet I needed? What was the cup thing? I'd need something with essence barriers, that's all I knew. But heavy flow, light flow, medium flow, heavy flow with medium essence level—I couldn't say the word flow in my head anymore.

It was going on a loop. I grabbed a gauze packet with medium everything. It was a safe bet. I turned it over to check the price.

The packet and my arm fell limp at my side.

The saphrite in my pocket was too light.

My body went rigid, a stiff, bleeding bag of flesh.

In ancient times, when an Ironskin girl became a woman, her mother would take her into the wild. They would spend her first week of womanhood together, hunting, fishing, protecting themselves from beasts, and providing for themselves to honour how their bodies protect them during their monthly cycle. During each month, while blood accumulated in a woman's womb, so did her essence in the red blood cells. Through the month, her body regenerates essence enough for her and enough for a child. When she sheds that blood, the essence she loses creates distress signals between every body cell. This leads to regulation of essence throughout the entire body. Each cell that generates essence decreases its generation. Each cell of the weak spot increases its generation. The body balances the essence distribution naturally to protect it from harm in this weakened state.

The mother and daughter would support each other. The mother would teach her the gift of self-sufficiency and autonomy.

That sounded about right. Almost.

Be strong, Rinnaya, for your brothers.

Don't cry, Rinnaya.

Mother taught this to me, but it was so fucking backwards—isolating instead of a comradery between mother and daughter like the Ancients.

"Hey." The barking reprimand from the cashier pulled me back to consciousness. "You buyin' or you standing there all night?"

He was behind me, and I didn't know if my jacket covered me enough. The fabric between my legs was wet.

I turned, my boots squeaking on the dingy tile. The man scowled at me as I walked straight toward him, bashing him in the shoulder as I passed.

"Bitch, you gotta pay for those."

A smile fluttered on my lips. *Pay not to bleed on myself.*

I just kept walking to the exit.

A meaty hand fell on my shoulder. I jerked my elbow back and sunk it into his gut. He grunted and wheezed, and I sprinted out the door. As fast as I could, I ran to a cruiser service station and locked myself in the public bathroom.

I sank down on the second toilet of the night. The light flickered above me. A syringe lay in the corner of the stall. My knees shook, causing my boots to send ripples through the yellow-brown puddle at the base of the toilet. Ripping open the package, I brushed at my eyes. The damn things weren't allowed to leak when I already had other bodily fluids leaking out of me. I sniffed and swallowed a gag from the nose-full of urine fumes. I stuck one of the sanitary gauze strips to my bloody underwear. It was crooked and the adhesive stuck to itself. It bunched up when I pulled up my pants.

I unlocked myself from the stall and stopped. There was something written on the wall opposite the lock. Dawnranfet. An address. It said to talk to Marco at the bar. Saphrite rewards.

Father had taught me basic Telando. That's all I needed.

I pushed the bloody stain from my mind and the sensation of bulging gauze in my crotch and left the stall.

Blood stains and all, I went to Dawnranfet. I was going to

get my saphrite.

2

JOHANNA

I HAVEN'T DROPPED MY GUARD since Jeff-Ray and I started sparring, but I haven't landed many hits either. Dodging his jab, I shift my feet and throw my fist at him. A pain pulls tight through my chest—the pain that's been there since Rin left the academy. With heaviness sitting on my sternum like a lump of clay, and the telltale headache of the Soul Tether being strained, a sting slices through my scalp and drills through my temples.

Jeff slaps my fist away. "Come on, Jo. You're pulling back." His breathy voice shuffles through my mind, hitting the pain, stirring a nauseating twist in my gut.

I inhale and focus on the tension in my muscles, my form, his movement, and strike as his guard slips. My fist clips his chin, but the nausea jolts through me and a wave of heat blisters over me, and my body hits the ground. I gasp, shuddering against the sting through my mind and body.

Fucking tether. Exams start in two days. I really need to figure out how to get rid of this pain before then.

"Hey, hey, hey," Jeff says, getting down on the floor next to me. He peers at me, brushing curls out of my face, eyes wide and attentive. "Damn. It's not like you to be beat after two rounds."

"Who said I'm beat?" I say, glaring at him.

"Uh, that does." He points at me.

"What?" I swipe the back of my hand over my sweaty forehead.

"That. Your face. It's all pasty. You only get pasty-face when you're beat."

I roll my eyes and shrug him off, shifting into a cross-legged position. I cradle my head in my hands for a moment as the heaviness spreads through my neck, over my cranium, and into my eyes. Holy fuck, I want it gone.

"So, what's going on?" Jeff asks, sitting down across from me. "Is this a Soul Tether thing?"

My cheeks prickle, and my hands go clammy. The way he says Soul Tether without hesitation, without hushing his tone, makes the tether's reality even more pressing. It draws my hidden reality into the open, where I have to talk about such an intricate and oddly intimate connection to another person.

A smile creeps across Jeff's dark-brown skin, sparking a glint in his eye. I run my tongue over my teeth, shaking my head at his amusement from my embarrassment.

"You shouldn't be embarrassed by it. You should be proud of your tether."

"I'm not embarrassed by the tether . . . I'm embarrassed that it controls so much of how I feel and what I do. The only time

I've been able to experience the tether in a positive way was when Rin and I were faced with a giant Ironskin clone."

"I don't think it controls all that much."

"Rin is literally an emotional time bomb, which means I have this constant tension inside me. How is that not controlling?"

"Because you're angry about it, as usual. You are always present and reacting to the tether in your own way, a consistent way, with concern and attentiveness. You are you, with or without the tether." Jeff wrings his hands. His eyes trail away from me. "And I like who you are."

The starlight is soft on his skin. Shadows define the hard line of his jaw, and his eyes are bright, round, and kind. He's handsome, the kind of guy Mom would pair me with in a heartbeat. I can almost hear her urging me on. But I keep quiet, just watching the subtle movements of his face—dark eyelashes fluttering, his lips pressing together.

He turns to me again. His eyes take their own account of me. Stiffness spreads through my bones so all I can do is stare back at him. If I look away, I might lose him, but if I keep looking, I might have him in a way that I don't want to.

His hand, so large it cups the entire side of my face, is warm and dry despite training. Leaning into me, his breath touches me first, then his lips. His kiss is as careful as he always is, not pushing into me too much, but lingering all the same. I wait for the moment to fill with desire, something inside me that wants to lean in, but it's just a moment. A moment of pause and reeling thoughts that make no sense with the way the world works. Shouldn't I want to be kissed by the handsome Jeff-Ray Warden? But my body is still, my lips have no sincerity, and my eyes, closed now, beg to open, beg for a space between our bodies again.

Shuddering, I pull away. I brace one hand on the grubby training room floor and raise one hand between us, warding off the uninvited change. My cheeks flood with heat and the Soul Tether pain stabs me behind the eyes. Tears swell and I don't know why, it's not the pain. I just know that this change between us isn't what I want.

"I'm sorry, I should have asked." His low voice is broken in a whisper. The hollowness of loss fills my stomach as I shrug off his arm.

I wrap my arms around myself.

"Yeah, you should have," I whisper back.

"There's someone else, isn't there?" he asks.

Licking my lips, tongue brushing against the scar from my fight with Rin, I draw in a long breath through my nose. Shaking my head, pressure builds inside me. "No, Jeff, there's not someone else. You just can't . . . you just can't do that."

Jeff holds up his hands. "I'm just trying to understand. I thought we had a good thing going. Thought we could take another step, but I guess I was wrong." Jeff rubs his hands together, slowly back and forth, a shadow of the movement he does when he's excited about something.

I clench my fists tight in my lap, stomach churning and my head spinning. I don't want to be angry about this, but I can't process it. It doesn't work in my brain.

"Why does there have to be another step?" I say.

Jeff shrugs. "I can't help that I like you, Jo." He catches my eyes. I can't keep the hold as my face heats even more and static buzzes in my heart. "And when I like someone, I want to be close to them, you know, romantically. Hasn't there ever been someone like that for you? Back in Senn, maybe?"

I used to think that I had just never met my match. None of the boys at school sparked anything in me, and I never thought the girls were attractive beyond simply being pretty. Now, with the most handsome man I've ever seen in front of me, I haven't felt the butterflies Mom described when she met Dad. Despite this indifference, it would kill me to see our friendship break—it would kill me to know that his feelings were so strong for me that he couldn't be around me if we couldn't be more than friends. But I don't think romance is more than any other feeling.

"Why isn't this enough? What we have now?" All I can do is breathe. Taking breath after breath, my chest rises and falls. I can't get any more words out to explain what I feel for him.

"I . . . It is enough, Jo. Don't worry." Jeff smiles, but his face grows long and tired as it falls. "I'm going to call it a night." He pushes off the ground. Crossing to the door and into the arena, he leaves me too fast.

Aside from Rin, Jeff is the closest thing I've had to a best friend, and he's walking away. His most powerful feelings have been rejected by me. I want him to come back, but I can't get my feet to move. I want to apologize, but how do you apologize for saying something that's true?

The green starlight blankets the empty training room in eerie light that makes shadows stretch and the room wider, taller, emptier—the blood-red punching bags are the only company. The silence creates its own energy that stirs around me.

Rin is a different type of friend. She makes me feel like there's challenge and meaning to life, and that it's worth fighting through it, to look for peace. We had companionship before we broke apart. Now she's my Soul Tether, a likeness and a complete opposite of me that I've bound myself to. Something profound that I don't understand.

She doesn't feel it though, I'm pretty sure of that. Maybe I should tell her about it. Maybe I can still contact her with Mind Fire, even at this distance.

I close my eyes and focus my thoughts, searching for her mind's aggressive cold like a snowball to the face. My body cools, but it's not her—I'm just losing heat from the fight, from the confusion. The hit doesn't come. I grunt and draw my knees to my chest, hiding my face in them to block out the light and the distracting emptiness around me. Focus.

I imagine my mind spanning the entire province back to Senn. Searching through locations we used to go together or ones she would frequent alone, but I can't find the cold. A dull pain pulses at my forehead like I've hit a wall.

"Shit."

If I can't connect to Rin's mind, then I can't get to the Wander Lands to find the Silver Wander Wraith. Maybe I can find her if I go back to where she first appeared to me.

I slap my hands to the ground and push myself up. "That fucking wraith is going to tell me more about this stupid Soul Tether," I mutter as I cross the training room to my coat and shoes. "She warned me"—I stuff my feet into my shoes—"and now she's got to follow through."

Throwing on my coat, I barge through the door into the snow. I didn't want to acknowledge the tether. It's not like I want it more now, but I need to understand it. For me and Rin.

I tromp through the snow, scrunching my fingers open and closed in my pockets to keep my essence flowing for the warmth against the cold all the way from the academy to the city centre.

Once the whitewashed walls become grimy and grey, I know I'm getting close to the underground train station. As the streets get tighter, an old melody haunts the back of my mind—an energy, mental energy. I follow the song as its weary trills stand my hairs on end.

Each step down into the train station brings the energy closer, the song louder. I shrug my coat tighter around me and breathe on my hands as I keep my eyes alert for the sparkle. At the platform where we met, in the absence of drunken students, the song is so much louder, and my mouth is dry with the taste of ash.

"All right," I yell into the tunnel, to the grey-brown stain of the ale I smashed against the wall. "Where the hells are you?" My bitter voice bounces all around me with its own energy and fades down the tunnel.

My heart thumps hard in my chest. I shake my hands. "Come on." The words crack through my throat and tears well inside me.

I can't be like this forever. I can't break down every time Rin leaves me—that's pathetic. How am I supposed to go into the Illysonian army as a Warrior if we can't be separated?

My stomach lurches and my pain pounds in a circle around my head as I step off the platform onto the tracks.

Flames burst to life from my palms as I shift my essence. I hurl a ball of fire down the tunnel. The tracks vibrate and the cold air blazes as the flames illuminate nothing but graffiti and rat shit.

But my spine tingles. A melodious chuckle wraps around my mind. I spin around and my hand burns with nervous energy and fire as I link with the wraith's mental energy. I thrust out my hand and grab the wraith by the throat. But silver mist doesn't flow around me. This wraith is blue, shimmering like sapphires. Her hair is dark and wild, and it snakes around me. Her piercing irises lock onto me with a raging sea behind them, unlike the endless, pupilless orbs of the Silver Wander Wraith I came here for.

The wraith struggles, shaking flecks of her shimmering body off like sparks. My grip on her is tight, linked from my nervous system to her mental energy like steel chains. A smile crackles on the wraith's lips as she stops her fight.

Her voice rings in my head without her forming words with her mouth. "She won't be back for a while, the Silver Wraith, as you call her."

"Where is she?" I say, my tongue thick and dry.

"How would I know? She's always on the go. Very determined that one."

"If you don't know where she is, then do you know anything about Soul Tethers?"

I let go of the wraith and she chuckles again, not sweet and rhythmically, but callous and pointed. It stings inside my mind, sending a string of nausea through my gut.

"Sorry, girly," she says skirting around me, hair rippling over my shoulder. "I can't stay much longer in the land of the living. You got yourself into a tether? Well, then I'm afraid you're going to be stuck with that pain in your head for a while."

I whirl around to follow her, but the tunnel shakes and my vision blurs as a streak of black slashes through the tunnel. A rectangular shape like a mirror reflecting shadows instead of light appears, and she vanishes into it with her voice echoing in my mind. "Friendship, what a pain." The black streak strikes again with a force that knocks me off balance. I land on my ass, gasping for air and head spinning.

Further away from anyone I give a shit about, and in more pain than before, I haul myself back onto the platform.

Fucking Wander Wraiths. There's got to be someone here on the solid Karess who knows more about Soul Tethers. I just have to find them.

3

RIN

The death affinity drains from my eyes like blood rushing from my head after sitting too long. It leaves my skin hot, rashy, and energized. Brand leads me down a long hall, her arms wrapped around me to keep me upright, away from the noise of the refinery and away from the stairs. My lungs are burning as I fight to keep air in them, my eyes are going spotty with black dots, and my feet drift like the concrete floor is merely clouds.

"How is he here?" I ask as Brand ushers me into an office. Everything inside me readies to run away from her, away from my father, and away from the prying eyes of the refinery workers in the hall. But I keep leaning into Brand.

"No one disturbs us," she commands and slams the door.

Brand helps me into a chair as my limbs start to shake. With gentle hands, she unzips my jacket and removes it from my arms like I'm a child. But I'm eighteen. I haven't felt like a child since I was twelve years old waiting for my father to return for my birthday party. Since then, I've been the one removing little helpless arms from dripping rain jackets, brushing off scraped knees, and wiping tears from one little face. I clasp my hands in my lap, urging my eyes not to cry any more.

Another small room, with not enough air and no way to see the sky. This one also has books; they're scattered everywhere— stacked on top of each other, lying open, papers sticking out of them. Files cover a wooden desk at the back of the room in haphazard piles along with an open journal and a handful of pens, none of which are in the empty holder that's about ready to fall to the floor. On the wall behind the desk are all kinds of maps of Illyson, the Vein, and Senn.

Brand moves to the desk, but I grab her arm. "How is he here, Brand?"

Letting go of her, my skin retains the pressure of his arms around me, and I rub at them. It is so different than the last time he hugged me in his newly washed Protector uniform. He said it was a simple escort mission, but usually for an escort mission, Johanna's dad, his partner, would go with him. That time he went alone and didn't come back. They said he was captured, that they'd found his weak spot.

"We had an open casket."

There's a small crack in Brand's cool façade as she leans against the desk in front of me—a flinch in her silver eyes, a quirk of her jaw. "What do you know about the afterlife?"

I have a hard enough time keeping myself out of the afterlife, so a simple answer would be great. Gripping the arms of the chair, I say, "Somethin' about an intermediate space that you pass through and then go on to the Beyond."

"It's called the Lesser Worlds. Your father found a rift from the Lesser Worlds back to Illyson instead of moving on to the Beyond."

A rift from the Lesser Worlds. Beastshit.

Did Mother move on? Did he see her?

I can't focus my eyes. They rove around the room, skipping from one pile of mess to another, slipping over the solid objects. Tapping my thumb and pointer finger together gives me just enough pressure to bring my mind back to my body, and my body back into the room. I slump back and allow the chair to support me.

"How long ago?" I ask.

"Three years."

I tap my fingers harder, and crack my knuckles, and shift my weight on the seat. Three years ago, I was fifteen, winning my first Dawnranfet match with blood on my hands.

"Three years and he didn't show his fucking face to me once?" Tears prickle my eyes. I tilt my head back and grind my teeth to keep them there. Glancing at Brand for answers, she just takes a long breath, folds her arms over her chest, and shakes her head.

Am I really that worthless?

The thought takes up space in my mind, right in the centre. It wasn't just me he didn't come back for, though, it was Stephen and Liam too.

"Fine." I swipe my hand across my face, energy building in my chest. "Why are we in a powerstone refinery?"

"I wanted to bring you here so you would be safe from the Revival. We think they have an Ironskin-Emberstead halfie with them. A collection of powerstones in one place protects against Mind Fire abilities."

Logical. Good, I can work with that. I can follow. "You called it the Vein."

Brand pushes away from the desk. The pen holder teeters on the edge as she moves to the other side to sit. "The Vein was created shortly after the Fourth Great War. It started as a place of refuge for Ironskins. A place to live, work, and to stay safe."

"But I'm Ironskin. Why didn't I know about it?"

"Your mother didn't want to raise you and your brothers in the Vein." Brand leans back in her chair, head tilting to the side. "The Vein was built with good intentions; it was supposed to be temporary. But safe became isolated and the mission to avoid war became an obsession. Some broke off because of this, leaving the Vein to live normal lives for themselves—your mother wanted this for you. Others believed that the Vein's methods were slow, ineffective. Threats to Ironskins were rising at the time. Geret Aronson took it upon himself to try to reverse the Death Ritual and many supported his efforts."

I press my lips together, expelling air through my nose.

"Your father went with him, Rin," Brand says, her eyes steady on me.

Heaviness fills my body. It shifts inside me, moving memories and pinching nerves.

"He went without your mother's knowledge. He helped find the Ritual instructions. But Geret and your father had their differences. Your father backed out of the Revival's plans and was going to report them to the LPs. Geret killed him for it."

The cold starts at the tips of my fingers. It climbs my limbs, weakening them bit by bit. My mind spins, trying to make sense of the truth about my father. Those times he went off alone, they were to the Revival. It's all worse than I had imagined. What's left of my lineage is completely divided, and my parents fell right in the middle of it.

Brand rubs her hand over her face and deflates with a heavy sigh.

My armpits are damp with sweat. I press my shaking hands to my eyes, breathing in and out through my constricted throat. The truth spreads out in the darkness behind my sweaty palms, sinking heavily inside me, slipping into my boiling blood.

"And you?" I ask. "How do you know all this, and why do I have this weird feeling about you?"

Brand nods. The blond curls around her face shake. Her sleepy eyes stare at me, a glint of light twinkling from the swell of tears. Why is she crying? I take a breath as her chest heaves and her thin lips part but make no sound. An ache stirs inside me as her silence overwhelms me. The way she moved during the ambush sparks my mind. She was so fast, just like my mother. The way she acts, the way she speaks, the cold in her presence. All like her.

Brand's lips move again, letting a whisper slip through. "Your mother was my older sister." A tear slides down her perfect face. "I changed my name after I graduated from the academy."

My brain is an ocean of memory with missing pieces like waves crashing against my skull. Heat envelops my face. I paw at my eyes with my sleeve to dry my tears.

"When I—"

"Stop." I'd intended to yell it, but the whisper makes it harsher as the air rips through my throat. The ice inside me sets a rattle deep in my bones. A broken laugh jumps out of me just as breathy as the whisper. "Stop talking. I don't want to hear any more."

My life has been battered and boiled in lies and it makes me sick. My stomach spasms and my tongue is heavy and dry. Brand, all muscle and poise, can no longer meet my eyes. She shifts in her seat and tears drip off her chin.

"I want to get to Liam." It's a direction away from the mess here. Backward again, to the one constant in my life.

"Liam . . . " Brand stops to rub her eyes.

Until now I thought the tired shape of her eyes was natural, but with the way she pauses to relieve the stress, it could be acquired. She has so many secrets on her shoulders, and she just unloaded them. I don't want to accept them. She can keep them. Let them weigh on her.

"I want to get to Liam." The words slip out, leaving my chest to cave in. I press numb hands over my heart, over the hole.

"Do you think Stephen would hurt Liam?" Brand asks. Her voice is strained, but the ice in her tone, full of Commander and full of my mother, pushes against the tension.

"No." I stare at the pen holder balanced halfway off the desk. "But he shouldn't be forced to be involved in this against his will."

"They'll use him to get to you. We can't give them what they want."

I snap my eyes back to Brand. They itch. I know why now. The death affinity is ready, and Brand makes the itch worse. That's as far as I can comprehend.

"They're not just using him to get to me, they need him for the Ritual too."

"Why?" A crinkle cracks the smooth skin between her

eyebrows.

"They need his blood for the Ritual to work. What if they convince him to do it?"

Brand averts her swollen, red eyes and her face pales as she straightens some papers. "We can't risk the Revival getting their hands on you too. You'll have to stay here while my team searches for him."

Burning fills my eyes and heat spills down my neck. I blink away the pain.

"Beastshit," I say, slamming my foot into the desk sending the pen holder clattering to the ground. I push away from my seat. The room is too tight, too full of the cutting truth, too humid, too close to Brand.

"Rin, wait," Brand says as I turn.

I throw on my jacket, hold my pinky finger in the air, and slam the office door behind me. The hallway shudders against the force, splinters skittering through the cement walls. As I run back through the hall, the stale refinery air is heavy in my lungs. She can't be serious. Liam is my brother, and I will find a way to get him home safe. I'll do it myself, so no one else gets hurt.

In the factory work room, sweaty and directionless, I stop. My breaths collide into each other, tightening my lungs, and my eyes burn with tears—I'm unwilling to let them fall again. The scent of earth and metal is intoxicating. The clang of machinery and chatter is as jarring as the new information about my family. My fists clench at my sides and my heart thuds in my chest.

It all rattles through my brain until it stills with a disorienting calm.

My father could still be around. He could walk past me any second.

I press my palms to my eyes. My pulse taps through my blood vessels in hurried bursts.

The heat of the room is heavy on my clothes. My heart sinks to my gut with pounding thuds, anchoring me to the hard slab of concrete beneath my feet.

If only my mother had known that he could come back.

The thought screams inside me. It rips through my veins, leaving them raw and burning hot under my skin. It bleeds through my heart like a scab's been ripped off a cut that never healed.

I can't urge my feet to move as my knees go weak and my vision blurs with the rush of blood.

Someone clamps their hands around my shoulders as I teeter. My stomach flips. They turn me around to face them.

It's not him.

"I don't want to talk to you," I say. My pulse shakes my body, but I remain upright with Brand's hands steading me.

"I know you don't." The chill that comes crawling out her throat with her words is so much stronger now that I know she's related to Mother. She drops her hands from me. I sway, taking a step back to right myself.

Brand looks straight at me, her blond curls circling her round face like a wreath. I used to think she was taller than me, but her eyes meet mine and our broad shoulders are level. We match. I don't remember if Mother was this tall or taller. She always stood with her back so straight, her hair was so sleek. Everything about Mother was long. Or maybe I just felt small in her shadow. My stomach churns at being so visible to her sleepy, silver eyes, just as she is visible to me.

I take another step back. "What more could you have to say to me?"

Brand casts her gaze away from me. Her teeth click together as she bites down on an exasperated huff.

Her irritation with me spikes red in my eyes and pressure fills my face. Red edges into my field of vision.

"That." She points her finger at my eyes. "I'm not letting you out of my sight until you have that under control."

I scoff, slapping her hand away. "I want out. Out of here, away from you. You all lied to me. This place is a lie. Shit. It's such a fucking lie."

Turning on her heel, her stray curls fly. "The death affinity is heightened by exhaustion," she says. "But it also drains you. More exhaustion. It's a cycle. You need to calm down and you need to eat."

"Where are you going?" I yell at her back.

"I'm going to get some food, and you're going to follow me because you can't go anywhere else."

Feet planted, I work my jaw with a wave of heat running over my body, making me sweat even more. The walls of the workroom are floor-to-ceiling concrete, metal rails, and water pipes—a cage, and beyond this cage is the Fōstrank, a mountain range filled with beasts. The heady aromas of grease and stone and mechanical heat mixed with the undeniable rumble of hunger in my stomach jar my gag reflex. I take a step after Brand with lead in my feet.

Brand leads me to an elevator, and we take a silent trip two floors down. We stare at our muddied reflections in the metallic doors with long frowns, the seconds drawing out endlessly. The door slides away, and Brand nudges me into the Vein's next dark corridor.

The smooth concrete ground slopes down to an intersection of tunnels. The ceiling is rounded and covered in white tile. Cutting through the white tiles are black ones with white, Slyvic script. The script trails from the right side, up over my head, and down to the left. The message repeats—up and back over to the right. It's always on an angle, so the script moves down the tunnel back and forth in front of me, guiding me. On both sides of the script are lines of alternating colour. They start red, circle back around in purple, and then continue on with the script in blue until they spiral again in purple and back to red. It's like a depiction of the continuous network of blood vessels in the hédin body. Red for oxygenated blood, blue for deoxygenated blood, and purple for the exchange of gases.

Our skin as strong as iron, our blood stronger, our hearts stronger still.

My throat constricts. Not only do these markings resemble the cycle of blood, but they're the colour of the spirit affinities, red and blue. And the purple reminds me of how the bright flashes in my blood aura at Registration merged into one purple hue.

I drop my eyes to the ground, focusing on Brand's feet leading me through the images clamouring for my attention. Recycled air, heavy with humidity, rushes through me, until at the end of the corridor its scent twists with spice and thickens with salt and a splash of ale.

We enter a bar lit with lightstones that cast an amber glow over the room. The walls are rough, red brick, the tables and the bar are dark wood. Music plays just loud enough to irritate my ears.

Brand walks with confidence through the crowd, nodding to those she makes eye contact with. "Commander," they say, returning the nod. Despite the noise, the rhythm of her heavy tread gives me something to focus on. Pulling my coat collar up around my face, I follow behind her, eyes on the rough tile floor, half blinded by hunger, saliva pooling in my mouth.

At the far end of the bar, she stops at a corner booth. Brand motions for me to sit and waves to the bartender. I slide into the booth, right into the corner where the noise doesn't reach me. Hands clasped between my knees, I shrink into myself, like a bag with the air sucked out. Brand takes off her jacket. She smooths the creased lines of her blouse and then hooks one arm over the back of the booth.

I swallow as she watches me. I run the back of my hand over my sweaty forehead. Sighing, I fan myself with one side of the open flap. It's still too hot. I shrug the coat off but have trouble getting my arms out of the sleeve in the tight space. A hand takes my jacket by the hood, pulling it away from me, allowing me more space to remove my arm. I jerk my arm out and whip my head around.

Hot breath escapes me as I stare up at a man with dark-umber skin towering over me. Not my father.

"Just heard about your brother," he says.

My jaw goes slack as I stare at him. He says it like he's known me his whole life.

"How are you coping?" he asks with one hand on his hip and rubbing the other over his scruffy white beard. He must be Eethian Ironskin, with his dark skin, silver eyes, and white hair.

I swallow hard. "Fine."

The man exchanges a glance with Brand and a sad but knowing smile pulls at his mouth. "Cold and blunt. No doubt she's related to you, Commander."

A hunger pang hits my gut and I ball my jacket up beside me.

Brand smiles back, just a show, a formality compared to this man's sincerity. She drops her eyes as I stare at her. I turn away from both of them, resting my eyes on the rusty red brick where there's no movement or expectations as Brand says, "Just bring us two specials, Devin."

"Two riijune coming right up."

"Make them big," Brand adds.

"Only for you, Commander."

The bright-red brick blurs, the noise is distant, my hands run over my knees—the only thing keeping me grounded. The fading of sensation around me is a menace and a blessing. My mind is stifled with information, so at least my body is filtering something out.

"Warrior Commander? Or Commander . . . of the Vein?" I ask.

With a slow turn of my head, I scan the bar. Some people wear Protector and Warrior uniforms, others ordinary clothes. A few tables away, two Nytrue girls are engaged in a conversation using hand signs.

"Both. I went to the academy. I focused on making my way through the ranks as a Warrior, a fighter, before coming back to the Vein."

My eyes jump to her. The way she says fighter stirs something in me, but I don't think we are the same kind of fighters. I shouldn't have asked. All the information she's given me is not enough, but also too much, because none of it helps Liam. The Revival always came to me since Stephen knew I was at the academy. He was talking to Professor Hans the first time he told me about the Revival. Professor Hans was the one to deliver the note from Stephen. Maybe he can contact Stephen the other way around. The only way for me to talk to Hans is at the academy. The winter break is two months, Jodvan and Fevron. I can't wait that long.

"Cassy and I grew up in the Vein," Brand says.

I draw an audible breath and lean forward, pressing my hands to the table for strength and staring Brand right in the eyes. "You are just another family member who left us," I say as a steaming plate of riijune appears in front of me, obscuring Brand's stony face. "I don't know if I wanna know your story yet."

I jam my fork into the riijune—a flat, fried-potato and egg mixture with mushrooms, keeta leaves, and fire-pepper sauce served over rice. Shaking my head, I shovel in a few scalding hot bites. Brand's silence is just as hot, hotter, pulling at my tears for the hundredth time. But I'm not crying in front of her again.

I down the whole plate of food in silence, every bite sinking heavy in my stomach and soothing my nerves.

Brand finishes her cup of water and says, "Cassy and I weren't close. When I found out your father was alive, you were his responsibility, and I had no say in the matter of bringing you into the Vein."

I set my fork down, the metal clinking against the porcelain plate. The moment I viewed Liam as a responsibility was the moment I made the biggest mistake of my life. My fingers go stiff with sudden cold. "Responsibility," I say in monotone, like an automated device providing the correct pronunciation of an unfamiliar word. Correct but heartless.

The blood drains from Brand's face. She lets out a small gasp and her eyelids fall. "Rin, that's not what I mean."

Squeezing my eyes tight and my fists tighter, I say, "I want to talk to Oron." It's louder than I meant to say it. The buzz of conversation falls for a moment and rises again as Brand passes her echo to me.

I snatch the echo and shuffle out of the booth. My fingers shake over the lightstone as I move through the bar and into the deathly dark hall. Flipping through the lightstone registry for Senn, a breath escapes me once I find Kruger. I select it and press the lightstone again. The connection tones wind my breath tight in my chest, as I count them.

"Hello?" Oron's voice is rough, frantic, tired. "Hello, who is this?"

"O-Oron?" I say.

"Rin, is that you?" His tone softens and my tears break free, streaming down my cheeks. I sniff and nod, even though he can't see me. "Thank mother fuckin' Carnity. The headmaster told me you were comin' home but got back from work and you weren't there. And . . . and Liam. He's gone. I don't know how this happened. I've been cussing out the LPs for hours . . . I . . . "

"The Revival took him. I tried, Oron, I tried to get to him before they did but I . . . Did you know about all this?" A sob escapes me and bounces around the tunnel. I clasp a hand over my mouth to silence myself and mumble through my fingers, "The Revival and the Vein?"

His heavy huffs crackle through the echo between swears. "The Revival and Vein I know about, yes."

"And my father? Did you know he was alive?"

The echo goes quiet. My mind goes quiet.

"Shit," Oron says, his bitterness punctuated by the static of the call. "No. No I didn't."

My eyelids fall closed. I find the wall with my fingers and rest my head on the cool stone. The dark is like velvet against all the cuts of truth. I let it brush through my mind for a little. I just can't shake the pit in my gut.

"Rin, are you still with me?"

I swallow, opening my eyes, still leaning my head on the stone for one point of contact with something solid. "Yeah, I'm here."

"Okay, I'm going to stay on the echo with you until you're ready to tell me more."

His voice is calm, still urgent, but where's the accusation? It should be in there somewhere. Might as well get it over with.

"Are you mad at me?" I ask. "F-for losing him?"

"Oh, my sweet girl."

He knows I expect it. He always gets mad first. When I got suspended, when I'm late, and so many other times when I just needed someone to understand.

Oron clears his throat. "He was under my watch. You don't blame yourself for this."

A draft through the dark hall freezes my body, but not the quivering tears in my eyes. I've never been good at doing what I'm told, so I'll probably blame myself forever. Without his anger, though, Oron becomes solid again, as if he's standing right in front of me and I could touch him.

"This is too much," he says. "I just want you safe. You and your brothers."

My knees give way and I drop to the cold floor, clinging to the echo. I take in a long breath of my musty jeans and the last hints of Eliote on my coat. Oron has always been rough, but deep inside, I know he wants us safe. He loves us. Me. I think. Does my father? Did my mother?

Oron's wish for our safety was Mother's too. At Father's funeral, she said we can't all be together, but she told me to be strong for my brothers. Right now, the Vein and the Revival are dividing us. I need to find a way to get me and my brothers back together. Maybe then we'll be safe.

4

ELIOTE

I SET OUT MY NOTES, colour coded by topic, and bring out a list of questions to ask the Guardian Basics professor during the review. I received a fine grade on the midterm, but fine doesn't cut it for my parents. Anything short from perfect shows them I'm not putting enough effort into Guardian training; it will confirm their suspicions that I'm not cut out for this place. It sets a lump in my gut, and for just a second, I wonder if maybe I'm *not* taking it seriously. Which is why I have to get as much understanding from this review session as possible. There can be no room for doubts.

But the Guardian Basics professor dims the lights. I grip my questions as he turns on the vision tech. Sitting straighter, I raise my hand, but he turns to a man standing by the door in a grey uniform. It's similar to the Warrior and Protector uniforms, but theirs are green and blue. I've never seen a Guardian in a grey uniform. Still, he has decorative metals adorning the thick, grey fabric of his jacket, a hat tucked neatly under his arm, ironed slacks, and polished boots. Everything about him screams Guardian. His gaze is measured and calm as he turns to the vision tech. Under that calm, his aura dances in rippling, pale-blue waves. The ripples are frantic but controlled, a constant vibration through his aura—he's excited.

As I glance around the room, my peers close their notebooks to give attention to the video. I drum my fingers on my desk, giving my notes a quick read through for as long as I can concentrate with the competition of the video. I read through one page, but the spike of motion on the vision tech draws my eyes.

An airship streaks through the sky. I've never seen any airship like it. It's sleek and compact, made for one pilot with no passengers. A shiver passes over my arms at the shock of the airship's speed. The pilot manoeuvres the aircraft with such precision, taking it further up into the sky, back down, spinning the entire ship upside down and levelling out to a smooth, sustained flight pattern. My stomach lurches and my heart thrums. A rush fills me from head to toe, constant and rippling— like the man in grey's aura.

The view shifts to show the inside of the aircraft from the pilot's perspective. His gloved hands are nimble, switching from steadying the aircraft and flipping switches. He hits a button, and a stream of fire and smoke projects from the aircraft and hits a drone dead on. The airship speeds past the wreckage.

I clasp a hand over my gaping mouth. My eyes are transfixed as the view switches back to the outside of the aircraft parked in a large, open garage. It pans over the glowing firestone connected to a tank of core energy that fuels the rest of the compact flight anomaly.

The pilot made that explosion with a button. No essence manipulation. A smile pulls at my lips as I imagine my hands on those controls.

The vision tech goes dark and the lights come on, bleaching my sight. I blink and turn to Ace sitting next to me. He's hunched over his open notebook, glasses sliding down his dark, crooked nose, and he twists one of the studs in his ears. My stomach drops. His aura is calm sapphire water with a midnight slurry of shadow glinting underneath, the shadow he gets when he's deep in thought.

The rest of the class rub their eyes from the shock of light, or lean back in their chairs, stretching, or prop their heads on their hands, eyes glazed.

I'm on the edge of my seat, my knees bouncing uncontrollably, my fingers still drumming as the man in grey approaches the front. I give him my full attention, putting the bored faces out of my mind.

"The world is always advancing, and the tools we use to protect our homes advance just the same," the man says.

I grip the green lightstone hanging from my neck. Running my thumb over one of the smooth surfaces of the stone, I cross my legs to contain my jitters. I can't remember the last time I had this much pure energy bringing life to my essenceless body.

Behind me, a blush-pink aura flares. I peek over my shoulder. Johanna stares right at me. Her high ponytail sends red, frizzy ringlets all around her head. As she raises an eyebrow at me, a snarky but sincere smile quirks her lips. The pink energy of her aura sparks into flame. She twirls her pencil between her fingers, then points it at the screen, leaning back in her chair.

The man says, "Airjet technology is the next step in Guardian advancement. As the High Commander of the new Flight Sector, I'd like to encourage you to consider how you will evolve with the times. Will you stay the course of a Guardian on foot or take the next steps of combat into the sky?" The High Commander nods to us. "The process to enrol requires no essence-manipulation demonstration. All that is required is a full, updated, physical exam with special attention on vision and reflexes. The Flight Academy in Lorisal is looking forward to seeing some new brave faces in its halls."

The entire class stands in unison to bow before his departure. I can't get myself to move. I'm drowning in adrenaline, stuck on the High Commander's words. No essence-manipulation demonstration.

We just got an invitation to go fly airjets for the Guardian forces of Emberstead, and no one is batting an eye.

I can barely focus on the review for the final exam. I keep imagining the controls in my hands, flipping switches, gliding through the air. An image of a fleet of enemy airjets in front of me. But in that image, my mother rolls her eyes at me. I already put so much work into coming to this academy. My parents wouldn't be surprised if I dropped it. But would they be surprised if I wanted to do something that's potentially more dangerous?

Class is dismissed, and I scoop my books up and plop them onto Ace's notes. He startles and pushes up his glasses.

"What did you think of the video?" I ask, giving him a kiss on the forehead.

"The video?" He brings a warm hand to my cheek and

stills me, kissing me on the lips. A tingle buzzes in my chest as I linger for a moment with him. "The tech sounds interesting," he whispers to me.

I nod to him, my head swimming in the sweetness of his voice. My face fills with heat. But my heart goes cold like the contractions have been paralyzed. Ace focused on his notes the whole time. He's on the Guardian track with no intention of leaving, and why should I? I got this far and I'm on the advanced team. How can I think about the Flight Academy? It's all the way in Lorisal. For Vin's sake. I'd be crazy to throw away my progress.

"What did you think?" Ace asks, gathering up his things.

"Oh." I twist my hair between my fingers. "Yeah, the tech is really cool. I've never seen anything move that fast before. It's nothing like those hulking passenger airships." I slide my books off his notes so he can reorganize them. "Kind of makes me wonder why they didn't have the tech sooner."

"Mechanics have always focused on elevation and sustaining large weight capacity for passengers and the powerstone trade."

"Right, right." I smirk at him, still searching for any ripples of excitement in him, something that might encourage me to keep up the conversation. His aura stays steady.

"Right," I mutter.

A final note. No more of this. I shake my head as Niko and Jeff come over to us.

Niko props himself with both hands on Ace's desk. "Study schedule, guys. Tonight, crank out history and elements and run some combat drills. After the exams tomorrow, we hit the books for calculations and Guardian Basics and bring the sweat for weapons training. Sound good?"

Niko looks nothing like his aura. His face is narrow, his eyebrows stark and mean, his smile is mischievous. And yet his aura is soft, pillowy, and white, with a sharp spike here and there like burs in bear fur. They say a Beastblood's beast form is their second soul, which explains some discrepancies between his wiry, sharp looks and the soft aura.

"Sounds good to me," Jeff says. "Food first though."

Jeff's aura has become clearer to me in the last few weeks. It's almost as if his aura is shy. But Jeff isn't shy—quiet and calm, yes, but not shy. His aura is bundled. It's layers and layers of pale-green and lavender held together by clay and bound in twine. The twine is thin, strained, as if pulled too tight, the load of his layers too much to handle. I inhale and the image takes on a sharpness that sparks all my senses. My nose tingles like the green is fresh grass cuttings and the lavender, not just colour, but tiny, fragrant blossoms. The clay is cool, earthy.

"Yeah," Ace says. "Food first."

The guys shuffle out of the classroom. I follow after them, but Johanna claps her hand around my arm and pulls me back.

"What the hells was that?" Johanna says. Her smile from earlier has vanished. The pervasive crinkle between her brows tightens, and her green eyes hold the weight of an entire accusatory jury.

"What do you mean?" I say, wiggling out of her grasp.

"You were practically drooling over that video." Johanna pulls herself up onto her desk and props her feet on the chair Ace was sitting in, her chunky black boots hitting the wooden chair with a thunk.

"I wasn't drooling. At least I don't think I was." I run the back of my hand over my chin just to make sure.

"Your head practically exploded when the pilot shot that missile, and all you can say about it is that it's cool tech?" Johanna scoffs, rolling her eyes and shaking her head at me.

"It is cool tech." I take the hair tie from my wrist and pull up my hair, providing an excuse to avoid her eyes and calm some of the energy skittering through my veins.

"Cool tech that you want to operate."

"Don't put words in my mouth."

"Am I though?" Johanna's head tilts forward, her eyes boring into my skull. "Am I really putting words into your mouth?"

"Fine." I drop my arms. "I want to fly the cool tech and shoot the missiles and not be at a disadvantage because I don't have essence. But . . . "

Johanna's boots slide off the chair and swing back and forth under the desk. She nods at me, curls falling forward.

I plant my hands on my hips. "But it's all the way in Lorisal. My boyfriend is here. All my friends are here. My parents would think I can't hack actual Guardian training and that I'm copping out." My chest heaves for breath. I clutch my lightstone. "And I chose this. I chose the Guardian system."

"Mm." Johanna clicks her tongue. "I think it would be good for you." She slides off the desk, hikes her backpack up on her shoulders, and heads out the door as she flips open her pocket gamer.

The din of voices and footsteps, the clouds of brilliant auras, all fade to a muffled buzz as everyone goes to dinner. I slump back down to my seat. Short winter days have darkened the sky already and let the green glow of the stars sift into the room. Neat rows of desks surround me, empty, but energy lingers in each seat. I've never seen auras do that before. I rub my eyes, but even a subtle aura lingers where the High Commander had stood. I get up. Moving down the aisle, my skin prickles. A force presses on me from one side, a heat from the other. Stopping in the place where the High Commander stood so proud and strong, the energy is gentle. Maybe just gentle enough to spark a level-one essence reading.

My mother had opened my acceptance letter to the Akinnera Academy for Guardian Training before I could get my hands on it. She didn't know I had applied. As she read it, her brow crinkled. Her magenta aura folded in on itself like a spring. She turned to my father. *"She's not going. She's not embarrassing us again."* She threw up her hands, letting the letter fall to the floor. My father picked it up. He read it through while I stood in the doorway, still waiting for congratulations. He frowned. The night-wing moths fluttered on his shoulder as his essence churned. The letter dropped to the kitchen table, and he said nothing about it.

For the first time, someone looked me in the eye and told me I could do something. But now, even with approval, I don't know if I can. Sending in that application was supposed to show them I can be a Guardian, receiving the letter was supposed to show me that I belong, but neither of those things have been confirmed.

RIN

I LOCKED MYSELF IN MY ROOM this whole week to study for exams. Brand was away in Akinnera to finish up the year's training with the advanced team, but she's back now to proctor me. I sit across from her at her desk. My knee bounces underneath and she sighs every time I bump the desk. But really, I'm kicking myself. I should have had Ace help me with calculations. I run my sweaty hands down my knees, stilling the shake. Eliote is probably a wreck. She studies more than any of us and puts more stakes into doing well academically. I wish I could be with her.

Brand glances at me from her files. I snatch up my pen and scribble in the last few answers.

"Done," I say, sliding the booklet over to her.

"That was fast." She slips on her round gold-rimmed glasses to look over the answers.

"Why? A girl from South Senn can't have a brain?"

Her silver eyes glare at me, magnified by the thick lenses. "You do realize I'm a girl from South Senn, right?"

I raise my eyebrow at her and slump back in the chair while she marks the exam. It's happening again. Building walls of petty jabs, sarcasm, and cold to distance myself against someone who hurt me. Just like with Johanna. What has Brand done to me? Nothing. She's done nothing except confuse me by keeping important information from me. More than that, the only reference for interacting with Brand is my mother. Brand isn't just my Commander anymore, and interacting with family members isn't my strong suit.

The air in the office is heavy inside me, too hot, after sitting in the windowless space across from each other for two hours.

Holding up the exam, Brand says, "What number is this?"

I lean forward to see the scribble. "Forty-nine."

She nods and puts a red check by it and then folds the booklet closed. "Well," she says, pushing her glasses up into her curls. "Guardian Basics was perfect, your history essay was well written, elements was really good too."

"What about calculations?" I ask, twisting in the chair to crack my back.

"Eighty percent. The work was a mess though."

"So, hand-to-hand exam next?"

"Yes." Brand marks her signature on the front of the booklet that is just as messy as my scribbles.

"Am I sparring with you?"

"Unless there's someone else you would like to spar against, then yes."

We leave the stuffy office, and Brand leads me through

the Vein to a training room where I'll do my hand-to-hand, essence-manipulation, and weapons test. Passing another small office, my nose itches. The rustic, sweet smell of my father wraps around me and I stop. At a desk lit by a lightstone lamp, he sits, studying a large book, his back hunched, making him small in the dark. My heart stutters. The ghost of him in my memory is large. If I think of him as a ghost, it's better, it takes the pressure away. But this ghost still isn't the man I knew. My father was a large presence, always working, always on missions. He taught me to fight. If he's going to be real to me, he has to make sense. Someone in this shithole Vein has got to make sense.

"Hey," I say, coming to a full stop. Brand is already halfway down the hall.

My father looks up from the book. Our eyes clash, and I take a step back.

"Rin," he says with a sharp breath.

He's why I studied so hard. I don't want to see him contrasting the ghost in my head. I squint and he blurs a little. If I keep his outline blurred and his face not so stark, maybe I can get within three feet of him.

"You," I say.

He blinks, holding a pencil over the book, but I can't speak any more words to him. I turn to Brand, who's made her way back to me. She peers into his office.

"Him?" she says, pointing her thumb at the ghost.

"Yeah, him." I nod.

"All right, Peter, you've been elected to participate in Rin's final exams."

The constant thrum of machinery is dampened by the wall of silence that falls between us. My father stands, bringing his full height back into reality as he ducks through the door. His smile is flat. He brings his hand up to my shoulder, but I turn away from him before he can touch it and make my way to the training room.

"I was preparing myself to get destroyed, but now it's on you," Brand whispers to my father.

A chuckle warms the space between us. I could linger in that warmth if it wasn't from a cold body, if it wasn't a conversation with a dead man and a stranger, if my heart wasn't still bleeding.

The room is long, about twice the size of the training room we use at the academy. There are a few sparring rings mapped on the floor, punching bags, and weights. Some of the Vein members practice with swords or spar hand to hand. They stop as they see us.

"Peter, you doing some training today? It's been a while," one of them says.

Brand holds up her hands to them. "Rin's doing her exams today, everyone stay quiet so she can concentrate."

They line up between our sparring ring and behind Brand, folding their arms across their chests, muttering to each other. Their eyes track me as I shake out my arms in the middle of the ring, waiting for my father to remove his coat. The audience brings a thrill to the air. My heart pounds and my mind conjures an electropulse song that gets played at Dawnranfet too often. It draws me back into the dimly lit cage, drunken shouts surrounding me. Haze fills my eyes as my father joins me at the centre.

"Rin," Brand says. "You'll need to demonstrate your specialties, Dawntimdato and Telando in this spar. One takedown will need to be demonstrated, along with defensive and offensive manoeuvres. Show me strength restraint and control over the life affinity, and you'll get a pass on your essence manipulation too."

I nod and raise my guard. My father mirrors me in a perfect Telando stance. The last time we matched like this, I was eleven. So much has changed since then. I've done so many things I wouldn't want that eleven-year-old girl to see. I bring the blue veil of the life affinity over her eyes and lock her behind the pulse of essence in my skin.

My father is painted in blue, and the cool electric rush fills my every cell. I jab at his face. He blocks and back steps. Steel sharpens in his eyes, and he strikes at me. Bobbing away from his reach, I sweep a crescent kick to his head.

My body knows these moves like it's a simple walk around the block. The impact of fist to bone is like a deep inhale, the rush of blood like a cool breeze. I just need my brain to connect with this effortless contact with my father.

"You were dead. You could have gone to the Beyond," I say.

His brow furrows as he takes heavy breaths and raises his fists to guard his face. "I found something. A Hold in the Higher Plane."

He tries to land a hook, but I block. He kicks low, but I counter, step back, and kick him in the gut, sending him stumbling back. As our audience applauds, I lunge forward, smacking my fist to his face. He hits the ground.

I prop myself on my knees and look down at him. "What's a Hold?"

Pushing himself off the ground and rolling his neck, his eyes never meet mine. "Angel and Demon Palm," he says. "They're supposed to send someone straight to the highest level of the

Lesser Worlds." I step back to give him space to reset. "The techniques keep their vital energies fully integrated, mind, spirit, and essence. They can go right to the Beyond from there."

The life affinity flickers in my eyes. He moves in with a combination of quick fist strikes. I block them, but he sneaks in a kick to my side. I jolt to the edge of the ring.

"What do you mean, they're supposed to?" I say, switching my feet to my dominant stance.

"The Fourth Great War, the Death Ritual, it made a Hold that traps anyone sent to the Higher Plane with the palms." His strikes come faster. I welcome them with my own, and we fall into a rhythm of back and forth that almost touches the memories stashed in the heart of the girl behind the veil. "I've been trying to get back there, studying to find a way to break the Hold so they can be free and make the Revival impossible. I've been looking for rifts back to the Lesser Worlds. The one I came through only takes me to the Silent Realm."

Blood and light course through me, faster as his words hit the same nerve that's been hit so many times. The war. It's never over, and the consequences linger. "How do you know that's what you saw?"

"I know because I recognized people in the Hold. People I sent there because of failed Revival Ritual attempts."

I draw breath and let it out slowly. My fists unravel, and I shift into a wide Dawntimdato stance. The light fades from my eyes. The girl, now twelve, kicks and screams inside me because she never did before. She screams as her father's face appears, no longer hidden by the life affinity. It is plain and pale, creased, with hard cheekbones and wide jaw. She screams, not for him, but for her mother.

"In the Lesser Worlds, did you see her?" The words wind me more than a hit to the diaphragm. "Mother, did you see her?" I say it loud, for the whole room to hear, kicking at him high and low. "Did you try to bring her back with you?"

Instead of avoiding the kicks, he stops and puts up his hands. My momentum sends me into his palms.

"I didn't see her," he says.

I back away. My breaths shake me as they cling to each other and pull my lungs tighter. What if he had found her? Would they have gone to the Beyond together or come back together? No, she wouldn't have chosen to come back. She made up her mind.

"She chose the Lesser Worlds over staying on this Carnity-forsaken planet, and you came back." My voice breaks, dipping low and filling the room as I stand with my arms half raised. "Why the fuck did you come back?"

Chest heaving, his face sours. That little girl who sat on his lap must be a figment of his imagination by now. She didn't swear in his face or yell at him. She was content to listen to his stories. That's all he gave her. Stories.

"I had to make it right." His conviction is thick in his voice. It's a protective force against the clashing realities between us. "I found the Hold. It was my duty to warn people, to do something, and save them from their fate."

Stories about heroes.

His little girl loved those stories. But now one thought burns inside her. If I don't let her say it, I might lose her too. It prickles behind my eyes with itchy heat. "You chose to stay away."

The room is a void. There's nothing beyond him, or beside him. His scent brings his memory back and merges with the ghost. Life strikes from his eyes and he becomes solid. I pound my fist on his chest and he doesn't budge. Warmth brushes my skin.

"Away from me, from Stephen, from Liam."

Father stands in front of me, breathing. A tear streams down his face, but he holds his chin high as he holds my fist back from striking again.

Brand steps into the ring. "You need to demonstrate a take down," she says in a quiet tone.

I twist my wrist out of his grasp and his fist snaps shut. "Hit me," I say.

"No." He shakes his head, letting the tear fall to the floor.

Heat crawls over my skin. I yank him forward, knee him in the gut, and send him to the ground. He lands on his back, and I pin him. Panting, I say, "Three years you stayed away. You broke your promise."

I wait for a light to hit his eyes, for a spark of realization. But his eyes are dull and tired—strange.

Every mission he went on, he came back stranger and stranger. I clung so tightly to the knowledge that he loved us and wanted to come back. He was protecting us out there. He kept Illyson safe. From beasts. From people who would harm others. And now, as he works to protect the world from our own people, he didn't come back to me. So, I let go of the idea that love comes back. The twelve-year-old girl's heart breaks, but that illusion isn't doing either of us any favours.

I hold tears in my eyes, cling to them like a child crossing the room with a cup too full of water. Careful and on guard, no drops hit the floor. I slam my fist next to his face, denting the ground, and push off him.

The Vein members file out of the training room in silence.

My ears sense the shuffle of their feet and then let the sense fade.

"High marks, Rin," Brand says to me with a nod, her glasses reflecting the lights above as she dips her head to her clipboard.

"Next test," I say. I turn my back to Father and grab an Illyson long sword.

Handing one to Brand, my fingers brush leather and metal and can't differentiate them. The materials are dull to my skin. But I recognize the tug of the little girl I used to know, who doesn't want to be forgotten. As a shadow paints over my mind, the little girl wraps herself around me.

When Mother couldn't sleep, Father would talk to her if he was home. Maybe he would just tell her stories or encourage her, I wasn't sure, all I could hear were murmurs through the walls. This time, Mother's voice wasn't anxious, it was full and heated. I crept into the hall, but they weren't in their room, they were downstairs. I sat down on the top step and hugged my knees to my chest.

"You're putting it first again. It's just a job," Mother said.

A thin shadow moved in the amber light at the base of the stairs and a thicker one moved with it as they paced through the kitchen.

"My job supports all of you, all of Illyson. It's not just a job."

"Support must mean something very different to you than it does to me."

"Cass, please lower your voice. You'll wake them. Just come into the living room."

Father's footsteps were heavy, already in boots, but Mother's feet slapped against our hardwood floors. I leaned forward, trying to stay in range to hear them.

"Rin."

I started and teetered forward. I braced myself on the wall and the banister.

"Why aren't you in bed yet?" Stephen looked down at me. He crossed his arms and leaned against the wall with a playful, satisfied look on his face, knowing he caught me.

I sighed and scooted back on the top step. "They're fighting about something."

"Fighting?" His eyebrows furrowed. "They never fight."

"Well, it sounds bad."

"Bad how?" He nudged my shoulder, and I shuffled over so he could sit beside me.

"He's leaving again."

Words formed on his lips and his eyes darted down the stairs and back to me. Shaking his head, he said, "You better get back into bed before Mom sees you, or you'll get in trouble."

"Not in any more trouble than Father already is."

Stephen smirked, making the shadows on his face rise and his eyes brighten. He chuckled, and it filled my chest with warmth as we sat close together.

"Think Mom's going to win this one, or do you think he's going to leave?" he asked, keeping his eyes on his hands.

I drew a breath and matched his pose with my elbows propped on my knees. A thin shadow passed through the patches of light that made it through the rungs of the railing. I dropped my whispers lower, not much more than air. "I hope she wins."

Lips pulling tight, Stephen didn't chime in on the bet.

"Has Rin showed any signs of the spirit affinities? She's old enough," Father said.

Stephen leaned closer. "You better not start developing new enhancements. You're still getting crap for the hole you put in the wall when you discovered your strength enhancement."

"I only put a hole in the wall because you moved your head," I said, scrunching my nose at him.

He shrugged. "Basic self-defence, Rin."

"You deserved it though."

"Yeah, I did." He ducked his head, hiding the grin that showed his teeth, and I clapped my hands over my mouth to stifle a giggle.

"I thought she would by now," Mother said. "But it's Stephen, he needs help, I-I'm not sure if I'm doing enough for him."

"He's still having essence surges?"

"Yes, that's why I need you to stay."

"You're too soft on him. He needs to learn to regulate himself. You learned to control the life affinity by yourself. Why should he be any different?"

"It *is* different, Peter. Which is why I need your help. He's only fifteen."

"Fifteen is old enough to know how to control his emotions."

For one shitty moment, I hated them both because Stephen's smile disappeared. The light in his eyes faded. They took away our moment.

"The station's been working you too hard. They can't deploy you on missions the day you come home."

"It's not the Guardian Department."

"What?" A chair scraped the floor. Mother whispered, but she might as well have yelled at him, her voice was so stern. "No,

Peter. No. You cannot get involved with the Vein."

"It's not the Vein, it's Geret. He wants to meet about something he's been working on."

"I don't like having you gone when Ironskins are going missing again. They say they come back without memory of what happened, but they all talk about a woman."

"I know, they're calling her The Captor. It's what Geret wants to talk about . . . "

His voice quieted, his urgency bringing depth to the shadows around me and Stephen. I held my breaths and Stephen was so still I imagined he did too. I shifted closer to him, but he didn't flinch. He was immovable—caught in some sort of trap.

"Has it really been that bad?" I asked, turning my knees to him to keep my words from spilling down to our parents. "The death affinity?" I wasn't supposed to be around when Stephen trained the affinity, so I just assumed it was going well.

Stephen blinked, and I let in some breath. He rubbed at his nose and my heart skipped a beat, then pounded hard, picking up speed. Our parents' whispers slipped through the silence, razor sharp. Stephen shuddered and he shook his head. As he stood, he said, "Go to bed, Rin," and shut his door to me.

I stayed where I was, curled into myself. Father would stay. For Mother, at least. Maybe to help Stephen. Liam has been growing so much and talking. Father would stay. He wouldn't want to miss that.

" . . . and I just want to talk things out. That's all."

"You'll be back for one day and then what? You'll have another assignment," Mother said. "Your children need you." The strength in her voice turned bitter too fast. "I need you."

I pressed my knuckles into the palm of one hand. My fingers

popped one by one as panicked breaths from downstairs drifted to the top.

"It won't be long. I'm doing this to keep us all safe, you know this. You're strong, Cassy. You know I love them. You know I love you."

"Then just stay."

The words exchanged next were too hushed and too heavy for me to comprehend. They were clear enough, but they didn't make it past the pounding of my heart and the tingle crawling up my neck.

The door clicked.

Cool night air couldn't have reached me that fast. Somehow the hall expanded around me. The pictures of our family stepped back, the shadows churned, inky and thick, and the outside and inside air traded places. Maybe Father felt too warm as he left.

It wasn't the last time I saw him, but it was the first time I felt him leave.

Maybe now I see my father as he was back then, all the ways he was that I didn't want to see. I only wanted to take what he claimed. That he loved us. It wasn't a lie, and it still rings true today, but the moments he showed it to us were so rare, so strange. Coming back from the dead gave him a new mission, a new way to be a hero, when just a little honesty with his children would have made him hero enough.

LANCE

I have to make it stick this time. Not just quitting smoking, all of it—following along, just like in this crowd. Crowds are always a sure path to me shutting up, letting the irritation build, then running to vices to take it away.

I clasp hands with yet another graduate. "Seena's blessings," I say, staring at our hands.

The graduate, a dude I've never even talked to, uses the handshake to pull me in for a hug. My wings flinch, unfolding to nudge the student next to me on my right, and on my left, my wing lifts my classmate's skirt.

"Watch it, Lance," she says, slapping my wing away.

"Sorry, sorry," I say, unfurling myself from the unsolicited beast-hug. My face swelters, and I run my hand over the back of my neck, drenched in sweat.

I'm nudged to the next graduate. The line extends the length of the dining hall. For Seena's sake, I still have to shake half the graduating classes' hands. Tension grips my shoulders so hard that my entire arm shakes as I extend it. Irritation stirs in my throat and presses on my chest. Instead of grabbing the next graduate's hand, I slap it down on his shoulder.

"Good luck, man." I turn on my heel, again mowing down the procession line with my wings. Coughing into the crook of my arm, I cross to the opposite side of the dining hall where there's food. My lungs rattle and seize with the effort to clear my airways.

At the food line, I fill my plate, hands jittering and lungs burning, as I hold back a cough to spare the buffet. I drop my plate at a table with the advanced team by the windows, rip off my blazer, and loosen my tie before melting into my seat.

"I can't believe Adrianne isn't going to be training us next year," Niko says through a mouthful. "I'll never forget our first session with her."

The group chuckles and exchanges a few teary glances. Johanna's tears are the heaviest as she looks back at the procession line. I follow her gaze to the very end where Adrianne stands with her face red from crying. There's a gold medal around her neck, marking her acceptance into Monitor training. Like she can feel our eyes on her, she finds our table in the crowd. Tears streak her face as she waves to the advanced team, long hair swishing behind her and the beads on her dress shimmering.

"What happened in your first session?" I ask, turning back around.

A grin spreads across Niko's face. "Adrianne punched Johanna in the face for being a bitch and then asked us what we were going to do about it." He leans back in his chair and folds his hands calmly over his stomach, the grin still flickering on his lips. "I, of course, wanted to save my comrade and went in swinging. Adrianne had me flat on my back in seconds."

Johanna rolls her eyes. "She didn't punch me for being a bitch, she punched me to make the point to think before you act, Niko. To defend before you attack." She presses her finger to his head. There's a smile under her defensiveness.

"Point well made," he says, rubbing the spot. "But it was also because you were being a bitch."

"It was not." Johanna brushes a rogue tear from her cheek. Turning in her seat, she gives me a once over with narrowed eyes. "Lance." She swirls her fork in the air at me, and says, "This is just an observation, but you look like beastshit."

"There she goes, proving herself wrong," Ace mutters from the far end of the table. More chuckles and a smile twitches my face.

Anchoring my hands to the table on either side of my plate, I nod, my knees dancing to two different beats under the table.

Jeff nudges me in the arm. "Smell a little rank too."

I huff and run a hand over my face. "Thank you both for pointing that out, but I am well aware of these facts."

"Probably because he's spent every free minute in the weight room," Niko says through a mouthful. "The dude's jacked."

"Yeah, well, what can I say. I can only concentrate on studying for fifteen minutes before the cravings hit, and the only way I've found to get rid of them is lifting things that are way too heavy for me." The explanation leaves me winded, and I cough into my sleeve again.

At the other end of the table, Eliote leans into Niko with

one ear turned to me, trying to hear over the extra commotion in the dining hall packed with the graduate's families. "Lance, did you just quit smoking?" she asks. Her silky purple hair slides over her shoulder and dips into a pool of gravy on her plate.

"The day we went to the festival." I stuff a heaping mound of potatoes into my mouth.

Jeff turns to face me with one arm propped on the table and one on the back of his chair. "You quit smoking the week of exams? You've been studying through withdrawal. Are you insane?"

I swallow. "I'm not insane. I'm exhausted."

From the other end, opposite Eliote, Ace peeks around Jeff. "One week, that's a huge milestone, man." His voice is quiet and calm, cutting through all the racket. He reaches across the table with a napkin to wipe the gravy from the ends of Eliote's hair.

Niko jumps up, bumping Eliote so her hair re-dips, and she frowns while Ace continues to remove the sauce from her hair.

"One week!" Niko bellows with his hands in the air, shirt riding up, exposing his stomach. "Right here."

He points at me. A few families turn to stare at us with confused faces and a few chuckles until Johanna grabs Niko by the blazer and yanks him back to his seat.

"Thank you for your enthusiasm." I cough twice and shake my head, dropping my eyes to my plate. "I'm just glad Rin didn't have to see me like this."

A low chuckle draws my eyes up to Johanna's smirking face. The smirk drops fast, replaced by pink in her cheeks as Jeff shifts in his seat and takes an unnecessarily long drink.

"Rin wouldn't have minded. She's been lower," Ace says.

I lean forward to look at him and so does the rest of the table, except for Johanna, whose smile has dropped, its absence brings a shadow. "What do you mean?" I ask.

"Hm?" Ace looks up at all of us. "Oh, I probably shouldn't have said that. It's not my place. All I'm saying is that she'd be sympathetic to what you're going through." Ace smiles at me with lips pressed together. The blue of his eyes seems to deepen, filling with something heavy.

I saw the same heaviness in Rin's eyes after I told her how I screwed up my life and screwed up Khalie's even more. She took it all in, watching me, listening to me, only responding when she had something to add. With the clone attack and her leaving, we never got to talk more about it. Maybe she had more to add about what brought her low and made her so sympathetic. But thinking about her makes my stomach turn and my face hot.

"Anyone got big plans for the break?" I ask.

Eliote claps her hands. "Yes," she says with a smile beaming on her dark lips. "My mom just became a priestess of Vin, and she's asked me to help set up the shrine for the Festival of the Heart."

"Is that a pretty big deal?" Niko asks.

"Very. Since I don't have essence, a lot of Luminee think I'm cursed or something, but if the priestess of Vin has her lightless daughter help her in the shrine, then maybe they'll see me differently."

My bites slow as I take in her excitement. Both of us have spent the majority of our lives without our lineage enhancements. I waited so long for mine and have only had them for four years, but Eliote's will never come. Even if I have nothing in common with another Lavarian, we can always talk about weather manipulation. But without that, the point of connection isn't there, and no one knows why. It's awkward and lonely—it hurt to be left out. I've heard Eliote mention how strict her parents are. This may be a huge deal by Luminee standards, but for Eliote, it must mean even more. I smile, too exhausted to look away when her dark-brown eyes catch me staring.

"You know, Lance," she says. "Your essence has really strengthened in the last week."

Clearing my throat, I shake the fog out of my head. "Yeah?"

"It's almost doubled in volume."

I lean back in my chair. Despite the surges in my essence channels, all the jittering, and the headaches, my essence-manipulation exam went well. But outside of those consciously controlled manipulations, the surges have caused a constant stirring of clouds in the sky. Every time I step outside, it rains or hails or the winds pick up. Both instances make what the Seer said to me sort of believable.

"About that," I say. "At the festival, a Seer gave me a mystery. She said Seena walks in my shadow now."

The whole table looks at me with wide eyes. Niko's mouth drops.

"What, uh, what do you think that means?" I say, running my hands up and down my knees.

"Seer's rarely give such clear mysteries," Jeff says.

"That's clear?"

"Yeah, usually they give images, one-word mysteries, like grace, peace, terror. Yours is so specific. We need to find this Seer."

My heart rate spikes. I grit my teeth as a wave of dizziness sweeps through me. I lick the phantom sensation of a cigarette from my lips.

Ace hands me his echo. "Recognize any of these Seers?"

I take the echo, and as I scroll through Akinnera's registry of Seers, echo glows light each face at the table.

Tension in my chest builds with each swipe of my finger. I hand the echo back to Ace. "Sorry, I don't recognize any of them."

The advanced team takes turns showing their echos to me. Shaking my head, I say, "Thanks for trying, guys."

"Hold on, don't get your titties twisted. I have one more listing," Johanna says. "No picture, but there's an address."

"What am I going to do with an address?"

The listing is just her name and her specialties: **Zy, Ancestral Seer. Energy imprints, Soul Tethers, and future readings.**

"You're going to *go* to the address, obviously," Johanna says chewing on her thumb nail. She glances at Jeff as he looks over my shoulder at the screen. Dropping her thumb, she grabs her echo back.

"When am I going to go? It's late, and I leave for Jiaan tomorrow morning." I grasp my tie and loosen it more.

Johanna stands. She pauses to pick a piece of food from her teeth then gathers her dishes. "Then we better go now. See you in the new year, guys." She walks away from the table. "Come on, Lance."

Jeff's eyes trail Johanna as she stacks her dishes. He rolls his shoulders and sighs. "She'll leave without you if you don't follow her now."

"Right." I shovel in a few bites and follow Johanna.

Thankfully, Johanna suggests we change out of our uniforms

before we head out, but once we meet in the lobby, she ushers us out the door. "It's close. We'll walk it," she says.

I stuff down the fact that I'm literally following her like a puppy, and just keep walking half a step behind her. Johanna leads me through snow-covered streets to a small compound right along the city wall. There are no motorways in this part of town, no electro lamps, only lightstones and candle flames lighting windows and sidewalks. The snow falls in hushed waves over the houses, chimney smoke curling to the dark-green sky.

"Almost there," Johanna says.

I take a gulp of cold air. My essence pulses in rapid chugs.

The light from Johanna's echo paints her in blue-white light so her curls are like lightning.

"This one." She stops and points at a small house with a low-hanging roof with green tile, a dark wood frame, and whitewashed panels. My essence rushes to my feet like two anchors. A flash of lightning streaks through the sky with a rumble.

"Maybe this was a mistake," I say. The snow turns to sleet as my hands tremble at my side.

Johanna raises her face to the turbulent sky. Her curls flatten and she turns to me. "Are you doing this?"

"Yes. There's no way that mystery was true—she was probably Eased and didn't know what she was talking about." I turn around and start walking back the way we came as the sleet turns to hail.

It can't be true. I'm not the guy people walk behind. I'm the guy people laugh at when I use first year essence-manipulation techniques as a second year, the guy who drinks too much in order to get a laugh out of them—miles behind with my head in the clouds.

Johanna grabs my arm and tows me back to the hut.

"Johanna, please, let's just go."

On the Seer's front stoop, Johanna stops, her hand clawing into me. Incense wafts around us. Clenching her eyes shut she says, "I'm not doing this for you." Her fingers lock tighter around my arm, blocking off essence and blood, making my hand go cold.

"Fine."

Johanna slams her fist on the Seer's door, as tiny white pellets collect in her curls. "Open up," she yells.

A light flickers above us. My essence jolts. The pellets dissolve into rain.

"I'm not open," a woman calls from inside.

"We're not leaving until you give us some peace of mind."

"Go away."

"No." Johanna pounds on the door, still clutching my arm. The lanterns around the door jangle.

The door flies open.

"You know him?" Johanna asks the Seer.

I let out a sigh and wipe sleet from my face. My hair hangs in damp strands in front of my eyes, my wings slump heavily behind me. I wave a hand to the Seer, but my lungs spasm, and I hack into the crook of my arm.

The Seer holds one hand tight on the door handle and the other clenches a half-eaten piece of toast. She wears suede slippers, night shorts, and an electropulse band t-shirt. On her wrist is a silver bracelet with every ancestor's charm tinkling in the wind that my essence is creating without my command. In place of the emerald-green head cover with gold tassels, she wears a colourful silk scarf tied tight around her head so all her hair and half her forehead is covered. The golden rings of her irises pulse like sunlight and the two-headed night snake slithers from her sleeve down her dark, slender arm.

She brushes at the toast crumbs on her shirt. "Thought you would have come by sooner."

Blood and essence flow hot through my arm as Johanna lets go of me.

"You were expecting me?" I take a full breath and release it. The wind calms and the rain quiets to soft snow. I shuffle my feet in a pile of slush.

"Mhm, most people I give a mystery to come knocking on my door the next day." The Seer eyes me up and down. My face floods with heat while icy rainwater trickles down my neck.

"So, are you going to help him figure out his mystery?" Johanna asks.

The door creaks open as the Seer drops her hand from the doorknob. The amber rings in her eyes are still bright. Her eyelids are lowered though, her head tilted, her lips pressed firm. "I guess, since you're here." She shrugs and steps to the side.

I flick the rain and sleet from my wings and brush some stubborn hail off a few feathers before stepping across the Seer's threshold.

Johanna grips her still-glowing echo, she opens her mouth but only a croak comes out.

"You too," the Seer says. "I see it." She folds her arms around her middle and shivers as she eyes Johanna.

She got me this far and now she's frozen. Whatever this Seer sees in both of us, it's going to cause a shift. I felt it when she looked at me the first time at the festival. Answers. Good or bad, Johanna and I both need them. I let out a breath, relax my shoulders, and smile at Johanna. Her eyes flick to me and her quick breaths calm. She steps inside behind me.

The Seer closes the door behind us and moves deeper into her home. "Coats off. Shoes and socks off," she says.

Our shoes and boots squeak over the clean tile of her entryway. As I struggle to get out of my wet jacket without bashing anything in the small space with my wings, the Seer goes to the kitchenette to the right. A kettle sings on the stove, and she pours herself a cup of tea. Lemon balm wafts over to me, soothing to my mind, and it doesn't irritate my lungs. I step out of the shoe well onto hard wood in my bare feet.

The home is one large room. Opposite the kitchenette, there is a fireplace and a reading chair across from a bed with various lightstones hanging overhead. Directly across from the front door is a sliding screen. The Seer shuffles to the screen, her slippers scuffing along the wood floor, muttering to her steaming cup of tea. She sets the tea on a table by the door and takes a veil from a hook above it. Beaded tassels tap together as she fits it over her headscarf. I glance at Johanna as the Seer slides the screen open.

Johanna's eyes are wide. She stands stiff as a board.

"You okay?" I ask, touching her arm.

"Uh, do you know that there are three Wander Wraiths just hanging out in here?" Johanna asks the Seer, her voice high and pinched.

My blood goes cold as I whip my head from side to side and take a step back. My wing drapes over a stack of books on a chair to my left, knocking them to the floor.

The Seer sighs. "Yeah, well, at least you can see them. I can

only feel them, and they never leave, which is weird because wraiths don't usually stay in the land of the living for long periods of time. Have a chat with them while I work with your friend."

Not even paying attention to the Seer, Johanna stares into the darkest corner of the room. Her face scrunches and she crosses her arms. She must be able to hear the wraiths, too, because she rolls her eyes and scoffs. "They always chat more when you don't want them to."

I can't see, hear, or feel them, but Johanna's facial conversation gives me chills.

My heart pounds in my chest as I follow the Seer.

I expect to step into a snow-covered courtyard with some extreme weather nonsense from my spike in adrenaline, but the Seer's courtyard is lush green grass. The Seer slips off her suede slippers at the door, takes a long inhale of the steam of her tea, and leads us onto the grass. Rocks, small bushes, flowers, and creeping vines cover the ground. The foliage is natural, not coaxed into pleasing arrangements around the small spring in the centre of the greenery. Nothing is trimmed down, held back, or fenced off. I breathe in the scent of fragrant blossoms and lush earth.

"I manipulate the vibration of the soil in a subtle pattern that creates heat, promotes growth, and attracts ancient, present, and future energy," the Seer says. She sits down cross-legged in front of the spring. "Sit."

I get down on the ground and run my fingers through the grass. A thrum of energy trickles up my body, warm and constant. Snowflakes fall overhead but turn to mist in the heat produced by the Seer's fine manipulation of the earth.

I open my mouth to ask what we're supposed to do. The

Seer shushes me.

"My name is Zy, as you probably know from my ad. I have three rules," she says, folding her legs in closer. She holds up her fingers to count her rules. "You sit, be quiet, and you get what you get because I can only see so much. Now to answer some questions that I know are going around your head. The veil blocks my energy from interfering with your energy and all of its ancient and future ties to the planet Karess. No, you don't have to pay. I don't have a formal listing in the registry because the clearest visions come to me when I'm alone, then I go try and find the people they're attached to at the Festival of Two Moons since they come from all over the province. Sometimes I find them, sometimes I don't. If I do, then with their presence so near, I can get an even clearer view if the ancestors allow it."

I fold my wings behind me, shifting a few times to get comfortable. "Do I need to—"

"You don't do anything. Just sit there."

Running my hand over the back of my neck, I nod.

Only the Seer's deep-brown eyes show through the slit in the veil. She blinks once and presses her eyes closed. She leans forward, planting her hands in the grass in front of me. The night snake slinks down her arm. It slithers through the grass, making rings around her wrists and flicks its tongues in and out of its scaly black faces.

The ground trembles. The air cools for a moment, letting a few snowflakes break into the heat. Another tremble and the heat bolsters. The energy in the earth radiates through my bones. My jaw vibrates even as I clamp my teeth. Energy that was intangible a second ago, becomes thick around me. The warmth isn't like the sun, not like fann heat. The thickness isn't suffocating either, it layers, but softly, like pieces of silk. It must have something to do with Earthkin essence being between unama and fann in energy alignment—a balance of give and take.

"Your energy imprint only appeared here on the Karess when you were sixteen. Another faded at that point as well." The Seer's voice lowers to a murmur, muffled under her veil. "Seena's energy imprint is with you. She's watched you since your energy imprint appeared. You've seen so much, so she urges your essence to calm, but also to grow."

My stomach churns and my fingers drum on my knees. I'm anything but calm right now. Khalie faded and I'm encouraged to grow. How is that fair? She faded because of me.

Sitting back, the Seer breathes deeply. "I believe Seena is guiding you to your Sage abilities."

"But . . . Lavarians don't have Sage abilities."

A moth flutters behind the Seer's head and the night snake makes its way up her opposite arm. "Seena is very attentive to her lineage. Her imprint visits many of her descendants. She's always waiting to see how they will grow. She sees it in you. But it will require that you reconnect with yourself and sustain that emotional connection."

The environment of the garden moves with Zy. As she leans to one side, the grasses sway. She blinks, and a moth flutters. She runs her fingers over the heads of the snake, and a moon beetle crawls over a core-energy boulder. Her energy connects with everything around her, and they push and pull against each other.

All my life I've wanted something to move toward me, to notice me, accept me. So, I chased acceptance and didn't make a lot of noise when I disagreed with people.

"The imprint that faded," Zy says and removes her veil, revealing a deep frown and dark bags under her eyes.

I swallow hard. *Khalie. She's not faded. I can never get her out of my head.*

"We can never say that death has a reason. But she did impact you, and now she's gone. Think about that."

"Th-thank you, Zy, for your time," I say, scrambling to my feet. Looking down at her, golden light glistens beneath heavy eyelids. Her chest rises and falls with deep breaths.

"People think that being a Seer is a blessing from the ancestors," she says. "But the energy the Karess is most familiar with is pain, and it provides it in abundance. Send your friend in."

I let out a heavy breath. It fogs the air as the heat in the garden falters. As a weight falls on my chest, my essence churns, and the snow breaks through the layers of heat.

7

JOHANNA

Tʜᴇ ᴡʀᴀɪᴛʜs ᴡᴏɴ'ᴛ sʜᴜᴛ ᴜᴘ, but they won't talk to me either. They whisper to each other, glance at me, and giggle. Why is every wraith I come across an absolute pain in the ass? As they glide back and forth along the wood floor, their hair and their hands and their ringing voices scratch through my mind. I clutch my stomach, pacing with them because the physical energy of my movement sooths some of the mental toll.

It will all be worth it if Zy can tell me at least something about Soul Tethers.

The screen door slides open and Lance steps in with snow flurries and a chill. His face is drawn as he stares at his feet.

"Hey, how'd it go?" I ask, trying to resist the urge to rub at the nauseous ache in my gut and still my feet long enough to make sure he's okay before running off to the Seer.

He shrugs. "Fine, I guess." He smiles but doesn't look at me as he steps into the shoe well to put his socks on.

Acid burns in my esophagus, spiking the pain in my head to full force. He might not have gotten the answers he needed, but he got something to think about, that's for sure. So what in the hells is coming for me?

"You can go," he says.

I dart out of the hut and pull the screen shut behind me. The moment my feet hit grass, my knees buckle. My blood is like gravy sloshing in a saucer, and my essence quakes, falling heavy like a rock tilting some invisible scale.

"Yeah," the Seer says. "This isn't going to be fun for you." She puts an arm around me and guides me down to the ground in front of a spring. The trickle of water sticks in my mind like pinchers, but Zy's voice is rich and confident, giving me something soothing to focus on, not like the wraiths whose voices crackle through me. "I keep the garden in perfect balance between unama and fann energy. You Emberstead with your pure fann energy are little beasts eating up any energy you can get. You don't like it when environmental energies balance away from you."

"Then can we make this quick?" I say, breathing slowly through my nose, fresh grass and fading cold stirs in my lungs.

Zy circles around me, taking sips of her tea. She scrunches her feet in the grass and waves her hand over me. "You're sick because the energy you're tethered to is too far away."

Letting my head fall back, I clench my eyes shut. "I got that already."

"You don't know why the tether formed. That's why it strains so much. It's a spiritual and mental strain as much as it is physical.”

“Okay, so why did it form?”

“I’ll only be able to see when it formed, maybe some surrounding circumstances, but not why.” She fixes her veil over her face. Crouching in front of me, she presses her hands to the earth. “Just try to relax and breathe.”

I banish any lick of shame I can find in my heart and release a heavy sigh. I unbutton my pants to let pressure off my stomach and I tie my hair up, steadying my breaths as my shaking hands get caught in the tangles. The sparkle of core energy streaming out of a boulder sends a pain through my skull and I shut my eyes again.

With the dark sheltering my mind from the sights, I block off the sound of the water and the wind whistling through the courtyard with Zy’s voice.

“It wasn’t too long ago, just over a year. You were disturbed by the possibility of another person’s energy being separated from you.”

The only reason Rin would have been separated from me, that I knew about at the time, was if one of us went to the Aria Academy. I suggested it. It was a stab at her, a joke, and not a joke at all.

A chuckle, warm like sunlight, spills from Zy and the ground trembles. “The tether became fully anchored when you punched this person in the face.”

Fucking hells. I’ve been more involved in chaining myself to her than I thought.

“You drain their energy,” Zy says.

“What?”

“Your hungry little fann energy molecules draw on the fann

side of your Soul Tether's jint energy."

"The fann side?"

"Jint essence molecules are neither a mix nor a balance of fann and unama. One molecule has signatures of both, a sidedness if you will. The signatures are present to create something other than fann or unama, whereas my Earthkin essence is a balance of separate fann and unama energy molecules."

If I'm constantly drawing on her energy, how is she even alive? Does she have that much energy to spare? I had just started trying out Mind Fire around Registration and it became easier afterward, especially after punching her in the face. This is fucking ridiculous. I've completely screwed us over.

"You absorb the fann energy their essence puts out into the atmosphere. It essentially doubles the amount of energy at your disposal for fire manipulations."

"So, she doesn't gain anything from the tether?"

"Not likely."

"But what happened when she was dying, was I dying too?" I ask, my own abrasive voice kicking at the pain in my head. "I felt just as sick, or even worse than I do now, but she was just across town."

"The shock of her dying, of the mental, physical, and spiritual energy between you breaking, could have killed you, yes, but . . . I think you were giving back the energy you stole from her to keep her alive. It's possible that you converted the physical energy you gained from her into mental energy. You sustained her mind to avoid death. You two have a very special connection. The most stable one-sided tether I've ever seen."

The ground stops thrumming. My eyes flutter open to stare at my hands. I want to know my thoughts and intentions, not be ruled by them. I don't want to be so removed from myself that I don't even know what I'm doing or know what I want. It screwed everything up. I've damned Rin because I wasn't able to let her go and then I fucking saved her. But if I was so mad at her for all those years, why couldn't I let her go?

Zy's eyes flare with golden light. Her lips part and her chin raises. The energy in the garden builds with heat and my stomach drops.

"I see a door," Zy murmurs. "Energy flows back and forth through it. The energy is warm and stimulating, sacrificing and accepting. But . . . the door closes. Energy on one side fades completely, and on the other, the energy starts pooling. It's trapped, it thrashes and consumes, and . . . it can't be contained on the one side . . . "

Her eyes snap closed, sending my head reeling from the shift of light exposure to the dark of the night. Zy shakes, leaning heavily on one hand in the grass.

"What happens on that side?" I ask.

"I-I don't know. I think it's best if you leave now, for both our sakes."

I scramble to my feet. The grass under my toes is like glass, the trickle of water a rush, and winter blankets me with a bitter chill. "Are you all right?" I ask.

"I'm fine. Future readings just take a toll on me."

My body protests against every breath and tears stream from my eyes. I turn from her and make my way back to the hut. At the screen door, my toes catch on the track. I land hard on my knees. The wraiths gasp but they keep their damned laughter to themselves, exchanging the mischievous glint in their eyes for awe. My mouth dries in their presence.

"Johanna, are you okay?" Lance offers a hand, but I push it away and crawl to my shoes. As I slip on one boot, he whispers, "She doesn't play around, does she?"

I hold the other boot, nodding. My mind is going to burn me alive if I don't get out of here. The boots ground me with their heavy soles and rustic leather scent. I don't want to have to put myself back together like this, one foot after the other, one experience, one thought—it's too exhausting. I just want to go home.

8

RIN

There's been no word about Liam. His absence brings the room's cold closer around me, and I curl deeper into the corner, bringing the blanket to my chin. After the physical exam yesterday, I curled up in bed, and I've been here ever since. Not really sleeping. I wish I could sleep. I wish I could escape the Vein.

I think I could escape, but it would be a matter of timing and a lot of luck. There's an exit by Brand's office, but she's the only one with a key. It leads into the mountains—the Fōstrank, also knows as the beast range. Bitterly cold, not well marked, and full of essence syphoners. They could suck my essence right out of my cells if they got close enough. A swarm of syphoners with razor-sharp teeth and long talons clouds my mind. An essence syphoner attack is survivable if they just drain essence channels. But I don't have essence channels. My essence would burst out of my skin cells, then my muscles and my organs, blood everywhere. The red of that image lingers behind my eyelids a little too long.

There's an exit by Devin's, but everyone knows I'm not supposed to leave. It's a popular traffic route, so I wouldn't be able to slip through, even though I know the code—nine, nine, five, zero, one, eight, seven—someone would see me.

I press my eyes closed and run my fingers over the smooth piece of curestone in the triangular pendant Adrianne gave me. If she were here, I'd tell her I don't know if I can go on. If she were here, she'd tell me she knows, and I'd believe her. She would also tell me I can beat my pain, and I'd believe that too. It's hard to believe when I tell it to myself though.

The dark is heavy, my mind goes blank, but my body doesn't rest; I just lie here, immovable. My skin is rough and dry from the recycled Vein air. My hair is oily at the roots but straw-like at the ends strewn over my pillow. The muscles and bones in my arms tense around my blankets, protecting me from something, anything. My feet are hot, tangled up in the sheet, pulsing with energy that could be used to run, but I can't go. With heavy beats, my heart keeps me conscious.

A knock rattles the door. I twitch, eyes opening. Air goes into my lungs and stays.

The knock sounds again.

"Rin."

The voice is stark and stale, with no pitch to inform me of intention.

"Rin."

Louder this time, still, even.

Brand opens the door. A rush of voices and footsteps follows her into the room before she shuts the door again. I turn back to the wall. Her presence prickles the back of my neck.

"It's past noon," she says.

Silence spreads over the room like wind, swiping her scent over to me, something I haven't picked up on until now—something sweet like a peach with a more abrasive tone like weckler wood. The prickle at my neck grows hot as she shifts.

"Come with me, we're going to train the death affinity today."

My stomach tightens, and I curl my knees to my chest.

"Come, just for an hour."

An hour. If only an hour was a short amount of time, or if time itself made any sense right now. It passes over me like a river. I move with it, but not as fast as others in the rapid current at the top. I'm stuck in a competing current that is slow and washes back and forth at the bottom near the cool soil below.

Brand's hand finds my leg. Through the tangle of sheets, it is a clamp that shakes me to life. I sit up, pulling my leg away from her.

"Get dressed. Training is the best thing you can do for Liam right now. I'll wait outside."

My throat grows tight as she leaves. Shallow breaths weave through me, in and out. Heat blisters in my cheeks.

Training. That's what I've been doing to keep him safe. Make sure I can keep my affinities under control. It's important, but I'm not sure it's the most important thing. I need to be close to him. I just don't know how to do both.

I stumble out of bed, cringing as my toes greet the icy concrete. I dress and scrunch my hair into a bun and meet Brand outside my door. Brand waits with her arms crossed.

Her glassy grey eyes flick to my shirt. "You like the Ease Beetles?"

I run my hand over my shirt, but I don't want to chit-chat. Mentally, I'm back in that tangle of sheets.

"Why haven't we found Liam yet?" I ask.

Brand lets out a controlled breath and her arms fall to her sides. "The Revival scatters when we're on their tail. We've checked their known hideouts, notified the LP missing persons units and our other bases. We're doing our best, but anytime we get close, they spook. Everyone knows everyone between the Revival and the Vein, so they always know we're coming." The muscles in Brand's throat twitch. Her eyes shift over me, like she's waiting for a response. I answer her eyes with a blank face. She nods and turns to the elevator.

I follow with an ache in my chest because I'm just expected to take her guidance and stay hidden. If I come out of hiding, then they'll come to me, won't they? I'm what they want. So, if they come to get me, they'll take me to Liam. We could escape together and leave all of them behind—both the Vein and the Revival. But what about the other Ironskins who are still out there? What if I don't escape and the Revival is a success? Won't everyone brought to life be divided, too, choosing between the philosophies of the Vein or the Revival? What if they don't want that choice? They could all just kill themselves again. What if I just kill myself? Then no one can perform the Revival. But there could be some seventeen-year-old Ironskin out there learning about their affinities and anxiously looking forward to testing and the next step of their life, just like me. The Revival could find them.

My breath gushes out of me, loud and harsh in the confined metal elevator. Brand turns to me.

"Are you okay?" she asks.

"Why would you think I'm okay?" I say, staring at the flashing lights marking the floors we pass.

Brand stares at me. Her chest rises and falls steadily. "Right."

The elevator reaches the very bottom level with a lurch that makes me sway from foot to foot. I continue to follow Brand through the bottom level of the Vein—the deepest vessel of this network of hidden corridors deep in the mountains. The corridor we follow is darker than the ones above, but the swirling patterns of reds, blues, and purples, becomes more elaborate. They fill the walls, cutting up and down, Slyvic markings telling all sorts of stories—stories that would take so much effort to read that they exhaust me just looking at them.

The markings weave a net around us and lead to a grand staircase of polished marble and iron railings. The room surrounding the stairs is cavernous, with a domed ceiling of white tiles and lightstones placed at even intervals throughout, like stars in an otherworldly sky. Our footsteps echo through the room, along with my breaths that swell through the majestic space. Twisted pillars of marble connect sky to ground and urge me to descend the stairs. Each step takes me closer to a red-tile circle at the bottom ringed by the spiral columns.

A whisper of wind circles around me. It comes from the far-left side of the room, from sliding doors with a sign for a garage exit.

I stop at the bottom of the steps, just before the white tile bleeds red. The circle glistens, colour shifting from blood-red to crimson and deepens to inky black as I shift my eyes.

Brand places a hand on my back, pressing me forward to cross the blood-like tile to a shrine embedded in the far wall. My steps slow and my knees weaken as the mosaic in the shrine becomes clear. Shards of yellow crystal, amber, and black onyx depict flowing hair. Iridescent opals of all colours shade her skin in varying hues. Grey slate stands in as a stark contrast for her eyes. Keena herself stares at me, modelled in stone.

Nolaria, with her ghostly complexion and powerful horns, sits in a gold frame in front of Keena surrounded by incense, dried herbs, and two pictures of affinity monks—one in sky-blue robes, the other in fiery red. She was the queen who fostered the community of Ironskins who had spirit affinities in ancient times, urging them to find balance in themselves to control their power. There's a softness to her intense blue gaze—the constantly engaged life affinity that cured her blindness.

A few cushions line the floor in front of the shrine for prayer. I take a final teetering step and drop to my knees. Every lineage ancestor is present on these walls, including the very first enhanced hédin, Carnity and Dien. Carnity stands tall next to Keena in glistening black onyx, pearls, and star crystals. On the other side is Dien in sandstone and copper. The circular structure of the room makes it so whichever ancestor you stand in front of becomes central, but they're always surrounded by the others.

Brand kneels on the cushion next to me. She touches her fingers to her forehead and then to her heart. I do the same with a shaking hand.

"We lost our way." With all the space in the room, Brand's voice, usually monotone, has room to spread. It's soft, broken. "Ironskins always had power, we always had pride. It took the collective effort of our ancient ancestors to keep that power untainted by pride. Everyone needed to know that they had potential for good and evil and they needed to steady themselves through the love and kindness of the people around them."

I run my fingers along the seams of my jeans, my heart beating in slow, heavy thuds, and I glance at Brand. She keeps her eyes trained on Keena, fingers still on her knees.

"One person's weakness wouldn't burden them because they were supported," she says and swallows hard. "One person's unique qualities were praised and used for the good of the community. Good things always get twisted though. Pride grew, desire for power grew, unique became individual, and kindness became perfectionism."

Her words ring through my ears as I stare at Nolaria.

"The world has reason to distrust us, and the Revival is exactly that reason." Brand stands and walks to the middle of the blood-red circle.

The murals of the ancestors bring the ancient world close. With Nolaria and Keena in front of me, I almost have comfort in my skin, a possibility of wholeness. With Brand and Geret giving me two conflicting images of rebuilding, the possibility is muddied. Geret told me he wanted Ironskins to be together, but I think together in his mind just increases numbers and builds power. I see Brand wanting to bring us back together, but she left all this once when she didn't want anything to do with the Vein or with me. Can I trust her to carry on Nolaria's dream of peace?

"We'll train here," Brand says.

All the ancestors follow me with their gleaming eyes into the centre of the hall.

"The affinities draw power from emotional energy and

physical control." Brand starts to pace around me. "Essence in the hands is highly active, so it's the easiest place to activate a select portion of your skin with the death affinity or life affinity. That's why the ultimate abilities, Demon Palm and Angel Palm, exist."

"You want me to activate Demon Palm?"

"No, the opposite. I want you to activate your red blood cells with the death affinity. I have a theory that projecting the energy inward, and having it flow through you, will change the effect of Demon Palm to a slow energy drain that won't result in death."

That seems logical, but also ten steps too far for me. Activating the affinity without breaking something would be step one.

"Has anyone even done that before?"

"No." Brand clasps her hands in front of her. The lightstones provide her with a halo of gold around her ringlets and give her features a sharp edge between warmth and dark shadow.

I run my hands up my arms, pacing along the red circle now that Brand has stopped moving. "Why do we call it . . . it?"

"What do you mean?"

"Why are the spirit affinities set apart from me?" I skip my boots along the smooth tiles and stare up at the twinkling stones. "The life affinity always felt like . . . " A taunting ghost, greedy. "Like a separate entity until Sii. In the story about Nolaria, her adviser, Renya, said the life affinity was a manifestation of goodness inside us. But in Sii, when I engaged it for the first time with full control, nothing I was feeling was necessarily good."

I let it all in. Every part of that day, of that moment, of me.

"The death affinity," I say. "It keeps coming up like it really is a part of me, oozing out of my veins." Stopping, I turn to Brand with the iridescent Keena behind her. "Doesn't separating the spirit affinities from the person confirm that old myth about the Ironskin Lineage being infested by demons and fallen angels? Like we're not in control?"

Brand nods. "Let's examine why that way of thinking exists. What made people think that?"

I sigh. The rush of air lessens the pressure in my chest but brings a surge of blood through my limbs. I shake them out. "We literally form angel wings and demon horns."

"Would you believe me if I said you could choose the form in which you project the energy of the spirit affinities?"

"Are you saying that we chose for people to see us like demons?"

Brand nods. "I'm saying the way you see yourself is how you project your energy. Whether you believe in them or not, demons and angels represent power. The ultimate spirit affinity abilities have always been to take and give life, nothing to maintain. Will you work with me to change that?"

I know what my father taught me about Ironskins and the Fourth Great War. How they used their power to hurt people. And now with the Revival, people will get hurt again. I understand the need for change.

"Yes," I say. The affirmation gets strangled in my throat. I can't separate the Revival so far from Father and Brand. Reform, change. It's taken them too long to bring me into that and now it's apparently on me to make the change. "But . . . There's so much. So much to learn and unlearn and . . . and I don't know if I can trust you."

Brand's chin raises as she watches me pace around her. I flex my fingers and crack them at my sides.

"For six years, all I had to depend on was Oron and myself. Just keeping myself alive along with another little hédin took all my energy. I didn't get time to learn about the affinities before I had to use them. Now you're telling me to change it. And you could have helped me do that already. You've been around all this time."

I catch her eyes for a second, but they run away, up to the ceiling and around the room. She touches her brow, eyes back on the floor. "Look, Rin, I told you your mother didn't want me in your life."

"Maybe she was right. Maybe she saw all that power and duty in you too. Or not enough. Not your responsibility, right?" I step off the red line. The room carries my voice and pushes me closer to Brand, my face and eyes blazing hot but not yet demonic.

Breath raises Brand's chest. Her lips press together and her eyes twitch as they meet mine. My stomach aches and the rush of blood stings inside me as her silver irises shy away from me again.

"You think that just because we're both Ironskin you can relate to me." I scoff, shaking my head, an incredulous smile playing on my lips. "But you know nothing about me or how I operate."

"I don't relate to you, I am you!" Brand bridges the gap between us so we're eye to eye.

Her scent washes over me and sinks into my skin. Chills crawl up my spine and the hairs on my arms stand straight.

I squeeze my eyes to shut her out and say, "Like hell you are. You're a prestigious Commander, and you have it all under control."

I jerk my arms to rid her presence from my skin, but she won't move. Her ghost face stares at me, grimacing, curls quivering around her face.

"The Vein was my parent's life. They lived and died for it," she says. Her smooth, cool voice jumps high, just short of a shriek. It shocks me into silence. "The Vein came first, and when the Revival broke away, my mother, your grandmother, left with them. It tore our family apart. My sister lived for it, too, until it broke her. Cassy was abused by the system. They used her speed to gather intel, but she was captured and tortured to give up her secrets. When she escaped, she came back to the Vein and asked for help. They didn't give it to her, said it was her problem to deal with, they had to keep moving forward."

A rush fills my ears. Drawing my arms around myself and turning my face to Keena, tears tempt my eyes. Keena looks down at me, a shadow falling over her face like regret. I always knew my mother was haunted, I just didn't know by what.

"So, Cassy left, and when she left, I left," Brand says, her voice cracking. "I became a Warrior to follow my own path far away from them." She crosses her arms tight around herself, causing her shoulders to pull forward and she shrinks. "My family was all gone when I came back. I was alone, and I was too stupid to realize you were too. Is that what you want to hear? I'm a stubborn bone head. But now"—she jabs her fingers at the ground—"now we have to fix it. We can't stay away."

My breaths are heavy, but hers are heavier. They crash through the grand hall. Brand's face blooms red, her eyes glisten.

My insides are like a wound broken open. Blood rushes, everything stings, and aches, and I can't tell where the pain is coming from. Her eyes make it so much worse. They're eyes that don't cry enough, like my mother. They're eyes that have seen too much pain, like my mother, and they're eyes that see too much of me, like my mother. And my mother isn't here, making Brand's eyes dead and intangible.

"Just . . . " Brand sighs, eyes pinching shut, head jerking to the side, finally pulling away from me. "Just work with me."

I take in a long breath through my nose. Tension crawls over my body and the lightstones might as well have been removed from the ceiling because the only thing I see is her and the exit to the garage behind her.

"Fine," I say, my voice nothing but breath.

Brand's shoulders lower by an inch and the colour drains from her face. "Focus on your blood flow and place your palms together. Set an intention for the . . . for your death affinity to match your blood flow. From your fingertips, through your arms, and your chest."

Blood is the only thing in my mind. It's rapid, warming, and colours the tips of my fingers pink. My arms are like stiff tree branches I have to force to bend. But I connect my hands and close my eyes. My intention is only to get Liam back, the one person I truly love.

The heat in my body elevates. It blisters over my skin like a spreading disease. My eyes burn and go dry, itching like sand has been poured into them. And just for a second, my blood vessels pulse through my skin with ruby-red light.

9

JOHANNA

I NEVER THOUGHT I WOULD BE SO RELIEVED to see the gates of Senn. The pain has settled to a dull pressure like the irritation of wearing a hat too long. Which means Rin must be close.

Mom rests one hand on the wheel and her arm on the window ledge as we wait for the gate to open. Her signature perfume has filled the cruiser with tones of salia wood, white-bean blossoms, and sugar. She set the heat at the perfect temperature and turns the audio player to a classical station—just like she would when she would drive me to and from school each day. All these things I didn't think I needed. Her most of all. That has to change, though, because the door closed, and I don't know which side the energy gets stuck on, mine or Rin's. I can't let it close without knowing what makes me just like Mom, what makes the Soul Tether to Rin so special, and how I'm still nothing like either of them.

I drink in Mom's scent and lean my head back, thankful for her silence and for letting me savour this mundane moment as Local Protectors yell back and forth over the screech of the metal gate opening and the patter of rain on the roof.

An LP waves us forward and we drive through the gate into the city. It's late and the haunting glow of streetlight spills over the rough roads. Buildings tower over us, stealing air and taunting the pressure in my head. The cruiser sloshes through puddles on the side of the road, splattering a street vender's cart.

"Fucking asshole," the owner yells after us.

Mom holds up her pinky finger to reverse the sentiment. I chuckle as she glances over at me with a smile spreading her ruby lips.

We pull into our garage just before nine. Mom sits for a moment in the dark after powering down the cruiser's firestone with her mind.

"Well, Joey," she says. "Why don't you put your things in your room, and I'll make us something to eat."

I nod to her. I want to say something. Our last conversation was after the winter formal. Which could be why she's so quiet. She told me about her and Rin's mom, how they were close and she lost her. My chest tightens thinking about it.

"Okay, thanks," is all I can say. I slip out of the cruiser, but Mom stays behind.

Inside, I touch my forehead and my heart as I pass my father's image. Switching on the lights in the kitchen, the smallest changes to the immaculately clean house spark my attention. On the tall stools by the kitchen island are round, mint-green cushions, and on the counter is a ceramic bowl filled with pinichu berries and yellow loa melons. A soft, cream-coloured rug bridges the wood floor connecting the kitchen to the living room. I squish my toes in the soft threads. It's the same one we looked at in the store a few months before I left for school. She said we didn't need it, that it would be something extra to keep clean. For a final touch, she has a small, round prickle bush in a terracotta pot on the centre table next to a scented candle.

All the new additions keep the house just as practical as before, but with a little added comfort.

"Do you like it?" Mom asks from behind me.

"Yeah, it looks nice."

She joins me in the living room and lights the candle with a flick of her wrist. "I had to get a little something to fill the space while you were gone."

I run my hand through my curls and stare at the ground. Mom heads back to the kitchen. Within seconds, my feet cross the strange carpet and I wrap my arms around Mom from behind. She tenses and relaxes, leaning her head against mine.

There are so many things I could say right now—apologies, thank-yous, guess whats—but I can't choose one. They are jammed in my throat so I just bury my face in Mom's silky hair. Her hands wrap around my arms.

"Go put your things away. Take your time." She rubs her smooth hands over my fingers and lets go.

My room is chilly, still, almost like it thought I wouldn't be back. The tech games in their plastic cases are rigid, the blankets on the bed are settled after a year of being unfluffed, the few pieces of clothes I left behind hang long and lonely in the closet. I flip on the light. Kneeling by the games, I expect dust, but each case is wiped clean. My heart aches. I can almost feel Mom's lingering presence, coming up here every week to make sure it stayed clean for me when I came home.

Maybe it's not the room that didn't think I would be home. Mom sure knew I would be. Why do I keep thinking I wouldn't be home?

I sink down cross-legged on the floor. I run my hands over the carpet, over my legs, and grab a controller to steady my hands.

Be careful, you're Soul Tethered.

Every time I experience the tether between me and Rin, I am incapacitated. Sometimes I wonder if it will kill me. I sure wondered if Rin would kill me when I started that fight in class. She was at full power, I know, because I was at full power. Our moves were stronger, brighter, and faster than even during the attack at Sii. Sii. That airbus back to the academy was never guaranteed once the attack started.

I press one of the buttons on the controller, revelling in the light click, the shape of the controller, and how the plastic makes my hands sweat. Turning it over, I run my finger along the little star sticker on the back. Rin put it there to mark it as the better controller when we were little, the one with the right bumper that doesn't stick when you press it in.

I put the controller back in the cubby next to the tech games, unpack my things, and head downstairs. Mom has set out two plates with keeta wraps for us at the island so we can sit side by side. There's a bottle of water for us to share, two glasses, and napkins by our plates. After my ascension tournaments when we would come home late, she'd always make us a little meal like this. She never lets us skip meals or eat too much.

"Hey," she says as we sit. "Are you okay?"

I nod as I adjust myself on the cushion. The fabric is still new and stiff. "Yeah, just happy to be home. This year was . . ." I shrug, "I don't even know what it was."

"Me too, Zenta knows. When I saw you on the news about the festival attack, I had the entire living room hovering with Mind Fire because I was so stressed."

I take a bite of my wrap and a dribble of lemon dressing trickles down my hand.

"It's not just the attack," I say through a mouthful of keeta and chicken.

Mom takes a dainty bite of her own wrap. She chews, ten times like she always taught me, swallows, and dabs her mouth with a napkin—all with a crease between her eyes. Her moment of thought sends a prickle of heat through my chest. She always has a reply. But as she lifts her eyes to me, the crease softens, her eyebrows loosen their tight arches. She's fought off her reply and she's waiting for me.

A gush of air spills out of me and my eyes prickle. "Remember in eleventh year ed at the end of the year? I had this massive headache that just fucked me up and I couldn't do anything?"

Mom nods. Her lips press together and her head tilts to the side.

"I found out that it was because I'm Soul Tethered to Rin. She tried to end her life and the pain was . . ." My heart pounds. "I gave her energy to keep her alive." My head is heavy with a rush of blood.

Pools of tears swell in her light-green eyes, but she takes a finger to each of them to collect the waters and save them for later. "Go on," she whispers.

"She has so much power and I just take it like a leech without knowing." My own tears spill down my cheeks. "It connects me to Wander Wraiths in the Wander Lands. I've spoken to one . . . and . . ." I try to swallow a lump of chicken, but it goes down slowly and I cough and sputter until I can speak again. "A Seer had . . . she gave me a mystery of our Soul Tether, of a door that connects us. But it closed." My body trembles. I brace myself on my knees, cradling my head in my hands. "Mom, it closed and energy on one side went away." The words shudder out of my mouth.

"All right, just breathe for a minute, okay? Breathe," she says, taking my wrap from me and pushing the plate aside.

I draw a slow, sluggish breath through my snotty nose and let all the hot air rush out of my mouth.

"What else?"

"I know you want me to find my person, just like you found Dad." Bracing my elbows on the counter, I hold my head in my hands. "But I won't ever feel those feelings. I had to tell a guy that really likes me that I don't want to be with him in that way. He was kind about it, but I could see he was in pain. He didn't get how I couldn't want a love like that. I don't get it either, but I know it. I-I'm sorry if that makes you uncomfortable."

The smile on Mom's face fades, but her ruby lips are safe from a frown as she buries herself in thought again. She takes a bite, chews, swallows. "Some of us have soul mates, some Soul Tethers, some of us just find people who fit. What gives me comfort"—she wipes a crumb from her cheek—"might not be the same thing that comforts you. So no, it doesn't make me uncomfortable."

My shoulders slump. I laugh into my hands as my face heats from all the emotional exposure that's new to both of us.

"Come," Mom says. "I want to show you something." She dusts off her hands and smooths her pants as she stands.

I follow her past Dad's memorial and wait for her to put on her slippers before she takes me into the garage. She walks up to Dad's speeder under a grey sheet. Hands clasped to her chest and back turned to me, she stares at it. The core-energy hub hums in the dark corner of the room. The cold of the cement bleeds through my bare feet and crawls up my shins.

"Mom?" I say.

"I got the parts we needed for the speeder." Slowly, she takes off the sheet. "I took it out for a test ride yesterday. It's ready to go."

I stare at the tight twist that holds her red hair on the top of her head with graceful accents of silver glinting in the light. She picks up a cloth to give the speeder a shine.

"He was always better at knowing what you needed or how to calm you or answer all your questions," she says. "He'd know how to console you about your Soul Tether."

"You pushed me to reconnect with Rin. I wouldn't have figured this out if you hadn't."

Mom smiles down at the greasy cloth in her hand. "I was only able to give you that call once I started working on the speeder, when I started learning from your father again." She takes a step away from the speeder and turns the soft smile to me. Looking right into my eyes and tucking a curl behind my ear with careful fingers, she says, "After we talked the night of the formal, I knew I had to learn from you about you, instead of pushing you into what I thought was right for you."

My heart pounds from her gentle touch. Mom moves over to the workbench and picks up a brand-new firestone charge-key with a silver chain.

"I'm allowing myself to remember him again." She wraps her fingers around mine, trapping the warm stone between our hands. "I forgot he always told me to enjoy the ride."

Her slippers scrape against the concrete as she takes a step back. I hold her hands tight. She stops, her hands curling back around mine.

Whenever Mom would give me driving lessons in the cruiser, she'd always have one hand clamped around the handhold, and the other would grab my leg if I sped up too fast or she thought I didn't see a sign. Her knuckles would go white. "For Zenta's sake, I'm holding on for both of us here," she'd say. I thought she didn't trust me. I would storm out of the garage and slam the door in her face because she never just let me do it myself. But I didn't realize that she held so tight because I was all she had to hold on to.

Taking the sleeve of her sweater, she wipes the tears from my face. "You can't ride with tears in your eyes. There. Now wear a helmet, and there's an extra in the compartment. Have fun."

I throw my arms around Mom, taking a deep breath of her overpoweringly sweet scent. "Thank you."

RIN

I WAITED UNTIL THE HALLS WERE QUIET before making my way down to the grand hall again. I took my wooden box with me, the box with the memories I care about, because I don't know what my intention is—get some air or leave entirely.

The ancestors' stony eyes follow me as I try to keep my footsteps light. I skirt around the edge of the room and come to the garage door. I run my sweaty palms down my pants and then punch in the code, holding my breath.

The lock whirs and the door slides open. Heart in my throat, I whip around to make sure no one saw or heard me, even though I know only the ancestors are with me. I dart into the garage. It's dark and smells of city grime, burnt-out firestones, and wet tires. It's filled with all sorts of cruisers, speeders, and trucks, but I ignore them with my eyes set on the trail of lights leading down a tunnel.

I fill my lungs with air and bolt into the tunnel. I don't know where it will lead me or how long it will take to get there, but it will lead me out of the Vein. Lights flick on a few metres ahead of me as I run, then flick off as I leave them behind. Only the path directly in front of me is lit. I push my legs faster as the dark behind me threatens to catch up with the dark in front. I run faster, breaths heavy, palms sweaty even though they swipe through chilled air.

The path of light expands down two different tunnels. I slow, but only for a second for my eyes to catch the sign to Senn. With the slowed speed, my ears perk up at a rushing sound. Is that the blood in my head or the sound of a cruiser or just my heartbeat? I toss a glance behind me, but I'm only met with darkness. I bolt down the Senn tunnel.

The air thickens with moisture. It takes on a familiar stink—hédin and garbage and burnt-out firestone cores. I'm getting closer to Senn. To home. Not home. Liam isn't out there. I have no idea where he is. And I don't know where in Senn this tunnel leads.

Voices join the cold and wet. I stop my feet and press myself along the tunnel wall. It's slick and greets my back like a greedy, slimy monster meant to keep me in the dark. My heart beats into it, melding with the cold stone as my lungs heave for air in one last effort to fight off the dark. The lights flick off. The light sensors may not sense my movement, but my body lurches with each pulse. My eyes adjust to the dark, taking in a wide tunnel and a light at the end. There's a door big enough for a cruiser. Two figures stand on one side of it. On the other side of them is a smaller door with an exit sign. There are a series of pillars on either side of the tunnel that—if I'm lucky, calm, and quiet—may provide me cover to get through the exit.

If I move.

If only my body could stop complaining and my mind could see a point to escaping this dark, a way to get to Liam. But even if I get out of here, I don't know if I want to be out there alone.

I wet my lips in an attempt to prepare myself, but my knees go weak, and I slide to a crouch with the dim light going spotty. I lean my head on my knees.

WHAT THE FUCK ARE YOU DOING?

Starting, I wobble on the balls of my feet with a sharp gasp.

The voices down the tunnel go quiet. I clamp one hand over my mouth and steady myself on the ground with the other. The silence is pierced only by the drip of condensation from the ceiling. My mind heats like Johanna is breathing her hot, intrusive breath all over my brain.

YOU'RE MAKING ME SWEAT AND I JUST SHOWERED THIS MORNING.

All scorn, but her voice doesn't bite as bad as it used to. Tension releases from my chest.

Wow, I'm sorry my distress is such a burden to you. You almost gave me a heart attack. A little warning would be nice.

WHATEVER. WHAT ARE YOU EVEN DOING?

I'm trying to get out of . . . well wherever I am.

IT'S DARK. ARE YOU GOING TO GO THROUGH THAT DOOR

OVER THERE?

You can see what I see?

IT'S NOT REALLY SEEING . . . IT'S KNOWING WHAT YOU SEE. SOUNDS STUPID BUT IT'S ANNOYING SO I'M COMING TO YOU. I ASSUME YOU'RE IN SENN. I'LL MEET YOU ONCE YOU'RE OUTSIDE AND I KNOW WHERE YOU ARE.

I don't know when I became so okay with Johanna being in my head. But none of this sounds stupid. Having her here makes the tunnel less dark and long and cold, the door not so far away.

The voices build again with a few chuckles and scraping of feet as the two meandering forms fall back into easy conversation. I stand and inch my way along the wall, placing my feet heel to toe to diminish the sound.

ANY DAY NOW.

Do you have to yell?

I'M NOT YELLING.

Well, it sounds like it.

IT DOESN'T SOUND LIKE ANYTHING. YOU CAN'T HEAR ME.

Then how do I turn you off?

YOU DON'T TURN ME ON.

The silence, that is not silence, from the lack of Johanna's not-voice, ripples. The double entendre hits me, and I roll my eyes as she laughs at me.

Did you just make a sex joke?

MAYBE.

I make it to the door. Still in the shadows, I glance at the two figures. Just two guys on guard duty, it looks like. No weapons, but most people are born weapons in Illyson. I press the handle of the door as slowly as I can. The door doesn't budge.

DO YOU HAVE A KEY?

No, why would I have a key?

I'M SO CONFUSED. ARE YOU IN PRISON?

They're just trying to keep me safe.

NICE TONE.

You're not yelling but I have tone?

CHOOSE YOUR BATTLES, RIN. NOW, ARE YOU BUSTING OUT OR WHAT?

They'll hear me.

YES. THEY WILL.

You have to know my eyes are rolling.

NOW YOU GET HOW THIS WORKS.

I press my eyes closed. My mind is fuzzy, my feet itch to move. The second I bust out, if I can bust out, those guards will know. They'll call Brand. I'm really not looking forward to her being mad at me. I have no clue what I'm doing.

Taking a sharp breath, I bash my shoulder into the door. It bursts open and my feet jolt into a sprint.

"Hey! What the hells?"

"Dude, call the Commander."

The alley is long and dark, but neon lights from the street guide me out. A cruiser honks, electropulse swells around me, moans and grunts from the next alleyway repel me, and I sprint in the opposite direction. I throw my hood over my head and keep my head down, just like any other night in Senn.

I KNOW WHERE YOU ARE.

This is never not going to be creepy, is it?

PROBABLY NOT. TAKE A LEFT AT THE END OF THE STREET AND MEET ME AT THE LAIR.

Senn is abrasive, like gravel in snow. Dirty, cold, but I know it. I know how it reacts. One cacophony after another. A flare of headlights, "Fuck you!", cruiser backfire, sirens. If I run fast enough, other pedestrians will move and then cuss me out. I don't like the way it operates, but I like that I know it. I know how to be in this world. And I'm thankful for someone to run toward.

JOHANNA

I'VE NEVER ACTUALLY RIDDEN A SPEEDER BEFORE. The moment I sit down on it, I know it doesn't matter. The firestone that powers the machine sends its fann energy coursing through every wire, every piece of metal, and the rubber tires. Kinetic energy runs from the pavement through my bones. My mind syncs my nervous system and my body, the firestone and the machine.

The speeder roars and the wet pavement sheds a constant spray of water behind me. The night air is frigid, but I am energy that can't be frozen.

I skid to a stop outside the Lair. The firestone loses its orange glow, taking its heat with it. I dismount, and the vibration in my bones continues, but it's alone, there's no response to it. The pavement is too solid, the cold catches up with me, and the lights don't match the clarity I had just moments ago, when my mind and my body had the same energy. I'm detached. Frayed nerves and frizzy hair.

Hand on the metal doorknob dripping with rainwater, I stop, staring through the smudged glass. Rin sits in her red rain jacket, hood up, under a dangling blue light at the end of the bar. My jaw hardens. I spoke to her just a moment ago. But it's one thing to have a conversation with someone in my head. Whether they can respond to me or not, it's idealized. I put up a front of sarcasm with Rin and kept control because I know how Mind Fire works and she doesn't. It's a whole different dynamic seeing each other's eyes and the scars we've laid on each other.

I run my tongue over the little bump of tight, new skin on my lip. When Rin's elbow broke through my fire armour and bashed into my face, I really didn't feel like she was trying to hurt me, it just always happens that way.

I push open the door to the Lair, silver wraith bells jangling over head. The ring is pure, right into my being like it's hitting the auditory processing centres of my brain without being collected through my ears. They resound inside my skull for a few seconds, and I swear they're stuck there—no, they're coming from inside me? I shake my head. I may not be a Wander Wraith, but the bells really are effective.

The thick soles of my boots squelch over the sticky, cracked tiles. Walls of grey cement, pitted and stained by bottles gone astray, close in around tall tables with stools of mismatched wood and the bar that stretches through the centre of the room.

My ears ring like the bells that have long since faded, and Rin's posture stiffens with my approach. She turns on her stool. Her narrow nose pokes around the rim of her hood and her piercing grey eyes catch me in a stare that's both haunting and calm. My skin crawls and I don't know what to do with my face.

I yank her hood down further over her face. "Keep your head down. You're still a wanted woman, for fuck's sake."

The barb is a reflex, and I'm not sure when I learned it. Was it before or after she refused to stand by my side at my father's funeral?

Rin's eyes stay focused on me as I take the stool next to her. This close, my essence fortifies. It's stronger, deadlier. I just don't know how to be myself around her. Mental and physical energy is one thing, but my spirit still withers when we're together. If my intensity pushed her away, then will I continue to do that over and over again? Am I even allowed to still be angry when I was the one who suggested starting over? My emotion is always contrasted by her emptiness.

That's it. What makes us completely different. I start fights and she reacts. I say let's start over and she says she'll try. I get energy from her and she is emptied. After all that, she's still here, still strong even with depleted energy. I am always the child throwing the tantrum. She just decided not to deal with me that day at the swings. I don't blame her anymore.

Rin bites her cheek, otherwise she is still, stone, unreadable. I'm a mess, one foot in one foot out, hot under her steel gaze and cooled by her mental energy. She opens her mouth. Breath goes in, her lips preparing to speak. I slam my hand on the grubby countertop. She jolts, clamping her mouth shut.

"You have to let me be angry," I say.

My face heats as she stares at me.

"At you . . . at me. I'm angry at me for being so . . . awful. Too much."

Rin cringes. I know she's back there. On the swings, in the cold, soaked to the bone. We're both there right now. Two sides of the story piecing themselves together in my head.

Rubbing my arms to ward off the cold of the memory, I say, "I forgave your stupid ass, and you forgave mine. But that doesn't fix the fact that I shut off half of myself the day you pushed me down in the mud. The only self I know is the one that's angry." The words ache through me, leaving my throat sore and hoarse. My breaths come fast, filling and emptying, trying to exchange the poison inside me for something cleaner. All I get is the stench of ale. "I–I want to be other things too. Happy, sad, and whatever other fucking emotions are out there."

Cool static fills me. Rin's dark eyebrows pinch together as she works her jaw. The beginning and ending of her thoughts twist around in the haze of my mind. My curls shake around the side of my vision as essence pulses through me. This time I open my mouth to urge her on or cuss her out, I don't know, but she shakes her head with one quick jerk and presses her eyes shut to cut me off.

She exhales and says, "I hear you." Shifting away from me, the fabric of her jacket crinkles.

Still taking too many breaths, I do the same, with my eyes brimming with tears. Those three words are like a hot poker to my heart to cauterize a wound that's been festering for years. The hot rush to my eyes is a pain, an annoyance. I hate it and love it all the same.

I scrape my fingernails along my scalp, into my curls and pull. "I want that for you too."

The wraith bells ring, heavy tread, Ease, and the smoky bite of firestone cores blister over my senses with the rowdy crew of men entering the Lair.

Rin ducks her head lower. Her arms brace on the counter and her knee bounces underneath. Her thoughts are so fast, like a recording being played on fast forward. The curses are the loudest. I can't get the context, if they're directed at someone, me, or herself. Her breaths are audible even over the men on the other side of the bar.

I press my eyes closed, letting some of the moisture trickle through the creases. I focus on Rin's ice, the raggedness of her thought pattern, until I catch on to the jagged shards of the mess in her mind and piece a few together.

HE'S STILL ALIVE.

The shard pierces her, melting and gushing over her mind like hot blood.

Who?

MY FATHER. HE'S ALIVE.

Rin hides her face in her hands, mine are slick with sweat. Her shoulders cave in around her, shaking.

AND HE DIDN'T COME FOR US.

The man who died and left behind so much pain that fell right on Rin is still alive. She broke because of him. Cassy broke because of him. We broke because of him. The blue light above her bathes her in a pale glow, but she is red. Energy boils around her. Hot embers burn behind her hands, lodge in her skull. With a flash of ruby-red, horns spike from her forehead. They pulse but fade in the pale-blue light.

I wrap my arm around the demon girl beside me and steer her out of the bar into the darkness of Senn where we both start to breathe better in the cold.

I WASN'T ENOUGH FOR ANY OF THEM. I'M NOT . . . FUCK . . . WHY WOULDN'T HE. I'M HIS DAUGHTER . . . AND STEPHEN. MOM . . . NOT ENOUGH.

"You're enough for me."

I hold Rin.

"You're enough for me, okay?" I say again, taking her face in both hands.

The whites of her eyes have gone ink black, her irises red—blood-red, fire, sorrow blossoms, but not the red of the demon she thinks she is. Her tears boil from the heat of her essence, and the veins around her eyes bulge. I run my thumb over the strained skin. "Your friendship has always been enough for me."

Our friendship was broken for six years. She was my only friend before that and hanging onto her through hatred and harsh words and unnecessary fights was the closest thing to normal I could get. It was normal to have her around me. We pushed each other and took each other's shit. No wonder I tethered us at Registration.

"That's why it hurt so much," I say.

Her teeth clench and her throat strains to swallow. She searches me. No matter how much more enhanced her sight is from the death affinity, she still can't see it. She can't see my truth. That's why the wire that tethers me to her doesn't go the other way. I don't think she's even tethered to herself.

"Rinnaya," I whisper, stroking the pulsing vessels beneath her eyes.

Tears crest her eyes and spill as steam into the air.

I take a breath. Rin's chest rises in a breath of her own. I breathe and she breathes. The blood drains from her face, bringing the pale, cool-eyed girl back to me.

The collection of societal norms I have stashed in my mind urges me to smile at her. I lock the stash away and light it on fire. My cheeks are heavy, and my eyes burn from the light that has left Rin empty again. I take her to my speeder and hand her a helmet.

"Put it on," I say.

She doesn't even hesitate and stuffs her head behind the tinted visor. I put on the spare helmet and get on the speeder.

"Where are we going?" Rin asks as she climbs on behind me, no spark of life in her voice.

"I don't know," I say, heating the firestone with my mind. "Just hold on."

The speeder lurches forward, kicking up pebbles and spraying water on the front of the bar. I accelerate as fast as possible. Rin screeches behind me and tightens her grip around my waist.

We are flying through the city, the lights blurring at the edge of my vision, the freezing air whips my hair around my face, energy coursing through my veins and pumping my heart. Weaving around parked cars and potholes, slipping in and out of streetlights and neon signs, the roar of the speeder could wake the dead as we pass the graveyard.

"Take a left at the intersection," Rin yells.

I don't know where she's taking us, but I turn, letting her guide me until we end up in her neighbourhood. Speeding through the dilapidated apartments of Rin's street, she doesn't make us stop. The street becomes dim as lights in the windows dwindle to none. We end up in the old, Ironskin quarter, which is said to be cursed by Ironskin energy. No one's lived here for decades and probably no Embersteads have ever stepped foot on these streets. This part of Senn is a scar on the city left by the Fourth Great War.

"Here," Rin says, and points to a towering archway. "Slow down." Her mind crackles as she loosens her arms, tapping me a little. I smile as her urgency sparks a thrill in my gut.

I pull in under the archway leading to the neighbourhood. The pillars are covered in graffiti, the stone top is shaded by a small, tiled roof jutting out on each side, tapering to a point as it curls to the sky. The tiles were blue once, now the colour is faded and only preserved in patches.

Rin slides off the speeder and moves toward the gate. Waving me over, she ducks under a chain blocking off the entrance. She leads me down the cobblestone path to a tall building at the end. The building towers over the small sector of the city, at least five storeys. It is built into the part of the city wall that climbs into the mountains. Wooden planks form a platform around the building connected with wooden pillars in the same faded blue as the archway. The windows are wide and low to the ground, a lattice of wood painted red separates panes of glass.

We stand for a minute in silence under a banner spread over the door with Slyvic markings on it, just an Ironskin and an Emberstead standing side by side in the midst of ruin. My shoulders fall. My people are the reason that her people aren't here. We're the reason why the paper lanterns have fallen to the ground, crinkled, torn, and dark, void of lightstones. We're the reason Rin lives three blocks away and not in the quaint peaked houses painted blue and red with quiet gardens in the back.

"Eenwa seya ha," Rin says.

"What?"

Rin motions to the banner fluttering above. She points to each black symbol painted on the red cloth and slows down her speech. "Ee-ne-wa se-ya ha. It translates as the path of life has brought you here. It means welcome."

Rubble crunches under my boots. Rin removes her helmet. A gust of wind blows her hair around her face and prickles my neck. The unfamiliar words roll around in my head. *Eenwa seya ha.* They have a warmth to them with the way Rin pronounces the syllables, the *ha* coming from the back of her throat. Her eyebrows knit together as she stares at the banner.

The wind whirs through the cracks of the door. "Why'd you bring me here?"

Rin presses her lips together and tucks her hair behind her ear. "Come," she says, prodding me in the side with her sharp elbow.

She runs into the building through the shattered glass doors. I follow her and she sprints up a flight of stairs. As we take the stairs two at a time, up farther and farther, I get a picture in my head of us when we were little. We used to play tag. I would always catch her right away but she would try her hardest. Rin never gave up on a challenge and she never did anything half ass. She ran into everything headfirst.

We come to a point where the stairs have caved in. We scramble over the rubble. There's no way to get to the next landing, but that doesn't stop Rin. She pumps her arms once then jumps straight up, a good ten feet in the air, and catches hold of an exposed beam. She pumps her body back and forth until she gets enough force to swing herself over to the next level, pinwheeling her arms to keep her momentum moving forward once she lands. She looks down at me and waits. Even if I propel myself with a burst of fire, I probably can't make that jump. Rin puts her hands on her hips as she waits.

Along the stone walls to the next level, there is a trail of holes all up the wall. She's been coming here for years, I bet, and those holes are probably handholds she made herself to get up there from a time when she wasn't strong enough to make the jump. I get it now. She's letting me into her space, showing me a part of her life that she lived alone.

Eenwa seya ha.

I start in the middle of the landing and push off, angled toward the wall, propelling myself with a stream of fire. I plant my feet on the wall and spring off to the other side, a little trick I picked up from Rin during that second day of training at the academy. I aim a little higher each time I push off and move my way up with little bursts of fire.

We head up a final flight of stairs and end up on the roof.

Senn spreads out ahead of us. The governor's tower and the Registration building stick out in the centre like a sore thumb amongst the common buildings stacked on top of each other. The city lights, caught by the smog, create a halo ringed in by the city walls. I take a deep breath, inhaling the same air I've breathed all my life, but up here it's easier to swallow.

Rin zips her jacket up to her chin and slips her hands into her pockets.

"You broke in half," she says. Her face is dark on this lightless balcony. "And I, uh . . . collapsed."

The screech of an LP cruiser fills the air from the city. Behind us, a howl bellows far off in the dark mountains. I take a seat on an old crate and wait for Rin to continue.

"I loved my parents," she says, shifting her feet. The past tense of her statement digs into my heart. Starlight accentuates the small flex of her jaw muscle. "But I always felt a little . . . lost I guess, even when they were around."

I nod with a shiver and create a small flame to float between us. Rin turns to me, the light of the flame flickering across her stoic features. She stares at her feet.

"Coming to this place made me feel connected to other Ironskins."

AND NOW THAT I HAVE CONNECTED WITH OTHER IRONSKINS IN THE VEIN, I CAN'T SEEM TO FEEL LIKE I BELONG THERE EITHER.

Her thoughts slip in, quiet, to fill in what she hasn't spoken.

"It's been so hard to connect with my own people." The muscles in her face tighten and her eyes squint in pain. She shakes her head. "Maybe you're my people." Her shoulders shrug as she turns back to look over the city just as a shred of red light sparks her eyes.

I take a long breath. The cold air bites my nose. Standing to lean over the railing next to Rin, it's clear now that this is where we start over. We didn't start over when I asked her to, it was too much right after the fight. It's here. I know because my spirit is still. I don't have to be any specific way around her anymore. We can just be.

We watch the city for a while, until I can't stand the cold.

"I should probably go back to the Vein," Rin says, looking down at her bare hands on the iron railing.

"Are you sure?"

She nods. "It's not that I want to go back, I just can't run. Not without more information."

There's more going on than her father's return. There's so much and it's overlapping. I can't attempt to read those thoughts.

"Okay, I'll take you back," I say.

Climbing down through the ruins, the route is familiar to my feet, even after one encounter. We replace our helmets. As we settle back onto the speeder, a face catches my eye in the dark across the street. A perfectly sculpted face with dark eyes and bronze skin. Tōmas, the boy who forced himself on Rin. My tongue dries like I just ate whisper weed. Why on the Karess is he in this part of the city?

I set my hand over Rin's, making sure they're clamped tight around me. I ignite the firestone with my mind, sending a jolt through the bike. The tires squeal and we speed away before she can see him.

12

ELIOTE

The early morning chill and the wash of green starlight revitalize my sleepy body as Mom and I shuffle in silence along the black basalt bricks to the shrine. Mom's aura sends tingles up my arms as it brushes over my skin. It is like a purple mist churning toward me and stretching to the shrine—her expectations are unreadable but not hidden from me. A flutter fills my chest, keeping my breaths quick.

Mom places her feet in reverent steps. I do the same and let the lush, traditional Luminee clothes swish around me in the quiet morning. Mom and I match in long, flowing pants of silver silk and a tunic that drapes down to our knees in magenta linen. Over the layers, she wears a crisp, black velvet robe with a gold sash. This type of robe is only worn by the ka'haletna Mavesh na'Vin—the priestess of our revered ancestor Vin. They are specially tailored, seams stitched with golden thread and blessed by the previous ka'haletna.

"So, why do you have to come so early this week?" I ask, as I hold my arms tight against the cold.

"The Festival of the Heart is an important time to thank Vin for his provision through the long nights of winter as we look forward to the light of the spring," Mom says. "I must say a prayer each morning as the stars and moon fade to bring Vin's attention closer to the shrine as many will come during the festival to pray."

I smile at her back as the layers of cloth flutter around her like flower petals. The early hour doesn't bother me, and I'm happy she asked me to help. I never thought I would get a chance to be so close to her world.

Mom stops at the steps of the shrine. She turns to me, handing over a wooden box of ever-lights. Her hands are covered in Luminee script. On her left hand are markings that indicate her mastery over level-three Luminee-essence abilities that she acquired while I was at the academy this past year, and on her right are the marks of a ka'haletna. Her skin is still red from the new ink.

I take the box. "The robe looks good on you."

Smoothing the heavy fabric and tightening the sash, she smiles to herself, head still bowed. "This is my first festival as ka'haletna. I want to make sure everything is perfect." Turning back to the shrine, she touches two fingers to her forehead and then her heart and bows deeply. "Exchange the dark-lights for ever-lights at the base of each pillar and then come inside. Don't forget to bow." She looks over her shoulder at me as the wind picks up her dark-purple hair and shifts it around her face. The wrinkles around her eyes deepen and her gaze wavers. Her aura swirls around her, tight as if to guard against the cold. It glints in hues of purple, like liquid amethyst.

"Of course," I say, nodding and holding the box with careful hands.

Mom nods back and heads inside.

The shrine is a five-sided sandstone building with a dome roof. At each point where the five walls connect, there is an outdoor pillar. There are more windows than walls, really, all intricately cut glass and crystal letting natural light into the shrine.

I breathe deeply, fogging the air with long exhales as I follow the path lined with yellow energy suckles, their petals casting a glow on the first pillar. Throughout this winter break, the dark of night has been a refuge to me. Luminee aren't as powerful at night, not even those with shadow affinities, since shadow phasing isn't becoming a shadow. Instead, it's travelling at light speed along the line of light and shadow, distorting light waves around them to fool the eye. Luminee manipulate the light of the sun and moon easily, but green starlight is a wavelength Luminee can't manipulate. It's the middle of the light spectrum, not aligned with fann or unama, and Luminee don't like in-betweens. Shadow phasing is imprecise at night because the green light is so prevalent. But since the last Festival of Two Moons, auras have become clearer to me with the night. My heartbeat is sure and powerful in my chest. Maybe this time is meant for me?

Kneeling, I unhinge the little iron door at the base of the first pillar. There are five dark-lights sitting in a contraption that swivels around the pillar. They have a dim blue glow as the dawn approaches and once the sun is up, their glow will fade completely. I open the wooden box and recoil at the bright light of five rows of ever-lights. One by one, I remove dim stones from the pillar and replace them with the bright ones, so the pillars will be lit day and night throughout the festival. Once I've exchanged all the lightstones, I clench the last dark-light in my fist.

There are many kinds of lightstones. The one hanging around my neck is a green companion light. Balance, my grandmother reminds me. It shines when a Luminee touches it. Its brightness is a direct correlation to a Luminee's essence strength. Companion stones are everywhere, in all different colours. Ever-lights are always bright, but they are rare. This dark-stone I hold is the only stone I can make shine by blocking out natural light with my hands. It reminds me that I've found something that lights me inside, just a little shine. I need all the strength I can get to tell my mom that I think I need to change directions.

I close up the box so the dark-lights can glow in peace. At the front of the shrine, I tap my fingers to my head and my heart and bow. I pray that Vin will bless my family with health and strength, that my grandmother will have joy in her last few years on the Karess. And for me? What can Vin do for me? My heart is heavy, bending me lower, and Carnity's name comes on a breath to my lips. Maybe she can bring me clarity, strength to change my course. I thank Vin quickly to finish my prayers, since it is his shrine.

Just inside the door, I slip off my flats. The cold stone shocks my toes, and I move into the centre of the shrine, where Mom sits lighting fresh incense. White tiles mark out a star on the floor, each arm pointing to a corner of the room. The slap of my feet echoes through the room. Draped in purple and gold, the shrine is lavish, everything gleams and has purpose. Despite the beauty of this shrine, the Grand Temple in Yugon is a fortress compared to this. My grandmother took me once when I was little, and we both agreed never to tell my mom that we thought Vin got too much credit.

"Set the dark-lights on the stand here by the candlesticks."

I set the box down and kneel on the cushion next to Mom.

She lays an assortment of lightstones in front of us around the incense. One ever-light, one companion light that glows as her fingers brush past it, and one dark-light. The incense curls to the high ceiling and into my nose, overpowering my senses and leaving me dizzy. Mom places her hands together in front of her heart. I clench mine in the folds of my tunic. Not sure if she's praying or what I should do, I clear my throat and the harsh sound reverberates through the room.

"Uh, Mom?" I say with my voice as low as possible to make sure I don't disrupt the quiet and have the walls yell back to me.

"Mm?"

She's so still. Her aura streams straight up, glittering and rigid.

"I wanted to talk to you about something."

"What is it?" she asks and moves the incense closer to me.

"Well, at school we were introduced to a new flight-training program."

Her brow furrows as she moves the ever-light closer to me. "Flight training?"

"Yeah." My heart squeezes inside me. It thumps and urges me to retreat. "Small-scale airships have been manufactured for speed and aerial combat and a new training program has opened. They're looking for applicants going into their third year of Guardian training."

Starlight spills through the crystal windows and glints off Mom's metallic-gold nail polish as she moves the companion light over by the ever-light, so there's one stone in front of each of my knees.

"I was thinking I would apply to the Flight Academy for my third year of training."

With the dark-light clenched in her hand, blue spilling between her fingers, Mom huffs a string of the Luminee tongue in a harsh whisper. "*Mavesh na'Vin visashaya to norshaya ke rishat visa.*" She places the dark-light over the incense, then moves it over my head, behind me, back over my head, sweeps it through the smoke, and continues to wave it over me so there's a constant arc of blue light over my head.

My toes are ice cold, but a wave of heat spills down my neck. My cheeks burn. "You're not even listening to me."

A clatter sounds from the door of the shrine. Mom's hand stops overhead. We turn to the door in unison. A young woman about my age, with the darkest-purple hair I've ever seen and a glowing companion light around her throat, watches us with wide eyes as she bends slowly to pick up the scroll she dropped.

"Ah, Kia," Mom says in an airy voice. A smile flickers on her lips, and she drops her hand and the stone to her lap like she's trying to erase the Ritual in progress. "I told Riaan I wouldn't need you here until seven."

"Oh," Kia says, fingers grasping the bright lightstone. Her wide eyes fix on me. Her back goes rigid. "Is this your daughter?" Her voice wavers and the walls catch the hesitation bouncing it all around me.

"Yes, this is my daughter, Eliote." Smoothing her robe, Mom says, "Come back in an hour, Kia."

Kia turns, arms tight around her scrolls, and eyes still trained on me. "*Belhalia Mavesh na'Vin*," she says, slipping on her shoes.

"*Belhalia Mavesh na'Vin*," Mom repeats, her brown cheeks flushed.

I keep my hands clamped in my lap and my eyes to myself until Kia's footsteps fade. "I can't believe you," I say, my voice ringing through the room.

Mom shakes her head and mutters her prayer again, waving the stone over my head.

"Stop waving your hands around and listen to me." I snatch her wrist, disrupting the stream of light. "You didn't bring me here because you needed help preparing for the festival. You brought me here to pray for my essence. And you didn't want to do it in front of your ka'onahalet."

Squeezing her eyes shut, Mom says, "They are worried—"

"You mean scared?"

"They're worried for your soul."

"You mean they don't trust me because I'm different. And you don't trust me either."

Mom's harsh sigh bites the air. She sets the stone down, the clack of stone-on-stone merging with her sigh. "How can I when you apply for the Guardian Academy without my knowledge, and now only a year in, you're thinking of changing paths? Without light, you have no guide."

"I have myself."

"What a selfish thing to say. Following your every whim doesn't serve the community. I serve the community by caring for their souls, your father serves the community by upholding the law, even your brother serves the community with his business."

"What about me as a Guardian?" I say, standing up from the cushion and planting my feet on the cold, hard tile, now relishing the way my voice is amplified by this sacred space that is not meant for the lightless.

Mom stands to meet my eyes. "Yes, what about you? Guardians hurt, they kill—"

"They protect—"

"They escalate matters that should be handled within the community."

"Am I not part of the community?" The words rain down on us and silence fills in.

The shrine trembles as if a thunder cloud has formed right above us, only for a few seconds, but the gold candle holders, the tiles, the sandstone all quake. Mom holds one hand to her chest and the other out to steady herself.

Those hands. They're marked with sacred scripts now, the only thing stopping her from striking me. Her eyes are dark with pride. Her jaw tenses.

"You say Dad blesses the community with his work? How did he bless you? By sleeping around with other women? And now he left you. You bless the community with your prayers of abundance, and for me, you say prayers to save my soul. Maybe say a prayer for yourself. Maybe you wouldn't be so threatened by me if you gave yourself the attention you deserve."

My face stings as her eyes narrow into daggers.

A terrible rumble shakes the shrine again. It's not a thunder from above. It's the ground—a stomp of wrath from Vin maybe.

I stand strong as it urges me to say my piece before it's too late.

"You're so concerned with what other people think that you're not serving them, you're hiding from them."

The blood drains from her face. Her eyes dart around as the earth continues to shake. "Eliote, please, something's wrong."

"And you're hiding me from them."

The tension inside me deflates for a moment as all the energy I had stored to tell my mom just one thing evaporates. I draw in a long breath, but a gold aura spills into the room. The aura quakes through me just as the ground quakes. The aura is blinking and rips at my senses until it's met with a dark shadow outside the shrine.

With an ear-splitting crack, the ceiling caves in. Mom throws her arms around me and shadow phases. We slink along jagged shadows to the farthest corner of the room, away from falling sandstone. My stomach flips as we reappear, and my vision is spotty. The shrine is shaking, and Mom's hands are vices around my arms. Stone blocks and shards of glass crumble to the ground, expelling dust into the air. A chunk of rock plummets, striking the back of Mom's head. I screech as she falls limp into my arms. The bitter words I lashed at her ring in my ears as their heaviness gnaws at my stomach.

I choke back the taste of metal on my tongue and a too fast breath. Gritting my teeth, I drag Mom into the archway of the back door, sharp rubble cutting my feet.

Through my stream of tears and the gaping hole in the shrine ceiling, an Ancient beast towers over us. Its eyes are golden slits like its aura, its face like a bird with snakelike fangs. Scales and feathers ripple over its ribcage as it heaves a breath and bellows to the sky. My body trembles with the scream, but

I keep myself upright. The beast's eyes dart left to right, up and down, locking with mine but then releasing. It keeps looking all around. Screeching, it lunges away from the shrine.

"Mom," I whimper, cradling her head, blood spilling over my hands. "Mom, can you hear me?"

Moaning, her head falls to the side. Her eyes flutter for a moment but seal shut. Her pulse is heavy. I put my hand beneath her nose, and her breaths are still hot.

A howl jerks my head up. A smaller beast prowls over the rubble—a Nodaha Downfōst. The Ancient wouldn't hurt me, they're not drawn to hédin, not to hurt them at least. The Ancient's beady eyes darted away from me, looking for something else that called it into Tien Bay. But this Downfōst, with its abrasive golden aura and sharp senses, is drawn straight to me. It growls, deep and wet, sending chills down my spine. I can't outrun it with Mom. I can't leave her.

With trembling hands, I reach up my wide pant legs and unsheathe two daggers. The steel blades fortify my bones and cool my skin. Wind gusts through the open shrine, putrid with the stench of beast and biting with cold.

I stand, tiny bits of rubble scraping against the tile beneath my bleeding feet. The beast prowls to the right. Knees shaking, I take a step to mirror its slow, arcing path, keeping the distance between us. This beast is just like the ones I fought in the forest outside of Akinnera. Which means it has a pack. That also means a swift swipe of my blade to its jugular will do the trick.

Breath pours out of the beast, billowing with its aura. The gold brightens, lurching forward, and I brace myself. I draw in a breath full of dust, incense, and the rotting smell of the beast's dripping saliva.

Claws dig into rubble. The beast springs forward and sprints across the shrine. I clench my daggers in front of me, heart in my throat and cold sweat slick on my back. It leaps at me. I jerk to the side, and it hits the ground behind me, the impact reverberating through my bones. Grunting and gnashing its teeth, it slashes its paw at me, light spiking off its claws. I sidestep, but red flashes behind my eyes as the burning-hot claws shred my skin. My fingers spasm and my body quakes like stars are exploding in my muscles.

Dragging breath through my teeth, I hold fast to my blades. A scream rips through my throat and I plunge steel into the beast's neck. I yank the blade and it grinds through bone. My muscles tremble as I lacerate the beast's tissue. Hot blood gushes over my fingers and down my arm and all over my front, sticking linen and silk to my body. The beast slumps to the ground. I gag as the blood steams from my clothes.

Black spots fill my vision as the beast's gold essence leaks from the wound and twists in the air. Its aura dissipates with a warm brush against my face. I shudder, holding my bloody dagger in the air, my skin itching with its blood.

"Eliote," Mom whispers from the dark corner of the shrine, dust settling around her.

The haze thins, and we stare at each other, like we are both becoming clearer to the other's eye. I swallow the acid in my throat and scramble over the rubble. My silk and linen smears blood over gritty sandstone as I kneel beside Mom.

"We have to get out of here before more beasts come." My fingers shake around her, tapping her head, searching for more blood, more breaks. I need to keep moving and figure out what to do.

Mom's eyes roam the shrine, unfocused and watery, skipping past my face. I squeeze my eyes shut and my tears wash blood from my face. *I can do this. I can get her out of here.*

"Come on," I say. I hold her head steady as I get her up, her blood trickling down my hand, mingling with mine and the beast's blood. Pulling her onto my back with a grunt, my knees shake and my arm stings. But I move forward, Mom groaning on my back.

The shrine is on the outskirts of the city, near the city wall which now has a gaping hole in it. The howls of the beasts and the pounding footsteps of the Ancient merge with my heartbeat. I move as fast as I can across the field, stumbling over snow and dips in the ground. My lungs burn and my body aches under Mom's weight, but I keep moving, teeth gritted and audible waves of air sifting in and out of my teeth.

Reaching the city limits with sweat trickling down my face, I stagger and brace myself against a supply shed behind someone's home. The laceration on my arm smarts as I shove the door open. Howls grow louder behind us. I set Mom down and push a crate in front of the door. Blood courses through me, rocking my body and stirring nausea in my gut. I drop to my knees and fumble for my echo. My fingers skitter over the numbers as I dial the emergency Local Protector line, leaving red prints across the glass.

"There's a beast attack at the south end of the city by the shrine of Vin. My mother and I are injured. We—" I breathe through the choke in my throat as tears streak my face. "We're injured. In a storage shed on Lotis Street."

My mind swims as the operator asks me for more details on the attack and sends a squad to come get us. The echo ends. Even with tears in my eyes and adrenaline spilling into my blood, my vision is steady. I track my hands as they untie Mom's golden sash with startling clarity. Tying it around her wound, the shadows don't distract me. Everything is clear, perfect.

As I work, an aura I've never seen glows in the dark. Green wisps the colour of starlight tangle around us. They shudder for a moment but then are whisked away through the slats of the shed. My sight is drawn with the aura. A vibration stirs in my eyes. I rub at it, but I can't shake the feeling that I need to follow the aura.

"Stay here, I'll be back." I lay Mom against the wall.

"Eliote, no," she rasps, but I'm out of the shed before she can convince me to stay. I smear the beast's blood from my tunic over the door of the shed to cover our scent and sprint around back.

The green energy curls and swirls horizontally, moving deeper into the city. Why did it come out of us? Where is it going?

I follow for about a block, stumbling every other step because of my numb toes.

In an open square stands a man. He holds his hand out with a metal contraption on his palm and a jagged, black stone set in it that trembles and jerks his arm. Tall, dark hair, pasty white skin, and eyes red like firestones. I know this man's face. The first time I saw him, he drained Rin of all her will. She met with him, and she broke. And now here he is, breaking my city. Stephen.

His blood-red aura snakes around him, oozing with power, turning almost black. I shudder as shadows reach around him. A stabbing pain hits my stomach as the ground trembles.

The Ancient beast locks eyes with the stone. It screeches and its eyes grow large, like they've spotted gold. It lunges forward, crashing through the street. The inhabitants flee their destroyed homes, green tendrils mask their auras and sweep through the dark over to Stephen. The quaking stone drinks in the light.

The stone splinters and another sharp edge grows from the mass of ebony spikes. The red glow in Stephen's eyes fades. A smile crests over his exhausted face and he clenches the stone in both hands. My blood boils as he lifts his head and locks eyes with me. His sick smirk sets my breaths on fire and twists my hands into fists. The Ancient beast crashes into the square but Stephen bolts. He sprints through the throngs of LPs. Even if I wanted to pursue him, I wouldn't be able to catch him in this chaos with my frozen feet.

An LP yells at me to get to safety.

I can't move. Green light from above me mixes with the green surrounding me. Seafoam, emerald, and starlight. The brightest stars in our sky are not pure, they're a mix of jint, fann, and unama energy, something called utanic energy. Why have I never seen it on the Karess before, and from other hédin? Why can I see it billowing out of my chest?

The LP grabs me and shoves me back the way I came. With burning lungs, I sprint to the shed. I lock me and Mom in and cradle her head on my lap. Waiting for Medics to find us in the midst of the wailing screams and howls and carnage of our city, I close my eyes to the cloud of green. But the sting in my arm forces them open again, forces me to keep Mom's head up, her eyes open, and my breaths even.

13

LANCE

My first birthday after Khalie was a nightmare. I had another year of life to celebrate, and Khalie had none. The guilt flooded me, so I built a dam with liquor and drugs to shut off my senses. I blacked out somewhere and my family didn't see me that day, a day I should have spent with them, cherishing them. I found my way home, slobbering drunk at two in the morning.

Dad had waited up for me that night. He opened the door for me because I couldn't find my key. In his night shorts and slippers, he made a pot of tea with scolya, ginger, and whisper weed to sober me up. I slumped into a chair at the kitchen table, smelling of ale and Ease and shit and Seena knows what else. I lit a cigarette because Khalie loved ginger, and the smell brought up her face, and it made my heart stutter.

Dad told me to put it out, that my sister was asleep in the

next room. I took another breath of smoke. He said that using so much liquor and drugs would only suppress my essence and I'd have more trouble controlling it down the road.

I told him to piss off.

What did he know about power and control? He barely has a level two essence reading.

I screamed at him and said so many things I can't take back or apologize for because I don't remember what I said. I know they burned my throat more than scotch, they tasted worse than bile, they hurt both of us more than any wound a blade could make. Before I knew it, I was on the floor screaming and sobbing, but he wouldn't let me get more drugs to calm the electricity that charged the air around me. It caught the curtains on fire. I clutched my heart, and my dad held me, his wings spread out around me, shielding the house as best he could from me, so my mother couldn't see me, and my sister wouldn't see her brother's intoxication.

He always just held me and used the kindest, softest tone. I shrunk, so unsure of anything under his wings. All I could do was cry. And for the next month, I cried and shook from withdrawal under his wings, all the while cussing him out for my mistakes, my pain.

Today, I cut off my tears with a tight necktie. I ironed the crinkles out of my shirt and pants, pressing at the guilt. I put on a dark sport coat to hide the tremors in my limbs. It's no longer the shake from withdrawal, just nerves that I used to control with a pack of cigarettes. Twenty years old is a big deal for Lavarians, but all I can do is tremble.

Dad holds the door open for people exiting the restaurant. He smiles at each one of them, jokes, and picks up an echo someone had dropped. I'm shivering from the early Fevron wind by the time he ushers me in, still holding the door.

Warmth washes over me and the scent of spices and oil fills my shaking body.

"Just the two of you today?" the hostess asks. Her wings are silver, like her long swishy dress. She smiles at us with two menus in hand.

"Yes, we should have a reservation for two under Hirra," Dad says, laying a hand on my shoulder. "Today is my son's twentieth birthday."

The squeeze of his hand tightens a knot in my throat.

The hostess dips her head to me. "Long life and blessings." She touches her forehead with two fingers, then marks out the shape of a square in front of me, blessing the environment with good energy. I bow my head in thanks and clear my throat.

Turning on her heels, the hostess leads us through a wide wooden archway. The restaurant only has a few tables spaced generously through the room with some paper screen dividers along them for privacy. The openness of the room allows Dad and I to walk side by side without our wings crashing into tables or toppling the screens. Conversations float around the room in low murmurs. The peaceful atmosphere takes a bit of tension out of the day.

We sit at a table with dark wood chairs, a white tablecloth, and a single candle in a crystal dish.

"Would you like to order from the menu today, or will you have a traditional *hosashu* meal?"

"The traditional," Dad says, his wings spread out between the screens comfortably. "But we would like to substitute the yizo liquor for a pitcher of water."

"Of course."

Once the hostess leaves, Dad unzips his wing-securers and drapes his coat over the back of his chair. I keep mine on, fiddling with the cuffs. Dad folds his hands in his lap and leans back in his chair, still with perfect posture. The candlelight flickers over his tan skin. For as long as I can remember, he's had the same hair cut—buzzed short on the sides and just a little longer on the top to see the thick, dark hair going grey.

I drop my gaze to my hands. This man is so familiar to me and yet I can't remember the last time I had a full conversation with him. I lick my lips and furrow my brow. I don't know how to express that to him, to express that he means more to me than I've ever let on. Disrespect and disregard were the way I chose to treat my dad. Every year of my life, he has supported me more and more and I keep letting him down, shutting him out, because I hate how my reputation rubs off on him. But he never falters.

He should know. Why should I keep my gratitude from him?

"Thank you for this, Dad." The shake in my voice makes me sick to my stomach.

"Oh, I'm sure whatever your mom and your sister are concocting at home will out-do this by a long shot." His smile spreads wrinkles through his face and hides his brown eyes from me.

"No, really, thank you. This means a lot to me, to be able to do this with you."

His screen of humility drops and his whole face brightens. Even with the fading smile his dark eyes shine. "It's my absolute pleasure."

The hostess and another server return to us with a board the size of the table filled with steaming food. While still balancing the board, the server removes the candle from the table and sets it in the middle of the board before lowering it in front of us. Dad thanks them as they wheel in a cart to sit beside the table with two crystal cups and a pitcher of water.

Taking the pitcher, Dad says, "We drink from one pitcher and separate cups because our energy comes from one source, yet we are separate vessels."

We each take a cup and sip. I'm not sure what I believe about the source of all energy, whether it's the All Creator, the Dual Pure Spirits, the Beyond itself, or something else. Only realizing my enhancements at sixteen left me wondering if the source of power was some sort of cosmic joke that I didn't have the punchline to. Now, if what the Seer saw is true, then the source has played a sicker joke on me than I realized.

I get mastery over my essence, but Sage abilities? It's ridiculous.

Dad picks up his silver utensils and uses them to point to each dish before us. "Tore fish with orange glaze, rice and sweet root, kechling fried in salia oil with sautéed keeta greens."

My mouth waters as the sweet, salty, and tangy scents waft around me.

"We have a responsibility to the environment. The environment and animals in it we use to nourish ourselves. In turn, we must nourish it, or it will perish. We eat animals from the sea, the air, the land. We take the seeds, the fruit, the roots of the plants. But we take great care to see that what we take is renewed." Dad puts a bit of everything on my plate. "The same goes for the relationships we have with other people. When we receive, we must also give in return."

"Thank you," I say, taking the plate.

"And when one has nothing to give, they must be nourished." Dad locks eyes with me. My throat bobs with this last instruction. He's not talking about the plants anymore. I shut tears behind my eyelids and bow my head.

Dad says a prayer, thanking the Dual Spirits, Ashnaho and Neuoa, for their provision and the ancestors for their care. We take a few bites in silence.

"How do you hope to grow this year?" Dad asks.

The tore fish with the tangy glaze melts in my mouth, but the question is heavy. He asks me every year. I've always brushed it off because I didn't know, and maybe I didn't want to know. This year I might have an answer. It scares the shit out of me.

I swallow hard. "A Seer gave me a mystery. She said I might . . . unlock Sage abilities."

Staring at his plate and chewing slowly, Dad's eyebrows draw together. My wings pull in, folding behind me. I shovel in a few bites of rice.

"But I don't know, it's stupid. Why would I unlock Sage abilities when I only manifested my abilities at sixteen? Not even scholars who have studied Lavarian abilities for their entire lives have figured it out."

Dad puts his fork down. With a deliberate, long sigh, he sets one hand on his side and points at me with the other.

"I don't want you to use that word. Stupid. Have you ever wondered why your enhancements came so late?"

Heat waves through my face. "Because I was high out of my mind?"

Dark eyes pierce through me. I set down my utensils.

"I think the lateness of your essence's development might be linked to the greatness of your ability. When you were young, you were always cautious, always listening. The environment spoke to you and waited for you to respond. You waited, contently, but your schoolmates made fun of you for your lack of enhancements. And you started to listen to them too."

"What are you trying to say, Dad?" I say, rubbing a hand over my face.

"Sorry, you're right, I'm rambling. What I mean is Lavarian abilities depend on manipulating the environment through charges in the atmosphere. You took your time and developed strength. It took longer than most children. When their negativity got to you, like an imbalance in the environment, your strength retreated. I-I regret that I did not give my emotions to you so that you could give your emotions to me. I'm sorry you hid them from me under ale and smoke."

The glistening tears in my dad's eyes are mesmerizing. I've never seen him cry. It triggers a release inside me. All my life, I've known the love of my family through their support, their closeness, and my parents' healthy relationship. But today it is inside me. It warms me, stabilizes me through my father's vulnerability and his ability to express what he's seen in me all these years. Taking a long breath, I lean back. My limbs are heavy with relaxation, my wings are widespread behind me.

I sniff, keeping my eyes low. "I'm sorry too."

"But remember that even when emotions are not given to someone, they are still valid. They don't need to be seen by another person to be true." Dad's voice is thick, but it lifts with a smile.

We finish our meal and, over a bowl of steaming scolya root tea, I say, "I'm not sure where to start. The Seer said sustained emotional connection could be a potential starting point but . . .

for the longest time I've felt all over the place."

Dad nods, setting his tea down. The restaurant has cleared out now that the lunch hour is over, but the hostess would never shoo us away.

"Sage abilities are nuanced. One might never believe a Nytrue with water affinities to take control of time. Emotions are all different, like all types of weather. Maybe she wants you to find something that sustains you through all your ups and downs." Dad folds his napkin and places it next to his plate. His eyes flick to me and then back down. In a soft, hesitant voice, he says. "Maybe it's time for you to go back to the first time it happened?"

My throat goes dry as steam licks my face. Sometimes scolya smells too much like Ease. They're both deep, earthy, sweet smells that get to my head. My stomach churns.

"If you're ready," Dad adds.

I twist my bowl, rippling the tea inside. "Whenever I was with Khalie, I didn't feel like I had to be on."

Her voice fills my head, sweet and high, caring as she whispered in my ear that night. Every word, every touch, was sincere. Who cares if the Ease amplified my perception? She was close.

"I miss her."

My face heats as I look up at Dad. I expect him to smirk or chuckle at such a cheesy thing to say. But he frowns in a way that fills his eyes with a world of understanding and care. "What I'm hearing is that you felt like yourself when you were with her. Is that right?"

"Maybe. I can barely remember what that feels like."

"Pay attention to what lets you feel like yourself and who

responds well to you."

The honesty between the two of us, it's tearing something down. I don't know what, and I don't feel like myself yet, but I can't dismiss chances like this, chances to tell people how I feel. Being open about my faults with the one man who has never faulted me and expressing gratitude, it's created a shift.

Now Dad smiles. He sighs, stretching his arms over his head and his wings out to the side. "Well, I think you'll serve this world well as an adult." He stands and folds his jacket over his arm. Setting his hand on my shoulder, he says, "I'm proud of you, young man."

I push away from the table and throw my arms around him. One of my wings drapes over the table, pushing the dishes dangerously close to the edge. I hold on to my dad and he holds on to me.

I came into this restaurant hidden and awkward with a man I've known my whole life, and I'm leaving with a connection to him like I've known him for two lifetimes. I couldn't have asked for a better gift.

14

R I N

A TREMOR VIBRATES THROUGH MY BED, the floor, the walls. I open my eyes with a sharp gasp. The air that strikes my lungs is hot. It moves through me, thick and gravelly. I cough and roll over to turn on the light. White curls of smoke breach the door. The walls shake. Shouts send chills down my arms and legs. The crack of a firestone rifle sends my stomach plummeting and my heart to my throat. Haunting and urgent, the sound of metal scraping metal resounds from deep within the Vein.

My door flies open, crashing into the wall. Brand bolts into the room, a firestone pistol pointed to the hall. Smoke snakes around her bare legs. Her night shorts and shirt are smudged with soot, scorched in places.

"What's going—"

"We have to leave now." Brand grabs my arm and yanks me

out of bed.

In the hall, the florescent lights flicker, sending bursts of ghostly light through the veil of smoke.

"Brand, what's happening?" I yell over the shouts, rifle fire, and metal.

"We're under attack."

"By who?"

"Emberstead radicals."

My mouth is dry, thick with smoke. Brand pushes me forward and down another hall away from the elevator. My feet slow and Brand blazes on ahead of me. She vanishes in the dark. My heart constricts, mind reeling. There's chaos all around me quaking the cement structure of the Vein, pounding through my skull. The lights go out, stealing tangible reality.

A light flickers behind me. I turn to it.

"Rin! Come on, we have to evacuate immediately." Brand's voice jolts through me and I cringe.

"I can't leave it," I say, starting to inch my way back to my room through the smoke and dark.

"Damn it, Rin. We have to go." Brand's hand clamps around my wrist. She yanks me again, but I yank away from her and run back to my room with more shouts behind me. Brand's pistol goes off with a crack. All I see is red. Red blood. The cashier's blood, Eshra's blood.

I stumble back into my room, hacking and wheezing, feeling around the dark for my suitcase, my box, my parents' wedding rings, and the note—the only thing I have left of her that made all this my reality.

"Mm, lucky me." A voice so smooth it makes me want to vomit.

I spin around with the box clenched in one hand, my other hand fisted and ready in front of me.

"If it isn't the Angel's Demon."

Tōmas' face stares back at me, distorted by smoke, dark, and the tears stinging my eyes, but it's him. I've never seen someone as beautiful as him.

I cough, and say in short, breathy bursts, "What are you doing here?"

He chuckles, unbothered by the smoke, as he saunters into the room in his silky, furred, black jacket. His cheek dimples and my head swims.

"Tōmas said he broke you. I see he wasn't kidding."

Did he just refer to himself by name?

The tears streak down my cheeks as I shake uncontrollably. "Why the fuck are you talking like that?"

He's sick. This can't be happening.

He swings his fist at me. I duck, sidestep around him, and push through the door. I pant and clench my burning chest. His hand grabs my hair. It's hot like embers. An orange glow burns behind my head. I twist in his grasp and jab his elbow joint. Tōmas yelps, backing away, plated in fire armour.

Fuck. Tōmas is Lifeblood, and I know he isn't an Emberstead halfie. Why is he using fire abilities? I'm dreaming, I have to be. *Wake up.*

More shouting, flashes of light, and rifle fire are behind me as I dodge this phantom's flaming fists. My body is trying to calculate for Lifeblood air attacks. I misread him every time, fire blackening my clothes and hands with soot.

I brace myself against a kick, but not with strong enough footing, and his fire plows me over. The box clatters to the floor, its contents scattering, the rings bounce and tinkle as they roll into the dark. I fall hard on my backside, scrambling away from Tōmas, clutching at any of the trinkets from my box my hands can find. My fingers graze a piece of paper—glossy surface and frayed edges. The memory of my team. I clutch it in my fist as Tōmas crouches over me, his demon smile splitting his face.

Everything dims. The flickers of light are just a faint aura around him. The shouts are muffled. A sob escapes me into the void. My limbs are stiff as Tōmas picks up my mother's suicide note. He stares at me with dead eyes as the note catches fire, the edges char, sparks sprinkle his face in orange light. As the note crumbles to ash and smoke, my mother's face flickers in my mind with the last spark. I blink. Paralyzed under the heavy dark, a suffocating hollow presses on me, stifling the urge to breathe.

Tōmas is yanked back by the neck, eyes bulging, mouth agape, his cry deadened as it reaches my ears. Brand flips him on his back, pinning him with her knees. She fires two shots into the ground, one on each side of his head, so fast that the two flashes of light merge into one, the second crack layering over the first. Tōmas screams. The sound is high, female. Tōmas' coat fades away. His body shrinks to a figure wearing full black leather. A woman with jet-black hair and pale skin clutches her ears.

Brand holds her pistol steady, but she breathes heavily. The woman's face curls into a smile. She chuckles, tilting her head as she stares at Brand.

"Found you, Daalza," the woman says.

But the cruel smile that twists her face drops in an instant and a flare like fire smoulders in her eyes. Breath shudders into the woman as shock and terror bleed from her. "It's really you." Sweet sincerity softens her voice, like she's a completely different person, and it sends chills down my back.

I squeeze the memory in my fist and pull myself on the ground away from them. Who is this woman?

The woman's head tilts with a violent jerk. The embers burn in her eyes, and she gasps. "I'm trying to stop her. I'm trying, Daalza, but she's getting stronger. You have to get away from me."

"Thea?" The name seeps out of Brand with a breath, and her grip loosens on her pistol.

"Get away from me!" The woman shakes Brand by the arms. Her eyes burn.

Brand slams the butt of her pistol to the woman's head and the light drains from her eyes.

Leaving the woman like a lump of coal in the darkness behind her, Brand kneels in front of me and takes my hand. Pulling me up, she brushes my hair out of my face. Her eyes are clear. They're alert, vibrant. Her hand is firm around mine. I grip it back. The only control I have over my body is in my finger muscles. The only feeling my skin registers is her warmth.

"We have to go," she says. Her hand brushes my cheek, and she keeps my gaze until I nod.

Brand leads me back down the hall. Smoke clings to me, the light is a phantom, the dark is inky black. As we turn the corner, my lungs spasm and I hack into my elbow. Shouts sound from the other end. Brand pulls me to her side, aims her pistol and fires. The bullet strikes an Emberstead man in the leg. He jerks back and collapses.

"There's a stairwell at the end of this hall," Brand says between breaths. "It'll take us down to the garage."

We stumble along, Brand's pistol ahead of us, until we come

to the door. The air is cooler, and it strikes my sweaty skin with chills. At the edge of the steps, Brand's hand loosens. I grip it harder. My eyes are on the steps, but Brand's arm jerks and her curls shake at the corner of my vision as she looks at me. I hold tight, taking the first step. She holds tighter and we descend the steps together, slowly, then gain speed as we find a rhythm for both our legs.

Footsteps echo from below. A fire ball scorches past my head. A man appears at the base of the next flight. He punches the air and another sphere of fire blazes toward us. I throw up my arm to block it. With a burst of energy, a plate of ruby red appears before my arm like a shield and my eyes are blinded with red. My whole body itches and Brand ducks behind the shield. I scream as the fire collides with the red energy and dissipates. Brand takes aim. The pistol cracks and my ears ring. I'm pulled along by Brand's firm grip. The man moans on the ground as I misplace my foot on his hand.

"Keep moving. We're almost there."

The stairwell sways, but there are no longer tremors shaking the Vein. I lose track of my feet. My body is just a leash on my mind as we make it to the garage.

A cruiser roars down the tunnel. A group of people scramble into one of the two cruisers left.

"Rin, Commander," someone says. My eyes lock with his. My father stares down at me for a moment and his hand moves to my shoulder.

"You should have been long gone by now, Peter," Brand says, her voice powerful despite being raspy from smoke inhalation.

Father ignores her. "Rin, are you all right?"

"I . . . " My breaths run together. The little light left around me is fading into spots. My skin heats.

"Go, Peter. I'll take care of her. Get the others out of here." Brand jabs her finger at the cruiser filled with people in their night clothes just like us, their faces blanched, eyes wide.

Father's face twists. He clenches his teeth and swipes his sweaty forehead. Grunting, he sprints to the cruiser.

Brand steers me to a red, two-seater cruiser, opens the door, unravels her hand from mine, and gently shoves me in. With the slam of the door, all sound is cut off. Breath catches in my constricted throat. I dig my fingernails into the skin of my bare knees, the memory of my team crumpled in one fist. Tires squeal as my father's vehicle is lost down the tunnel. Brand's pistol fires, flames flicker from the stairwell.

"Damn," Brand says as a muffled clicking sound pricks my ears. She throws open the door and climbs in, dropping her smoking pistol at my feet.

As Brand jams her key into the ignition, the cruiser rumbles to life. I jerk back and forth as Brand steers us out of the garage. The lights flick on and off and shouts fade behind us.

We take the turn away from Senn into the mountain pass. There's a ringing in my ears and they pop as the cruiser bolts out of the tunnel onto the open motorway. Green starlight spills in through the windshield. I drop my eyes to my knees. The light is too normal compared to all that's just happened. It's too striking.

Brand lets go of a shaky breath. Her hands grip the steering wheel so hard that it scrunches against her skin.

My lips part. "Who"—I cough and clear my throat—"who was that? What did she do to me?"

There is no colour in Brand's face, no life, as her eyes lose

their vibrance again. "She's a powerful Mind Fire user. There are different Mind Fire abilities. Johanna can read minds. Some people can just read memories. Others, like . . . her, can make you see them as someone you have an emotional connection to. But she has to have seen that person too." She glances at me. "Sound can disrupt Mind Fire. Without her hearing, she can't keep her hold on you. That's why I shot by her ears."

I lick my dry lips and retract my nails from my knees. "Who is she?" I whisper.

"Her name is Thea." Brand's voice is ice.

"How do you know her?"

The question leaves her frozen, only her breaths move her chest. Her eyes are forward, but they twitch, seeing into the past. "She was my girlfriend." She blinks. "S-something happened to her. I fell in love with her sweet nature, but one day, she became harsh and possessive. She manipulated me by disguising herself as my other friends, doing things to make me distrust them and rely on her only."

So, Brand and I have both been manipulated by people who we thought cared for us, even momentarily. I shake my head. "Why did she call you Daalza?"

"I changed my name and my appearance to hide from her. Now that she's found me, I have no clue what she wants from me." Brand's eyes flick to me and back to the road. "What did she burn?"

I swallow past the soot and dryness in my throat. My eyes sting, but no tears come. Opening my mouth, only air passes through in heavy rushes. I swallow once more. "My mother's suicide note."

"Rin," Brand says. Her hands loosen on the wheel, and one

slides off, hovering between us as if to touch me.

I shake my head as a dizzying lurch fills my stomach. "It was the one place I remember her telling me she loved me."

My head lolls back as Brand's hand leaves the air between us and slams the wheel. My body doesn't startle. I'm thankful for her outrage. Because I have nothing left. A moment is what I need right now. Just a moment to really rest. I don't think I've had any of those, not real ones at least. They always take on a tinge of darkness.

Oron sat in the armchair in the living room reading a book. Stephen, fourteen at the time, was upstairs, but I hadn't seen him all day. I was in the kitchen working on a colouring page as I snacked on cookies and milk, enjoying the fire warmth behind me. It was the month of Fevron, and the house was decorated for the Festival of the Heart. A copper bowl of cinnospice sprigs and dried plums sat on the table next to the staircase, spreading a sweet and spicy aroma through the room. Purple snow blossoms were wrapped around the banister with strings of lightstones draped through them.

Once I was finished with the page, I slipped off my chair and made my way over to Oron. In the entryway above my head hung eleven wooden stars, one for each lineage's revered ancestor as well as Carnity and Dien. Keena's star had cut-outs lined with iron and filled with clear crystal. It caught the glow of the lightstones throughout the house and spread tiny dots of light through the other stars.

"Oron," I said.

"Mm." He kept his eyes on his book.

"When will Mother and Father come home from the hospital?"

Oron closed the book. With shadows in his eyes, he set it on his lap. "Well, sweet girl, they'll be back when the baby is born." His words were heavy, not filled with a lightness and joy like a new baby should bring.

"Why is it taking so long?"

"Sometimes babies just take a little time to come out into the world."

I hopped up to the couch and wrapped a blanket around me. I squished my toes in the carpet, knowing Mother would scold me if I put my feet on the couch. Father had rushed home to be here for the birth of my new sibling, and I was anxious to see both of them. Father would have to leave to get back to work, so if he wasn't home soon, I wouldn't get any time to see him.

Oron's eyes softened as they stayed on me. "You're just going to have to be patient, sweet girl. They'll be home as soon as they can. Why don't you go get Stephen and we'll figure out something to eat?"

A smile crept to my face. I ran upstairs with the blanket trailing behind me like a cape.

"Stephen," I called, but the sound of my voice didn't reach him over the music that pounded through the door. I knocked. "Stephen."

Still, he didn't answer me, so I took both my fists and rapped my knuckles on the door repeatedly until the door opened and a bleary-eyed Stephen appeared in a sloppy t-shirt and gym shorts. His dark hair was pushed up on one side.

The room was dark behind him. It was clean as it always

was, but the blinds were closed and the only light in the room came from the audio player in the corner.

"What?" he asked, rubbing his eyes.

"Were you sleeping?" I peered around him and a waft of stale air and boy smell slipped out from his lair and hit me in the face.

"Yeah."

"Why?"

"I don't know." He smirked and poked me in the forehead. "Why do people usually sleep? I was tired?" He pushed past me to the staircase.

"I meant, why are you sleeping during the day?"

"Why do you have to ask so many questions?" His voice was still playful as he headed down the stairs, but with his back turned, he hid his smile and whatever made him so tired.

"Whatever," I said. "You want to help me and Oron make something to eat?"

"No. Mom and Dad aren't home yet?"

I hopped down the steps behind Stephen one at a time, careful not to smoosh the flowers on the banister. "Not yet. Baby's slow."

In the kitchen, Stephen grabbed the last cookie and dumped himself into a chair. Oron pulled out a big pan from the cupboard.

"What are we going to make?" I asked.

"I found some frozen tore fish in the icer, so I think we'll make fried tore fish with garlic broth and salted fire peppers. You like fire peppers, right?" Oron looked down at me with an eyebrow raised.

"Mhm!"

Oron turned to Stephen.

 156

"Yeah, whatever," Stephen said through a mouthful of cookie.

"Rin, can you chop the peppers for me?"

I pressed my lips together. "Mm . . . can you show me?"

With a heavy sigh, Oron nodded. "Grab your mother's apron over there and I'll show you."

"It's Father's actually," I said, taking it from the hook.

Oron chuckled as he eyed the pink flowers on the apron and adjusted the neck strap to fit me. From another cupboard he found a cutting board, and from a drawer I had never looked in, he pulled out two knives. He took the larger for himself and handed the smaller one to me. Placing the pepper on the board, he began to chop. "We'll cut six of these and make lots of fish, so there's enough for your parents if they come home, or you'll have leftovers for tomorrow." He set the rest of the peppers in front of me.

I took the pepper in one hand and made a tentative cut. Juices spilled out of the flesh and the spice prickled my nose. After I had chopped one of the peppers just like Oron showed me, I turned to Stephen. "Look, Stephen. I'm cooking."

He leaned his head on one hand and held his echo up to his face with the other. Blue light accentuated the dark bags under his eyes. He yawned.

"Stephen, look."

He lowered the echo just enough to take a peek at me. "You're cutting peppers, Rin, not cooking."

The smile on my face melted, and I lowered my eyes back to the oozing peppers. "When do you think I can get an echo, Oron?"

Oron glanced at me as he cut the fish into even portions.

"I'm sure your parents will get you one when you're Stephen's age."

The room went silent as I focused on the peppers. Oron attended the fish and Stephen was pulled back into whatever was so fascinating on his echo. As I worked on the last pepper, my eyes were drawn to the window. A big fluffy snowflake floated down in front of me, the first and only snow Senn saw that year.

The front door opened.

"Is he okay, Peter?"

"Yes, Cass, I've got him." My father's voice carried into the kitchen in soft, even notes to contrast the tired worries of my mother.

"Do you have my bag? I don't have my bag. We left it in the pay-cruiser."

"I just left it on the curb. I'll get it once we've got you and Liam inside."

"I'll take him. We shouldn't leave it there long."

"Of course, Cass, I'll get it."

"They're back," I said, and dropped the knife to rush to the entryway.

Mother stood under the wooden stars, the door open behind her, letting in flurries that swirled at her feet. She wore a pink shawl and a loose-fitting grey dress. Her shoulders hunched over the little body cradled in her arms. A line formed between her eyebrows and her eyes were sunken, her tight lips dry.

My father came in behind her.

"Peter, the door," Mother said.

"Yes, dear." He kissed her white-blonde hair, his eyes closed tight as he lingered with their closeness. Setting the suitcase down, he shut the door. "Rinny," he said with a wide smile.

I rushed over and wrapped my arms around his legs, taking a deep breath of his scent of sawdust and pinichu berries and cold.

"Rinny, you remember how we welcome new people to our home?" He picked me up with strong arms.

"What's his name?"

"Liam."

The name was short, sweet in my ears. "Liam," I whispered.

My mother held him out for me to see. Her face remained blank and furrowed. With my index finger and my middle finger, I touched my head, my heart, and then Liam's tiny forehead. "Eenwa seya ha, Liam."

Liam wiggled, opening and closing his mouth.

Stephen and Oron joined us and gave the greeting to the new little hédin.

The moment was perfect. We stood together, huddled around Liam under the memory of our ancestors. Lights twinkled around us, spice and heat filled my nose, and Father kissed my cheek. But Mother shifted. The crease deepened between her brows. A sharp breath slipped into her body, pulling warmth from the small space. Her shoulders shook and a gleaming tear rolled down her face.

I grabbed her shawl. "Mother—"

"Peter," she said quickly. "I'd like to go upstairs." She squirmed away from our circle and hurried through the kitchen to the stairs. Liam began to cry, and my mother hunched tighter around him. A deep sob escaped her as she was swallowed in the dark of the upper level and Liam's cries.

My heart raced in my chest as Father set me down. He planted a kiss on my head and put a hand on Stephen's shoulder. "She's tired," he said, and his larger-than-life frame walked away, following Mother's sobs and his new son's helpless wailing.

I held my arms around myself, my jaw slack and my eyes wide. Tension settled on my forehead. Oron cleared his throat and ran a hand over the scruff on his chin and went back to cooking. Stephen walked over to the banister, his bare feet padding over the hardwood. Leaning into the stairwell but not moving a foot to climb the steps, he listened.

"Cass, it's okay . . . shh . . . I'm here . . . shh . . . breathe . . . I'm not going anywhere tonight."

Feet frozen in place, I stared up at the stars. One twisted right on a piece of twine, another left. Left, right, left, right. Each one was unique. Carnity's was painted white, Dien's charcoal black with shiny edges. Red for Zenta's with intricate swirls of gold wire to fill the carved-out centre like flames. Sobs filled my ears, the sizzle of fish cut in, Liam's screams faded to whimpers. I stood alone, clinging to the small beauties above me, like I've clung to the documentation of my mother's love all these years.

RIN

I NOD IN AND OUT OF SLEEP FOR THE NEXT FEW HOURS. The course of the cruiser is soothing until I cough smoke from my lungs and the ash in my hair prickles my nose. The reality of why I'm not in bed comes crashing down on me.

Oron needs to know what happened. I should have gone to see him instead of Johanna. Carnity, how is he going to cope now that I'm even farther away? Someone must have seen me when I escaped for those few hours into Senn the other night. I shouldn't have left the Vein.

Brand's been on an echo call for the last forty-five minutes with the Senn LP department. From what I comprehend within my bouts of consciousness, the LPs detained fifteen of the intruders trespassing on the East-side Refinery property. She ends the call once we clear the gates of the city of Vensya.

The emerald night is fading and the city of Vensya, sprawling and modern, with tall buildings made of dark metal and bronze finishes, is coming to life. Outside the city gate stands a giant Ancient beast challenging the mountains in height. With a long body, neck, and lizard-like tail, it wraps around the city. Its silhouette sways against the backdrop of pale morning light that sifts through the clouds and mist. Eyes of pure white slowly open and close. Its body is encased in thick, armour-like scales and is peppered with snow and moss. A cloud of its breath smokes over the city.

I've read about this beast—Utōnyo, is its name. It never eats, all it needs is its feet firmly planted on the Karess to absorb core energy. The steady thrum of traffic doesn't seem to bother it. Vensya has very low crime rates and has always been a safe haven because of this monster. Violent disturbances only aggravate Utōnyo. The wall is all different shades of brick and mortar, telling the story of angry legs smashing it down in protest of the commotion. I wonder what my life would have been like if I had grown up here.

There are monsters on every part of the Karess. Funny how this one, so fucking huge, is more content to take up a small space of land than the hédin who kill each other to assert their dominance, burn down safe havens, and attempt to bring back the dead to finish a war. The Vein is Utōnyo, steadfast for all these years. Or are the Vein and the Revival two heads of the same monster, each head fighting to lead? This two-headed monster is not a monster I identify with, and I've always felt monstrous inside.

Brand drives us off the motorway and deep into the sprawling city. I keep my eyes on the road, not blinking enough, but not noticing the effects either. She takes the cruiser down into an underground parkade. We get out of the cruiser and Brand leads me to an elevator. As the elevator rises, I rub the blood back into my arms. The smoke has clung to us and fills the small space.

Brand turns to me. "This is one of the Vein's bases. We'll need to discuss safety for you, Liam, and the Vein before I call a council meeting. Are you up for that?" She pushes a curl heavy with soot out of her face.

I fit somewhere in all this. Stephen decided I would do the Ritual for the Revival. Brand decided I would stay in the Vein to be safe. My father decided it would be better to stay away. I decided to leave the Vein the other night and got no further away from this mess—I might have even made it worse.

The elevator keeps going up, no longer hidden underground. I swallow hard. Why hasn't she said anything about me leaving the Vein the other night? The guards gave me a lot of shit for busting out when I got back. They must have relayed that shit back to Brand. And someone must have seen me and followed me back to the Vein.

"It's my fault, isn't it?" With all the smoke inhalation, I sound like an old woman, but my question is childish.

With feet planted shoulder width apart, hands on her hips, Brand is solid. Her long, even breaths raise her chest in an easy rhythm. Her toned, light-brown arms have smudges all over them. My breathing stops. A cut, dried and crusted with blood, slashes across her shoulder. Brand's skin isn't enhanced. I had no idea. The bright-red shield of my death affinity could have saved her from major injury.

Breath expels from her nose as if all the energy inside her is exiting as steam. Her jaw sets with a twitch of muscle. "You made a choice." Her eyes sparkle with tears. "An action. For yourself and no one else. To get out of a place you didn't want to be. Someone else capitalized on that choice. They chose harm when you chose freedom."

I drop my eyes to the ground but Brand yanks my chin up. I meet her eyes.

"You think I'm mad at you. Every one of our actions affects other people, whether it has malicious intent or benevolent. I don't see a reason to attribute fault to you here. It was reckless to leave like that, but you're not hurt, and we all got out of there safely."

Our smoky smell fades away and the weight of her words fills the metal box. I motion to her arm, the rusty red blood. Brand glances at it with a short huff. "My skin isn't enhanced. Just my muscle. And my eyes have more essence than normal, making me a great shot. Incredibly farsighted though."

I laugh, an awful, dry sound. "That's why you wear those terrible reading glasses."

"Terrible?" Brand says through a laugh as she picks a piece of rubble out of her hair. "I like them. I think they're cute. This is us." She turns to the door as it slides open with a smirk on her smudgy face.

We enter a long hall filled with the Senn Vein evacuees. My father is in the middle of it all, helping hand out clean clothes and food. He crouches down to hand a juice pack to a little kid. My stomach rolls over and I keep my eyes on the ground. Brand strides ahead in her shorts and bare feet.

"Devin, Peter, conference room."

I follow Brand and my father follows me, his huge form casting a shadow over me.

The conference room has one long table in it and the north-facing side is ceiling to floor windows that look over the city with a grand view of Utōnyo. The table has the familiar twisting etching of blue, purple, and red through the centre, spanning from one side to the other. There are ten chairs around the table. An older woman with grey hair tied in a tight knot on top of her head, russet skin, and a flowery robe wrapped tight over a nightgown, meets us at the door.

"Rin, this is Beda, the Vein's Beastblood representative," Brand says, nodding to the woman. "She oversees the Vensya branch of the Vein."

Beda nods back, raising her chin and keeping her back straight as she clutches the robe together at her neck.

Brand moves to a PAT at the desk in the corner of the conference room. Beda and I, along with Devin and my father, follow her, gathering around the desk as she works on setting up the communication with the council.

"Commander," Beda says, her voice gravelly and dismayed. "How on the great Karess did this happen? After all these years, how did they infiltrate us?"

"Right," Brand says. She sits straight in the chair but lets her eyes wander past us, icing over. "I knew one of the attackers from my academy days. She must have tracked me down."

I shift on my cold, bare feet. The simplified truth. If Thea has to have seen the person she disguises herself as, then she no doubt used Tōmas to watch me. But why would she need Tōmas to do it? Was it to make me vulnerable? If Brand hadn't come back for me, I'm not sure if I could've defended myself.

Father lets out a heavy sigh, rubbing his hand over his scruffy chin. His eyebrows furrow and his lips twitch like he might say something in response to Brand's vague answer, but Devin lays a hand on his shoulder, quieting him. Beda and Brand share a knowing look, still cool as ice, but its softness is not lost. She lets it fall to me as she nods.

Beda folds her hands in front of her. "Although it's nothing short of a catastrophe, if we can identify their target, then we can evaluate their motive. No casualties?"

"Right, no one was seriously injured. Most of their attacks were meant to stop us or block us, not kill us," Devin says, sticking his hands into ashy sweatpants.

Father folds his thick arms over his chest. "Did they take anything?"

"Yes, as a matter of fact," Brand says. She holds the PAT at arm's length and squints down her nose at it. "Our files on the Revival have been wiped from our systems."

Father's forehead creases, his grey eyes are focused. His face is a mask to me, hiding his past, hiding all the twisted things he's done. "So, their target is the Revival, not the Vein itself," he says.

Brand nods and sets down the PAT to prop her elbows on the desk and rub her eyes. Clasping my hands together, I pop my knuckles on one hand. The creases in my father's mask lessen, and his eyebrows draw down as he eyes my fingers.

"And what was in the file?" I ask.

"Detailed directions to their previous hideouts, all recent activity that we know about, and the information that we just received about Stephen's appearance in Tien Bay."

I snap my head up. My feet go numb and my stomach lurches with the loss of contact with the floor. Eliote lives in Tien Bay.

"So the Emberstead know the Revival has a utanic Death

stone," Devin says, rubbing his forehead. He steps out of our semicircle around Brand and paces behind us.

"Utanic Death stone?" I say. "Utanic like the stars."

"Yes," Devin says. "The green stars in our galaxy are compact sources of utanic energy, chaotic energy. Utanic energy forms when jint, unama, and fann energies mingle in perfect balance. With so many celestial bodies of different core energies, there is no shortage of utanic energy out in space, and it causes an erratic orbit for our second moon. Year round, the sustaining force of the Karess' jint core keeps utanic energy out of our atmosphere. But when our second unama moon approaches, the energy balance shifts and utanic energy builds."

Geret told me that there needs to be enough jint, unama, and fann energy in the atmosphere for the Ritual to work. He meant utanic energy.

"For utanic energy to have an effect, it needs to have a certain concentration. Death stones can absorb a large amount of utanic energy and stabilize it," Devin says. He braces his hand against the window and watches Utōnyo sway over the city. "The Revival gathered utanic energy into a Death stone during the Festival of Two Moons."

The sway disrupts my perception, inducing a sense of falling. My stomach growls and churns with the shift, and I drop my eyes back to the floor. "So, they literally have a battery to power the Revival Ritual at anytime now?" I ask.

"Yes, but they still need the affinities, and they still need *enough* utanic energy to perform the Ritual. It seems they didn't gather enough from Sii, and Stephen was spotted in Tien Bay with the stone."

Tension seizes my muscles, blood pulses hot under my skin,

and I press the heels of my hands to my eyes to keep back the itch.

Devin's voice lowers. "Death stones draw in beasts, and large-scale beast attacks create fear. Mix fear with fau beast energy, add a little jint from the Karess, and you get crude utanic energy."

"Eliote. Is she okay?" I say, still hiding my eyes. "Shit." My body sways, just like the beast watching us from outside. The wheels of Brand's chair squeak and something drags along the carpeted floor.

"I checked the obituaries. I believe she's still safe," Brand says from behind me. Warm hands guide me into a chair, and I let my icy fingers fall to my lap. "Right now, we need to focus our energy toward the things we can control. We move forward even when we have been knocked down. Our current priorities are Rin's safety, finding Liam, and keeping the Revival from happening."

So not only did they attack a festival full of people in order to force me to use my death affinity, but they also created a utanic Death stone. To top it off, they destroyed my friend's home.

"To make sure we're all on the same page here, the attack was to obtain information," Beda says. "They found information on the Revival which threatens the Emberstead position of power."

Red spots crackle at the edges of my vision. A bottle of water appears in front of me, a light-brown hand holding it. Brand's hand, with soot caked under her nails and smudges of blood and ash on the back. I take the bottle, but my hands tremble and my arms are stiff. Brand nudges the bottle to my lips.

"But why did they destroy the powerstones if no one used Mind Fire on us?" Devin asks.

"Thea, the woman I told you about," Brand says. "She used Mind Fire. Rin has been staying in my personal room, so I'm not sure if she was looking for me or Rin or if she just happened to be there."

"A woman with powerful Mind Fire abilities showing up when there are so many Ironskins disappearing can't be a coincidence. Some have been going to the Revival, but not all of them."

"What are you saying, Peter?"

"I'm saying that there's a connection to The Captor."

The Captor. I know that name. Mother and Father fought about it before he left that one night. It has something to do with Geret. Did the Revival form to combat The Captor? Thea said she's trying to stop someone. Was that the "her" Thea talked about? Either Thea is The Captor or she's trying to stop her.

"Thea isn't old enough," Brand says. "We know now that The Captor was already working during the Fourth Great War, fifty years ago."

"Then maybe The Captor hasn't just been one person," Father says.

I pull my eyes away from the ground and glance at Brand as she stiffens. She wets her cracked lips and says, "Beda will revise our security detail, making sure it has no flaws. And we'll be doing psychological evaluations as soon as possible. Peter, get a team ready to track Stephen."

Father crosses his arms and huffs as the Commander shifts focus.

"His last sighting was in Kyo," Devin says.

"Good, start there."

"What about the team following the lead in Toreth?"

"Keep them there."

Each voice fades to static. The only voice I hear is Brand's, not as she currently speaks, but just what she said earlier, that they'll focus their energy toward the things they can control. I can't control anything here. I have no say in the Vein. The Revival only wants me to start a war. The Vein won't let me look for Liam. If I get to the academy, I can focus on training. I can find my own way to the Revival. I can get Liam out. The Revival spooks at any sight of the Vein. Their trail goes cold. So, the Vein can't be a part of this rescue. It has to just be me.

"I want to go back to the academy." Blunt. No question. No hesitation. My chosen words and chosen path, split their attempts to work around me. But just in my mind. They keep talking.

My exhaustion leaves no room for what ifs or a gentleness that quietly resigns and waits for my elders to finish. That kind of respect costs too much energy.

Heat crackles through my face, drying out my eyes, filling them with itchy pain.

"I'm goin' back." I raise my voice so it's sharp, abrasive, and full of Senn.

The first voice to quiet is Brand's. Her eyes turn to me as my vision clouds with red. My breaths grow and energy crawls down my spine and my limbs.

I breathe in. The scent of the wood table tingles my nose, morning breath and body odours mix through me attempting to cut off my air, but I fight through it taking each long, greedy breath with my full lung capacity.

"With the Revival gaining power and the Emberstead taking strikes at us?" Beda asks. Her lips purse and her dark, beady eyes challenge me. "That's absurd."

What's absurd is constantly learning bits and pieces of important information days late. If they're not going to be upfront with me, then I might as well leave.

"Not really, actually." Devin runs a hand over his short white hair. "As long as we keep a close eye on her, the academy might be as safe a place as any. We know they want to disrupt the Revival and the Vein, so keeping her away from both might be a good idea. Besides, they wouldn't attack a Guardian Academy filled with Emberstead prodigy."

"Shouldn't the girl be with her family in these trying times?" asks Beda.

I shift my eyes from Brand to Father, both unable to meet my gaze. "My leave of absence will expire soon anyway. I'll need to go back to get my last weeks of mandatory essence training."

Once that's fulfilled, I'll find my way to the Revival, get Liam, and we'll run.

The red energy of my death affinity grips my muscles. I lean back in the chair and tilt my head to the ceiling and imagine the red energy pouring from my head down my back. It clears my eyes and loosens my muscles, but the heat remains.

Brand says, "I came back to transform the Vein. To connect the Vein to the Guardian system. The goal is peace with the other lineages." Her pause commands attention and each of us shift our bodies toward her. "The goal is letting Rin pursue her own goals, as an Ironskin and a hédin." Her affirming words swim through the dark in my mind. "We can't connect if we hide," Brand says.

The hush of quiet gnaws through me. The thrill of energy teeming through my skin takes a nasty turn, sparking thoughts in the darkness of my exhausted mind. This is still a woman who kept herself from me. My father stands beside her, a man who came back from the dead, but not for me.

"She should go back to the academy," he says.

Every inch of me hates the words now that they fall from his mouth. Those are my words.

In the glass walls of the conference room, Utōnyo's reflection sways beyond the city. Its form shifts, and as it raises its head, snow and debris crumbles off its neck. It blinks its brilliant eyes as the whole city trembles from its movement. I stare at the reflection of the white light in the window, keeping the image of the red waterfall down my back until all the heat in my body has drained and Utōnyo settles with the retraction of my hostile energy.

I tune out the rest of the discussion until Brand dismisses me as she starts the council meeting. Leaving the room, I fall in with the last of the Vein evacuees filing around a table with used clothes. My stomach is in knots and my hands tremble as I try to find something that will fit me. The fabrics are all well-worn, which gives them a familiar, soft texture for my fingers to cling to. But they have too many smells. Each one's been washed in a different detergent, with a lingering whiff of body odour on one and perfume on another.

"Rin, may I speak with you?" The smooth, deep voice sends prickles down my spine. I grip whatever item my hands come to first to hide their shake.

My father rounds the corner of the table as the rest of the clothing hunters gather their pieces and leave us alone. His shadow spills over the clothes and onto my hands. I step to the side, dropping the shirt and continuing to browse.

"Rin, we need to talk."

I glance up at him. His grey eyes are storms, like Stephen's, there's a smile in them like Liam's.

Keeping his eyes captive in my gaze, I say, "Now's not a great time."

I throw up my hands, still holding the last thing they came across, leaving me flailing an old bra that would fit three of my breasts in one cup. I drop the bra with a scoff at him and shake my head at myself.

Father follows me as I keep moving around the table. "I just want to talk to my daughter."

Daughter. The word rings through my head, blocking out the rest of the voices in the Vein.

"Please, Rinny. When is there ever going to be a good time?" His words take a direct path to my ears, like he's speaking down a tube.

He towers over me. I turn on him, clutching a grey flannel button-up shirt. "A good time would have been before I started wearing your shirts instead of buying myself new clothes to save money."

All those shirts are gone now. All of my mother's shirts, too, and her pants, her ring, her note, and the beautiful shoes Eliote gave me. Tōmas' face flashes through my mind behind the flickering flame. I wince and press my eyes shut, nausea whirling in my gut, and too many scents stinging my nose.

"A good time would have been when you stepped your feet back on the Karess," I say, opening my eyes and steeling myself for the millionth time in my life, forcing the tears down, and straining my voice over the lump in my throat.

Father runs his hand over his scruffy face. His hair is dishevelled, and his barrel chest caves in, eyes no longer smiling.

"A good time would have been before Liam was taken away. But you didn't take those chances to come talk to me so, yeah, I guess this is as good a time as any, when I haven't slept, I smell like a fucking bonfire, and I have the emotional control of a toddler. So, go ahead, talk." I face him dead on, folding the flannel under my arm.

Father sighs. Planting his hands on his hips, he paces around the table.

"I said talk. Oh, and don't get too scared if my eyes turn red."

With a stifled grunt, he slams his hands down on the table. "I made mistakes."

"I don't know, but I think abandoning your children falls in a different category."

"Before," he yells, his head bent, arms still braced on the table but shaking. "I made mistakes that cost me my life and the life I found after death."

My heart shakes with his heavy breaths. I stare at his tight forearms, the wrinkles on his face as he lifts his head to me. "I was involved with the Revival early on. I helped Geret find the ancient Slyvic texts about the Death Ritual and came up with a way to reverse it. We tested our theory, but that only lead to the death of the individuals willing to perform the Ritual. We worked endlessly to find a way to bring back our people. Sometimes a few people were brought back, sometimes healthy, sometimes catatonic. It always led to the death of the one who performed the Ritual, usually an Ironskin with only one affinity."

I snap my jaw shut as he pauses, and I drop my eyes back

down to the table, taking hold of a pair of pants that might fit me.

"I had enough. Too many lives were being lost for the sake of our Ritual. Geret insisted I stay, saying that he found the location of an ancient text recording a Ritual that was successful in bringing back the dead. I refused. But since I knew too much and was going to tell the LPs, when I tried to leave, Geret took my life. The Emberstead government was watching us, and they wanted us dead. If Geret found out that I made my way back to the land of the living through the rift, he would take my life again. If the Government knew I was alive, they'd terminate me too. Hiding myself in the Vein was my only option if I was ever going to see you again."

Tears stream down his pale face. Energy fizzles through me. I swallow hard and sniff. The muffled voices swim around us.

"What the fuck have you been doing all this time?" I say, barely loud enough for me to hear myself.

"The Hold."

I hug the clothes to my chest, breathing in the scent of the other hédin bodies.

"There's something in the Lesser Worlds that calls to us all. For some, it's the Beyond, for some it's something back on the Karess. For me it's the Hold." His hands are at his sides, fingers limp, muscles relaxed. "If I can just get to the Hold in the Higher Plane, we could find a way to break it without reviving them into this world." He beats his fists on his chest. "The lives I trapped inside because of failed Revival attempts can be released to the Beyond. I did what I thought was right when I worked with Geret. Again, I thought it was right to leave. I've had to pay the consequences of my actions for six years." He keeps his eyes on me.

I take a black hooded sweater from the table. I turn my back to him with my eyes on the ground. Father's shadow catches my feet. Standing in his shadow, his darkness, draws my darkness out of the depths of my heart. The dark that drove me to try to take my own life when my little brother needed me. The dark that led me to dingy Dawnranfet rings and drove my fists into bloody noses for cash prizes.

Walking out of the room with my arms full of someone else's clothes, I wonder if we needed him to come back at all. Maybe we didn't need that. Stephen, Liam, and I, we needed him with us, present, the first time around.

He thinks his darkness deserves distance, atonement. What does my darkness deserve?

Maybe I wouldn't have come for me either.

16

JOHANNA

Ever since the fire at the East-side Refinery, I've been able to connect with Rin's mind but not hear her thoughts, which means she's not at the refinery anymore. She's far away. A fire. That's all the LPs told the public. But that's where she had me drop her off. My stomach has been in knots ever since I saw Tōmas' pretty face in the dark. Wherever Brand took Rin "to be safe," I'm not sure it's safe anymore.

I throw a few more pairs of shorts and leggings into my bag. I zip it closed and sit down on the floor beside it. Lemon pepper and the sizzle of frying vegetables wafts up the stairwell to my room as Mom cooks us our last meal together before I head back to the academy. My stomach lurches. The last day in Akinnera, Lance and I went to see that Seer. That damn mystery. I tried to put it out of my mind. But the image of energy flowing back and forth has to be the Soul Tether. The door closing though—a break in the tether. Maybe that's why I can't connect with Rin? But whenever something drastic happens to our tether, like when Rin tried to end her life, I am dropped on my ass.

None of this makes sense, and to top it off, every time I think of seeing Jeff, I feel like I've done something wrong. Like I made a mistake, that maybe I do want a relationship. But I don't, not like that.

I push off the ground. I don't need to be second-guessing myself. Grabbing my bags, I chuck them down the stairs, muttering to myself.

"Joey," Mom says, coming to the steps and peering up the stairwell with a spatula in her hand. "You okay, hon?"

Sucking in a breath and running my tongue over my teeth, I hold up my hands. "I'm fine," I say, keeping my voice as even as possible. The urge to tell her to butt out of my business is right on the tip of my tongue, but her voice lingers in my mind as she stays still, eyebrows raised. Just the slightest lift in her voice says she could put down the spatula and come help me at any moment. All I have to do is say the word. I nod to her and march back to my room, closing the door behind me.

An ache taps into my head. I rub my temples and pace my room in the pale-green light of early evening. As I wear away my rug, chewing on my thumbnail, my mouth goes dry. The smell of dying embers prickles my nose.

"Is now a bad time?"

I jolt and whirl around with my fist plated in embers, heat licking at my face.

In the corner of my room, on the console that holds my vision tech, sits the Silver Wander Wraith. Her voice is wispy and echoes in my head, mirroring the lightness of her glowing form. The bright orbs of her eyes bore into me as she sits primly, leaning back on one hand with her legs crossed.

My fists drop, the plating dissipating into steam. "You. Where the fuck have you been?"

Her brilliant form shudders, brightening and darkening, yet leaving the shadows in the room untouched, the green light of the stars unbothered. Her head dips and her hand touches her lips.

"Oh, for Zenta's sake, you're embarrassed that I said fuck? You barge into my space, and you're embarrassed by me?" I roll my eyes and hold up my pinky finger.

The wraith's silvery brow furrows.

I look down at my pinky. "It means the same thing as fuck. Zenta, you must be ancient."

Her sigh is like a rush of wind in my head. She slips off the vision tech stand and moves toward me. "So, it is a bad time."

"Yeah, kind of. But you're here now, so we're going to talk. No more random pop ups."

"My appearance is not random at all. I've only appeared to you twice. The third time you came to me."

"All those times felt as random as this one."

"Again, not random at all. You are getting stronger. As your energy grows, it allows me to converse with you with far less risk."

"Well, you're not wasting my time, so since you can see the Soul Tether, you can tell me if she's okay."

"The one to whom you are Soul Tethered?"

I flop down on my bed, curls spraying wildly over the sheets, and I stare at the ceiling. "Just call her Rin, it's less of a mouthful."

"Yes," the wraith says, a quiet murmur in my head. "Soul Tethers are not just one type of energy. They are spirit, mental energy, and physical essence. They can be sensed in all the realms. The Lesser Worlds, the Beginning, and the Beyond."

I rub my eyes. I can't believe I'm sitting here casually talking to a wraith.

"Why do I feel like I'm in a pew in a cathedral for the All Creator?"

The Silver Wraith's chuckle ripples through me. "Rin is safe at the moment. Her power grows just as yours grows."

I open my eyes to find her perched on my bed frame, staring down at me. It makes me sick that Rin's power grows with mine. We should be able to grow separately, at our own pace. If I hadn't tethered us, then maybe she'd already have full control over her affinities. Maybe I'd be further along with my Mind Fire abilities, or maybe the other way around. Gaining power from her through the tether might be the only reason I'm as far along as I am now.

"Why did you contact me?" Way back on Registration Day I saw her. I know it was her in the alleyway. She's been teasing me this whole time.

The wraith shifts. "I need your help."

"No," I say. "Not unless you agree to helping me untangle the mess I've made with this tether. You told me about it, so help me get rid of it."

"Fine, I will help you figure out how to break the tether." She folds her glowing hands in front of her. I glance at the mirror across from her, like it might flip her face around and give me more information, let me know if she's telling the truth. But not even a glimmer of light reflects off the glass.

"What do you want me to do?" I ask, crossing my arms.

"Come with me to my Wander Land."

"Go back to the Wander Lands?"

"Not *the* Wander Lands, *my* Wander Land. To my captivity. The mental energy that binds me to the middle realm of the Lesser Worlds, the Silent Realm."

I work my jaw as I glare at her. She still has not given me any straight answers. "I'm supposed to be going down to dinner in like two minutes."

"It will only take one." The wraith smiles and glides off my bedframe to stand before me, her hair snaking in long silver strands all around her and dress billowing with a thrum of energy. She holds out a sparkling hand to me.

The clatter of plates coming out of the washer sounds from downstairs. This is ridiculous. I reach out and grab her hand.

The breath in my lungs evaporates. My room disappears and darkness expands all around me. Pink light flows from me, energy pulses in my fingers, still clutching the wraith's silver hand. She keeps hold of me until the void around us shifts, filling with shapes and colour. A dirt path fills the space beneath me. But my pink toes don't touch it, and the Silver Wraith hovers above the dirt too. The path leads into a bustling town. People are dressed in all sorts of long, colourful dresses and robes, not a cruiser or speeder in sight. Some of them carry firestones, lightstones, or waterstones, embedded in intricately carved staves. Wooden buildings with peaked roofs and vermilion-painted columns surround a cobblestone square.

The sky is bright blue, and an easy breeze shifts the long grass around the path. A shudder of energy pulses through me. I want to touch and smell and hear the noises of this place, but it is deathly quiet, and my senses are not in touch with this reality.

"This is the moment I died." The wraith stands with her back to me as she stares beyond the town, head tilted up to the grand palace on the hill. "At the time, all the lineages were at peace. But I knew there were seeds of hate and lust for power over others under that guise of serenity. I died knowing what I worked for would not last. My intention, my true goal, was never realized in the Beginning realm, your realm. And now I am trapped in the moment of my demise. My Wander Land. Wraiths can move through the Silent Realm and even into the Beginning, but the energy of our Wander Lands keeps us from moving on to find our spirits and our essence. It keeps us from moving on to the Beyond."

I wrap my arms around my glowing pink body as I hover with the mind of a dead woman. My energy squirms inside me. The Silver Wraith is calm, or maybe not calm. Her energy moves freely around the boundaries of her womanly figure while my energy is tight in her world.

"You can't see mental energy in the Beginning," she says. "You can't touch it. If wraiths touch hédin who don't have Mind Fire in the Beginning, they run the risk of killing them with the mental shock. Only a very strong individual can hold two minds at once."

Her wide glowing orbs brighten, taking in my energetic form. I hug myself tighter. She wears clothes in this form. I am only a form—a woman, just as in my world.

"After my death, I watched the peaceful world I knew fall into chaos, one war after another. I tried contacting many Emberstead women to urge them to peace. They all resisted me. But you"—she turns fully to me—"your mind already wanted peace."

The energy where my heart should be prickles like static. It's becoming clearer to me why she keeps invading my space, but I still have so many questions. "You want me to help you make peace in the Beginning. So you can be free of your Wander Land?"

A silver smile lights her face.

"Who are you?"

Vibration stirs through me as she prepares to speak. Heat spikes all around me. The scene of the serene village wavers, colour bleeding into dark again. The wraith's eyes grow, her mouth falls agape. Pain pierces through me at every point of my body. I crumble to my knees, still hovering in the void. My hands go to my head like a vice on the splitting pain that might dissipate all the energy holding me together.

Shuddering, I lift my head. The void of darkness shifts to a green forest, a shimmering full-figured woman of vibrant red stands before me. Her eyes glare at me with bright-red irises. My body shudders, and the world falls apart again. It pieces back together in the heart of a nightclub. Light and bodies flash around me. A woman of brilliant purple stands stone-still in the middle of it all. Another scene filters on top of this one. I turn in circles, surrounded by people and strange buildings.

The Silver Wraith appears in her Wander Land again, but then vanishes as a woman of inky black takes her place.

Short, tall, large, skinny, bright, and dull, wraiths flash all around me, their individual Wander Lands layering infinitely.

I scream, but it is caught inside me. The accumulation of the mental anguish of each wraith and my terror ricochet against the boundaries of my pink form. Trembling, I curl in on myself, but it doesn't take away the clash of worlds.

Overtop of it all, an image clearer than the rest breezes through me. It's me, me and Mom. I lie on her lap, eyes closed. She strokes my head. Tears streak her face, and she squeezes her eyes shut, a halo of fire above her head.

I grab hold of this image. As a few of the Wander Lands fade, another clear image appears. Rin lays in bed sleeping. She's on her side, curled in on herself just like me, hair soaked with sweat. She trembles as deep burgundy light filters through the skin of her eyelids. My hand twitches toward her. But the image of Mom comes back to me.

The image brightens. Her hand runs through my hair, tangling in my red curls. Her fingers graze my cheek and my skin shivers. I breathe in, her sweet smell fills my lungs, and the lemon pepper prickles my nose. The beat of my heart fills my chest as the fog of Wander Lands clears.

Gasping, I shift in Mom's lap, my shirt clinging to my body with sweat.

"Thank Zenta," Mom says, propping me up and wrapping her arms around me. Her arms shake, but she is strong and holds me until we can both breathe again. "What happened? I was just about to call you down for dinner when I heard you fall."

I unravel myself from her grasp. My stomach is heavy with hunger, my essence rages with my splitting headache. Pressing my eyes closed, I shake my head at myself, preparing to tell her what I had just done.

"I went to the Wander Lands," I say, my words muffled and tinny from the thrum of pain inside me.

Mom's usually tan skin is blanched, her eyes wide.

"I went with a Wander Wraith," I say quietly. "She needs

my help."

A sound escapes Mom's mouth, but she presses her lips and expels a breath through her nose.

"I don't know if I can help her. And when I was there, I . . . my mind . . . It's like my mind started to connect with all the wraiths in the Wander Lands."

"Johanna, this is very dangerous," Mom says.

"I know."

"If you get stuck in the Wander Lands, your mind could fracture and get lost in the nine hells."

I force myself to swallow the slimy lump growing in my throat and I rub my clammy arms. "She said it was safer now, my strength is growing—"

"Just *shh*." She pinches her eyes closed and presses her hands over her face, taking a long breath. "I am not mad." She holds one hand up to me. "I'm just worried. Helping a Wander Wraith is not a joke."

"I know."

Bracing her hands between her knees, Mom goes quiet, looking off into the dark corner of the room where the wraith materialized just minutes ago. I bring my knees to my chest and lean my head on them.

After a few breaths, I say, "How did you pull me out?"

"I have a unique Mind Fire ability. I can cause a person's mind to centre on one moment in their life. I chose the present."

I peek out at Mom. Her red hair is brilliant, even in the dark, with subtle wave and grey streaks. Her eyes are lost in the dark of the corner, still but quizzical.

"Why have you never told me that? I mean, I knew you could move things with Mind Fire, but never anything like this."

"Mind Fire," she says, pausing to shift off her knees and lean to the side. "It's dangerous. It's manipulative. I choose not to use it unless I absolutely need to. My will should not hold command over another person."

I nod, leaning my chin on top of my knees. My head is still throbbing, my essence pulses and shakes my body. "Why did I see Rin?"

Mom tilts her head to the side as she looks me over. Running one hand down my back, she says, "If you are Soul Tethered, then my ability would show you her present moment too."

Somewhere out there, she's curled up in a bed alone, restless, and exhausted.

"I don't understand, Mom." I run my hands into my curls and pull the roots. "All this about the Lesser Worlds. I thought it was all just religious crap."

Taking my hand into hers, she says, "The realms themselves are far from religious. They're our reality. In this realm, the Beginning, we spend our lives becoming whole." She places my hand on my chest. "When we die, our spirits, our minds, and our essence remain without our bodies. If someone became whole in the Beginning, they go on to the Higher Plane, where they move on to the Beyond. If someone is not whole before they die, they have to find a way to unite themselves before moving on. Some might be aligned, body and mind, and have to find their spirit, others might not be aligned at all. But they always have a chance to become whole with their missing parts."

"And wraiths?" I ask, still holding my hand over the beat of my heart.

"Their intentions were so great that their minds created an anchor between the Beginning and the Silent Realm, the anchor is their Wander Land."

The Silver Wander Wraith's intention was peace. But as long as the Karess revolves around Ōna, will there ever be peace? Will she ever move on to the Beyond? Will I?

My skin cools as my sweat dries. I run my hands over my arms. "All the wraiths I see are female."

A warm smile spreads over Mom's face. She makes a gentle arc with her fingernail down the side of my face. "Our minds use sounds, language, words to make sense of this world and communicate with each other," she says. "Minds only know what they learn. Your mind understands yourself as a woman. But if you identified as a man, you would see others who identify as men. If you identified as neither, you would see others who identified as neither man nor woman. We see the wraiths who had a similar understanding of the world, similar mental energy. Spirits are different. They don't need made-up words to learn. They already know what they are."

My skin prickles. The first time I saw Rin's life affinity, it was like seeing an entirely different person. Each time it shines out of her, Rin seems to know it a little better, she knows herself a little better, and I get tethered a bit tighter.

"How do you know all this?" I ask.

"Because I've been to the Silent Realm. I've listened to the wraiths. Very few of them have good intentions." Fire burns behind Mom's eyes as she leans into me. "Which is why the next time this wraith contacts you, you make sure you get her name."

RIN

I WENT TO BED EARLY to try and regain the rest that has been taken away from me by sleepless nights in another new bed, in someone else's clothes. I drift in and out of sleep, waking when other women stir in the dormitory, falling back to sleep, and waking again with energy. Energy and heat all over me. My body shakes and the bed is soaked with sweat. Stars fill my head twisting and turning and reflecting. All I can think about is those stars. I didn't hang the ancestral stars in the window of my little apartment with Liam.

Here in Vensya, the air is dry. It is heavy in my lungs. The darkness pinches me. I throw off the sheets and sit at the edge of the bed, running my hands over my knees. My skin is clammy. A drop of sweat trickles down the side of my face. I wipe it away with the back of my hand. My cheeks burn with heat. I've never been this hot in my life.

As I sit in the dark, chills crawling my scalding body. I fling a blanket around me. I'm not sure what time it is. The cots are all full now. It must be late. I get up and move to the door. My vision flares with red. I snap my eyes shut and sway into the doorjamb. Clutching the frame for support, I slowly open my eyes again. The room is dark. No, it's red.

I suck in a breath of dry air into my dry mouth. I cough, cupping my hands over my mouth to keep it quiet. My steps are tentative as I leave the dormitory and head down the hall to the cafeteria. The tiles are cold under my feet, my head burns, my shoulders quiver as if they were being shaken by a beast. At the small kitchenette that everyone is free to use, I pour myself a glass of water. The building trembles. Utōnyo. The beast can feel my energy. Water spills over the edge of the cup and splatters my feet. Red light breaks into the sides of my vision with hot, itchy tendrils. "Shit."

The cup tumbles out of my hands. As the glass smashes to the ground, the blood-red light covers everything around me. A sound slips from my mouth—a whispered scream.

Everything is wrong. I don't know how to stop the rage of power inside me. It boils inside as memories spin through me. Every dark thing I've done, every lonely night, every nasty lie pokes at the beast inside me. It wants out, I want out.

Waves of energy pulse through me. Every cell in my body itches to rip out of my skin and destroy something—destroy me. My hands grasp the ridge of the kitchen sink connected to the counter. The metal contorts under my grasp, the wood splinters and cracks down the counter. I focus on my breath. It cuts and rattles my lungs. Sinking my awareness into my muscles only makes them shake more. None of the training for my life affinity serves to cool the surging essence inside me. My stomach spasms and I gag over the sink, coughing up acid, and forcing tears out of my eyes as the building shakes again.

A moan escapes my lips as I stumble over to one of the long tables in the hall. Barely making it onto the bench, my stomach spasms again but I clasp my hand over my mouth with my other arm around my middle. My breaths come in rapid drags. The table shakes. Which beast is it this time? Me, my pounding heart? Utōnyo?

I collapse onto the table, unable to control any movement my body makes or any thought in my brain. My eyes remain open, staring at the icer that's supposed to be yellow but glows ruby red under my demon gaze. I can't do anything. My death affinity might rip me apart, I might die right here—in the safest city of Emberstead, a failure who lost her brothers, who wasn't worthy of the truth or to be fought for.

I watch the clock on the wall pass the hour mark and my body still rages. Finally, my eyes fall shut and I wait for sleep or death, whichever comes first.

"Rin."

It must be a dream. Her voice is too urgent, too sweet, too much like she gives a damn. My eyes flutter open, and Brand's round face appears in front of me. I stare at the small cluster of freckles below her eye.

"Rin, can you hear me?" she asks, brushing hair out of my face.

I lift my head, but as soon as I move my mouth, my stomach clenches and I gag.

"Okay, okay. Don't move." Her hands hover directionless

around me, flitting like moths over my body.

My eyelids fall heavy, and a scream threatens to tear through me with a jolt of red-hot energy.

"Let's just get you somewhere you can lie down." The voice has no body attached to it in my swirling mind.

"I-I can't." The muscle of my heart burns.

"I know."

Those two last words are whispered, almost nonexistent.

My body is lifted from the bench. I pry my eyes open as my head falls heavy on Brand's shoulder, but I squeeze them shut with her face so close to mine. With a jerk, I draw in my limbs. I could resist her touch; I know I could—there's enough power inside me to level the Vein.

Brand's arms tense, holding me tight. "Shh."

The soothing sound slips through the thick fog in my mind. My head falls back to her shoulder and my arms cling to her as she takes me somewhere.

Brand's voice swims around me in the darkness behind my eyelids, and my breaths are like fire in my lungs. Time is nothing to me. I open my eyes in a private room, my vision still painting every little detail with vivid red strokes. Darkness falls. Again, my eyes light Brand's face as she kneels by the bed.

She runs her hand down my arm.

My breaths come easier with her fingers soothing my skin. The sweat coating me dries, leaving me shivering. The flood of fever still spreads through me. I close my eyes.

"It's going to be okay, Rin." Brand's voice matches her touch on my arm, tender and strong.

Why is she here?

My first clear thought, and I cling to it.

Why is she here with me?

One by one, my muscles relax into the terrifying refrain. My chest rises and falls easier now. Opening my eyes one more time, the room has lost the red and takes on muted tones. Brand's camisole is no longer bright, but pale in the night.

Brand folds her arms around herself. She sighs and hangs her head. Turning, she takes hold of the door handle.

"Don't go," I whisper.

Her eyes grow wide, shining silver.

I can't believe I said it. I don't know what I mean by it.

"Don't go," I repeat as an unwanted tear slips down my cheek, betraying any other request in my mind for Brand to get away from me, as far as possible, to stay away like she's done all these years. Like my father has done. Like Stephen does. Why would Commander Brand Highcaller stay with me? There's nothing I can give to her. I don't think I can even form the words to thank her.

She drops her arms to her sides. Her lips press together as she takes a few steps toward me, eyes on the ground. Sitting down on the chair next to the bed, she lays her hand on my leg.

Stay.

Light breaks through my eyelids. It's cool—bright and white. My body is heavy and weightless, the blankets have a texture that my skin can't identify. The quiet fills my ears like cotton. Staring at the ceiling, I blink. The movement is sluggish. I wish I hadn't done it because the dark is magnetizing. As I open my eyes again, bits of dark vignette my vision.

Images flit through my mind. Red ghosts. I cringe and

sit upright. My eyes are slow to track with my body, yielding streaks of light through my vision, like starlight, so close and so, so far away. I take a few breaths, but it all goes to my head, fogging up the space for thought instead of my lungs and limbs. Wrapping my arms around myself, I wait for warmth to fill me. My mind knows my torso is a strong, living form, but my arms hold a dense, cold mass.

Eyes on the ground, I don't have the strength to look around the room to figure out where I am. There's a pile of clothes on the ground. The flannel I picked up the other day and the black sweater is there. A few other worn items and a few with tags fill the stack. Beside the stack is a new backpack.

My dad's old Guardian pack, the one I've used for the last six years, was lost in the fire.

My memories infused into the fabrics of my mother's old clothes, her note, all gone. I have to rely on the foggy images of her face that haunt my mind.

My fingernails dig creases into the skin of my knees. I retract them and rub my legs. The rough skin of my hands shifts over my dry legs. I capture the sound in my mind. I focus on the texture of my body, long enough for feeling to spike my nervous system.

The city of Vensya greets me, and Utōnyo sways in its peaceful stupor.

It's morning, and if it's morning, then that means I'm going to the academy today. If I'm going to the academy, then that's one step closer to Liam. The Vein and the Revival repel each other. Being on neutral ground might be the only way to get in touch with the Revival. And getting to Professor Hans might be my best bet to contacting Stephen. All this leads me to Liam.

I urge my stiff body off the bed, forcing it to engage with reality. I dress, layering the grey flannel and the black sweater to surround my body with warmth and weight. I pull on a pair of black pants that're baggy and have big pockets on the sides, but they fit.

Sitting back down, I put on the one pair of shoes that are no comparison to the beautiful running shoes Eliote gave me. I don't know where she was during the beast attack, my brother's attack. Carnity, please let her be okay.

My eyes catch on a package next to the clothes and my fingers freeze with the laces of the shoes still untied. Feminine hygiene products. My eyes brim with tears and my nose prickles. I didn't even think of it, but my cycle should be starting soon. I'll need those, and Brand anticipated that.

The door opens and I jerk, sniffing and rubbing the tears from my eyes.

"Good, you're awake," Brand says in her Commander voice—full and loud without raising her volume.

I focus on my laces. They blur together and I lose my fingers. I swipe my eyes again, wishing the numb would come back.

"How are you feeling?" she says, moving into the room. She sits down on the chair she sat in last night.

"Fine," I say to my shoes.

She nods and leans forward on her knees, holding onto a coffee. "How long were you down there before I found you?"

I pull the loop I've managed to make too far and end up with a knot in my laces. Fumbling with the knot, I say, "I don't know."

It couldn't have been long. Not with the beast throwing a tantrum and shaking the city.

Her silence pulls my eyes. Brand shakes her head and looks off to the side. "Do you know what brought on the essence surge?"

She said so herself, exhaustion and emotion fuel the death affinity. I've had a lot of both lately. Sleep's been hard to grasp in the Vensya barracks over the last two weeks that we've been here. I've kept to myself and trained a little, avoiding Father. So, the overwhelm seems random. A panic attack maybe? Probably.

I wet my lips and tie up my hair. Every strand is tangled and greasy but there's no time for a shower. Losing patience after already tying and re-tying my shoes, I leave my hair in a knot on the top of my head.

"I . . . Everything's just been a lot, okay? I woke up and I couldn't breathe right. Felt like I ran up a mountain and back. I was really hot, so I went to get water. Everything just got worse."

"Are you sure you want to go to the—"

"Yes. I'm sure." I crouch beside the pile of clothes and move them into the backpack. "Aren't we supposed to be leaving now?"

Brand clears her throat. "Yes. I just wanted to talk to you about something first."

"Okay, what?"

"While you're at the academy, I want to set up some sessions for you with a Psychological Health Professional." Brand stands and holds out the coffee to me. "I would make sure it was someone the Vein can trust, so you can talk about related issues."

"Uh . . . " The muscles in my neck twitch as my hand jerks up to push a stray clump of hair behind my ear. I zip up the backpack and take the coffee. Psychological help isn't something I was ever able to afford. Looking back to shattered glass and hospital rooms, Carnity knows I've needed it. "Okay," I say in a small voice.

I put on the new backpack and take a few awkward steps in the shoes that are a size too big to the door.

"Hold on."

I look over my shoulder at Brand.

"I've talked with Evelyn. You'll need to check in with her every night at nine p.m. And you won't be able to leave campus without a staff member. We just need to know where you are at all times."

Brand's face is blank. No sign of the tenderness from last night. But the restrictions make sense. The Vein has kept me captive for the last two months, it's been my prison, so why wouldn't I be treated like I'm on parole?

Nodding, I leave the room. In the hall, I freeze. My father is at the other end talking with Devin. His face is shaved and he wears a clean white shirt. His dark grey eyes find me. A prickle surrounds my heart, as if a layer of ice is splintering. Frown lines fade as the corners of his mouth pull up. Crinkles fill the skin around his eyes. Warmth fills the hall, and he lifts a hand to wave at me.

My fingers twitch at my side, otherwise, I am still. Tears well up in me again, taking away the detail of the hall and pinning my focus on my father. I've longed for that look on his face for so long, to see him smile at me as I go off to Guardian training. The thump in my chest invites me to run to him and have him embrace me with his strong arms, to breathe him in. But my mind fills with long nights alone. Nights where Liam got sick and I stayed up with him. Nights where I bled through my sheets and had no one to help me through the confusing feelings. Nights where I fought my hardest to make a little extra cash, coming home with blood on my hands. The night I got my acceptance letter, when Tōmas touched my body and called me names, when I couldn't sleep.

I sniff and wave back at my father. The motion is one step. An acknowledgement of his presence and a barrier of space between us. I don't think that's a bad thing. Turning back to Brand, we take the elevator to the garage and get in her cruiser to head to the academy. Ice settles in my veins again as we drive in silence, and I fight with the part of me that hates my father—the same part of me that hates myself. It knows that he wouldn't be proud of me if he knew how I lived without him.

"Liam, this is the last time I'm going to tell you to get ready for bed," I said, snatching the wet towel he had left on the floor after his bath. He sat by his bed, in nothing but his underwear, playing with a new toy Stephen had sent him.

I threw the towel over my shoulder and put our dinner dishes in the sink. My bare feet slapped the hardwood floor as I marched over to Liam.

"Liam, now. Put your nightclothes on." I planted my hands on my hips.

Liam moved the toy through the air, making wind noises with his mouth. I rolled my eyes and grabbed him under his arms, lifted him, and plopped him on his bed.

"No, I just want to play with it," he whined. I grabbed his shirt and pulled it over his head. He poked his head through, shaking it back and forth so water droplets flew off his hair and into my face. I flinched, pulling his arm through the sleeve.

"Tomorrow, okay? Time to go to bed."

"I don't want to go to bed. My eyes are all funny." He rubbed his eyes with the back of his hand still holding Stephen's toy.

"Sleeping will help them feel better. You're probably just tired."

"No." He held the note. It was long and shrill, and he shoved my shoulder so he could put his arm through his sleeve himself. "I have funny dreams."

I put a hand to his head. He squirmed but let me check. His forehead was cool, and I planted a kiss after taking my hand away.

"Well, buddy, dreams are just our brains processing the day. So, I bet you'll dream of your toy." The winter chill blew through the crack in the seal of the window. "Where are your bottoms? You're gonna get cold here soon."

Liam shrugged, pouting his lower lip.

"'Kay, go brush your teeth and I'll look for them."

Liam slipped off the bed, and I got on my hands and knees to peer underneath, feeling around with one hand. There was a dark lump all the way back along the wall. I flattened myself onto the floor and reached for it.

A knock sounded at the door. I grunted, finally reaching the bottoms. I wiggled out from under the bed and pushed my hair back. Pausing on my knees for a moment, I pressed my eyes shut and took a breath. The knock came again, louder. I sighed and shook my head.

"Brush good, Liam," I said, pushing up from the ground.

"Rin," Oron said through the door, tone gruff and echoing through the hallway.

I hated when he would show up late. It never meant

anything good. He would come to let me know the coin-operated laundry was eating the saphrite without turning on again, or to stay inside that night because the LPs were looking for a sexual predator in the neighbourhood. Sometimes he didn't come to tell me anything, he'd just rile Liam up before bed.

I unbolted two locks at a time and then the third. "What?" I said, pulling the door open.

Oron ran a hand over his dry face, leaning against the doorjamb. His pale eyes were glazed and bloodshot, he had dirt on his hands and face, and his hair was mussed. He squinted at me in our dim apartment light. I shivered from the draft in the hall.

"What the hells are you wearing? You know we can buy you some new clothes."

My face flared with heat as Oron's eyes looked me up and down. I was in a tank top and sweats. I had taken my overshirt off when I helped Liam out of the bath so we wouldn't both be soaked by the end of it. The tank top had ridden up when I got onto the floor and apparently the neck had ridden down too.

I bit my cheek. Placing a hand on my back over my weak spot, the raised scar was just barely tucked under the hem of my sweats. "Save your cash for Liam, he's growing. There's still a box of Mother's clothes in storage I can look through."

"We can get you a few new things. Your mother's clothes weren't necessarily on trend when she wore them."

"It's okay. They work fine."

"Rin—"

I sucked in a breath and pitched my voice a little higher so it was pleasing. "How about I get a few things once Mrs. Khatari pays me?"

Oron sighed and dragged a hand through dirty hair. "Fine."

"Why'd you stop by?" I asked as he slumped onto our couch, his knees cracking, and he let out a long sigh. "Pants, Liam." I held them out to him as he trotted out of the bathroom.

"Hi, Oron," he said, stumbling into his pants and then over to Oron, jumping up onto his lap. Oron held back a grimace and shuffled Liam onto his other knee.

"Rin," Oron said as I closed the apartment door and moved into the kitchen to clean up dinner, giving Liam just a few minutes to sit with Oron before bed. Even if I had almost had him tucked in, it was better for them to sit together than for Liam to get to sleep on time. "I just got word from Stephen."

My throat became thick, so I swallowed hard, scraping food scraps into the garbage and tying it up, hands dripping soap suds all over the floor as I transferred it to the door. I cleared my throat. "Yeah? What'd he say?"

Oron draped one arm over the back of the couch. Liam slumped into his other arm. "He's not coming home for winter break."

Liam squirmed, pulling his head away from Oron's shoulder and blinking his sleepy eyes. "What do you mean, he's not coming home?"

Breath worked its way into my lungs even though they were tight and the air made them pinch. The lights flickered and shouts sounded in the hall. I moved over to Liam and took him by the hand. "Bedtime," I said softly.

He slipped off Oron's lap. All I had to do was pivot as he crossed the two feet of space between the couch and his bed, and he slipped under his covers.

"Why's Stephen not coming?" Liam whimpered.

I pulled up his covers to his chin and shifted my eyes to Oron.

"He said he wants to work with one of the professors on his death-affinity control."

Liam's new toy sat on his nightstand—a little air bus with a button you could press to make the fake firestone glow. If Stephen wasn't coming home for winter break, then he'd miss the Festival of the Heart and Liam's birthday. No wonder he sent Liam the gift. He wouldn't be here for his own brother's eighth birthday.

"Beastshit," I muttered under my breath, turning away from both of them and resting my arms over my head.

"Watch your language." Oron huffed. It wasn't a reprimand, just a half-hearted suggestion to keep curse words out of Liam's ears. We both knew Oron swore enough for the both of us around Liam.

I stared at the ceiling as tension grew through my jaw. I couldn't say all the names I wanted to call my brother in front of Liam. Liam saw Stephen the way I saw our father. Perfect, hardworking, dutiful, good. I hated that Stephen would force distance on Liam, on me. A break was supposed to be a break, but I guess a little extra time to study one on one with a professor was better than spending it with your family.

"Thanks for coming by, Oron." I jolted to the door. "I think you should go." I rested my hand on the doorknob. It shook and my skin was flushed. "I-I'm tired."

Oron pushed off the couch, the springs squeaked, and he left the cushions smooshed and one falling off. Motioning to the bag of garbage I had set by the door, he said, "Want me to take this—"

"I'll do it."

Oron held up his hands and stepped out. I closed the door behind him and leaned my head against it, my breaths coming fast.

"He's really not coming?" Liam said.

I sucked in as much air as I could and plopped down on the bed beside him. Eyes to the ground, I set a small smile on my face. "Yeah, I guess not. But we'll have a great winter together. We'll hang the stars for the festival, and we'll have a little party with your friends for your birthday. Now, you have to go to sleep so you can have a fun play date with Jakeson tomorrow."

"Okay," Liam said. His cheeks were flushed and he frowned into his pillow.

Leaning over him, I kissed his forehead three times. "Love you, buddy."

"Love you too," he mumbled, eyes already closed and breaths getting slower.

I turned out his light and sat on the edge of his bed, rubbing his back. After the clock hit the hour, and Liam's breaths were heavy, and he hadn't stirred in a while, I stopped. I sat in the cold dark, elbows on my knees. Sirens sang through the night and drafts curled around my bare toes. Every breath pulled me tighter like an elastic ready to snap, building friction in my lungs, energy in my muscles.

I stood and found my shoes and my jacket. Headlights from a cruiser passing through the street below flashed through the apartment as I took one last look at Liam sleeping so soundly. My stomach churned, but I closed the door on him and locked him away from the world I'd head to next. I marked the sign of Keena over the door to protect him and headed off to Dawnranfet.

I waited in the crowd, sweating and inhaling the noxious fumes of blood, piss, ale, and who the hell knew what else. Icicle hands pocketed, hood up, I kept my head down. Standing in the crowd was like a sick sort of dance. Someone was always moving; I moved with them to avoid touching someone else. I shuffled in about a foot of space, building more friction with nothing in my head but a throbbing desire to punch someone in the face.

It had taken me three years to get really good at Dawnranfet. I couldn't go too often because it would be suspicious coming home with so much saphrite. So, I fought when I had to, once a month, usually bringing home 200 to 300 saphrite each time— about as much as I would make if I actually did clean for Mrs. Khatari every week. There were only a few things to keep in mind to be a good Dawnranfet fighter—hit hard, hit first, and don't stop.

The fights were a necessity. Sure, I needed the saphrite, but another need reared its ugly head every once in a while. Letting tension out around Liam would kill me, and if I told Stephen off it would push him further away. And Oron, Oron got the most of my frustration in sarcasm and slammed doors. I needed somewhere I could break.

I waited for my match on the lowest level by the bar. Leaning against the counter, my hood slipped back. In the second it took me to right my hood, the damage had already been done, and a man a few feet away turned. His eyes narrowed at me and he sneered. He had leathery skin and a shaved head, tattoos all along his lanky arms, crawling out from under his dirty tank top. Shouldering his narrow frame through the crowd, he pulled up in front of me and spat at my feet.

"The fuck you doin' back here?" he said, loud enough to draw most of the eyes around the bar. The vibration of electropulse fused with my heart so they pounded together, taking away a dimension of separation of myself from this Carnity-forsaken shithole.

I let my head loll to the side and gave him a bored, glazed look, half out of self-preservation and partly because everything was blurring together in a hot rage inside me. I held up my pinky finger to him.

"I'm here to fight." I stepped away, my boots ripped off the concrete and stuck back down, some unknown sealant between my shoe and stone.

"Get fucked, cutch," he said, and the crowd echoed him, tossing ales at the ground that splattered my pants.

My vision spun, churning my stomach, and acid lurched up my throat. I swallowed the burn and my body stiffened as my alias—Jin—boomed over a speaker along with my opponent's name and some sort of introduction, but it was all static. I swallowed a gag and bolted for the ring.

Stumbling through the bodies, my skin froze over, fingertips to toes. I entered the ring, lights blaring over head, and kept walking. Each step closer to my opponent.

My fingers were ice until they struck flesh.

My ears rung.

Heat blistered through my skin, and I struck again and again and again.

Dark covered me as everything poured out. All I knew was my arm striking, my bones colliding, red-hot energy coursing through my veins.

I blinked. I straddled someone, blood gushed from their nose and broken lips. It trickled down my hand, tangled in a silver web of essence. Red. Red. Red. Not red like the death affinity, no, it was never that. Just red, until my skin became cold again.

My first win by knockout, and I missed it.

I left with my saphrite.

Outside, I drew wheezing breaths into my spinning head. I collapsed in an alley. Leaning against damp wooden crates covered in snow, my breaths became a cloud around me. My teeth chattered as the cold let go of my skin and became a force against my body.

I rested my reeling head while images of my younger self flashed through my mind.

They didn't let me fight the first time I showed up at Dawnranfet, but they fought to get me out. I refused to leave without money. Three men grabbed me. I'd kicked, thrashed, bit one in the ear, salty blood trickled between my teeth. They threw me into a pile of garbage bags in an alley. One of them kicked me from behind and chucked a stack of single saphrite coins at me. The pain was dull, but it pumped my blood and gave my muscles a reason to tense. I survived that fight. I could fight another one in the ring. So, I went back the next week. And each time after that, I went home with money in my pocket and another memory that didn't sit straight in my head. Each match was always the first and the last, and I just kept going because the beatings pumped my blood.

LANCE

I NEVER GET ANYWHERE ON TIME, always too early or too late. But today I decided to arrive at the academy early. Everything is unpacked, and I am thankful for the quiet. Between Mom's cooking and not having daily training, I thought it couldn't hurt to get a gym session in before orientation. I took a jog and then hit the weights. Not too many reps, just enough to bring a sweat and bring me some focus.

I sling a towel around my neck and leave the weight room with a clear head and a slight buzz in my essence.

Shower, eat, orientation, read a few chapters, then bed.

I trot up the stairs, and as I come to the landing, a cackle of laughter prompts me to take out my echobuds. In the lounge area between the halls, Mycul, Aris, Litha, and a few other third-year students gather. Adrenaline pumps through my blood, sending it rushing through my head. I stuff my echobuds back in and round the corner, but it's damn near impossible to go unseen with wings sprouting out your back.

"Lancy boy."

I stop short, still tempted to keep going and ignore the jackass entirely, but I turn around. "What do you want, Mycul?"

Mycul sits with his arm draped around Litha. Aris stands behind, leaning against the wall staring at them. His eyes have lost their sparkle and his dark curls fall over them. My gut stirs, and I clamp my jaw as Mycul's arm curls tighter around Litha's neck, drawing her closer to him. Litha's legs are pressed up against his.

"Come sit," Mycul says.

"I thought I made it very clear that we are no longer friends." I yank the towel from my neck and clench it in my fist.

"Come on man, team meeting," Mycul says, gesturing to the crew gathered around him.

"And that concerns me how?"

Mycul chuckles. "Haven't checked your third-year team yet? It's us. You, me, Aris, Litha, Ira, and Kal."

Sweet Seena, this can not be happening.

Kal and Ira turn to look at me. Kal is an Emberstead with jet-black hair, tan skin, and a lanky frame. Ira smiles at me. She's Luminee, like Litha, and has a round face and short, spikey, purple hair.

"Come sit with us for a while," Litha says, leaning forward to pat the cushion of the free chair next to her. Mycul's hand draws her back to his side.

Litha keeps my stare even as her face flushes, purple braids framing her light-brown face. "Please," she says. Her long eyelashes flutter. Her teeth show in a smile, but the smile doesn't reach her eyes.

I could sit with them for a moment. For Litha. But what good would that do? Classes haven't even started, there will be plenty of time for "teamwork," whatever that will look like. But Mycul's grin cuts like a knife. If I back away, he thinks he's won. If I sit with them, he can make fun of me the whole time. Not if I just keep talking though.

Dipping my head and holding my breath as essence skitters through my body, I cross the room to Kal. I hold out my hand to him in the formal Lavarian fashion, because why not.

"I'm Lance," I say with a smile.

Kal's eyebrows scrunch as his eyes dart from me to my hand and back to Mycul behind me.

"I know," he says. He raises his hand, but not to shake, and drapes his arm over the back of the couch, like Mycul.

"Yeah, but we've never met, like formally met," I say with heat rising up my neck. Kal just stares at me, nodding his head, Mycul snickering behind me. "Well, we'll catch up later then." I slap him on the shoulder and shift to Ira.

She smiles and scoots to the edge of the couch and primly offers her hand to me. "I'm Ira," she says, giving me a delicate shake and gesturing to herself with her other hand, gold nail polish on display.

"Nice to meet you, Ira. You have a light affinity, don't you?" I cross my arms over my chest, still standing in the centre of the group, my head swimming, and my wings most likely—and hopefully—in Mycul's face. It takes way more concentration to capture people's attention in the middle of the crowd without a few ales in my gut.

"Yes, that's right."

"Well, that will be a nice balance to Litha's shadow affinity."

"Do you have any special talents, Lance?"

"Me?" I point at myself. "Not really. I make it rain a lot."

"Rain?" Ira's smile lowers to an uneasy grin.

I motion to the window. Tree branches sway back and forth beyond the speckled windowpanes. "Like now."

"Oh, well, I'm sure that can come in handy . . . " Leaning back, she wraps her arms around her middle. "Sometimes." She nods, still forcing the smile.

I turn. Mycul raises his eyebrows in disbelief and a mocking smile sits on his face. I stride over behind the couch to Aris. Slapping him on the shoulder, I say, "Good to see you, Aris."

He presses his lips together, flattening a smile and his curls hide his eyes. "Nice to see you too," he mumbles and shakes my hand.

I suck in a breath through my teeth. Rain taps on the windows, filling the awkward silence as I pat Litha on the head from behind. "Lith."

"Lance," she says, giving my hand a little pat in return. Her lavender perfume hits me, and I skirt past Mycul before the smell can trigger any type of embarrassing memory we shared from our partying days in basic ed.

Back in the centre of the sitting area, I plant my hands on my hips, and taking way too many breaths, I give them all a final dopy nod and say, "Good chat, I'll see you all for training tomorrow."

My feet can't take me fast enough without a literal sprint to the bathroom, shaking my head the entire way.

What was that? What was *that? Whatever it was, it wasn't for me. Nope.*

I turn on one of the showers to full heat and take my shirt off. Sweaty hands to my sweaty face, I wait for the water to heat. I don't know how I'm going to make it through these last two years with those guys without a lot of Ease. We've already had some practice together, so hopefully that will be enough.

The door creaks open behind me and the scent of lavender fills the room.

"Lance?"

Litha's voice makes me whirl around and scramble for my shirt. "Litha, you can't be in here."

"Oh please, I've seen you butt naked before. No one else is in here." Litha bends to check under the toilet stalls.

Steam from the shower licks at my back. Litha leans against the wall by the shower stalls. I rub my forehead, and I hold my hand over my eyes to hide her from me for a minute while I get my head straight. "What are you doing with him, Lith?" I drop my hand.

Litha crosses her arms, her sultry, purple eyes looking off to the side. Her collar bone is sharper, and her arms are thin. Thinner than last year. I know Mycul likes thin girls.

She shrugs. "I don't know."

"Are you sleeping together?"

"Fuck, Lance, you're the one who wanted privacy." Her words put a bitter sting into the mist.

"Lith, he's not a good guy."

"He's been nice to me, okay?"

"Yeah, he might treat you nice for a time, but I'm telling you to watch out. He's not nice to other people, and the moment you want your way, he's not going to like it."

"Come on." Litha groans and throws her head back. "It just happened and I'm riding it out like everything else. Seeing where it goes."

"I just don't want it to go somewhere bad before you realize it."

Litha pinches the bridge of her nose. "Look, I didn't come in here for a lecture."

"Why did you come in here?"

"I don't know . . . I just missed you, I guess." Leaning back on the wall, she drops her eyes to the ground.

Litha's always been confident, but in the moments where I lose her eyes, I know she's being sincere. The realest things have always been the hardest for her to say. I'm not sure she's said many of those realities to anyone but me. We've been in the same class since sixth-year ed. Yeah, we got caught up in bad crowds, but she never made fun of me for developing enhancements late. She was with me before and after Khalie—meaningless sex, dared kisses, and too much gossip—but the moments I lose her eyes are the reason I've never let go of her.

I reach through the scalding water and steam to turn off the shower. The quiet settles enough for a clicking sound to take my attention. Mindlessly tapping her nails together, Litha sucks in a breath. "I know you, Mycul, and Aris had a falling out last year and . . . we've had our stuff and maybe you don't want to be reminded of all that, but I really like having you around."

Without the heat of the shower and the pump of adrenaline, the sweat has dried, leaving behind a chill on my skin. "I just have to keep my distance from them, that's all. I have to do what's best for me, and they don't make me feel good."

Litha nods. "I understand."

"I'll always be here for you though." I set my hand on the top of her head again and leave it there. It pulls easy smiles to both our lips.

Sliding my hand off her head, she holds it in front of her and traces a vein. "I should have been there for you more when Khalie went to be with the ancestors," she says. "I know what really happened."

Breath catches in my throat and my hand stiffens in her grasp. I shrug, squeezing her hand. "We both didn't really know how to deal with that. It's okay."

The door opens and Mycul's sour face sneers at me. He scoffs. "What the hell?"

With a start, Litha pulls away from me, eyes finding mine as she backs up. Without a smile, her lips are always drawn and sad. Her narrow eyes are piercing. "Mycul—"

"This the way it's going to be, Lance?" Mycul says without acknowledging Litha, whose hands have switched over to him, one on his chest to keep him back.

"Babe, we just haven't seen each other in a while," Litha says.

My face fills with heat and my fists clench. I close my eyes to Mycul's glaring red hair and swamp green eyes. Energy surges through me. The steam in the room thickens.

"Why don't you keep your hands off my girl, Lance," Mycul says.

I open my eyes just as Litha wraps tendrils of shadow around him, drawing him to her. She presses her lips and her body to him, eyes shut tight, while Mycul glares at me with a side eye. I turn around to get the shower ready again but don't get the water on before the smack of their lips and Mycul's satisfied grunt fills my ears.

"I'm going to go get changed into my uniform. Meet me for dinner, babe?" Litha's voice is breathy and seductive.

"Yeah," Mycul mumbles.

My muscles tense and I shake my head, eyes rolling. I hate everything about this—their relationship, this team—it makes me sick.

Litha leaves behind her heady lavender perfume in the humid room. I turn to Mycul. He grabs me and thrusts me against the wall, arm pressed to my throat. My wings are pinched behind me, and the thickening fog accumulates above me as my essence surges in my chest.

"Don't screw around, Lancy boy," Mycul snarls, his breath hot on my face.

The cloud of steam flashes and rumbles around us, letting loose a deluge of rain. Mycul jerks away from me, hair plastered to his head. "Fuck. Get your shit together. Weird essence manipulations like that are going to screw this team over."

Shoving me again, Mycul tromps back to the door, shaking his hair out and muttering to himself.

Once the door shuts behind him, I let go of my breath. Slamming my hand against the wall, sparks crackle over my skin. Each breath drags through me. He's so toxic. And Lith got involved with him because I was involved with him.

Finally showered and changed, I head downstairs. A walk before dinner might be good to regain the focus I lost through whatever that was with my new team.

In the lobby, I stop short. Rin stands in the middle of the

room talking to Commander Brand Highcaller. Rin is dressed all in black, nothing I've seen her wear before. My rain has cleared, and the afternoon light spills through the stained glass, casting dots of green, blue, and yellow over her. Her face is blank, staring off to the side as Brand talks. Nodding, she runs her hand over her face. Dark bags hang under her eyes and her hair is in a tangled mess on the top of her head.

I can't breathe, I can't think, because I am absolute garbage. All that talk about wanting to be better with my dad, and then stuff with Mycul comes up all over again. I don't want Litha in that mess, not alone. Staying on the team might be bad for both of us though.

Rin's eyes find me across the room, and I feel small under her stormy gaze. For a moment, she just stares at me. Brand squeezes her on the shoulder and leaves her alone. Rin's dark eyebrows are heavy with a furrow between them. But as she draws in a breath, she raises her shoulders and straightens her back, life sparkles in her eyes and a small smile comes to her pink lips.

I cross over to her, my footsteps and the echoing voices going dull in my ears. As I get close, the smell of coffee fills me with warmth. I open my mouth to speak, but Rin's brow furrows again.

"Are you okay?" she asks. Her voice is low, with that distinct little rasp and sincerity knocking down my guard.

I drop my eyes to the ground to give myself a moment away from her intense gaze—hiding again, just for a second, maybe for the last time. "It's just been a day. Are you okay?"

Her lips part with a sharp breath. She shakes her head, squeezing her eyes together, then steps forward, leaning into me and resting her head on my shoulder. "No, but I'm happy to see you," she says into my new, blue, third-year blazer.

My arms are slow to embrace her. Under all the dark layers, she's so small. She just leans against me, her messy hair in my face, broad shoulders and her head the only parts of her that touch me. I put one hand to her back. She steps closer, inviting my other arm. I squeeze her tight with my mouth pressed in her hair. Even though her arms don't find their way around me, she fits. My throat tightens and tears sting my eyes.

I don't ever want to let her go. If I let go, then time has to keep moving and time will take me to combat classes with Mycul, Aris, and Litha.

But familiar voices sound from behind me and Rin steps away.

"Guys, it's Rin, she's back." Niko comes up behind me, drums his hands on my back and then gives Rin a huge hug.

Rin laughs, spreading colour through her cheeks, and the rest of her team surrounds her.

"Ace, you're on time, look at you go," Rin says, transferring a hug over to her friend, arms and everything. She hugs Jeff, and Johanna gives her a long stare, arms crossed.

"You have a lot of explaining to do. What the fuck happened?" Johanna says in a half whisper through her teeth.

Rin tries to fix the hairs that have been displaced by the hugs, and says, "I'll explain later. Where's Eliote?"

"Upstairs, I think, seriously though, we need to talk. Dinner." Johanna narrows her eyes at Rin.

The team drags us over to the couches to sit and talk. Their conversation is a whirlwind of jokes and laughter, but I barely get a word in. I'm still in Rin's hug, her not-a-hug. She hugged Ace, Niko, and Jeff, but she's never given me a full hug. I want to feel her embrace, but maybe she doesn't care for me that way. Her eyes though. Her eyes roam between her teammates and come back to me, stormy grey. They leave and come back, brighter. Storm raging, she embraces me with her stare. My heart relaxes. I let go of Mycul and Litha and this rowdy crew and find a sense of calm deep inside me.

19

ELIOTE

My fingers fumble over the buttons on the green blazer. I pick every speck of lint off the lapel before turning to the mirror. I fix my lipstick with a smile and touch up my eyeliner. *Mom's home from the hospital. She's okay.* I dash a bit of highlighter on my cheekbones. *I'm okay.* I tuck a stray hair into my bun with a pin and smooth the edges.

Turning away from the mirror, I fix the pillows on my bed, give myself a spritz of perfume, and sit, drumming my fingers on my knees. I never sent in an application to the Flight Academy. After my talk with Mom, I'm not sure it's worth it. This year, I need to find a deep love for Guardian work. It bothers me that I should have to look for it when I already worked so hard to get here. Flight training is new and exciting, so maybe I'm just bored after a year of training. If I don't stay here and don't go on to flight training, what else is there for me? I can't become a priestess like Mom, but maybe a ka'onahalet. I could be a lawyer like Dad or invest in a business like my brother. Every one of those paths serves others in some way, but they don't feel right to me. I'll stay on this course I've chosen for now. I'll do my best. But what has the Guardian system done to stop people like Stephen from getting their hands on Death stones? And what will flying an aircraft do to calm conflicts?

Rin's schedule is on her bed. That means she should be here this year. The staff make sure all the returning students' schedules and uniforms are ready in their room for when they return. It's almost dinner. If she's coming, she should be here soon.

The hairs on the back of my neck prickle. Energy sweeps around me, tremulous and warm. My stomach sinks as Stephen and his bleeding aura, backed by a giant beast, enters my mind. He destroyed my home. He smiled about it. And here's an energy so close to his, spiking in intensity, as the door opens.

"Eliote?"

I swallow and set that smile on my face again. *It was her brother. Not her.*

"Hey," I say, turning to face her.

Burgundy haze surrounds her swirling aura. Red and blue birds dive in and out of the whirlwind of energy around her. I stand still a moment and blink a few times to clear out some of the light from my eyes. Rin smiles, and I force my feet forward. My bones become heavy and the air around me becomes stale as exhaustion covers my heart like a dark, heavy blanket. I swallow and give Rin a hug, pressing away her emotions to form a clear path of thought for myself.

"Seems like you've had a rough couple of months, chicky." I

hug her a few seconds longer just so I don't push away from her suffocating aura too fast.

Her wide silver eyes grab me. "Eliote, is your family okay?" she asks, hands gripped tight around my arms, hindering my escape. "Tien Bay, my brother . . . I'm so sorry."

I take a breath and clasp her arms in return as the red and blue streams of her aura settle into waves. A pressure settles on me. My skin goes cold. Releasing her, I rub my arm where my flesh is still tender from the healed gash from the beast's claws.

"Yeah," I say with a breathy laugh. "We're all fine. Tien Bay will rebuild."

"It must have been so scary, so . . . I wish I . . . "

Her rambling spikes a hot gush of blood through me. "I don't really want to talk about it," I say, unable to keep the bite out of my voice.

"Oh." She pauses, tucking a stray hair behind her ear. Lips parted, and eyes wavering she takes a step closer. "I understand. If you ever need to talk about it. I'm here. I'm really sorry about what happened." Her voice is soft. It conflicts with the rage of colour around her.

All I can do is nod and soften my eyes, while my gut clenches.

Dropping her head, she crosses her bed to set down her bag. "Um," she says holding out her uniform. "You want to meet up with Johanna for dinner?"

Fiddling with the cuffs of my blazer, with eyes pressed closed, I say, "That would be nice." I exchange my bitterness for sweet.

Just focus on Rin and not the energy.

I wait for her to change. Each time my body shudders from her aura, I bite the inside of my cheek and focus on the physical forms in front of me—my desk, my shoes, Rin's face. We walk down to dinner, and I push her aura out of mind. But as we enter the dining hall, my peer's auras shift together, muddy, and thick. They're not as bright as they normally are, the colours that I've identified as excitement are absent even though all the faces I come across are spread wide with smiles and laughter, eye twinkles, and cheek flushes. But every aura is laced with dark tendrils, beads of ebony, lit like fire. My heart pounds and my palms go sweaty as tension builds inside me, pain around my eyes pulls them closed for a moment.

I ram into someone, opening my eyes again to the abrasive light flowing through the room. *What is going on?*

Rin takes me by the arm, steering me back into the food line. She tilts her head to me as she piles potatoes on her plate. Her tired eyes give me something to focus on. A bit of the light from her soul shines through the maroon fog surrounding my eyes. I nod to her, smiling and urging her forward.

We join Johanna at a table along the wall. I take a seat across from her with the rest of the dining hall to my back, and Rin sits next to me. Johanna raises her chin to us as we sit, her mouth full of food. Strangely enough, the space around Johanna is clear. I blink, clear my gaze, and settle on her blush-pink aura. Blinking again, the pink fades leaving behind Johanna's freckled face and frizzy red hair. So why am I seeing everyone else in such a negative light?

"What the hells, Rin?" Johanna blurts, and I jolt, dropping my fork and knife. "After I left you at the refinery, I couldn't get a hold of you. I thought you died and then . . . I connected with you but couldn't . . . call you."

"I could've died," Rin says with a shrug, and pushes her

potatoes around.

"You could have?" I say.

"Well, yeah—"

"Rin, some really fucked up shit happened, and I get a little weirded out when our mental echo connection doesn't work." Johanna taps her forehead.

I hold up both hands, silencing any response from Rin. "Okay, first of all, why can you only connect to Rin's mind and no one else's?"

Johanna's face turns beet red. "I just connect with her better."

"Fine. Now why did you almost die, Rin?"

Rin shovels in a mouthful, chews, and takes a sip of water. Leaning forward she says in a lowered voice, "Brand took me to the Vein, a secret Ironskin organization, so I would be safe from the Revival. We were going to pick up Liam, but the Revival got to him first. Seems he's actually part of the key to the Ritual. They kidnapped him. So, I was forced to stay in the Vein, finish exams and train, while the Vein searched for Liam. Last week an organization of Emberstead attacked the Vein. We escaped and went to another Vein hideout location thingy." She pauses for a breath. "My dad is alive. Brand is my aunt. Don't tell anyone this, I probably shouldn't have told you guys."

Rin slumps back in her chair. Her aura pulses like a heartbeat as she takes another bite but dribbles bits of potato down her blazer. She scoops them up with her fingers and pops them in her mouth.

"Why is everything so fucked?" Johanna asks, slamming the tines of her fork into the table.

The dining hall buzzes with voices and the clatter of forks and knives. Energy waves over me from Rin's churning aura. I cringe and shrink around myself, but Johanna is a clear space for me to breathe in, even as she mutters curses at the ancestors.

"That's awful, Rin," I say, turning my eyes to my plate.

With a churning stomach, I try to eat. But in the space between Rin and Johanna, a light appears. It hovers and twists in a patterned dance like it means something. It floats from Rin to Johanna, and then another appears, dancing from Johanna to Rin. My vision fogs around the edges. Johanna's head tilts to the side. She smiles. The smile is mirrored on Rin's face. They're talking to each other right now. Right in front of me.

My food goes sour in my mouth.

Strong hands wrap around my tight shoulders. I tilt my head back to find Ace's sapphire eyes and an inviting smile on his warm-brown face. He leans forward, pressing a kiss to my forehead. I let my eyes fall closed and wait for the calming waves of his aura to wash over me and take all the others away. But it never comes. Nothing is there, only static, a void, deep and dark like the depths of the ocean.

"I missed you," he whispers.

I wrap my fingers around his, clinging to the warmth in his words that I can't find in his aura.

"Are you doing okay?" he asks, trailing one hand to the back of my neck as he pivots around me to find my eyes.

Bright, ocean eyes, ocean soul. Why can't I see it? I am tight inside. Is that my feeling or someone else's at the moment? It's in my chest. It blocks the truth from my lips.

I nod to him, and his hands loosen on my shoulders with a smile. He moves around the table to sit across from Rin.

I take in air and hold it. Ace hands Rin an extra roll. Her face relaxes as she takes it from him. A bright-blue string mingles between them, even in the dark space around Ace and the red-hot shadows around Rin. The connection is effortless and leaves my stomach churning.

"All right," Ace says. "We've got geography, Beasts and Plants, and Guardian pathfinder for our academic classes this year, right?"

The switch in conversation from Rin's troubles, back to the present, far away from Tien Bay and beasts in shrines, is a leap for my heart. It thuds inside me, urging me to keep up. Johanna eyes me, and I drop my eyes back to my food.

"Guardian Pathfinder, how is that different from Guardian Basics?" Rin asks.

"I think we'll learn specifics about the history of the Guardian divisions, Protectors, Warriors, and Medics. You know, learn more about what they do so we can make a decision about which path we want to focus on for next year."

"Okay, about that," Rin says. She motions with her roll as she chews. "Johanna wants to be a Warrior, and I'm pretty sure we all want to be Protectors, except for maybe Niko. Does our team split up?"

Ace's brow furrows. He's surrounded by indigo. I can't make sense of it. It should be pure blue, bright, peaceful. "Well," Ace says. "I guess we would have combat classes together but maybe not field study. But that's still a year away. We can—"

"We were in the middle of a conversation," I say. My voice is high, tense, like everything inside me wants to burst out.

Ace's cheerful smile drops. His lips part and blush fills his dark cheeks. "Sorry," he says.

"Why don't you go find Niko and Jeff."

The static from his aura is breathtaking in the worst way. It shimmers, tempting me to enter it but repels me as I reach for it. I'm not sure what's doing the repelling, the aura or me. Ace's kind eyes search me, wondering what he did to deserve this, which is nothing. Maybe that's my answer.

Ace nods, gathering his plate and cutlery. "Okay. I'll see you all in combat training tomorrow. Enjoy your time together." He stands and squeezes Rin's shoulder. "Glad you're back."

I press my lips together and pick up my fork again, my heart tearing with his departure.

"Eliote," Johanna says, blunt and accusing. "Why did you just banish your boyfriend?"

"We were in the middle of something," I say with a shrug.

"I was finished," Rin says. She scoots her chair back so she can turn to me. "Is there something you wanted to say?"

Cold and strong like a harsh wind, Rin grasps my arm. Her eyes grasp me tighter. She just left a bomb on us about all the things that happened over the break, and she moves on just like that. Her pain festers in her aura, but she looks to me. It hurts to be the focus of her attention. It's not fully centred, like she's using me to block her pain. Usually, I'm the one to see pain first and probe her about it. I don't know where to begin now that she asks me about mine.

Her aura claws at me, power hungry and seething. This is my chicky, I love and care about her, but these new colours I'm seeing paint danger on my eyes. I push away from the table. "Actually, I think I just need some air."

"What is wrong with you? You're not acting like yourself," Johanna says.

"I'm fine." The words jump from my mouth. My brow is so tight. My heart pounds. I turn and stumble through the tight space between the tables, eyes on the ground, aura's licking at me.

At the door to the dining hall, tears break through the haze, and I bolt down the hall to the inner courtyard. Cool air brushes my hot cheeks. I bend over my knees, panting. Every part of me feels like sandpaper has rubbed the nerves ragged. I crouch down and hug myself, waiting for my eyes to trust my surroundings.

Today is the first day of training. If I'm not acting like myself, and I'm not seeing the way I normally do, then I need to focus even more on what is right in front of me—what I can do, what I can control. Right now, I have hand-to-hand combat, so that means control over my body.

I draw in a long breath, stretching one arm over my chest, as Rin and I wait for the others to join us. Reminding myself of all the things Rin told me and Johanna yesterday, I take in her tired gaze and the slump of her shoulders. Touching her arm, I smile at her, and she smiles back—the space around her is clear of her aura. But in a split second the space fills with a red haze. It whirls around her and my heart leaps to my throat. I snap my eyes shut and turn away from her.

That's not right, that's not her aura. Where are her birds?

I take a few steps away from Rin and grab Johanna by the arm. "Jog with me," I say.

"Ow, okay, spider arms." She pulls out of my grasp and falls into step beside me as I start a lap around the training room.

Her pink aura glimmers around her, like candy fluff with sugar sprinkled on top. It brushes my arm, sending a wave of warmth over my right side. Everyone else in the room is wrapped in new colours, dim greys, fire red, and dark, dark blue. But she's still the same.

I swallow hard and set my eyes on the ground and the lines that cross over each other mapping out different training areas. "Distract me." I cringe at the words.

Is this what Rin was doing just yesterday? I do want to know how Johanna is doing, maybe I judged Rin too soon.

"Distract you from what?"

"I just have a headache. Tell me about your break."

Johanna shakes her head. "Well, I had some good chats with Wander Wraiths."

I snap my eyes to her. "What? Like spirits of the dead?"

As she jogs and pumps her arms, her fists unfurl, and she gestures with her hands. "They're not spirits, okay, they're mental energy. Their intentions bind them to our world."

Mental energy, intentions. Maybe that's what I saw between Rin and Johanna as they spoke to each other through Mind Fire. Mind Fire is the purest manifestation of fann energy. "Is that how you read Rin's mind? Intention?"

Johanna's face scrunches. Cocking her head to the side, she nods. "That might be a good way to put it."

"What did you talk to the wraiths about?" I ask.

"I'm still trying to figure that out, actually. Wraiths are cryptic little bitches."

I chuckle, a real full chuckle that bubbles from my gut. I've missed her bluntness.

We take another lap around the room and come back to the centre with the rest of the team. I move close to Ace, grounding myself with a breath of his lemongrass scent. He has his nose stuck in a book and one palm held before him, ice coating his fingers and flurries sparkling around them. His glasses slide down his nose and his brow is tight.

"Guys," Niko says, spreading his arms wide as if to encompass us all in greeting. "I missed you all so much."

I lean into Ace. A smile plays on his lips as I kiss him on the cheek, but his eyes don't leave his book and a grey void fills the space between the highest flurry and the base of ice on his hand. It's an essence manipulation, so I think any of the team can see it, I doubt they see the dark static that shuffles around him though, clawing at him.

I blink, it stays, so I turn to Niko. "We missed you too, Niko."

"Speak for yourself, Eliote," Johanna says.

"Yeah, Eliote," Jeff says, slapping a hand on Johanna's shoulder. "'Cause Johanna missed Niko the most. Could barely get through the last two months without him."

Johanna glares at him. "You're such an idiot sometimes, you know that?"

"I missed you too," Jeff says, nudging her with his shoulder.

Johanna rolls her eyes, a smile twitching her lips.

I take Ace's arm and give him a little shake. Slowly, his eyes tear away from the page.

"What are you working on?" I ask, keeping my face turned to him but my eyes cast away, searching for a space where the fuzzy colours don't linger.

"Oh, uh, just some time orbs. It's so fascinating. I definitely can't use it in combat. That time-scape I made in training last year left me with a massive migraine. But I've been working on matching essence with blood movement because it says here that—"

I rub my hand on his arm and nod, propping up a smile with intense eye contact.

He looks back down at his book, lips tight. He sighs, closing the book and runs his hands through his hair. "I'm rambling about essence."

"It's okay," I say.

Ace frowns and takes me off to the side. The tension in my chest relaxes away from the team.

"Am I doing this right?" he asks. Holding both my hands, he dips his gaze to me.

"Doing what right?" I raise my face to him, a smile gracing my lips.

"You and me. Am I giving you enough space? Too much space? I've never been in a relationship before."

My heart jumps and I squeeze his hands. I was awful yesterday, like I had lost a bit of myself and lashed out with the tongue of a beast, banishing him, as Johanna said. "Oh, Ace. Yesterday. I'm so sorry for pushing you away."

Shaking his head, he says, "Don't worry about it."

"You've never been in a relationship, ever?" Letting go of one of his hands, I trace the smooth line of his jaw, swimming in the blue of his eyes, while static spikes around him and it fizzles over me.

"Ever. Never met someone who captures me like you." He steps closer.

"But you've had crushes before, right?"

"I guess I've found people attractive, but nothing like what I feel for you."

Heat fills my core and my eyelids flutter as he bites his lip. "And what kind of people do you find attractive?" I ask.

"Well, anyone, and no one." He tilts his head to the side, face softening and lips moving closer to me. "Just you," he whispers.

Resting his hands on my waist he presses a kiss to my lips. I let my eyelids fall closed to hold back my sight for one precious moment and sink into the soft pull of his lips. His touch always settles me. The skin-to-skin contact is almost as informative as looking straight at him, and far less confusing than an aura. My face is hot as Ace ends our kiss.

Taking me by the hand, he leads me back to the group.

"So, where's Marcus, Brand, and Professor Hans?" Jeff asks.

"Hey, check this out. There's a bunch of vests over here," Niko says.

Ace and I wander after the team to go check out the row of vests embedded with star crystals, my hand sweating in his.

"They're those supercool, go-all-out-don't-get-hurt do-dads!" Niko holds up one of the vests, grinning from ear to ear.

"Yes, that's the technical term. Protector Vest works too," Johanna says, also picking up a vest.

"Think we should put them on?" Niko asks, picking at the contraption holding the yellow stone.

"No duh. Why else would they be here?" Johanna says, and slips her hands through the armholes.

"'Kay, but I thought there were gloves and helmets to go with them too," Jeff says.

"I think the standard Guardian equipment is just the vest," says Ace.

Johanna smirks. "So, Brand must be instructing us today. She always likes to give us the real Guardian treatment."

I strap on my vest. The crystal and durable materials make it heavy. But this is why I insisted on training with the med kit last year. I knew, as a Guardian, I'd have many experiences of carrying heavy loads on my back, so I carried the heaviest. I don't want to lag behind with a lighter load. I adjust the straps and my posture so the weight won't strain my back. Glancing at Rin, her veiny fingers trace the vest as she stares into space. My stomach drops, but I urge her to secure the straps.

By the time we all have our vests on, the instructors haven't even shown up. They're already ten minutes late.

"Well now I just feel stupid," Johanna says, untucking her curls from the back of the vest.

"This is kind of weird don't you think?" I say, tapping my fingers together. "I understand Brand being late, she's a busy lady, but Professor Hans and Marcus? I thought those sticks up their butts didn't let them be late."

With a click, the mechanical shades descend over the windows. The lights go out.

The dark wakes me like cold water. My face relaxes like pins have been removed, letting the pleasant look on my face drop. Heaviness lifts from my eyes as everything around me becomes clear. The clarity I should have in the brightest daylight hits me like a wave in the absolute darkness. The familiar auras of my team dance around me and their essence shines like crystal through their essence channels and cells.

"Woah, guys huddle up," Niko says. "Backs together."

My teammates fumble through the darkness turning their backs to each other and patting around to know who's who. I come up next to Ace, nudging him into the circle next to Johanna. Rin's eyes flash with blue life affinity light but it crackles and fades. "Shit," she mutters, her hand wrapped around Jeff-Ray's bicep to keep herself steady.

"Are they going to attack us in the dark?" Ace whispers to me.

"Shut up, I'm trying to listen," Johanna whispers.

There's a storage closet on the wall farthest from the door to the arena. It has a door to the outside but no door to this training room, just an opening in the wall. The arena door screeches too much. If the professors are coming in to attack us, they'd come from the storage room.

Breaths build pressure in my chest and my blood pumps faster. For a moment, I have an easy existence in my skin, the calm I have during the starlit hours of the night.

I keep my eyes on the door, the seconds ticking by.

A flash of light bolts through the storage room. It streaks past our huddle. The light, silvery like essence, slows, creating an outline of a woman, the full form like Rin. The light moves so fast, I barely catch a glimpse of blond curls. If Brand's Ironskin, she must have a speed enhancement.

"Brand is here, heads up," I say.

Brand's light darts toward us. In a split second, Rin is thrown on her back. Essence pours out of the storage room as Professor Hans and Marcus sprint toward us, along with Headmaster Evelyn and two other professors. They all have special eyewear on, it must help them see in the dark because their movements are so sure.

I can see them, but the rest of my team can't. The lights. I need to turn them on before we engage with the professors to make this a fair fight for all of us.

For most of us. The second I flip that switch, I'll be at a disadvantage.

It doesn't matter. Do what's best for everyone.

I dip my head and draw in breath as the smack of bone and skin spike around me. Streams of light slice through the dark as fire manipulations smoulder and star crystals absorb energy. Sprinting toward the light switch, I get all of a few metres before the ground splinters under my feet and raises into a ramp. I whirl around to find Evelyn targeting me with a hovering boulder. I drop and slide down the ramp, rolling and kicking at her legs. She manoeuvres around me gracefully, but I push off the ground and body check her. She stumbles back into Jeff. He turns in a fury, smashing his fist into her swirling sphere of earth.

I vault over the stone ramp and push myself as fast as I can to the switch. Three metres to go and flames burst behind me. I turn, squinting against a huge flame hovering in the air. Heat billows over me. Sweat breaks over my forehead and heaviness grips my eye sockets. Under the orange glow of the flame, every instructor, every teammate is wrapped in a vivid tangle of colour that contradicts the aura's I've come to know and love. An intense force grips my heart. In the burning fann energy of fire, only their fann energy meets my eyes—their intentions.

"Someone get the lights," Johanna yells.

Blood drains from my legs and I drop to the floor, my eyes trained on one blond hédin in the middle. Red surrounds her. It strikes like a whip and lashes like claws. I can't tell its direction; it moves too fast. It shifts with every move she makes. So much of the red rakes at her own skin, the rest crashes down on Brand as Rin's death affinity fills her eyes, and Rin readies a hit.

The flame extinguishes and shivers run rampant over my sweaty skin. I turn my back to the team and hit the lights.

20

J O H A N N A

T HE LIGHTS COME ON AS ICE BATHES MY MIND, streaking from temple to temple in sharp pricks. But another hot light washes the room like blood. Energy surges through me, urging me to the light. I wrap Marcus in Mind Fire. My nerves sing as they connect with his, and I throw him to the side. I do the same to Professor Hans—heart pounding and eyes fixed on the light.

Rin is at the other end of the room, eyes bleeding red, fist burning bright like fire. Eyes wide and mouth agape, Brand's face is illuminated by the demon girl before her. Rin draws back her hand—Demon Palm.

"Fuck. Rin," I yell.

Rin's mind melds with mine as essence surges up my neck and builds pressure in my head. I plant my feet and thrust out my hands, wrapping Rin in sparking tendrils of Mind Fire. My stomach drops and my limbs shake as Rin's raging thoughts becomes my own. Heart in my throat, all I see is red. All I know is that Rin's love for her mother is steeped in darkness. It's buried deep under hatred—Rin's own hatred for herself. And the most chilling thing is, behind all those distortions, to Rin, Brand looks just like Cassy.

I can't let her keep doing this to herself—drowning herself—when there's already so much hate in the world to sink us all. She's suffocating, exhausted. The death affinity makes it so much worse.

I breathe out and push images of Cassy out of my mind, focusing on the bleeding red girl. I yank my hands toward me. Rin jolts back, just as her palm illuminates Brand's chest. Rin's feet leave the ground, and she flies back through the air straight toward me. Her body collides with mine. I catch her in my arms, and we slam against the wall, three metres back. Breath gushes out of me, dull pain replacing it.

Rin screams, red light blistering around us. She grasps at my arm, pulling it off her, but clutching it back to her chest. Blood pools where her nails dig into my skin. I wince and plate my arms with embers, clamping them around her writhing body. She screams again, not pain, not rage, but something else resounds through my being with her cry. I dip my head between her head and shoulder, squeezing her tighter.

"It's okay, Rin," I say in a shaking voice into her hair.

She grunts and whimpers and her energy contracts her body into a ball around my arms. Her face hides, pressed into my shoulder, and tears stick my shirt to my arm. Shaking, she sobs into me.

The light in her eyes flickers to a dull glow until a few hot breaths extinguish the light all together. My embers die, but I keep my arms tight. My heart thumps and Rin's pulse taps through her neck.

Feet rush toward us, vibrating the training room floor. Rin's breaths are quick and laboured. I keep her close, even as the team and instructors tower over us blocking out the light.

"Rin, what happened?" Ace says, crouching down next to us.

"Rin?" Eliote says, hands cupped to her chest, her brow glistening with sweat.

"Johanna, what's going on?" Jeff says.

I sit up a bit, loosening my grip around Rin to shift her upright. She sits up but her head hangs low, face cupped in her hands and hair draped around them.

"Give us some space, guys," I say. My throat is tight and my mouth bone dry.

The team shuffles back, all but Ace and Brand. Ace keeps still in his crouch, elbows braced on his knees.

Brand crouches down, too, stretching her hand to Rin. "Rin, are you okay?"

Rin flinches away from her, catching her balance on Ace's knee.

"I'm sorry," Rin whispers as Ace steadies her shoulders. "I didn't mean to do it."

Brand licks her lips and presses them together, breathing out through her nose. Standing, everyone's eyes are on her. "We'll break for today. Take some time to gather yourselves before weapons training." Her words are dull, void of command.

Rin's shoulders hunch tighter. My mind prickles and my vision swims. An image of Rin's family shivers through me—

Mr. Burgheim, Rin's mother, and Stephen all with their backs turned. Pain stabs me through the chest as a brighter image sparks my mind. Mr. Burgheim and my dad shake hands in the traditional fashion. Mr. Burgheim clasps his hand around his own arm and my dad puts his free hand over their clasped hands. A smile spreads Dad's tan skin, reaching all the way to his bright eyes. This is a memory, but it's not mine. It's in Rin's old neighbourhood. The wooden peaked buildings are covered in white and the air is foggy, snow drifting around our fathers.

He's so clear. My father, he's right there. I could touch him. His mischievous laugh fills me, and he smells like sweet-and-sour candy. A crinkle of candy wrappers tickles my ears. It's like it's been locked inside me, and Rin's memory clarifies all the things I've lost of him. She fills in the gaps.

But the clarity of the image pixelates. It splinters and is swept into the fog.

"Jo, you okay?" Ace asks.

"Yeah." I rub my face. "Yeah, I'm okay. Thanks, Ace. I'll take Rin."

I help Rin up and support her as we head to the bathroom.

"Wash your face," I say, turning the cold water on full blast. I lean against the wall while Rin puts her hands under the spout. The water sizzles as it strikes her skin. "Someone is going to get hurt if you don't give yourself a break."

Still with her hands soaking under the spout, she says, "A break? Someone's already hurt. Liam. He's been taken by people he doesn't know, for a cause he doesn't believe in. I have two weeks to fulfill my requirement for essence training, then I'm out of here. I'm going to get him."

"Rin, you can't regain the sleep you've lost in two weeks, let alone control the most powerful essence manipulation a hédin can achieve." I cross my arms and stand behind her, our faces staring back at us from the mirror. The whites of her eyes are pink and her veins are still pulsing around her face. "It took you a full year to control the life affinity. Mind Fire has taken me even longer."

Bracing herself on the vanity, face dripping, she catches my eyes and cringes. Pushing past me, she pulls a wad of paper towel from the dispenser and dries her face. "It's not just Mind Fire that links us, is it?" She peeks at me through her stringy hair.

I avoid her eyes, crossing my arms tighter. I don't know what tipped her off, what she feels from the Soul Tether. The words to tell her why are on the tip of my tongue. But the Seer's mystery overwhelms me. It was a mystery from the future. If the door is going to close, if I want to intentionally free us of the tether, what good is it to tell Rin about it?

Without another word, Rin throws away the towels and leaves the bathroom.

21

RIN

WEAPONS TRAINING WAS A BLUR. We reviewed some basics from last year and went over some safety and handling for firestone rifles. Johanna was handed some forms to sign stating that she understands the moral responsibility of her growing Mind Fire abilities when it comes to operating firestone weapons. That's the part I paid attention to. The part that concerned her. Just for a second, my mind cleared as she took her time to read the form and sign it.

The team takes up one of the tables in the dining room by the window. My stomach rumbles like I haven't eaten in days. My hands are cold, though, the warmth of my body all drained by the clutches of my death affinity. Pressure lingers behind my eyes with an itch I can never scratch. Keeping my eyes on my plate, I shovel in mouthfuls of fried vegetables and sautéed meat.

Each bite heralding another to fill the empty pit in my gut.

Marcus takes a seat with us too. "I know this day hasn't gone as we all had hoped. Brand wanted the drill to prepare you for the unexpected that you're most definitely going to experience on the field."

The team chews silently, glancing between their plates and Marcus.

"I think you all did really well." With one arm leaning on the table, he points his fork at us. "Grouping up, casting the flame, responding to each others' commands. You guys did great."

I stab a bean. I did absolutely nothing to help my team. Just like with Johanna last year, I let my own shit whittle away my patience, causing a scene. I stifle a sigh, leaning my head on my hand. I don't know how to take a break. I just break.

"This is why you guys are in the running for the Guardian Academy tournament. We get to put two of our strongest teams into the tournament to represent Akinnera."

Niko bounces his knees, sending a jolt through the table. "That's so cool. Who else is going to be in the tournament?"

"We've chosen a fourth-year team, and we're looking at you and a third-year team as our best choices for the second. You'll have a chance to compete against each other for the spot if you guys want to be in the tournament." Marcus' deep-brown eyes glance over to me.

The buzz of voices around me is distorted by my heartbeat. My pits are sweaty, and I've bent my fork.

"Guys, guys, guys," Niko says. "We've got to do it."

Ace rubs a hand over his chin and leans back. "Do we get any kind of credit if we enter?"

"You'll all get a full extracurricular credit, and the tournament helps with the academy ranking. Accreditors come and give marks to each school," Marcus says.

"How often do we have these tournaments?" Johanna asks. "Why haven't I heard of them?"

"They happen on anniversary years. This year is the seventieth anniversary of the Akinnera Academy, so we'll be hosting."

I set my fork down and sit on my hands. Everyone chats and asks Marcus questions while my stomach drops. If we are chosen for the tournament, it's a big deal for our team, for the whole school. They'll need me here. If I figure out some way to contact the Revival, should I even go before the tournament? I can't leave Liam with them that long. But maybe the Vein might get to him first.

Pressure builds in my chest. I press my eyes closed. I can't just wait for the Vein to find him, not when the Vein and the Revival are polar opposites and know everything about each other. And then there's me. I almost killed my professor today, a Warrior Commander. The dark was so bright, so close, so tight around my lungs—I couldn't shake it. *Please just take me out of this picture.* Out of the Revival, out of the Vein, out of the tournament. *Please, someone, I can't do anything here.*

I breathe, clear my throat, and ask, "When's the tournament?"

Jeff and Johanna are already talking strategy, Niko is so hyped up he's singing one of his Beastblood drinking songs, and Ace and Eliote are turned to each other.

Marcus pulls his chair closer to me at the end of the table. He leans over his knees. "The tournament's going to be the first weekend of Jen." He runs a hand over his short, rusty red curls. "All of you will have to pass an essence stability exam to be eligible to compete." He drops his voice just so I can hear him.

I swivel to face him, pressing cool hands to my hot face, and nod.

"If you're not up for this, then you need to tell your team. You've been through a lot, Rin."

I smile at him and turn back to the team for a moment. Johanna's face is rosy and there's a smile in her eyes. Eliote's eyes flutter their long lashes as she looks to each of us for our opinions. Niko drums a beat on Ace's shoulder—Ace doesn't even flinch. They all want this. I want them to be happy, to help them be the best they can be, but that means I have to be my best. Liam needs me to do my best. If I agree, we'll train harder than ever. Maybe that's what I need to get control of my death affinity. Once I figure out how to contact the Revival, telling them I've mastered my death affinity like they wanted will be more enticing for them. They'll believe I'm on their side.

As I hold my smile, my lips twitch. Tension pulls my shoulders close.

Eliote turns to me. "What do you think, Rin?"

"Uh yeah, it sounds great," I say, raising my voice as much as possible against the din in the dining hall. I turn back to Marcus with a nod. "It sounds great."

Eliote's eyes darken. Her smile remains, but it's plastic, moulded, and perfected to stay in place even though her eyes see everything, and the slight crease of her brow displaces her good humour.

Jeff throws an arm around me, and I let him pull me in even though I'm stiff from head to toe. He releases me and I drop my gaze back to my food. I take a bite, chew, swallow, jaw working in rhythmic rounds. The bite slides down my throat and the noise around me dims to a hiss in my ears. The colour of my vegetables fades away. Eliote's hair darkens to violet. I blink to make sure it's not my death affinity creeping over my sight again. But there is no red, everything is just picking up shadow, my senses numbing, my world fading around me. I've been here before, it's never good, but at least I don't have the urge to cry or yell or hurt someone. At least for right now.

The team gets up to put their dishes away. As I pick up my plate to follow them, blood rushes to my head, and Marcus puts a hand on my arm. My knees give way and I slump back into my chair.

"Adrianne would be better at this," he says, his voice low, his eyes looking off to the side.

I tap my numb fingers together. "Better at what?"

"What happened today, somehow, she would be able to know what caused it and how you were feeling without spirit sight, Mind Fire, or anything else. She just knows people like that." He smiles to himself.

I swivel my knees to face him again, a bit of warmth thawing the ice inside me. "You two are close?"

Marcus nods. "We're dating, actually."

Pressing my lips together, I stifle a giggle. If anyone could knock the stick out of Marcus' ass, it would be Adrianne. His face flushes, and he rubs the back of his neck.

"What I'm trying to say is that Brand recruited me to the Vein to be their first Emberstead representative. I know what's been going on in the Vein. It's scary, the attack and seeing your dad again. I can imagine the strain it's putting on you and your affinity control."

I sit stiff on my chair. Marcus is a representative for the Vein.

I can't think of anyone better, a good fit, bittersweet though. I didn't know about the Vein and Marcus did.

I swallow the taste and say, "I'm happy for you and Adrianne," because I don't know what else to say.

The dining hall is quiet now and Marcus leans back in his chair. "Me too. I just knew I had to talk to you today. Adrianne gets in my head. I could almost hear her cussing me out for waiting this long to talk to you."

I smile. My body is numb, my stomach still grumbling, and my eyes are hazy, but his concern reaches my heart. Of all my professors and instructors, I never expected Marcus to be the one to check in on me. Maybe I just didn't expect any of them to.

LANCE

WE'RE A SIX-MAN SQUAD, joined in the arena by five other squads, all assigned to a Protector Volunteer. The arena is bright with spring light pouring through the skylight, the stands are clean since it's still the beginning of the year, and each team murmurs to themselves as we wait for instruction.

Master Lotera is talking to the Protector volunteering to advise our team training. She glances over at our squad, her eyes catching mine. She nods, and I nod in return.

Shuffling my feet, I ring out some of the tension in my arms. I take long breaths of the arena air filled with cleaner and rubber-soled runners. Kal and Ira stand an awkward distance apart, but still closer to each other than to the rest of our team. Litha and Mycul are the only ones talking. They whisper and snicker back and forth, leaning into each other. Aris stands off to the side, too, facing Master Lotera, waiting for command. He wears a dark sweater under his Protector vest with his hood over his head. His hair hangs long in his eyes again, and I've been missing the glint in his eyes.

Yesterday I made a fool of myself trying to upstage Mycul. It wasn't me. My body is still recovering from the colossal cringe. There has to be some other way for me to create some kind of working order with this team.

Aris glances over his shoulder at me. He catches my eyes, sniffs, rubs his nose, and turns back to Master Lotera.

I step to Aris, running my hand through my hair. "Hey," I say.

Aris turns his head to me with a blank face. He takes a breath and the void in his eyes fills with a little warmth. "Hey, buddy."

Mycul's fiendish cackle bristles my neck. I keep my eyes on Aris. It's been so long since he's called me buddy, but I can't allow myself to be friendly with him outside of class. There's no denying that what Mycul did to Rin was unacceptable and Aris just stood by, and Litha chose Mycul. But in class, being an encouragement to the others might be the best thing I can do.

"Learn any new techniques over the break?" I ask.

Aris' brown eyes waver around me, tracking, calculating. They twitch behind me as Mycul and Litha's voices drop to whispers. My name hisses out of Mycul's mouth.

Aris' throat bobs. "Yeah," he says, brow crinkling in contrast to the shy smile that lights his dark features—dark eyes and eyebrows, dark sweater, and a darker shadow in his eyes, and yet he is still kind, trapped in the dark, but kind. "Hopefully I'll get to show you them today. What about you?"

I stretch my arms over my head and give my wings a flick.

Feigning a smug smile, I say, "Not at all."

Aris laughs and gives me a nudge. "You're too modest. You're way more talented than you think you are."

His quiet confidence sinks into me as Master Lotera claps her hands together, drawing our attention.

"This is Protector Syo. She works with a small beast patrol unit and is quite familiar with teamwork, utilizing her unique skills against a myriad of threats. In this time slot, you will be coached by her and I to become better teams. You will be on this team this year and the next, so you best get comfortable because your field study next year depends on it." Master Lotera stares us all down standing like a sentinel, muscled arms and legs straight, shoulders back, weathered brown face stern. "Syo, please explain our first drill."

Syo steps forward. She's a foot taller than Master Lotera with variegated blue hair that matches silky blue and black Lavarian wings. Her face is pale and eyes narrow.

"Sometimes, when beast slaying, it can be good to attack in unison, other times it's best to attack in a cycle. Since we all have unique abilities, using them one after another disorients the beast, giving your team an advantage." Syo's voice is smooth and low. "We'll work on both during the sessions I have with you, but today we'll try out individual, cycling attacks. One teammate will stand guard against your other teammates. Each teammate will attack the one on guard until one of you gets a hit below the neck, then the next will attack. After three cycles, change the guard. You may begin." Nodding, Syo steps back with Master Lotera.

A heavy hand clamps around my shoulder and squeezes. "Why don't we start off easy and put Lancy boy on guard first?"

Mycul's slick voice slithers into my ear just loud enough for our team to hear.

I let it sink through me and let it out in a breath. I turn to him, sliding out of his grasp and say, "Sure, I'm up for it." I nod to him.

Mycul raises his chin to me, sneering, swamp eyes scrutinizing me. I walk past him to the weapons rack to choose a blade for the exercise. Mycul laughs behind me.

"He was still using first-year-level essence manipulations in second year," he says to Ira and Kal as I turn back to them, an Illyson long sword in hand.

Kal crosses his arms and looks down his nose at me but says nothing, brown eyes squinting.

Ira hasn't looked at anyone or acknowledged Mycul yet. She stays that course and grabs herself a short sword.

"Don't mess up, Lance." Litha takes a staff from the rack.

I try to catch her eyes, but she keeps them to herself, moving back to Mycul's side. It's always a show with her.

Master Lotera and Syo come over to our group. "Before you all begin, I have something to tell you. As you know, we put teams together based on skill sets that work well together. You all are very promising students with high control over your abilities. The professors and I have chosen your team as a possible contender in this year's seventieth anniversary tournament. You'll compete against one other team to take your spot in the tournament. Do you all agree to engage with this competition?"

Ah, wonderful. Now I have a tournament over my head with a joker who hates my guts, two people I barely know, my friend with benefits, and only one guy I can stand to have a conversation with. This is great, so great.

Despite the sick in my gut, we all nod, agreeing to do our best to represent Akinnera.

"All right, then, let's see you do the drill." Master Lotera crosses her arms, and she and Syo step back to watch my team wail on me.

I adjust my Protector vest as the rest of my team lines up before me.

"This will be a breeze. You know his enhancements only developed when he was sixteen?" Mycul says to Kal.

Kal gives me a disappointed stare and shakes his head, probably wondering why he's stuck with me if we're all supposed to have high control over our abilities.

I take a breath and let the tip of my sword rest on the ground for a moment. Tilting my head back, I take in the cool light from the skylight. The sky is bright blue and clouds swirl through it. I focus on the blue as my essence lurches through me. The clouds darken with my crackling energy. But I take another breath, drawing the calm of the blue inside me. The dark seeps out of the clouds, leaving them white and fluffy again. I exhale.

Drawing up my sword, I say, "Let's go."

The air around Mycul warps with heat, the clang of swords and voices fill the room. Mycul slams his hands together and a bright stream of embers grows from his hands, forming his preferred weapon—a massive claymore. His pimpled face, swamp eyes, and red hair flare behind his burning sword. Taking a few steps, his muscular frame tenses.

He'll attack overhead.

Mycul's steps grow faster, my essence rushes and a streak of lightning crackles from my hands, following the line of the blade until the metal is engulfed in white-blue energy. Mycul lifts his fire sword over his head, teeth clenched. I drop at the last second, crouching low, and slam the full width of my blade on the ground. The electricity spills off my sword in waves of flashing spidery tendrils. Mycul grunts and leaps headfirst over the pool of energy tumbling behind me. As he stands, I swing around and land a hit to his leg.

"Next," Master Lotera says, clapping her hands. "Keep it moving."

I give Mycul a nod, and say, "Good technique," but all I get is a scoff in return.

I swivel back to Kal, sword outstretched. *Emberstead. More fire.*

Kal focuses a breath and swings a whip around himself, beating the air in a rhythmic motion. I keep my eyes on him, waiting for his lanky frame to make a move. Smoke trails from the end of the whip and sparks skitter around it. Kal flicks his arm, and the whip strikes at me like a snake. I dodge right. Kal commands the serpent again, low, and I leap over it. Kal's eyes are dark, simmering coals. I loosen my grip on my sword, rolling my shoulders back. Kal steps forward, striking again. The whip sails toward me. I thrust my sword into it, letting it coil around the blade, fire and electricity crackling. I take one hand off the hilt, flip my grip, and rotate the sword downward and to my left, yanking the whip and a cringing Kal toward me. I thrust my right leg out just as Kal's knees hit the ground. My foot smacks his chest.

Ira lunges toward me, barely letting Kal step out of her way, and attacks with quick thrusts of her short sword. I step and she parries my attack, manoeuvring easily into another quick jab. I step back but with a flick of her free hand, Ira manipulates the light reflecting off her blade. The slashing movement of her sword is trailed by blinding light. Stars flare in my eyes and her blade whacks my side.

"Nice, Ira," I say, getting back into my ready position, wiping the sweat from my brow. Ira grins and bounds to the back of the line.

I home in on Litha's smirk as the stars fade. Tendrils of her own shadow writhe and wrap around her staff. She spins her staff at me, moving forward with long strikes. I back away, guard up, unwilling to connect my sword with her staff teeming with shadow that can anchor me in an instant. She jabs the staff at my feet. I leap over it, but she's moving me closer to the edge of the arena where the floor isn't touched by sunlight.

She strikes at my chest. I step and flap my wings. My feet leave the ground, and I tilt to the side, tumbling through the air back to the centre of the room, staying in the light. But with our positions switched, Litha dodges into the shadow. Her form melts into the dark.

My heart pounds. I rotate my guard from left to right, along the line of shadow. Ira directs light rays; Litha directs light boundaries—merging with the shadow's edge to move between pockets of light. I know she's still corporeal, but if I hit her with my sword while she's merged herself with the shadow's edge, she'd pull me right into the dark. I steady my breaths, keeping my guard up and feet in place.

Litha lunges out of the dark to my right. She leaps, staff overhead, shadow swirling around her, and she plummets toward me, swinging her staff down like a hammer. I dash out of the way just in time, and her staff crashes to the ground, shadow billowing out like a wave.

I swing around and tap my sword to her side.

"You almost had me there," I say.

Litha chuckles to herself and sprints to the end of the line.

My breaths are long and essence warms my entire body. I take a few steps back to my original starting point. Aris mirrors me with a long sword, and we circle around each other. As we lock eyes, Aris is cautious with his feet. He shifts his grip with every one of my movements, calculating the grip strength he would need to counter any possible combination of attacks. My other teammates attacked right away. They underestimated me because of Mycul's trash talk. But Aris knows me. We've fought, hand to hand, blade against blade. I adjust my grip and nod to his respect.

Aris strikes fast, his blade cutting through the air like it weighs nothing. I block and Aris pulls back for another attack, forcing air around his blade to push and pull the heavy metal in rapid strikes. I counter and block, my blade hammering through the air compared to his swift, easy movements. He pivots and dips down as I swing high. His sword slams into my side. I gasp and stagger.

"You good?" Aris asks, hand on my shoulder to steady me.

"Yeah, I'm good. Thanks, man."

We slap hands and Aris trots back into line. Mycul breaks his claymore into two separate blades and slashes them at my neck. I swing my sword to counter. A clang claps the air, my blade crackling between his. He presses them forward. My arms shake as I force my essence through me to counter his strength.

Static fills my mind, my fingers, my feet. Mycul just keeps pressing forward, sparks and electricity flaring all around us. I grit my teeth against the waves of heat wafting over me. Sweat trickles down my neck and a metallic tinge coats the back of my tongue.

Sound wavers in my ears. My skin is as hot as fire. My eyes close and I grunt, forcing my arms to keep pressing against the dual blades.

Mycul's force gives way. My sword drives forward and I stumble with it. Mycul trips over his own feet and I tumble after him, catching myself, planting my sword tip to the ground.

Mycul's eyes dart all around me. "What the fuck is happening?"

Electricity crackles around me, but my eyes don't find flesh. My skin is translucent. The long sword clatters to the ground as I stare at my nonexistent hands. Breath rushes in and out of me. I force it in through my nose, out through my mouth.

My team clambers around Mycul, offering him a hand as I stagger back from them.

Where are my hands?

"Lance?" Aris says, looking straight past me.

They can't see me. Why can't they see me?

My vision fills with spots, the clatter of swords and duals slipping away from me. I drop to my knees, clutching my pounding heart, staring at my team. Litha's face is the only thing I can keep in focus. She has one hand on Mycul's shoulder, one on her staff. She looks left and right, eyebrows crinkled and teeth clenched, looking for me.

She's seen it all, she knows it all—what happened to Khalie— why does she keep looking?

A blurry party scene fills my mind. I had drunk past the boisterous monstrosity that I had become known for and was at my limit. The crowd moved away from me, uninterested. I stumbled into one of the bedrooms in the house—I'm not sure if I knew whose house the party was at in the first place. I'd arrived drunk without Khalie on my arm for the first time. The bed tripped me and then caught me as the room blurred. Litha's silhouette appeared in the light from the hall. There were people all around her and she turned her head from person to person. When someone would look at her, she would make sure her chest was out, her eyes were sultry, and her hair just right. But they would look away from her. She shrunk in the crowd, waiting, looking, until she gave up. She moved into the bedroom where I was slowly becoming one with the dark. I don't think she knew I was in there when she entered. She just seemed to be looking for a place where she didn't have to be unseen, where she could just be invisible in peace. Her eyes never caught me in the dark—she just found a chair in the corner, sat down, and curled into herself.

I grab the calm of the blue sky, letting my head lean back and my limbs rest, breaths still agonizing.

The electricity around me fades, my essence calms, and my skin fizzles into existence. Chest throbbing with heavy heart beats, I fall to my knees, sweat sticking my shirt to my body. One hand holding my heart and the other planted on the gritty arena floor to hold me up, my team stares at me.

"Lance, you were completely invisible," Litha says through a breath. "It-it's almost like you shadow phased but not. You were just gone, in broad daylight."

Master Lotera steps up to me, silhouetted by the skylight. "That's impossible."

23

RIN

This visit with the Psychological Health Provider has my stomach in knots. I don't know what to expect. So, I'll just let the PHP guide the conversation, and I'll give simple answers. Maybe it won't be long. It will be fine. Once it's over, I can check a week off, and I'll be another week closer to making steps to Liam.

Evening starlight casts a minty glow over the path around the arena to the Psychological Health Professional's office. The gravel crunches under the soles of my new shoes. The texture is a comfort, even if the shoes pinch in places and slide in others. Beyond the city wall, evening doves call out, and the low rumbling growls of far-off beasts bring chills to my skin. On the other side of me, beyond the arena, waves crash in a soothing hush.

The PHP's office is at the edge of the academy campus. It's in a small house the same style as the rest of the houses in Akinnera—whitewashed with a blue-tiled roof and light glowing from within.

My steps slow as I get closer to the house. I rub my arms and stand on the stoop in the glow of a lightstone. With my gut sinking, I am still, unable to move my feet onto the front step. I don't want to talk to a stranger. I don't want to have to explain myself. Digging my nails into my skin, I turn away from the door.

Moon beetles trail the path all the way from the arena to the steps. Their wings buzz as they flit around, sending flares of white light every which way. Three of them swarm me. I bat at them, only striking air. One buzzes past my ear and my shoulders flinch. Another lands on my hand and crawls up my sleeve. I shake it out and bat at the third as it comes at my face.

The door opens. Yellow light spills over me, and the moon beetles scatter, buzzing in unison as they fly to the sky. I turn on my heel. A woman stands in the doorway holding a long, orange cardigan closed at her chest as she gazes at the beetles twinkling above.

"I've never seen so many at once," she says, with a fond smile. "You know beetles symbolize that you're on the right path." She straightens and turns to me. Her eyes are gentle under hooded eyelids, her skin is warm brown, and her dark hair hangs in a loose braid over her shoulder.

"I thought they just liked my essence," I say, rubbing the cold from my arms.

The woman chuckles. "That too. You must be Rinnaya."

I nod.

"My name is Sovya. Why don't you come in and take a seat?" She moves to the side and I step into the warmth of her office.

There is a low, leather couch in the centre of the room with an intricate tapestry blanket thrown over the back. Pillows of all shapes and colours are scattered on the wood floor and one cream-coloured armchair sits next to the couch.

"Sit wherever you like," Sovya says. She moves to the right side of the room, where a kettle is boiling on a small tea stand.

I sit in the middle of the couch, perched on the very edge of the cushion with my hands sandwiched between my knees. On a side table sits a flame with a dish of jaden-lily oil overtop. The sweet aroma is light and disinfects my senses.

As Sovya pours us tea, I pick at my nails, the silence spinning in my head. I've never been to a PHP, but I know from vision tech shows and conversations from classmates that they often ask about family. My stomach churns and an itch presses into my eyes. Drawing in a breath, I hold it. All I have to do is get through fifty minutes of potentially triggering topics and keep my death affinity from getting the better of me.

Sovya hands me a bowl of tea. I take it placing my fingers around the rim to avoid touching her, but my fingers graze her skin and tip the cup too much, dribbling tea down my hand.

"Sorry," I mutter, but Sovya just smiles and hands me a napkin before taking her seat in the armchair.

Crossing her legs, Sovya says, "I've had a few encounters with Commander Highcaller. She's had me come into the Vein for those who need it."

I stare at my tea cupped in shaking hands, then peek up. Sovya watches me, head tilted. I nod to acknowledge her.

"The fire," Sovya says, dropping her tone. "The attack on the Vein, how are you processing that?"

I sip my tea. The scolya root attempts to keep my nerves and essence calm, the ginger bites at my tongue. The night of the attack blurs through my mind, all orange and dark shadows. I grab hold of one of the fuzzy images. Tōmas one second, too close, too beautiful and vengeful, and then that unconscious woman. They both played with me in different ways—Tōmas with my heart and Thea with my mind. I swallow.

"I'm not sure I have processed it," I mumble and take another sip.

"That's very understandable. Did you know much about the Vein before? Did you know that they had experienced attacks like this?"

I shake my head, unable to keep my eyes on her. Her eyes are golden, face perfect with few wrinkles. She's Lifeblood, beautiful like Tōmas and Aris. They both showed me such ugly cores though. I shift a little down the couch cushions for more air between us. I don't know where her tenderness comes from. "No, not really."

Sovya hums in acknowledgement and jots down a note on a notepad. Taking a moment to take in the scribble she's just written, she plays with the two healing rings in her ear. Her brow furrows. "Your team is in the running for the tournament this year. How is training going?"

I set down my tea bowl, heat growing under the collar of my shirt. "It's fine. It-it's going fine. I had one slip up at the beginning of the week. Why's everyone so concerned about me doing the tournament?"

"Are you concerned?" Sovya asks, raising an eyebrow.

Long, beaded necklaces clack together around her neck as she straightens her back.

"No, I just"—I dig my fingers into my knees—"no. Marcus is concerned that I won't be able to handle it." I shake my head. "And Eliote doesn't seem to believe that I'm okay with it either. She's barely talking to me these days."

"Does that—"

"I want to do it. My team wants to do it, so I want to do it. I can learn to control my death affinity before then. I learned to control my life affinity already."

"Have you been able to activate the life affinity lately?"

The warm light of the lightstone lamps in the room fades around my eyes as I stare at my feet. Tension bristles in my chest. "What's the point of not doing the tournament? I need to focus anyway. I can't just sit around while my brother's kidnapped."

"You don't think Commander Highcaller, your father, and the rest of the Vein is capable of finding him?" Sovya asks, leaning forward on her knees, notebook still on her lap.

All these questions are making my head spin. "I uh . . . no." My voice is gaining volume that I can't control. It's high, sickeningly desperate. "I don't. They don't care. If they really cared, they would have found him already." Heat and itchiness and moisture envelop my eyes. I don't know if crying in front of a stranger is preferable over the fire-hot demon inside me.

In every spare minute I've had this week, I've used the library PATs to search news feed for Revival activity, for sightings of Stephen. I've searched lightstone registries for echo companies in city after city, searching Stephen's name, Burgheim, and Aronson. It's all I can think of to help find Liam faster while I'm stuck here, but I've come up short and wouldn't know where to go if I left.

"The Vein knows the Revival," I say. "Their plans, their people, but they don't understand them."

Kind eyes stare at me. Sovya nods, a smile perched on her lips. "So, you empathize with the Revival."

My throat is tight and my heart pinches in the vise of my body. "Yes. So much so that I hate them. They want to drag up the past, and that's where I've lived for so long. I live in my past so much that I can't tell when I'm in the present. My body doesn't get it. But the past is where I broke. It's safer there than having it happen again. It would be even safer to rebuild the past, to erase all the broken bits."

My heart beats and it echoes in my ears like I have two hearts and not enough blood for both.

Sovya hands me a tissue, but I just clench it in my fist, refusing the tug of the tears in my eyes.

"Thank you for sharing that with me, Rinnaya." She moves her notes to the side table without writing anything down. "I would like to leave you with one thing before I let you go. The life and death affinities are spirit affinities."

"I know they are."

"But spirit affinities are not just a name for essence manipulation. They are real interactions between your spirit energy and your essence. Your emotions are the bridge between the two." Sovya holds up both her hands and them places them together. "Physical essence and spirit are linked through mental, emotional energy. This union occurs when you activate one of your affinities. It is completely separate from your physical body. That's why you may not be able to connect to the life affinity at the moment. Your mental energy and spirit energy are not aligned with unama."

I swipe the rogue tears from my eyes. "I don't understand."

"What you are feeling that connects so strongly to the fann-sided energy of the death affinity is not good or bad. It is you. Take your time with the death affinity. It doesn't need to be banished."

The heat built up in my body goes cold and I sit stiffly on the edge of the couch. Jint is a complex energy. It's hard to wrap my head around a pure energy having sidedness, but it makes sense for those with spirit affinities to be able to utilize the unama and fann in isolation. I just didn't make the connection that the two affinities were unama and fann aligned—give and take.

"Take care this week. I'll see you next Freeday."

Sovya walks me to the door and thanks me for coming. Her thanks has come to me twice today, as if I had given her something instead of sucking up energy and spewing angry words.

The cool night air sinks into me. I wrap my arms tightly around myself as I take the path back to the academy. Halfway to the main building, a red light catches my eye across the outdoor training field. I blink a few times and rub my eyes, dropping my gaze to the ground to clear my death affinity. But there's no itch. My eyes are clear. The red was something red, not just an interaction between my spirit, mental, and physical energy or whatever Sovya was talking about.

The red glow wavers in the dark. I squint until the form of the glow solidifies. The shadows of campus grow and deepen with inky darkness as the glow becomes a face under a dark hooded jacket, dark pants and shoes connected to it. My breath sticks in my throat. The face is Stephen's face.

Acid churns in my gut, crawling up my chest and onto my tongue. I swallow, but a burning bitter trail coats my throat. The itch spikes my eyes, fire crackles over my skin. I bolt across the training field, my feet taking me faster than I've ever gone before. The world is a blur around me but for Stephen's face. I leap and tackle him to the ground, one hand pinning his arm and one barring his throat. His leather jacket scrunches under my grasp.

"Where the hell is Liam?" I say through heaving breaths.

Every inch of Stephen is pure, glowing red energy, not just his eyes. He has no skin. The energy glows and moves. Liquid, solid, energy, whatever he is right now, maybe this is what Sovya was talking about. It's like Stephen's spirit energy is here and his flesh is somewhere else.

"Too afraid to show me your face? Fucking asshole."

Stephen laughs. "I'm not afraid of someone who can't control their own spirit."

I grab his coat and slam him on the ground. The light of my death affinity casts an outline of horns above Stephen's head instead of a round shadow. I cringe at the deathly image and shove off him.

"Where is he?"

"He's safe," Stephen says, brushing himself off.

"Safe, Stephen?" I shake my head and scoff. "You kidnapped him."

"You think we're going to hurt him?" Stephen tilts his gleaming head to the side, hands in his pockets, slivers of red poking out from his sleeves.

"You are hurting him. He's not in school, and he loves school. You're keeping him from his friends, making him stay with you to do something he doesn't want to do." The trees rustle with a breeze in the dead quiet. The itch and my own light have faded, but Stephen's eyes are piercing. "Say something."

He turns his face away.

"How many times do I have to call you an ass before you stop acting like one? Come on, prove me wrong."

The dark-red line of his mouth quirks. He sighs, if it's even possible for energy to sigh. "What do you remember about our childhood together?" His voice is his own, but the quality is off-putting with a waver and a tinniness like he's talking into a can.

"You just—" I huff and kick the ground. "You just always preferred to be alone or with Mom. Not much to remember."

Stephen lets out a short laugh, bending his head so his hood hides his face.

He was so distant. I just wanted to be with him, but he always had something else he had to do—study, his own projects, training. He trained his death affinity with Mother a lot before she died—hours on end. When I needed help in school, I'd ask mother, but she would be busy helping Stephen with something, or too tired. I know he had it hard at school, never brought friends home, never had friends for that matter. He was bullied, I know that.

"You and Johanna were inseparable," Stephen says.

I snap my head toward him. Why would he bring her up?

"You always had each other from day one," Stephen says. "Mom just let you two do whatever you wanted."

"She didn't care what we did. She never had energy for me."

"Yeah, but I saw it. I knew it would happen at one point or another."

"What would happen?"

"That Johanna would limit you."

"What are you talking about?"

He paces around me. "Ever wonder why Johanna can only read *your* thoughts, why it's taking you so long to control the affinities, even with full essence maturity? I may have struggled, but my essence wasn't mature yet."

I clench my fists. "How do you know she can read my thoughts?" Who is giving him this information?

"She limits you," he says with the depth of thunder, and the cold of winter. "And you can't see yourself clearly. All those years with no friends, no distractions, gave me time to see who I really am. It was a gift to hone my strength, extend my power. You'll never have full control over your abilities if you keep letting her drain you."

"Drain me? She doesn't—" My mouth just stops. I don't know what he's saying, and this is getting me nowhere. He's never going to tell me where Liam is unless he knows I want to be on his side. I can't convince him I'm on his side if I keep arguing with him. Taking a step closer to him, he stares down at me.

"I don't want her to drain me," I say, evening out my breaths. "It's like how I felt in the Vein, trapped, no way out. And I don't want that for Liam. That's why I'm so pissed about this."

Energy is harder to read than a flesh face, but the outline of his brows raises a little, and the line of his mouth softens. He says, "I know you want what's best for him, Rin. I really believe it's best for us to be together for the Revival. Don't you want to be together?"

My mouth goes dry, the bitter vomit crawling up my throat again. My arms prickle, going numb at the fingertips. I have to agree to everything he's saying, that the Revival is the right choice, then he might tell me where they are keeping Liam, where the Revival will happen. My heart pounds and my head is light.

"Yes." Breathless and quiet, I almost sound sincere, at least sincere enough. It's almost the truth. I've always wanted to be together, not the way he thinks though. We could have always had it.

"The Vein is following us, so we're on the move. I can't tell you anything now." His red eyes bore into me. "You've never done what you're told, and it's always been hard to get the truth out of you, so forgive me if I'm not quite ready to believe you've changed your mind on this. Just know that Liam is safe."

I swallow bile, stifling a gag. I've told him so many half-truths and full-out lies in my life, but this one is a stake to the heart. I can't even comprehend everything he's told me tonight, the way I feel, what Sovya told me. The Revival is supposed to bring back Ironskins who have died from Angel or Demon Palm and those who died from the Death Ritual. For both Stephen and Father, it's been more important for the nation to be rebuilt than to help what still remains.

Does he know that he's finishing our father's work? Stephen told me himself he wanted to do things differently than our parents. Did he mean different than Guardian work? Or does he know that Father didn't follow through with the Revival, and Stephen's ideals are to make it happen? Does he know that he is alive?

The night chill doesn't touch me as Stephen's brilliant energy form leaps up onto the city wall. He turns and looks down at me. "Johanna limits you. Remember that, Rin. You'll need your full power for the Ritual."

He steps off the wall, disappearing beyond the city limits in a brilliant red flash. A beast howl wavers through the dark and the cold. I stagger over to a tree. Bracing myself on the rough trunk, I double over and barf into the grass.

The drizzle followed me into the house, dripping off my coat and pooling at my feet. The lights were off, so it was just as grey inside as it was outside. I set my bookbag down and hung my jacket, listening for voices. Mother's voice pierced the silence as she talked to someone upstairs. My muscles tensed as I took off my shoes. Muddy prints carried from the door to the shoe rack. I swallowed hard. If Mother was talking to someone, she might not be down for a while. Maybe she was on an echo call with Mrs. Kingsman or Father had called. It would give me time.

I hurried into the kitchen on tip toes. I took a towel that hung by the sink. The towel with soft new fibres and pretty pink lines. I froze, turned back around, and refolded it so it would hang nicely. I looked through the drawers for something else. Every dishtowel was folded a specific way. If I messed them up, I'd have to refold them, and I wouldn't do it right. My fingers hovered over them.

Another voice sounded upstairs. Out of breath and rising in tone, Stephen said, "I can't stop it."

My fingers stopped their dance over the towels as a red light filled the stairwell. It bled through the dull grey light, chasing the cold away like fire. The floorboards creaked. I lurched for the cupboard under the sink and found a rag there.

Rain splattered on the windowpanes as I tiptoed back to the muddy prints. On my hands and knees, I slowly wiped at the puddles. Little grains of dirt scraped between the wood floor and the rough cloth. Wood cleaner tingled my nose as Mother and Stephen's voices grew. Stephen's voice was choked. A sob found its way down to me, and I froze.

A tremor shook the house, and my wet jacket dropped off the rack. I waited for lightning, but there was no thunder as the house shook again.

"Stephen, breathe," Mother said, but Stephen cried over her.

I dropped the cloth and bolted to the stairs. I clung to the rail, taking tentative steps up through the glowing red light filling the dark. My breaths were short and fast as an odd heat brushed my face.

I padded across the landing in my socked feet, fists clenching my sleeves, and peered into Stephen's room. In the light of his lamp, he sat at the edge of the bed, hood thrown over his head and face in his hands. Mother sat on her knees in front of him. Her hair was tied in a perfect knot behind her head. She wore a checkered, button-up shirt with a white turtleneck underneath. Holding Stephen by the shoulder and taking his chin in her hand, she said, "Everything in you is trying to come out right now. Take control of it."

Stephen groaned and red light blazed from his eyes. It spilled over his black pants and painted the white checks on Mother's shirt. He jerked his head up. I stepped back into the hall. Stephen's blood-red eyes rimmed in black were wide and his mouth hung open.

"Rin, get out of here," he yelled, his voice cracked and distorted. His eyebrows rounded before he grimaced and threw his arms over his face.

A pulse of light brought forth a whipping tail behind Stephen. It thrashed through the room.

"Rin, downstairs," Mother said, turning to me. Her grey eyes were stone, her mouth straight and strong, dark eyebrows arched.

I backed away to the stairs and clutched the banister. But I leaned forward to see into Stephen's room. Mother put her hand on the back of Stephen's neck. The veins along her wrist and through her face pulsed and glowed through her skin with pale-blue light.

I knew I should go downstairs, but my bones were stiff. Why was he home early from school? My knees bent and I crouched down on the steps. My mother's cold light swept over Stephen like frost. Between the two of them, their red and blue lights melded into violet.

A cool sweat broke over me. The transformative light swept through the dark, cold house, coating everything violet and dreamlike. Stephen's breaths became easy and my eyelids drooped. I slumped against the wall, huddled on the step. My eyelids fell closed.

Mother shook me awake. I jerked and immediately turned to Stephen's room, but the door was closed.

"Rin, I told you to go downstairs," Mother said. Her eyes were bloodshot, and a single stray hair dangled between her silver eyes. "Come." She took my hand in her icy grip.

"Is Stephen okay?" I asked, stumbling down the stairs behind Mother.

She was quiet and her fingers loosened their grip on my hand at the bottom.

"Is he sick?" I asked, clenching her limp hand.

Mother looked around the kitchen and over to the entryway. I had left the drawer open, my puddles were spilling together, the dirty cloth soaking into them, and my jacket lay in a clump on the floor. She wiggled her fingers free of my hold, leaving behind the cold of her skin.

"Wh-What did you do?" I asked.

Mother's back straightened. "Rin, how many times have I told you to clean up after yourself?" She turned to me, dark shadows under her eyes.

I tried to swallow the lump in my throat. "Where's Liam?"

Her eyes snapped shut, and she sighed, rubbing a hand over her face. "I had Oron come pick him up when Stephen came home from school early. I have to go get him." She moved into the kitchen, and I followed her, wrapping my arms around myself.

"I don't understand. What's wrong with Stephen?" My lip quivered, and the lump strained my voice into a whine.

"Rinnaya, please, I-I can't deal with you crying right now. It's been a long day." She kept moving through the kitchen to the entryway, a shadow through the lightless house. She slipped off her house shoes and put on her loafers. Looking in the mirror by the door, she smoothed the rogue hair back into her bun.

I sniffled and mother's arms became stiff. She snatched her jacket and her keys. "I want this mess cleaned up by the time I come home. I'll bring dinner back with me," she said, staring at her keys. She moved them around the ring, counting silently but mouthing the numbers. As I pressed my sleeves to my mouth to calm my shaking lips, she took a breath and counted the keys again.

She snapped her head toward me. "Clean this up and start your homework." Pocketing the keys, she pulled the door open. A gust of cold, damp air swept at my feet, and the door slammed.

I dropped to the ground and grabbed the cloth. I wiped up the puddles the best I could through the slurry of tears in my eyes and purple fog in my head. I took my jacket and my bag, closed the drawer, and ran up to my room.

My heart was in my throat and my lips were salty with tears. I dropped my things on my bed and swiped my sleeve over my face, pressing the heels of my hands to my eyes to soak up the swell of tears. My breaths quieted and my heart sank lower.

I couldn't get myself to open my bag to find my homework. My feet took me across the hall. I stood in the dark, hand on the doorknob for minutes, replaying the lights in my head. Twisting the knob, I peered into my brother's room. The lamp was still on. Stephen lay on his side, echobuds in his ears, hood still shielding his face, and his room a disaster around him. I held my breath. His body rose and fell in an even rhythm. The beat of his music drifted over to me through his echobuds.

Backing out of his room once again, I sat down on the steps, the tap of rain overhead. Shivers prickled my skin, and I put my head on my knees. My heart beat heavy inside me. I hugged my knees closer to keep it inside.

24

L A N C E

I BALANCE A MUG OF SCOLYA ROOT TEA ON MY BOOK and hold a bowl of cat food in the other. I've been drinking scolya root tea like I drank ales in my basic ed days. It seems that every second without the tea to calm my essence and something to focus my mind on, my body starts to shift. It starts as static over my skin and grips my heart. I force myself to read or work out or listen to music to redirect the energy, but I'm left with aching joints.

At the back door, I step into the cool spring night, set down my book and my tea, squat low, and shake the bowl so the hard pellets of cat food shuffle and clink against the ceramic.

"Ravi," I say softly to the bushes. "Here, boy."

The wind rustles through the leaves and moon beetles fly through the trees and hop between core-energy boulders. I take a long breath of the fresh air, watching them and waiting for the greedy little grey cat to come find his food. The quiet wraps around my heart and the wind clears my lungs. Just as my body becomes completely relaxed, the static prickles my fingers. My skin flickers in and out of existence.

I set the bowl down with shaking fingers and sit next to it, cracking open my book. Folding the cover over, I read the first page as fast as I can. Reading another page and taking a sip of tea, the prickle drains from my skin and settles just in the tips of my fingers. My hands reappear, gripping my book.

After a few pages, Ravi slinks out of the bushes and sniffs his food.

"Hi, little boy," I say, giving him a long pet from the top of his head to the tip of his tail. He sits down beside me and gobbles up the food, crunching loudly and licking his lips.

Turning back to the book, I freeze at the sound of someone throwing up in the tree line by the city wall. Ravi looks up at me, green starlight glinting in his wide eyes. "Should we go see if they're okay?" I ask.

I stand and dust off the back of my pants. Ravi trots next to me as I move out of the light of the academy and into the tree line. Bent over, Rin braces herself against a tree with one hand and barfs at the base.

I run over to gather her hair away from her face. She jolts and teeters a bit. I hold her still with my hand on her back, shaking my head at myself. I should have said something so I wouldn't scare her. She groans and tries to shrug away from me.

"Are you okay?" I ask.

Trying to stand up straight, she keeps one hand around her stomach and wipes her mouth with the back of her hand. Her skin is pale and clammy. The edges of her eyes are red.

"Sorry," she says, just loud enough for me to hear.

"For what?" I tuck a hair behind her ear. My fingers linger for a moment, tangled in the soft strands as she stills under my touch. I smile and my stomach flips.

"I don't know, I just . . . " Her eyes go wide as she stares at the ground. "What is that?"

Ravi winds through my legs and brushes his face against Rin's leg. She goes stiff as a board, eyeing the little creature as it loves on her.

"This is your cat," I say, bending to pick him up.

"My cat?"

"Yeah, your very special gift from two very special jackasses."

"Oh." Her eyes squint at the fuzzy kitten. A smile quirks her lips as she takes me in. My face flushes, but before I can smile back, she grimaces. Her shoulders jerk. She slaps her hand over her mouth and doubles over. I put Ravi back on the ground. Rin shakes as I put my arm around her and lead her over to the bench.

She sits with her elbows braced on her knees and her head between her hands. "I hate this, I hate this." Her words sting the fresh air as she shies away from my touch now.

"What do you hate? What's going on?" Holding my hands together, I bend forward a little to see her face. She scrunches into herself more.

"All of it, everything. My death affinity. Feeling like I can't control myself, barfing in front of you."

I lean back. I know forcing her to look at me won't be beneficial. If I forced her to do anything, I would never forgive myself. "You don't have to worry about barfing around me. I've done my fair share of that around other people." And in those instances, I didn't want anyone to look at me, to see my insides come up, but I also didn't want to be left alone either. It's harder to go get yourself cleaned up when no one's there encouraging you. I didn't want anyone telling me it was okay or making light of whatever nonsense I had got myself into, because that always made it worse. I was a mess, and people I thought were my friends didn't care. But I care for Rin. So, I keep my hands to myself and my gaze into the night.

A few minutes pass, and Rin lifts her head, leaning back with me.

Running my hands together, fingertips still tingling and threatening to disappear, I say, "Are you safe here, Rin?"

She stretches her fingers and clenches them into fists, popping her knuckles with her thumbs. "I don't know. Which is why I'm supposed to go check in with Evelyn." A wind blows and her skin rises with goosebumps. Her face is still blanched and blotchy red. Touching her fingers to her mouth, she stares blankly at the door.

"Sit a little while longer. Don't want you barfing on Evelyn's desk."

Nodding a little too fast, her chest heaves and her eyes flash red. Snapping them shut, she says, "Can you just talk to me? About anything?"

Of course, I should have done that in the first place, given her something to think about so she can relax. The air around us heats, and she slides another foot away from me on the bench.

"Third year is going just as well as I expected. Training is kicking my butt, and I have my nose in my studies at all times, except for now. I try to keep my mind occupied in the evening, too, since my essence has been acting weird lately. It helps to concentrate on something." Ravi nuzzles me, so I bring him up to my lap. Rin watches the cat with glassy eyes. "This little guy helps me stay on track with my new routine. He gets very testy if I forget to feed him." I rub his tummy, and he rubs his cold, wet nose to my chin.

What else? Oh yeah. I really like you, and I feel so happy every time I see you.

"Do you want to pet him? It helps the nerves."

Her face sours, but only for a second. Ravi yawns and the sour turns sweet as Rin smiles. "Ok." She holds up her hand.

Her back is stiff, and she pulls away a little as she reaches across the bench. Hand wavering over him, she closes her eyes. I cup my hand over hers and press it gently onto Ravi. He mews. She flinches but keeps her hand on him. I lift my hand, and she smooths her narrow fingers over his soft fur. They linger where the fur is thickest. Stroking him a few more times, her spine curls and her head tilts to the side, eyes still closed.

"Do you think you want to do some weapons training in the evening again this year?" I ask, as the red blotches drain from her cheeks.

Sliding her fingers from Ravi's head down his back one more time, they settle on my hand. They're cold, and I wrap them in both hands.

"No," she says, shaking her head. "I think it's too much right now."

I nod, and even though she is blind to me with her face turned to the trees and her eyes pressed closed, her fingers grip mine. A frown pulls at my face as we sit in deep silence. I have nothing on my mind to distract me except for her. My fingers are warm, staying visible and still.

There's something I haven't told her about my week. I shouldn't hide it from her, not the way I hid the fact that I was hanging out with her last year from my friends. It made me nervous to tell them I was spending time with an Ironskin when I knew they wouldn't like it. It was awful. I was awful. Starting this year off with total transparency is the right thing to do.

"Mycul and Aris are on my team this year," I say.

She breathes in response. I wait for a twitch in her hand, for her to pull away, shut down, but her hand is still.

"Do you want me to transfer teams?" I ask.

Opening her eyes, her hand leaves mine, and she wraps her arms around her middle. "You don't have to make your decisions based on me."

"I'm not—"

"It's fine, Lance."

My chest tightens with the sharpness of her words, sharp enough to cut stones to build a wall. The honesty had kept her hand in mine. Trying to appease her, though, tiptoeing around her to make sure I don't make mistakes, that took her hand away. She's right, I can't put it on her to make this decision.

"We're trying out for the tournament," I add.

"Mm." She taps two fingers together. "Then I guess I'll have another chance to beat Mycul's ass."

Standing, she smooths her pants and turns to the door. As she steps around me, her cold hand trails over my arm, up to my shoulder, and squeezes. I hold her there for a moment. Maybe I shouldn't have said anything. No, that's ridiculous. I don't want to never talk about the past and shove it away. I want to make myself better each day, in all aspects of my life.

I kiss her fingers, and she leaves me.

25

ELIOTE

"THE TERM 'BEAST' REFERS TO ANY CREATURE THAT IS NOT hédin that has essence," the professor says.

I squeeze my eyes shut for a moment and rub the pinch in my temples. Opening them, I stare down at the text to follow along. I keep my eyes down most of the time these days. Intentions are not as easy to read as auras. At night, my normal sight returns, showing me auras and essence channels, but in the day it's all muted tangles.

"There are five classes of beasts, and these classifications refer to how the beast generates essence." The professor writes the classes on the board. "First, Ancient beasts absorb environmental energy and convert it to essence. They always find sources of pure jint, unama, or fann. Main sources of these energies found in nature are core energy, vegetation, and molten rock respectively.

These beasts, since they draw on constant, replenishable sources, grow large and armoured, but are generally noncombative."

I browse through the images of Ancients in the text. Running my fingers over them, my finger wavers over a beast identical to the Ancient that attacked Tien Bay. Noncombative. But that beast was aggravated and out of its natural habitat. Did it have something to do with the green energy? Or maybe that weird stone Stephen had. Both? I shiver.

"Peaceful beasts also draw from their environment, but are generally small, fast, and strong. Beasts that have their own essence channels and don't absorb environmental energy are also smaller and more hostile because they have a more primitive variation of fann-aligned essence called fau. We call these Rovers. The most hostile beasts are known simply as Feral. You are probably familiar with a subclass knows as Downfōsts—death beasts. Ferals have their own fau essence supply but also draw in energy from the environment. The mix of fau and pure essential energy makes them hostile. Finally, Ravagers are the most threatening to hédin communities because they have their own supply of fau essence, absorb energy from the environment, and syphon vital energies from hédin. Therefore, there are three types: essence syphoners, mind syphoners, and spirit syphoners. But mind and spirit syphoners are extremely rare."

Rubbing the smooth, new skin on my arm, I stare at the hideous Downfōst that I've become way too familiar with. The Nodaha Downfōst.

"Your assignment this week will be to write a five-page essay on your assigned beast with a partner. I've handed out a list with your beast assignment and your partners. Take this time to begin preparations for your essay."

I scan the list. Ōneera, Ancient classification, and Rin is my partner.

"As you research, you might come across some exceptions to the standard beast classifications like the Ōneera. The Ōneera migrates and absorbs natural energy from multiple sources. The mix of the three pure essential energies means that they are aligned with utanic energy."

A chorus of gasps from all the Luminee in the room makes me jump. They all mark the sign of Vin over their heads. The professor chuckles. "Yes, quite shocking, but it gives the Ōneera a very interesting ability. Those of you assigned to this beast, I'm looking forward to seeing what you find about it."

Utanic energy is unpredictable. Vin is the only Luminee to have ever manipulated its rays—the only tri-power sage recorded in history. Luminee believe that Vin's soul comes close to all hédin during the Festival of Two Moons to protect them from the utanic energy that accumulates in the atmosphere. But if someone is hidden from his sight, cursed some might say, their essence can become corrupted by utanic energy. I may not have much faith in Vin's divinity these days, or care much for Luminee superstitions, but energy is energy.

Rin is already scooting her chair over to my desk, juggling her text, notebook, and bag. She's wearing a pair of dark, high-waisted pants and a blue t-shirt. The blue is bright, new. I focus on it, pushing away the churning red flash around her. I shut my eyes, drawing a breath.

"I've read about this beast," Rin says. "The special ability the professor was talking about is that it can see in the dark, but it's blind during the day."

I freeze, mouth parted and tongue going dry. She did not

just say that it can see in the dark. There is no way that this corrupted Ōneera beast has the same eyesight problems I'm experiencing. I may not be blind, but I sure can see better in the dark. I'm just making the connection up. What energy would there be in me for utanic energy to corrupt? I've never had any problems around the Festival of Two Moons, but the strange energy I saw when Tien Bay was attacked was green. Green like starlight. Like utanic energy.

Mavesh na'Vin visashaya to norshaya ke rishat visa. I mark Vin's sign above my head.

"Hey, are you okay?" she asks, tying up her hair.

"Me?"

She chuckles. "Yes, you. What are you doing?"

"Oh, there was a fly."

Rin clasps her hands between her knees. Her shoulders slouch as she looks down at the ground. "Are we okay? I feel like you've been ignoring me."

I wet my lips and take a long breath, still praying in my head. "No, don't be silly, Bird Brain. I've just been feeling a little off lately." I smile at her, bringing my eyes to meet her cold steel grey. Clearing my throat, I say, "Why don't we start by reading the short synopsis of the beast that the text provides."

Rin nods. "Sure," she says and opens her book. Stray hairs dangle around her face as she reads.

All this talk of beasts, all these images of them with their horns, claws, and fangs, all their stats, makes my decision to be a pilot even more enticing. I have the advantage of not being sucked dry by an essence syphoner, but in all other battles against beasts, essence gives a definite edge. I never want to stare down a Nodaha Downfōst with only a blade again. I really only think

I made it out of there because my mom was there too. I couldn't let the beast hurt her.

Mavesh na'Vin visashaya to norshaya ke rishat visa.

I should tell Rin about the Flight Academy, that I want to go. She's my roommate and should hear it from me first. I have to apply by Registration Day, which means my decision has to be set in stone by then. Talking about it might be good.

I close my book and turn in my seat to face Rin. But she's already looking at me, her own book closed in her lap. "I need to talk to you about something," she whispers.

My pulse skitters through me. I fumble for words, rubbing my arm. I need to tell her something, too, but what am I going to say? I'm leaving? Leaning forward, I say, "Uh, sure, what is it?"

Rin glances around the room. Everyone is bent over their texts, auras a little less abrasive, just shifting clouds through the room. "Professor Hans. Have you ever noticed anything weird about his essence?"

My brow furrows. "His essence?"

"Yeah, like something"—she licks her lips—"different from other Emberstead's essence?"

I flip my hair over one shoulder and run my hands through it. "Come to think of it, I've never been able to see his aura really, and I'm having a little trouble seeing essence lately."

Rin shifts forward. "Really?"

"Yeah, some auras are just harder for me to see. Like Adrianne. I wasn't able to see hers until she transformed in class last year. Why do you ask?"

"He knows my brother. When Stephen wanted to contact me last year, he sent a letter through Professor Hans. And when

Hans gave it to me, he seemed to . . . care . . . about me."

I cock my head to the side. "You know that it's not weird for someone to care about you, right, Rin?"

"It is when it's Professor Hans. Whenever we're in public, he's cold and harsh to me, you know, like a normal Emberstead would be. So, I'm thinking, if he can get in touch with Stephen, he might even know where the Revival is and how I can get to Liam. I also . . . I have this gut feeling that he might be a halfie, an Ironskin-Emberstead halfie."

"Rin, why are you telling me all this?"

"I need you to help me find out if Professor Hans has Ironskin essence. Brand said the Revival might have an Ironskin-Emberstead halfie. It might be him. He might be able to help me get to Liam."

I stare into the haze around her as we sit knee to knee. Its red hue is thick, pressing into me with pinpricks raising the hairs on my neck. I don't know what any of this means any more. Auras are so much more intuitive. I used to know Rin's feelings like they were my own. Whatever her intention is, it rattles my core.

"I don't think it's a good idea." I turn my knees back under my desk and open my book.

"What's not a good idea?"

"You trying to do all this without help."

"I am asking for help for once." Rin grabs my shoulder. "Your help."

Her hand is a vise pinching my skin. I shrug her off, the pinch in my head digging deeper. "I mean like the Vein or the Local Protectors."

A few of our classmates turn to look at us. My face burns hot and Rin dips her head.

"This is the only way, Eliote," Rin says, her voice barely audible. "They need to trust me, or they won't let me anywhere near them."

"I just don't think it's a good idea. Especially since you're—"

"I'm what?"

Blush paints Rin's pale cheeks and her steely gaze fills with shadow. Her head tilts to the side as she leans back in her chair, knees spread open, arms crossed, challenge in her shadowed eyes. I swallow hard, straightening my shoulders, but it's so much easier for her to drop into that offensive posture. My gut twists as her protections solidify. There's so much I don't know about Rin—where did this girl learn to be so abrasive, so strong, menacing at the drop of a hat?

"Y-You're just a little . . . unstable," I say.

"What's that supposed to mean?" The rasp of her voice turns from sweet to a warning like she just flipped a switch.

I twist one of the studs in my ear. "You don't have control over the death affinity."

Rin scoffs, looking off to the side. "I left my brother to come here and control my affinities, and now look what happened. He's been taken away from me. I think the most important thing right now is to get him home." She drops her arms and leans onto her knees. "I'm doing my best to tame my death affinity enough so I can do that."

Heat washes over me, not a heat on my skin or that anyone else in the room can feel, just a heat in my soul. It wafts off Rin and smothers me like a rough bag over my head, itchy and rubbing my skin raw.

Someone in the room coughs. I jerk away from Rin.

Rin flinches. Her gaze wavers, lips parting and eyes

softening, but stricken with pain. I turn away.

"Can we just work on this?"

Jaw tensing, Rin nods and opens her book.

I read through the aspects that the professor wants us to hit on in our essay. "I can do the introduction and a paragraph about the history," I say. "Then there's the essence conduction physiology, which might be difficult. I can just do that too—"

"Okay, that's it. I don't care what you're pickin' up in your sight, but what I'm pickin' up is that you're being a bitch to me for no reason."

I inhale a sharp, cold breath. The murmurs of our studying classmates quiet. "Excuse me?"

"I'm way more capable than you think I am." Her tone is deep and dark, and she jabs a finger at me. "You've no idea what I've been through to get to this point."

Tears flood my eyes as red soaks through the grey of hers.

"Your aura is just like his. I don't trust it," I say, a waver in my voice.

"Whose?"

"Your brother's. I saw him there in my city, watching it fall with a smile on his face."

"I'm not like my brother." She takes a long breath, working her jaw, but feverish red lines crinkle away from her burning eyes. "Fuck Stephen and fuck you." Shielding her face, she pushes away from my desk, chair scraping the floor, and marches out of the room.

My heart pounds and I grip my textbook. Johanna glances at me with a raised eyebrow before jumping up to follow Rin. I glance over at Ace. His dark void shimmers with blue as his eyes follow Rin and Johanna out of the room. Jaw tightening, I dig my fingernails into the hard spine of my textbook. Ace's sapphire eyes find me. Tears spill down my cheeks. Dropping my head, my hair falls forward. I prop my head with my hand, barricading myself around my text.

I don't know if I can help her anymore, if I can't see what she wants me to see. Getting involved with stopping the Revival is ridiculous. The Guardians barely know what's going on. Right now, my goal has to be training for the tournament. That will be my marker. If I can compete well with the other schools, if I can keep up with my team, then I'll stay. If not, then I'll apply for the Flight Academy.

Mavesh na'Vin visashaya to norshaya ke rishat visa.

26

JOHANNA

"Hey," I call after Rin. "What did you do to make Eliote cry?"

Rin stops in the middle of the hall, her head tilted down to the ground. The stretch of hall is windowless and dark. The shadows swarm around her, breathing as she breathes.

"What'd I do?" A red eye peeks over her shoulder.

My essence and blood are hot like the Soul Tether has syphoned Rin's anger into me, and now it's my own. But it's not. I have to give it back to her. I press my eyes closed and let out a long breath and press my hands to my forehead. This has gone on long enough. We are two people. I need to tell her what's going on with the tether.

I need to remember that Rin doesn't strike first. I know she wouldn't make Eliote cry for nothing. Rin just retaliates, but most of the time too hard. Leaning to one side, I look down my nose at her.

She turns to face me, just her irises glowing red, casting a faint pink glow around her eye sockets. "She was being a bitch, so I told her."

I cringe. "Mm, yeah, she wouldn't respond well to that. But you know as well as I do that Eliote's intentions are always good, so what did you do to make her bitchy?"

Rin throws up her hands and lets them slap down on her thighs. "I—"

She paces, her lower lip quivering. Mumbles of lectures drift through the hall. I tap my foot.

"I just asked her—"

A group of girls turns the corner. Rin paces into them. She grunts, and her eyes flare like the sun. The girls scream. One shadow phases to the end of the hall. Rin throws her arms over her face with a sharp gasp as the other two girls huddle together along the wall, transfixed by the ruby horns on Rin's forehead. I roll my eyes and grab Rin.

"Come on, outside. You're growing horns again."

"Yeah, keep moving, demon spawn," one of the girls says behind us.

"Piss off," I say, glaring at her.

Rin shakes and her arms are feverish. I steer her to the central garden. My hands are close to burning, and I'm sweating as I let go of her to open the door. I push her through, a wave of icy-hot sweeping through my head.

I JUST ASKED HER FOR HELP.

Rin stops and stares at me. Her irises are blood, the whites of her eyes dark ink. Her veins bulge and pulse, and her skin is speckled with blotchy pink. The ruby-red horns grow from her forehead, smooth, no ridges, just sharp points curving together, each about three inches. Her dirty blond hair shifts around them, curling in wisps around her face, moved by the energy radiating from her. She swipes the back of her hand across her face.

My heart pounds inside me and I can't get my feet to move, but my essence heats. I draw in a long breath, expanding my lungs to full capacity and letting it all out. My muscles relax with the energy of my essence running through me. I smile at her in the light of the sun, with jaden lilies dancing happily in the wind.

"Why are you smiling?" she asks, her voice full and deep with energy.

You're not that scary, Rin.

A flare-wing moth flutters between the two of us. Its little, black body bobs up and down and its wings, orange and yellow at the tips, flit fast like flames. Rin's demon eyes follow it as it loops around her head and over to me. Her brow crinkles and her lips part. It flutters down to rest on my shoulder, creeping close to my neck to enjoy the fann energy of my essence.

"So, what did you ask her to help you with?"

My essence calms and the cool breeze soothes my skin, blowing my curls over my face. I push them back and guide Rin over to the bench by the trickling fountain. Rin sits, hands on her knees and eyes on the ground. The rash of red on her cheeks fades and the ink in her eyes clears. Like a flame extinguishing, the two ruby horns vanish.

"I asked her to keep an eye on Professor Hans." She sniffs and pats her fingertips to her cheeks. "I think he might have been the professor that my brother used to train with over the breaks sometimes. He gave me a note from Stephen last year. I just think Professor Hans is mixed up with Stephen in a way that doesn't make sense for an Emberstead."

I lean forward on my knees. "What doesn't make sense about it?"

"Why would an Emberstead help train an Ironskin with the death affinity? Why would he be standoffish around me most of the time, but when he gave me that letter, he was almost kind. I-I think he might be a halfie."

"You asked her to see if she could see anything about his essence?"

Rin nods. Her eyes have cleared to grey. They hold my gaze, stormy and gripping.

"You're trying to get all the information you can before you go after Liam."

She nods again.

"Eliote might not be ready, Rin. She probably does want to help you, but we have to trust her when she thinks something's off. She sees more than we do."

Rin shakes her head, her eyelids drooping. She's always been blind to how her actions affect others. My mind tingles as she comes to the same conclusion.

"She said she was having trouble seeing essence," she mumbles to her hands.

I SHOULDN'T HAVE PUSHED HER.

"I'll help you," I say. "I don't know what I can do, but I'm here for you. You need to get this under control though." I circle my finger around her head where the little horns keep popping out.

Rolling her eyes, she leans back on the bench, cringing and rubbing at her eyes. "She doesn't trust me. After all we've been through. I trust her with my life. Why can't she do the same for me?"

"Because you're not trustworthy," I say.

Rin drops her hands. Her lips press together, her whole body tenses, and her dark brows furrow.

"You're not. Never have been. You're not predictable, trustworthy, or a good person. But you are loyal, you always try your best, and you love people. Makes me feel okay, you know? I mean, I am mean, selfish—"

"An asshole."

"Yes, an asshole. But I like to think I can still be kind when I need to be, stand up for people, find some peace. With you around, I feel like I can be myself."

Gravel grinds under my feet as I shift on the bench. I run my hands over my knees, a knot forming in my stomach. Rin looks off to the side at the swaying tendrils of the sorrow-blossom tree.

"But I didn't always let you," she says in a quiet voice.

"Yeah, well, work in progress."

The flare-wing moth walks down my shoulder onto my bare arm. It sends shivers over me as it opens and closes its wings.

"Um," Rin says, rubbing her eyes again. She glances at me and then turns her eyes back down to her feet. The trickle of the fountain and the whisper of wind through the plants fill in her silence. "Stephen said something to me. He said we, you and me, were inseparable when we were young but that"—she shakes her head—"he said that you limit me."

I snort and cackle. A smile sparks on her face.

"He's not wrong."

"What does he mean? Like there's something—"

"It's called a Soul Tether."

"What? There's actually something . . . I just thought he was being a dick."

"Probably was but, yeah, I've known about it for about a year now."

Her eyes grow wide as she finally turns to face me. "What is it?"

"When two people have high essence levels and an emotional connection, they can become connected. I can't read anyone else's mind except yours because of it."

"Why didn't you tell me?"

"I didn't know if you . . . would want it or feel comfortable with it. It um . . . it's one-sided."

"What does that mean, being one-sided?"

"You're not tethered back to me, so I just drain energy from you."

Rin's eyebrows pull tight. Her jaw twitches like she's chewing on the information. My face is hot, and my hands sweat while I wait for her.

"What does it mean for us?" she asks.

"It means that if you hurt, I hurt, but if I hurt, you'll be just fine."

Rin stands. She wraps her arms around her middle, slightly bent at the waist. Sighing with her back to me, her shoulders scrunched to her ears. "Does that mean at the party when I-I tried to . . . die, did you know?"

I swallow hard as the memory floods over me—my body screaming in pain as energy left me, as it felt the effects of Rin poisoning her body with Ease. "A Seer told me that I was actually giving you back the energy that I had stolen from you with the tether."

Rin turns slowly, still holding herself together. "So . . . you kept me alive?" she whispers.

I nod and tense my fingers in the folds of my pants. "You would have died if I hadn't. I think I would have died too."

Rin hides half her face with one hand. "How do you know I'm not tethered back to you?"

"Because you kept getting farther away from me."

A frown falls deep on Rin's face. My mind fills with the crackle of icy static as Rin's eyes cloud. Even with her static, my mind is clear. The knot in my gut unravels and my chest fills with warmth because I finally said everything I needed to say. I know it hurts her, it still hurts me, too, but it's on the surface. The pain is skin deep, and I can soothe it instead of having it poison everything I do. I don't have to feel like I'm going crazy if I believe that my soul is inexplicably linked to another individual. It's almost like the tether has lengthened even though its grip is tighter.

I push off the bench and take a step toward Rin. She shrugs away. Thoughts are meant to be private, so even though I know I can find them through her storm, pick them out one by one, I'd rather her choose to share them with me.

"And after that night? Did you feel anything in the two months before we left for the academy?" Rin asks.

"I just felt a little achy, sometimes dizzy. Why?"

She holds a hand over her mouth and shakes her head. "No reason."

I put a hand on her shoulder. Her body shakes under my touch. "I'm going back to class. I think you should go to your room and get some sleep."

Rin sniffs. "We have two classes left today."

"I know. We'll catch you up. I think you should rest."

Lips pressed, she nods and pushes a hair out of her face. I turn to the school, this damn place that brought us together that has taught me so much and has more to teach me yet. The sun glints off the stained glass and warms the white walls. Vines twist around the entrance back into the hall. I squeeze Rin's shoulder and head back inside.

RIN

"Her eyes have been glowing for an hour. There's so much energy in the room, I can't sleep." Eliote's whispers burn through my ears.

The itch fills my eye sockets, it runs down my face, my neck, prickling and stinging. I keep my eyes shut, and my body still.

"Have you tried waking her?" Johanna's voice comes through the dark, warm and calm.

"No. I . . . I was scared to."

Heat sweeps through my body. My covers are pulled to my chin, and it takes everything in me not to throw them off. I don't want them to know I'm awake. I don't want to talk to them.

"Rin would never hurt you. You know that, right?" Johanna asks.

"I know. At least I think I do. I just can't get what happened on the first day of training out of my head."

Needles of heat spike through my eyes and tears spill through my pinched eyelids. Their feet pad away from me, and Eliote's sheets shift on her bed. I draw a breath, pressing my eyes tight as the dark behind my eyelids burns deep maroon.

"That was different. She's mad at Brand."

My heart twists inside me as the pause grows long. "But she's mad at me now too."

"She's not mad. A little, but you should be glad she's expressed being mad at you, because it's worse if she doesn't."

"I-I just don't understand why this is happening. I feel so much from her, but it's *too* much. I can't distinguish what's going on with her."

"Rin's had a bad life, and she's kept it to herself. It wasn't healthy. Even when her family was around, she didn't really have them to support her either. Her dad was always away on missions and her mom had a lot of trauma. It made her mom anxious, depressed, paranoid. Not a lot of room for hugs and comfort and self-expression. All that anger you feel from her, it's not directed at you or me or even Brand, really. It's at herself, unfortunately."

There's a wet sniff and a sigh. "I'm sorry. I'm just tired and stressed," Eliote says.

"I know. You can stay in my room tonight. If Rin's asleep, then let her sleep."

I count the seconds as the sheets rustle and their feet pad over the carpet, my lips quivering from strain. I bite down. A few more rustles and the door clicks. Breath expels from my lungs. My eyes flutter open. Red trickles along my sheets, over the floor, and mingles with the shadows in the room. The sky is overcast, unwilling to grace the world with the light of the stars.

I push off my covers and peel my hair away from my sweaty neck. The cool of the night brushes my skin. I shiver but swing my legs out of bed and fan myself with my shirt. Another shiver, and a wave of stinging heat chases after it. Nausea slithers through my stomach and up my throat. I bend over my knees, arms wrapped around my gut, drawing in long breaths.

Tears stream down my cheeks. She's terrified of me, my own roommate. She can't even sleep because I'm a fucking mess. And Johanna. How on the Karess could she have tethered herself to someone like me. She could have died because of me.

My shoulders give a violent shake, and I curl tighter around myself. I focus on the air going in and out through my constricted lungs, my muscles aching with energy. After a while, I unravel and prop my elbows on my knees. Lifting my head, I catch my reflection in the mirror.

My stomach lurches and I slap my hand over my mouth. I am ghostly, with jagged red lines breaking my skin. My under eyes are dark and hollow, my eyes red like rubies and black like the moonless, starless sky.

Two red flashes of energy spark above my head. Like wisps of red smoke, they curl on my forehead and solidify into horns. With shaking fingers, I reach for the horns, wrapping fingers tight around them. They pulse and vibrate. Brand said we can choose what the affinities can project. So why is this the form I project?

I snatch my hands back to my chest, heart pounding. Everything I know about the affinities now says that this is me. This red energy and the blue of my life affinity, it leaks everything I want to hide into the cold of this world. My body craves the release, the rush, the thrill of power, but mourns the consequences of its unruly nature—my true self has no experience in this world.

The heat brings the dark and the smoke and the chaos out of the Vein where I left it and into my room. The blood-red coaxes memories of stained sheets and bloody hands.

Those points of pain strangle me. I gasp, tears streaking my face.

I wish I had some way to just let all this tension go, redirect it somehow, so it wouldn't come out to harm those around me, make them fearful of me.

My mind wanders to the shard of glass, and my hand wanders with it. It moves along the skin of my back to the raised scar. I run my fingers along my skin and find a spot where it stops resisting the sharp edge of my nail.

I press it in.

Pressure grows into an ache until it spikes with a prick. All my attention builds around the spot on my back and I dig the nail in further, gritting my teeth. The heat on my head dissipates like smoke and cool air kisses my forehead. I dig just a little further until my nerves twinge.

I pull my hand away from my back, letting my shirt fall down. Hands in my lap, I stare at them, my eyes still painting everything red—along with the dark crescent of blood trying to hide under my nail. I blink, my world fading from black to red, black to red, black to red.

My blood tingles my fingertip and my eyes itch. I move my hand back to my weak spot. One more time might make the itch go away. I lift my shirt.

No. I can't. I can't do this. If I hurt, Johanna hurts, and she doesn't deserve that. If I keep hurting myself, barricading myself from who I am, from my emotions, then I hurt Eliote too. It does the same for Liam.

My life affinity is cold. It sustained me as I moved into this new environment last year—a cool frost that preserved the decay underneath. My death affinity sheds that armour. My body is too much. It heats and pulses and shakes the room. I don't know it. I stepped out of it long ago and now I squirm in unfamiliar skin. The pain of the finger pricks, the glass, is a connection and a disconnection—bringing me close to my body when I am far away and taking me out with a single point to avoid all the unrest settling into my limbs.

I drop my shirt and shake out my hand, bringing it to the tiny stone hanging around my neck. Emotion and physical discomfort are two points of pain Adrianne touched with gentle fingers and deep understanding. She touched my pain and then locked it in this stone where it couldn't hurt me anymore. She touched it first, removed it, but she didn't throw it away.

I stand and cross the room to the door. I'll go for a walk. I'll stay in this moment as long as I have to, letting the red stains on my spirit bleed out. I'll walk until the entire academy is painted red by my eyes. Maybe once they run dry, I can sleep again.

28

LANCE

MY SKIN REMEMBERS EVERYTHING, and now it found a way to hide it.

Yesterday was a good day. I didn't have to train with my team. I got a good workout in, classes were interesting, and I had a few spare minutes to read between classes at lunch. In the last class of the day, I left to use the washroom. Coming back through the halls, lavender perfume wafted over me. At the end of the hall, Mycul and Litha were making out. I clenched my fists. I just had to walk past and ignore them. So, I did, hands in my pockets and eyes on the floor. As I passed, their kissing slowed.

"Is someone there?" Litha asked.

I froze, and I've been frozen ever since because I looked down and couldn't find my hands as static crackled through me.

No one has seen or spoken to me since then. Ace stood behind me in the food line at dinner, didn't even notice that one of the plates moved on its own in front of him. I don't know if that's Ace just being Ace, but I'm hard to miss with my wings and all, so if I were visible, he would have seen me. Take away the wings and the body and he doesn't notice.

My essence is still running but like a river of ice, cutting through my body, creating friction that I can't shake. I pace my room, eyes on my window. Each time I pass, the glass only reflects the rest of my room.

Come on, one more time.

I shake out my arms and give my neck a crack. Standing right in front of the window, I close my eyes and focus on my breath. One long drag, like inhaling Ease, I imagine the air as a cool fog filling my body, calming my nerves, relaxing my limbs. I exhale and open my eyes.

"Damn it." The window holds the image of my unmade bed behind me.

I flop down on my bed and hold my arms up above my head. A small bolt of blue electricity skitters around the boundaries of my fingers and down my arm, but as it fizzles out, the outline of my arm fades with it. Even as I touch the bed, nothing goes up in flame from the sparks of electricity, nothing else goes invisible, just me and the clothes I'm wearing.

Maybe some scolya root tea would help, or a tonic. Hopefully there's a Medic in the infirmary.

I leave my room and wander down the stairs to the ground floor like I've done so many times in the dead of night. The academy is more familiar in the dark than in the day. I look through the glass window of the infirmary, but a Medic isn't around. They keep the tonics in a locked case with other sedatives and sleeping tonics that students might abuse if they got their hands on them.

Sighing, I lean against the wall. My eyelids are heavy as I stare down through myself to the tile floor.

Sustained emotion. What beastshit.

What does emotion have to do with any of this? I was having a good day before I saw Mycul and Litha. And then I was gone. I don't know what triggered it. Did I not want them to see me? Litha knows my skin better than anyone, and it disappeared when I knew she was there. I wish she could unsee all of me. If only Khalie could have unseen me.

"Lance?"

I jolt, and my essence coils through my arms that I still can't see. Despite the blood and essence surging through me, I keep still in the dark. Maybe the invisibility fell for just a moment, and if I stay still, keep hidden, I won't have to explain my disappearance.

"What are you doing?" The voice is soft and raspy, but it doesn't come close. I follow it to the end of the hall near the glowing, green exit sign. Pale as a ghost, with red eyes like sorrow blossoms, Rin stands in the shadows.

"You can see me?" I ask, the words sucking the breath out of me.

Rin sniffs. "Of course I can see you."

I run my hands over my arms. Holding on to the warmth of my skin, I say, "But how? I'm completely invisible."

Rin blinks and the hall goes cold. She blinks again, her eyelids filtering the sorrow-blossom light in and out of the hall. "What do you mean?"

"My essence. It's been doing weird things lately, making

me . . . invisible. So how can you see me?"

"I can see weak spots with my life affinity. I guess I can see things I shouldn't with my death affinity too."

I take a step toward her, and she shuffles back.

"You should probably stay back." Her eyes glow brighter, warming her skin. "I can't control this."

"And I can't see my own hands." I take another step toward her.

"Please, Lance." She holds up a hand and hides her face with the other, but her steps waver and she veers into the wall.

"Woah, are you okay?" I run over to her.

"I'm fine, just lightheaded."

I put my hand on her back, steadying her. She radiates heat through her clothes, and being this close, the red in her eyes is more dynamic. It centres in her irises and crackles over her skin in blotchy patches. She shakes in my grasp.

"Have you slept at all tonight?" I ask.

She shrugs, turning her head away from me, her fingers patting the feverish blotches on her skin. "Yeah, I slept all afternoon. Just didn't sleep much the days before."

"What's going on?" My voice drops to a whisper as my hand curls around her waist, a tremor in my fingers.

Rin tenses in my grasp. "Just a lot." Her voice quivers, and tears build in her eyes but vanish with a wave of heat. "Nothing I knew about my family is true, it's all lies. I'm worried about my brother"—her breath hitches—"both of them. Eliote is afraid of me. And Johanna . . . It's all fucked up. I fucked it up."

Red energy pulses around us, brushing my skin. Rin presses the heels of her hands to her eyes, shoulders shaking.

"Okay, I understand," I say. Heart thumping and stomach

twisting with the surging energy in me and around me, I rub my hand over her back. She draws a shaky breath. "Rin, come. I don't have a roommate. You can stay with me. I probably won't be sleeping tonight either, so you won't be keeping me up if you can't sleep."

She shifts away from me, wrapping her arms tight around herself, dark brows furrowed as she searches my eyes. Heat spills into my cheeks as tension steels her jaw. My hands rest on the slight curve of her waist. My invisible hands want nothing more than to keep holding on, but it's the dead of night, we're both in distress, and my offer has more weight than I intended. I drop my hand and focus my eyes on the ground.

"I don't want anything you don't want. Just stay with me," I say, electricity skittering over my concealed hands.

Rin is still and I can barely breathe. A wave of exhaustion passes over me in the long pause until I say, "I don't want to be alone right now."

Letting go of a breath, Rin steps closer. She reaches for the hand that I can't see—her fingers take mine with an unexpected chill. I stare at her hand interlacing with thin air as new energy races up my arm. Rin grips me with such strength that my bones ache.

If someone were to see us walking through the academy in the dark, I can only imagine what they might think. And what happens once Rin is able to let the death affinity fade? She won't be able to see me anymore—the one person I want to keep seeing me. The haunting memory of last year makes its presence known, piercing my mind to never let me forget that I have already hurt her because I was too afraid to stand up to Mycul.

I lead her into my room and loosen my grip on her hand.

She lets go and watches me from the doorway as I fluff a pillow for her and take one of them to the floor for myself.

"Try to rest," I say, nodding to the bed.

Rin sits as I get down on the floor with an extra blanket. The dark room is pink with the light of her eyes. She runs her hands over her bare knees. Sitting down, I flick my wings out behind me.

"Lance?" There's strain in her neck and her hair falls limp around her face, fingers tight in her lap. "I know I just said you should stay away from me but"—she takes a steadying breath and shakes her head at herself—"would you lie next to me?"

My heart beats hard as I nod.

Rin brings her legs up on the bed and shifts to the far side. I lie on my side so my wings don't bother either of us. Lying on her back, one hand on her stomach, she plays with a triangular pendant on a gold chain. A shuddering breath comes out of her, and she closes her eyes. The room goes dark, but a faint glow of red shimmers through her eyelids.

Her chest rises slowly, as if she's counting the length of her inhale. I try to match the rhythm and even out my heartbeat. The room is chilly, but Rin is warm. I leave the blanket off, just being close keeps away the cold. My essence still runs wild inside me, but not as urgent as I match her breaths.

My eyes are heavy, but the room brightens. Rin stares at the ceiling, tears streaming from her eyes and curling back up as they vaporize from the heat of the death affinity.

"I'm scared of myself too," she whispers.

It takes a second for me to backtrack to when she told me Eliote was afraid of her. This whole time, the thought never crossed my mind, that this energy surrounding her might be hostile toward someone, to me. It just seems so Rin. It's powerful but keeps fading to gentle pink and keeps me warm.

"I"—she swallows—"hurt myself."

Pressure builds inside my chest as my heart rate speeds. I press my lips together, straining to keep my hands tucked beside me. Rin's fingers fidget. There's a dark line under one of her nails. She hides it away in a fist.

"Different ways. Cutting my weak spot. Taking on fights I shouldn't. I went too far once." Her voice chokes and she presses her hands over her face.

"Why are you telling me this?"

"Because I'm scared that, with all this going on, I'll do it again." Wind howls outside and rain sprinkles the window, shattering the outside light over us. "I've been walking around for an hour fighting off the urge, trying to convince myself that I don't deserve pain."

I reach for one of her hands, pulling it away from her face. She lets the other drop too. I stroke the back of her hand with my thumb.

"It's hard to trust ourselves when we know the worst in ourselves," I say. "I try not to fall into my bad habits because it makes me a person I don't like to be. Sometimes it's like I have no control over myself. But I like to think that I can be a little proud when I catch myself. Some people don't know the worst of themselves, and that hurts others."

Rin turns onto her side and faces me, our hands clasped between us. "Why do some people go through hard times and have the will to fight, and I just want to give up?"

The heat from her is fading and my back becomes cold. "Is it okay if I don't know?" I say.

She lifts her head, bringing her eyes level with mine. The shadows clear, the ruby-red energy calms, leaving behind her cool silver eyes. Nodding, she shivers as the last of her heat dissipates, her gaze unfocused on my invisible body next to her.

I let go of her hand and, with the utmost care, run my fingers over her shoulder and down the curve of her back. I pull her close to me, and she dips her head into the crook of my neck. As I softly press my lips to her head, she shudders. Her breaths are warm on my chest and my arm rises and falls around her. My essence is calm and cool inside me. The thump of my heart has faded, and my skin reappears in the dark.

I squeeze Rin and kiss the top of her head again, breathing her in. All the regrets of my past seem so small compared to this moment with her.

29

R I N

The golden light of morning pulls my eyes open. Shadows play over the wall, all free of red. Lance's arms are tight around me and his body is pressed to my back. I stare at his hands—his smooth, light-brown skin, the lines of the tendons, and the veins in his arms. Deep breaths warm my neck as he sleeps. My fingertips trace the lines and planes of his skin. Just the tips. The rest of my skin is hesitant to know his, maybe not curious at all. My chest is tight as I syphon off the small pleasure of that point of contact, unable to shake the feeling that I've done something wrong to end up in his arms.

The moment my death affinity drained from my eyes, Lance vanished from my sight. But his arms were tighter, his presence nearer as he kissed my forehead. Closeness has always escaped me. It wasn't something I could afford from those around me and then those who didn't deserve it tried to take it from me. I let down my guard and found a hand down my pants. I've never been able to figure out if what I did that night with Tōmas was actually wrong. Should I have not let him touch my face or kiss me? It was sweet to be touched like that, to be desired, but it turned rotten so fast. Now with someone who is kind and gentle and just as dark inside as I am, there are so many things that could go wrong, and it's scary to want him close.

As I press away from the mattress, Lance's arm trails down me and lingers around my waist like a security belt. The tips of my fingers keep to his skin, gliding up and down his arm until shivers appear and he stirs.

I turn and Lance smiles at me, his other arm behind his head.

"I can see you," I say, tapping him.

"Good. I have a terrible headache though." He sits up straight, now with one arm behind me and the other around me. The feathers of his wings are mussed and he gives them a stretch. "How are you feeling?"

His shoulder presses up against me and my gut twists like it's confused which touches are allowable and which are too far for me right now.

"I'm okay," I say. "Still sleepy, but not tired."

"Good." His arm twitches on my lap and his hand moves to my side. I can't ward off the tension filling my torso under the warm strength of his hand. I flinch and pull away from him, crawling out of his bed.

"I should go though." My face burns with my back to him.

"It's Freeday. You can stay awhile, if you want."

"No, I asked if I could do my sessions with the Psychological Health Provider in the mornings instead of the evening so I'm not so tired. I have to go."

I know I need these sessions more than ever. Something's broken in me and it keeps cutting jagged gashes if I move too fast, and then I spill blood on my friends.

"Okay, uh, here." Lance climbs out of bed and goes to his closet. "It's still chilly in the morning these days," he says, taking out a sweater.

He holds it open for me and I press my lips together, trying to hide a smile, already warm enough from the blush flooding my face.

"Thank you," I say, scrunching the too-long sleeves in my fists.

"Rin, about what you said last night." His wings block the light from the window, and I stand in his shadow, small, unable to look at his face. "I'm always here for you."

I bring my fisted hands to my chest and draw a breath. "I think I know that. Thank you . . . for holding me last night." Heat spills down my back, and I bolt for the door.

I cross the campus, wrapped in Lance's sweater—in his scent of pine and a lingering tinge of smoke. After a few sessions with Sovya, I've learned to enter her office without knocking. She sits in her chair, two cups of tea steaming on the side table. A smile crosses her face and fills her eyes as I sit on the couch cushion closest to her. Today she wears a cream-coloured sweater with a string of red beads around her neck and wide legged pants, feet bare.

"How are you today, Rin?" she asks with a head tilt.

I take the pillow from behind me and put it on my lap so I

can sit back. "Okay."

Letting a pause fill the space, Sovya waits for me to expand, to share my thoughts, like she always does. I don't have any words though, a lot of thoughts, but no words. The ones I said to Lance last night still burn in my throat. Sovya nods. "Have you been sleeping well?"

I keep my eyes on the pillow and run my fingers over the silky edging. "Not really, but I slept a little last night." Once Lance's arms were around me.

"When you were younger, did you ever have trouble sleeping?"

"Sometimes. It was more that it took me a while to fall asleep. I could always hear my mother moving around late at night, or I would be afraid to fall asleep because I had bad dreams the night before."

"And what would you do when you would have bad dreams?"

I glance at Sovya. She has her pen in her hand and her notepad on her lap, her eyes are narrowed and focused on me, the pen and pad ready but nowhere near each other. Her eyes are patient, like she's listening with them, hearing things I'm not saying and seeing pictures I haven't painted yet. I lock my eyes on the threads of the pillow. "If I couldn't get back to sleep, I'd go lie on the couch downstairs."

"So, you'd be alone?"

"Well, no, most nights my mother would fall asleep in the chair downstairs, so I'd be in the same room as her."

"And did you ever wake her?"

I shake my head. "She didn't sleep much either. I didn't want her to lose her rest."

Just being close to her, seeing her sleep, helped me rest too.

Sovya hums a low note and looks down at her notepad. Tapping her pen a few times, her brow crinkles and she makes a note. "Brand mentioned to me that when the Vein was attacked, you went back for something, a box with a few items in it. Your mother's suicide note being one of them."

A weight sinks in my gut. My pulse is quick, but my heartbeat is shallow. I turn to the window as a ring of shadow fills in the perimeter of my eyes. I nod.

"You've told me a little about your father's funeral, how the moment felt so real even as it's faded. Would you be comfortable telling me what it was like to find that note?"

Outside the window is another building and a garden between the two. Scolya and golden energy suckles sway in the breeze. Two little moon beetles crawl on the windowsill, one outside and one on the inside, making its way down the wall and crawling along the floor toward me. My hands are tense, and my knees stick tight together, but my body between the couch and the pillow is like smoke—nebulous in its physical boundary and my mind a locked vault. I blink. I blink again, the only movement I can achieve.

"Rin?"

My eyelids close and open, haze on one side and haze on the other.

"It must have been terrifying," Sovya says.

I strain for the key to unlock the vault. Pressing my eyes closed long and hard, I lick my lips and flex my fingers. Silence stings in my ears. A touch of breath hits my tongue and I say, "I stopped breathing."

The pull of the heavy, eerie air drawing me down the stairs

that morning to find Stephen, frozen in time, and the note that changed everything, latches onto me.

"My body breathed but I didn't. I always just wanted to be with her. When she stopped breathing, so did I."

Whatever held Stephen so still, broke. He broke with a sob that cut his throat. She was all he had. All he thought he had, all he thought he needed, and I was a ghost in his house—a ghost of her, and of myself, one that didn't need breath anymore. And who wants to live in a haunted house?

The space between my thoughts was infinite. I drowned in the swirling script of her last words. My eyes clung to only eight of them like they were a life raft—*I love you three with all my heart.* The words were a jumble, but I told myself to memorize them.

A vibration in the floor shook my eyes away from her words. Stephen still held his head in his hands, but red light spilled out of him. His body shook, the table shook, the house shook. I took a step away, clenching the letter in my numb hands.

Letting go of his head, his fingers tensed. He crumpled them into fists. With a scream, he slammed his fists to the table, and it splintered into bits. Tears drenched his face and steamed from his eyes. He clutched his heart and leaned forward, falling off his chair into the pile of splinters on his hands and knees.

Heat poured off him and the room was filled with bloody red.

"Why," he screamed, hands hovering around his eyes.

I stepped forward, splinters crunching underfoot. Down on my knees, sweat on my brow, I put a hand on my brother's shoulder.

"Get the hell away, Rin." He jerked away and pushed my shoulder, energy clawing out of him even with his restraint. I stumbled back and huddled against the wall.

"Mama?" Liam called from upstairs.

Through the rails of the banister, his feet appeared on the steps, then his legs as he crept further down. At the bottom of the stairs, red light pulsed over Liam's face and his eyes filled with tears.

"Rin, Stephen," he said between sobs, but I couldn't go to him, my body just collapsed smaller against the wall.

The door flew open. Stephen spun toward it like a feral animal, teeth clenched, and burning eyes wide. Oron walked straight to Stephen and grabbed him by the arm, yanking him off the floor. Stephen thrashed and threw his free fist at Oron. Oron caught the fist with an open hand. My mouth dropped at the display of strength Oron had never shown before. He threw aside Stephen's fist and with gritted teeth, he grabbed Stephen's collar in two fists and thrust him against the wall.

"You need to get a hold of yourself," Oron said, and grunted.

Stephen gasped for breath and his head lolled forward.

The air was ash on my tongue and my eyes stung from the energy permeating the room.

"If you can't get a hold of yourself, then you have to get out. There are children here, you understand?" Oron shook Stephen so his head lifted.

Trails of blood vessels accentuated his long face. His lips parted and the tension in his body left like breath. His death affinity raged on. Stephen shrugged out of Oron's grip and left.

He left, and I broke. All the darkness my mother left behind

crept in through the crack.

Oron knelt before me. "You're okay, sweet girl. You're okay." I didn't know the tears had fallen until he held my face with both his hands and wiped them away with two rough thumbs.

Even though my lungs couldn't feel breath, my nose picked up the stench of ale on Oron's breath. Was it a few drinks the night before because he knew about Mother, or maybe that morning, numbing himself for the day? Either way, he was there. The smell curdled in my gut, but I let go of my strength and fell into him. He wrapped strong arms around me, the last strong arms I would know for a long time.

Father's funeral was planned by the Senn Guardian station. The Kingsmans came, and his other Guardian comrades and a few Commanders too. Mother's funeral was traditionally Ironskin—just family.

I can't bring the day back.

It wasn't a day. It was a moment. A long inhale to collect one last breath. It's like I blinked and smeared tears over my eyes so I can't see it properly.

My hands remember a match. I rolled it between my fingers. I struck it and lit a candle. Holding it, I shook and crouched by her grave, setting it on her headstone. The flame flickered and the melted wax trickled over the edge, down my fingers. Oron knelt beside me and put his hands over mine to guide them and set the candle in the votive.

For an Ironskin mother's funeral, it is customary for the oldest child to speak on behalf of the younger siblings.

Fog sunk deeper into the moment, trying to hide it from me.

Oron brought Liam between us. I took his hands and placed them together. Oron placed his own hands together and bowed his head. Finally, I placed mine together in front of my heart, bowed my head and Liam followed with a bow.

My body swayed with my pulsing heart. Leaves crackled under our knees. Our breaths curled around us and built the fortitude of the fog. The cold was challenged by a heat drifting through the graveyard. Stephen was close, but not with us, not where he was supposed to be, finding words for something so tremulous so me and Liam wouldn't have to.

I bent my head low to my shaking hands. All I could say was, "*Hee oona heeut.*" I love you, because maybe she didn't know.

Hollow and dark, my chest aches.

I lift my head, face slack, and find Sovya's eyes. They are round and gleaming, a world of knowledge and understanding. I shiver as the little moon beetle makes it across the floor and crawls up my leg.

Sovya sniffs and puts a steady hand over her mouth, looking off into the corner of the room.

The air is thick as I pull it into my lungs.

"You miss her," Sovya says, still lost in the dark of the corner. "Sounds like there wasn't a time when you didn't miss her."

Something splashes into the hollow inside me. I draw my knees to my chest and hide my face in the pillow as it fills. The stuffy air filtered through the pillow is lighter in my chest.

I always sought closeness from my mother, even though she continually shied away. I know why she did that now. She expressed her needs to the Vein, and they ignored her. She expressed her needs to her husband, and he told her she was strong enough to handle it on her own. So that's what she did—stuffed it down and made me do the same.

Adrianne insisted that Mother left us because she was in pain, and I would always carry that pain with me too. But maybe the way Mother showed love was by taking away other people's pain. She used her life affinity to neutralize Stephen's death affinity so he could rest. At Father's funeral, she wiped my tears and let them fall down her own face. My mother held everything for us, for Father, for Stephen, for me, for Liam.

Since she took our pain, Stephen and I never learned how to comfort each other. He pulled away when I tried to comfort him, as his emotions got the better of him and his death affinity lashed out. But when I first saw my father in the Vein, Brand wrapped her arms around me and I didn't shrug her off. When my death affinity raged in the night, it calmed with her close. As Lance comforted me, I calmed.

Sovya clears her throat as I stay hidden in the pillow. "This is just an observation, but I think you're angry at Brand and your father because it was your mother you wanted to come back to you."

The hollow caves in, letting tears seep from my eyes.

"You didn't know Brand was around and you thought your father died in the line of duty. But your mother was always there with you and never close enough. You've always missed her."

I lift my head to wipe my face and the moon beetle settles on my hand. It flicks its wings, flashing white light through the room.

Sovya comes to sit next to me on the couch. With her back straight and feet planted on the ground, she demonstrates the position she's taught me over the last few months to relax. I uncurl from the pillow, place my heavy feet on the floor, and let the back of the couch support me. Narrowing my focus on my feet, I breathe, curl my toes, uncurl them, and let them still. I inhale again, moving my focus up my legs, up my torso with more breath, all the way to the crown of my head.

Full of real breath, the breaths of my heart are still shallow and broken.

Sovya asks me, "Is there something you would like to say to her?"

What I want to say to her hasn't changed since the funeral.

I love you.

I can't speak to my mother anymore. There is someone I can speak to though, someone who has always been there for me, who tells me hard truths and doesn't let me get away with anything.

"Sovya, I have to go."

"Rin, hold on—"

"I'm sorry . . . I need to talk to someone else."

Someone who kept me alive.

I bolt from the couch and fling open the door, leaving it open as I sprint in my bare feet across the gravel path to the main building. Slowing in the lobby, I hold my hands wrapped in Lance's sweater to my chest and keep my eyes open for her. Where is she on Freeday mornings? She doesn't like to sleep in, so she wouldn't still be in her room. Maybe she's at breakfast.

My feet slap against the marble floor, matching the thump

of my heart. The dining hall is empty but for a few students taking a slow breakfast. Johanna sits at the farthest table, tucked in the corner by the windows. She has her knees to her chest and a coffee mug cradled in her hands as she stares out the window. I cross the room, tears brimming in my eyes.

I don't know what to say. I came to talk to her, but my throat is too choked. I've tuned my ears to all the negative things she's said to me and have always chosen to shut them out or let them shut me down. So, I didn't believe her when she told me that I'm enough.

Careful not to scare her and spill her coffee, I wrap my arms around her shoulders from behind. Her warm hands trap my arms like she knew I was there all along, because of course she did, probably knew I was coming the moment I thought of her.

Burying my face in her frizzy curls, I let my thoughts run freely as her mind links with mine with a warm thrum. All the times she just showed up for me. All the times she paid attention. She always told me when I was pushing away, and she's always fought to keep me close.

I heard you when you said I was enough.

YOU DON'T NEED THE PART OF YOU THAT KEEPS TELLING YOU YOU'RE NOT.

I am untrustworthy, because just like Eliote said, I am like Stephen. We isolate ourselves because we are proud like our father, and we hold our pain in like our mother. How would anyone know what to expect from me?

ELIOTE

TESTS ASSESS HOW ONE IS DOING IN A SPECIFIC FIELD. I did really well on my final exams in hand-to-hand combat, weapons training, and academics. But I haven't had a test that brings the knowledge and action together like real Guardian work. This tournament will be my test, and just like any test, I'll need to study.

"Marcus, can I talk to you about the tournament?" I say, rushing over to him as he wheels the weapons rack into our training room.

"Sure," he says. "Are you feeling okay about it?"

I nod and wait for something to spark around him. An aura, an intention, an essence channel, anything. There is nothing, just him. Last year I would be relieved because I would have had to work to clear the aura away. It would be an accomplishment.

Now, all the energy is hiding from me or taunting me with a language I don't know how to read yet.

"I'm excited," I say. Avoiding his eyes, I clench my fist around my lightstone. "I'm just wondering what you think I could work on before then."

I am excited, aren't I? It's a challenge and I can take it. Even if the one unique gift I have is, well, I don't know what is happening to it. Beasts corrupted by utanic energy can see in the dark, but that's not what is happening to me. I'm not corrupted. What I need to do is refocus for this challenge.

"Today we'll be working on beast-slaying manoeuvres." He stops wheeling the rack in the middle of the room. Turning, he squares his shoulders to me as he crosses his arms. "That's going to incorporate essence and weapons. It might give you some ideas about how you can counter essence abilities with a blade."

"Will I be allowed to carry a blade during the tournament?"

Marcus tips his head to the side, his eyebrows furrowing as he tries to catch my eyes. "Technically, no, it's not allowed."

Voices sound behind me, raising the hairs on my neck as they hit my ears hard. Usually, auras brush up behind me before I hear anything. The harshest, most volatile energies sink into my skin before their voices enter my mind. Even soft, unintrusive auras make an impression before a breath leaves their lips. Auras are states of being. They inform me of who a person is before they interact with me. An intention blocks a person's true self. There's so much contemplation, pain, and information that has to be processed before an intention is set.

Marcus puts a hand on my shoulder. "I'll talk to Evelyn about it."

"Thank you." I smile at him with a brief glance and a nod.

Jeff and Niko appear to my right. The sudden invasion in my field of view makes my shoulders flinch. I cringe, shaking my head, and say, "But is there a routine I can work on or a specific skill?"

Watching Niko and Jeff for a few seconds as they joke together, Marcus taps his fist in his hand. "You want to be able to notice an opponent's patterns and then get in to strike first with your skill set." His eyes turn back to me. My skin crawls. I don't think I know how to read someone's eyes anymore without their aura. "You are the perfect fighter, Eliote. You don't need to worry. You want to work on your own terms. Get past essence manipulations and bring your fight to them."

Heart pounding and eyes prickling with tears, I turn away without even thanking him.

Bring my fight to them. It's different advice than I thought I would get. I wanted a technique I can practice, a strategy maybe.

"Everyone grab a partner," Marcus says once everyone has gathered.

"We're going to warm up with some weapons sparring with essence incorporation before we move into slaying manoeuvres," Marcus says. "Master Lotera, Professor Hans, and I will be around to instruct while you spar using essence and weapons. Please begin."

A light flashes to my left. I snap my head to it, hoping for an aura. Rin and Johanna pair up with lights dancing back and forth between them. One long string slinks through the air from Johanna's temple to Rin's. It tightens, flaring with light, and my heart understands its meaning—*you and me?* I don't know how I know that, but it seems right as they grab swords in silence, heading to the far corner of the room.

Moving to the opposite corner, Niko and Jeff bump fists and start to spar.

A warm draft from the door open to the outdoor training field wraps around me and a gentle voice pricks my ears. "It will be nice to work together, hey?"

Keeping my eyes on the ground, I turn to him. There is no colour around him, no darkness either, but my skin is gripped with static. I shiver, raising my eyes just high enough to see his mouth, and he smiles.

"Yeah, it'll be nice." I put my hand to his shoulder and run it down his arm, taking in his solid form, smooth skin, and let those sensations sink into my fingers to fight against the static.

I move to the rack and select a Lavarian weapon with an elegant, curved, single-edged blade called a *rahanaso* that I've enjoyed working with lately.

"What kind of essence techniques do you want me to use?" Ace asks.

"It's up to you," I say with a shrug.

"Are you sure?" he says, giving his neck a crack. He readies an Illyson longsword with a sturdy stance.

"Yes."

I set my feet in an easy, comfortable stance. It is similar to what Rin uses for hand-to-hand. My feet aren't too far apart, one with a slight turn for balance. With a calming breath, I open my eyes and focus them on Ace. I nod. "Ready."

Focus, Eliote.

Ace's sword crackles with ice and flurries swarm the blade.

I blink a few times, searching for the lines of essence in his body, but they are swallowed by the void around him. I can't see the void, my skin knows it's there though, and my hairs stand on end.

Ace steps forward, swinging his blade. I step and counter, blades clanging, but his flurries shift and blast me to the side, denying my own attack.

I keep my movements easy and simple, trying to relax. Maybe if I loosen my focus on advanced techniques, I can allow my sight to latch on to his essence.

I strike with a smooth overhead stroke. Ace counters and nudges me back with his flurries of ice. Shivers crawl over my body and I shift my grip. My eyebrows cinch together as tension pulls down my back.

This isn't working. I can't see his essence flow so every time he moves the ice crystals, I'm caught off guard. The only way to avoid that is to not give him time for his essence to flow back for the next manipulation. I have to be fast. I have to bring my fight to him.

Ace circles around me. The overhead lights glint off his glasses and his mouth is drawn tight.

I huff, take a few steps back, and shift my blade low. Searching for strength in my breaths is like scooping from a near empty bowl, each one brings me less and less strength. I strike. The clang of swords trembles through my arms and I strike again. I spin, evading Ace's next strike, and attack again, never allowing him time to manipulate the chill around his blade.

Ace is flushed. He pants hard and advances. I counter and back up. Ace's hand leaves his blade. I step and strike, taking advantage of a chance to disarm him. But his free hand thrusts forward. A silver orb bursts into being with a flash of light. Cold rushes over me and breath expels from my lungs as I'm shot backward. I land flat on my back, head cracking against the floor, sword clattering across the room.

I yelp as pain smothers my head, rolling onto my side, my vision swimming.

"Eliote!" Ace yells, shock shaking his voice. "No, no, no." He scrambles down to the ground putting a hand to my shoulder.

Tears blister in my eyes and my stomach lurches. Distorted images flood my eyes, sending sharp pains through the ache in my skull. I jerk out of Ace's grasp.

"Don't," I say. My voice is choked and too harsh.

"El, I'm so sorry. It wasn't supposed to work like that," Ace says. "I just meant to make a small time gap to avoid your attack."

I grunt and press my hands to my pounding skull. "You and these time tricks."

Ace hangs his head. "I know. It was stupid. I got ahead of myself."

My heart shakes in my chest and my face swelters as everyone stops what they're doing to look at me. I push away from the ground. Stumbling out of his void, I steady myself on the weapons rack.

"Why would you use it if it wasn't ready yet?" I ask, turning to glare at him.

Ace's sword lies beside him as he kneels on the floor before me, hiding his face in his hands. "I know, I know. I'm so sorry, El."

"Essence is so much more powerful and harmful than you all think it is." I take a few steps toward him, vision spinning and legs shaking. Marcus rushes over to steady me, letting me wrap my arm around his shoulder.

"Come sit down," Marcus says, propping me up.

He steers me away, but I urge myself back to face Ace.

"None of you have to think about it and that's how people get hurt." I jab a finger at him. "But it isn't as important as you think it is. All this time studying essence techniques when we could be spending more time together."

Picking up his sword, he rises from the floor. "This is exactly what I was trying to figure out," he says, eyebrows pinched. "I feel like we're out of sync."

Tears trickle down my face. "I . . . I guess I do need a little more from you sometimes."

Ace nods. He presses his lips together as his eyes gloss over and he turns away. "But what does that look like, El?"

My lips waver around words. I don't know what it looks like. I was raised to be helpful and self-sacrificing. Asking for more is too much. I want the words back. What is more? Why am I not provided with what I want when I've chosen him, chosen to be at this academy? What I've chased should be right in front of me. It's out of sight now, and I've forgotten its shape. All I can grasp is static.

"Okay, Eliote." Marcus turns me to the bench along the wall. "You need to sit down."

Heat blazes in my cheeks as I sit, head hanging and stray hairs sprawling over my face.

Marcus hands me a bottle of water and an ice pack. He crouches in front of me while he waits for me to drink.

In a low voice he says, "Look, it's common for people with level-one essence strength to experience energy surges with the increase of environmental utanic energy during the Two Moons."

It takes a moment for him to lift his head to me and I'm grateful because he said that word again. Utanic. My breaths speed up as his attentive eyes fix on me.

"There have been reports of Luminee with low energy levels from Tien Bay having surges since the attack," he says. "I'm wondering if, I don't know, maybe the energy affected you too."

"I don't have essence, Marcus, how could it affect me?"

"I know. It's just not like you to not see an essence ability coming like that." Marcus pats me on the knee and leaves.

As I stare at the ground, Ace's feet come into view.

"I don't want to talk right now."

"El, things have been weird between us this whole semester. When are we going to talk about it?"

"Come to my room tomorrow evening after nine. We'll talk while Rin goes to check in with Evelyn."

"Okay. I'm really sorry, El."

The Medics checked me out in the infirmary. It's just a bruise. With a few tonics and curestones, it's like the injury never happened, the pain has been stolen right out of my body. There are still sore spots on my ego, so I stayed away from all my teammates today. Every time I saw one of them, my face would burn, and I couldn't look them in the eyes. They all heard me. I made a fool of myself today.

But now, in the evening, my heart slows. My shoulders unfurl, and I follow a pull of energy outside. In the open training field, I raise my head to the sky. The vast expanse of darkness is cooled by green light. I shudder as I drink in its bewitching calm. Darkness and chaotic energy should not calm me. I shouldn't see so well. Even so, I am strong in the night, free.

I set down the sheet of paper with the new training routine I've come up with for myself. I'll start with sprints and then work on some shadow boxing. I'll need to be fast in the tournament. My reflexes will need to be quick.

Starting with a jog around the field, I push myself harder and faster each time I pass my sheet of paper. I sprint, my lungs pulling in air, and my arms pumping like a Nodaha Downfōst is right behind me. No fear is in my heart, and I have no direction as I sprint back and forth across the field.

Finally, I stop, bent over with my hands on my knees. Sprints like this would leave me dizzy in class, with spotty vision, but under the light of the stars, my eyesight sharpens. The darkness layers in crisp lines instead of a nebulous haze. I take in rough lines of bark on trees metres away, individual blades of grass at the other end of the academy grounds, birds far beyond the city wall in the trees on the hills. The world is breathtaking at night. And I've never taken enough time to enjoy it.

Within everything I can see, there's something I can't. My pounding heart hurries me to move against a threat. I turn in a circle, but there is no one around. The forest beyond the wall is quiet. The wind brushes gently against my skin. Something only my heart can pick up is here though. It is needy and hungry. A beast on the other side of the wall, maybe?

I clutch my lightstone and take a step back and pick up my workout sheet. Tonight might not be the night to stay outside.

The academy door opens. I straighten as light spills out the door. Professor Hans comes down the steps with his briefcase in hand and some books tucked under his other arm. As he crosses the campus, silver essence courses through his body and a crystalline structure of essence sparkles through his skin. Just like

Rin's essence. Professor Hans Griven is an Ironskin-Emberstead halfie. She was right.

Rin being right about Professor Hans, doesn't make me any less wary of Rin's plan. What will this mean for her? Will she approach him about the Revival? What if she gets sucked into something she's not prepared for? Maybe those questions don't matter, not when her little brother is her goal.

I pick up my paper and head back to the academy, rubbing the cold from my arms now that the sweat has cooled. The lobby is surreal, bathed in seafoam-green light streaming through the windows. The pictures on the walls seem to levitate with their crisp edges, and my eyes pick up every eyelash and every freckle in the portraits.

Rin is at the stairwell to the dormitory. She turns, holding a stack of papers in her arms. Her lips press together, and she comes to meet me in the middle of the lobby.

"Hey," she says, the soft note echoes through the large room. "I was just coming to talk to you. Can we sit?"

I nod, letting her guide us to one of the couches. We both sit on the edge of the leather cushions. I plant my feet on the floor, letting it support and steady me as I am wrapped in Rin's aura. Streams of red and blue flow infinitely around her. The birds burst from her and dive back in, crossing paths and fluttering their wings. I blink and her aura vanishes. I blink and her essence shines throughout her body like diamonds.

It's still here. My sight is still here, stronger than ever, just only in the night.

I keep letting myself be pushed down to make room for other's expectations of me. I haven't been able to tell anyone that I've been thinking of leaving because I'm afraid they won't think I can do it, or that I shouldn't do it, like my mom, or that they'll need me here or forget me when I'm gone. All this time I've built up an image of myself just for others to want me and think I'm worthy to be in their space—a Guardian space, a Luminee space—to convince them that I move at the same pace as everyone else.

Clearing her throat, Rin says, "I found a few articles we can use." She hands them to me, important information highlighted, each one separated with a clip, and notes written in the margin. "They've all been peer reviewed, published in the last five years. I even checked the sources." She bends down and pulls another stack of papers from her bag. "Researchers are exploring how utanic energy affects passive and active energy. Active energy can use utanic energy to change something to a desired outcome. In the presence of enough utanic energy, passive energy is changed to utanic. Since the Ōneera absorbs all energy types, it has utanic energy. It must interact with the physiology of the eyes, making them respond to utanic light instead of fann light."

She holds out the stack and the papers quiver in her grasp. I take them from her, and she clasps her hands between her knees. The papers are warm, damp from where her fingers clutched them.

"I don't really understand how it all works yet." Rin's silver eyes shimmer, and she tries to give me a smile.

My stomach sinks and my thumping heart cracks down the middle. She's doing what I've always done, overcompensating for one little thing.

"Could the physical structures of bodies be considered passive—"

"Rin, stop," I say.

She holds up her hands, clenching her eyes tight. "No, no, I can't stop. This isn't really what I wanted to talk to you about." I grip her research as she scoots closer. "I pushed you when I should have been more sensitive to what you're going through. You told me you didn't know if you could help, and I should have respected that." Her throat strains as she swallows, rubbing a hand over her face.

Setting down all her meticulous research, I clasp my hands on her knees and say, "Thank you for apologizing." Her boney knees raise as she flexes her feet. I give them a squeeze. "But can you just listen now?"

Rin slumps forward, taking one hand and putting it over mine. "Yes, of course."

Letting my eyes go lazy, I stare at her pale hand and my dark skin beneath. Her thumb strokes mine as she waits for me. I blink a few times to keep all the light out and just look at her, right in her eyes, to learn them again.

"I've done so many things just to make people believe that I was as good as them. My parents made me eat a strict diet to boost essence regeneration and keep my weight down. They thought that if I didn't have essence that I wouldn't be able to burn fat as easily, which was complete beastshit, but I did it anyway because I thought that it would please them. When I never developed essence, I focused on weapons training and my extra curriculars all while making perfect grades."

Rin is still and the lobby is so quiet, I can almost hear the portraits blinking.

"I just wanted to make up for what other people saw in me—darkness, flaws, weakness. I wanted to show everyone they were wrong. I'm still catering to everyone else, trying to prove that

I'm worthy to keep around. It's too exhausting."

"Are you thinking of leaving?"

"I'm going to decide after the tournament, but yes, I have been thinking about it."

Rin sits in front of me just her flesh and bone. She tucks her hair back and her mouth turns up in a small smile. It wavers but the effort sticks.

"I just have to do what's right for me," I say.

She nods. "I know."

"And you have to do what's right for you. You have to find your brother. Professor Hans might be your best bet. He's Ironskin-Emberstead."

She is quiet for a moment, breathing and tapping her fingers together. "Eliote, I don't think I know how to actually care for people."

I capture her whispered words in my heart before I can lose them to the open space around us. She's been a caregiver for all this time and doesn't know how to do it. I've been fighting to stay relevant in people's lives and don't know where I fit in my own.

"I just know how to protect myself," she says. "I don't know how to deal when I've done something wrong. That is harmful. I want to do my best to support you. I know you were hurt because of my family, and I want to stop that from happening again. Thank you for getting that information for me. But I shouldn't have asked you without making sure you were okay. Which you weren't."

Over a year of living with this girl and I've never felt so connected to her. Her hand grips mine, and I couldn't let go if I wanted to. Leaning forward, I pull her in to a hug with my free arm.

"I want you to find the place where you feel your best," Rin whispers.

My body relaxes in her tight hold as she supports me, rubbing her hand on my back. "Thank you so much, chicky."

RIN

I STAND OUTSIDE PROFESSOR HANS' office. I was going to talk to him today after essence training. It's taken me all day just to get this close. It's nearly nine p.m., but light glows beneath the door. I pace the hall. Each time my feet near the light, I veer away, making a half circle around the light and back straight to the end of the hall. I turn on my heel, toward the light again, nausea sinking in my gut.

Everything makes sense now. Professor Hans was the one who insisted on extra training for me last year. He gave me general instruction that always seemed like it could be applied to any other essence manipulation, like a projection that doesn't focus on the flow of essence. It was always correct, helpful. Stephen and Professor Hans know each other well, so he must be the professor Stephen worked with when he didn't come home during the school break. Stephen trusts Professor Hans, and that's why he sent the note through him when he wanted to meet with me.

Stopping in front of the door, my toes sit at the edge of the light. Stephen might trust Professor Hans, but I don't trust Stephen. Can I trust Professor Hans? No, that's not the question I need to be concerned about. If he's a part of the Revival, I need him to trust me.

I give each finger a crack and flex them, shaking out my arms. Inhaling, I knock on the door.

"Come in," Professor Hans calls from inside.

Pits going sweaty, I turn the handle.

Professor Hans sits at a dark hardwood desk, working in the light of a single lamp. It smells of dark roast coffee and a half-empty cup sits beside the notebook he works in, the brown rings circling the inside of the cup mark long periods of time between sips.

Hans looks up, his glasses at the tip of his nose. His hand pauses and his dark eyes shift past me, into the hall, and back to me. "Rin," he says, removing his glasses.

My feet are stone as he leans back in his chair, folding his hands in his lap. I swallow the thickness in my throat.

Clearing his throat, he asks, "Is there something I can help you with this evening?"

A neat stack of books sits on the right sight of his desk and a stack of journals sits on the left. The rest of the small office is just as tidy. Books on the shelf by the window are ordered by author, the rug is clean and soft. I shift my feet, sinking into the fibres. I open my mouth with only a breath and no words.

"Your shield projection today was very well done. It seems

that the sessions with Doctor Sovya have been an asset to you this year."

"Uh, yes, they have." I dip my head to the rug, scrunching my toes in my shoes.

"Rin, would you like to sit down?" Hans' head tilts to the side. His stare is hard and quizzical, tone gentle but low.

I take the seat by his desk, cracking a knuckle as I clench my fist. "Professor?"

Hans responds silently with attention. His face is long in the shadows, wrinkles by his eyes deep, and the grey in his hair stands out in the dark like silver.

"Why do you hide?" I ask in a quiet voice.

"Mm." Hans lowers his eyes, lips pressed as he examines the gold watch on his wrist. "Hide what exactly? We all hide many things."

"You're Ironskin."

Pressure weighs on my chest like it's trying to quiet my pounding heart.

"Yes," Hans says. His inflection raises the hairs on my neck, as if without saying, he accuses me for not knowing.

"Why do you hide it? You and Brand, why do you hide that you're Ironskin?"

Hans crosses his legs. "Rin, let me ask you a question. Why do we put so much stake in our essence? Emberstead, Ironskin, Nytrue, Fyrra." He shrugs. "Our essence is different, but we're all hédin."

Running my palms down my legs, I nod. "I guess you have a point."

"Our emotional experiences, our passions, our energy, it's not so different, really."

The pressure fades and my heart calms. A smile twitches my lips as my professor practically transforms in front of me. A man who once looked down his nose at me, regards me with respectful eyes and a steady, level gaze.

"Why did you really come?" he asks.

"Did you train Stephen how to use his death affinity between the school years?"

"Yes."

My breath hitches. "And are you part of the Revival?"

Looking down at his desk, Hans picks up his coffee cup. Swirling is slowly, he says, "Stephen was a dedicated student, always looking for ways to hone his strengths. But I saw that he was unsatisfied with the Guardian system, restless, searching for something. Taking him under my wing, I wanted to help him focus to control his death affinity. I was searching for something too. Something that would make change. Geret provided all of that for us, and it gave Stephen exactly what he needed to gain full control over his death affinity—the Revival is a goal fuelled by anger."

Stephen has been searching for guidance for so long. I don't blame him for clinging to two men who gave him that. And a plan to rebuild a nation after our family and our lives had been broken to pieces? Of course he would pledge himself to the Revival. My heart pounds a heavy beat and I rub my eyes. "Do you still have contact with him?"

Hans gives me a slight nod.

Whether it's the cool night light of the stars, or the calm space he keeps in his office, the turmoil I expected to erupt inside me with his answers is nowhere to be found. My shoulders relax and my fingers uncurl. "You knew I would be at the Festival of the Two Moons. You helped them make the Ironskin clones. How?"

It was all speculation until now, that there was an Emberstead involved in the Revival, and that the Revival used the clone attack to draw out my death affinity. I should be more specific— how could he hurt all those people, how could he put me in that position?

Pulling his crossed knee closer to him with linked fingers, Hans sighs. "I have a Mind Fire ability that allows me to understand a person's memories. I cannot read their current thoughts. So, I was able to restore the memories of our mission in the cloned subject, but not a conscious state to comprehend his current situation and make his own choices. All the clones knew was to destroy and attack you."

I swallow hard, rubbing my hand over my chest as the storm of rage that I syphoned from the giant Ironskin clone fills me. He remembered more than that. He remembered his pain and regrets. I know that feeling—to be consumed by all the wrong that has been done and the only thing you can grab on to is violence.

"Which is also how I know that you have no good will toward the Revival. What I don't know is if you are angry with me," Hans says with calm and a genuine curiosity in his tone.

The question takes me by surprise, only because no heat rises in me, my jaw doesn't clench, even though I know what he and the Revival are doing is wrong.

"I am," I say.

"Mm." Hans turns his gaze to the window. "As am I." He scoffs and shakes his head. "My good will for the Revival vanished on that day. When I saw that monster come to life because of my doing, I realized how far I had let Geret take me down into his obsession."

A shadow passes outside the door along with the whir of a mechanical cleaner. I shift in my seat as words rise and form on Hans' lips, then vanish. The soft tick of a clock behind me on the wall fills the silence.

"We're all hédin," he says, "and we all deserve the lives we have been given. We owe it to each other to make amends and have our nation take responsibility for our poor actions in the past. But the Revival's disregard for the lives of the other lineages reminded me that we each have a seed inside that loves the idea of inequality in our favour, and raising the dead only allows that seed to grow." Hans' eyes turn to me, he leans forward, setting a fist to his desk. "The only way true growth in our communities can flourish is by dousing that unholy seed in the only thing that poisons it. Humility."

I plant his words inside me, allowing their weight to sink them deep and never be forgotten. Taking his lessen, I offer him a challenge in return. "So, what are you doing to stop them now?"

Professor Hans' jaw twitches. "I am relatively powerless against them. They would take my life if I defied them. The Emberstead essence inside me is something they are very willing to extinguish, and I am no match for the death affinities of Geret and Stephen or Adia's life affinity."

"Then help me do it. Help me infiltrate the Revival and get Liam out," I say, shifting to the edge of my seat."

"There are many variables to think about here, it will take time. We need—"

"Teach me to control my death affinity."

Professor Hans' stare is steady on me, his chin tilted down slightly so his brows shade his eyes.

"If I want to get myself to the Revival, I'll need to convince them that I'm willing to help them with their cause, and a sure way to convince them is having the abilities they need for the Ritual honed to perfection." I stand, not willing to walk out on him but not willing to just let him sit around and think. "It's the only way."

Hans nods. Standing with me, he removes his suit jacket and smooths his vest.

Heart racing, I nod back. "Brand was teaching me to activate my death affinity through my blood cells, so I might be able to sort of drain a bit of energy as opposed to taking life all at once. And I think I saw my mother do something similar with her life affinity once too. Can you help me do this?"

"Well, I've done much research on that technique. In truth, it's one that I never understood until now. Your brother is unfamiliar with it. But I do wonder if you will be telling Commander Highcaller about our training, about your plan."

My brow furrows. "Wouldn't she arrest you for your crimes, for the clones?"

"Yes, that's my point exactly. I am willing to pay for my crimes—"

"But then I'm out a teacher."

"Exactly," Hans says, stepping to the door.

"For now, this is between us."

"Right." He nods, smooths his vest again, and opens the door. "Follow me. We'll train outside."

Hans leads me through the academy and outside to the patch of trees on the far end of the outdoor training grounds—where

Stephen's spirit energy met me. As I follow a few paces behind, the thought that Hans might be lying about all of this still stings my mind. He might just want me to gain control and hand me over to the Revival so they can do the Ritual. But the way he talked about the seed and humility is still heavy in my chest.

"Here," Hans says once we're shrouded in the shadows of the trees, with green spring grass underfoot and cool breezes sifting through my hair. "The technique you're talking about is similar to a projection, but the opposite. A projection is a controlled release. Energy with intention and direction. What you want to do is go inward."

I hold my arms close, rubbing the cool night from my skin.

Hans' eyebrows furrow but his eyes go soft. "You want a fine understanding of what dwells within—both your physical energy and your soul's energy."

"Okay," I say with a waver in my voice. I spread my feet a little wider and place my hands together like Brand taught me.

"Good. Consider the course your blood takes through the circulatory system. From the heart, it takes a path through the aorta, where it is directed both up through the head and down through the body. A single chamber, two directions. You are one being and yet you can choose to activate your two spirit affinities. Imagine a block in the aorta, directing the blood in only one direction. To activate one affinity, you must compartmentalize your being."

His instruction is clear, but it's a lot. I close my eyes, blocking out the sights around me, and focus inward. My skin prickles with the tap of Hans' feet on the earth. My heart thrums in my chest. I grab hold of the pulse through my limbs, letting it guide my attention inward. And then I block it, redirecting my awareness to my head, where my neck pulses with blood, my jaw tenses, and my eyes itch with fire. Heat fills my body as I light the emotions I feel with my death affinity.

My anger anchors through my feet like deep, dark roots, my love only grows through my arms and to my cold hands like frail leaves. My core shakes. It is barbed with thorns, cracked under a crushing weight. A thistle, a weed. I've always let myself grow that way.

The image is so ugly. The thorns are like my demon horns. The straggly ridges in the leaves of the weed are like the pulsing, grotesque veins that bulge around my eyes. Lance saw all of that and wrapped his arms around me and kissed my forehead. I don't know how he did that, but I am so grateful. I wonder if I can allow myself to be held like that again.

Tears rush from my eyes as I open them to the red glow of my veins. I part my hands and stare at the thin lines of light tangling underneath my skin. Professor Hans bends a tree branch down to me, so a leaf lies on my palm. The leaf quivers. The green colour pales at the tip. It fades slowly through the body and through the veins, until it is left grey. The lively green and earthy brown of the bark fades away through leaf after leaf and branch after branch.

"Well done," Hans says, clasping his hands in front of him.

He lets the branch bend back into its natural position. The tree is still alive, the branch will grow back. The glow in my body fades, the itch clears, and I shiver, swiping a tear from my cheek.

"I-I think that's all I can do tonight," I say, averting my eyes.

"Very well." He nods to me, a stiff smile tugging his lips. "Tomorrow evening then?"

I nod with a sniff and turn back to the academy.

The haze was so deep in my head that I handed my exam sheet in, unaware that my body had moved from my desk to the front, unaware that my hands still had muscles to move. I left the classroom. It was quiet with the haze. It filled my ears with static, blocking out the whispers of my peers as I walked down the hall to my locker. I hadn't been to class in a week, only came for the final exams that day. A few more to go and I would be rid of Senn public school.

As I took a few books out of my locker, my eyes caught sight of Ace down at the other end. I peered around my locker door. Ace was talking to a Fyrra boy a few inches shorter than him. His skin was warm brown with just a touch of pink to it, his short curly hair was pink as well. He talked to Ace with his hands up between them to demonstrate as he spoke. Ace held his hands in his pockets, his face flushed, and eyes sparkling as he listened. A smile broke over Ace's face.

It made me smile to watch Ace, to see my friend happy after I had made him so miserable. I clutched my locker door. The light in Ace tingled my skin, the haze around my eyes thinned, and voices in the hall met my ears. I blinked, taking a breath to settle myself as it all rushed through my nervous system.

"Do you think she knew it would kill her?" someone whispered behind me.

My grip tightened around the locker door. Palms sweaty, I turned my eyes into my locker. Six textbooks. I counted them. Over and over again I counted them, trying to drown out their words with the numbers in my head.

"Probably," another person whispered back.

"You really think she tried to kill herself? At a party?"

One, two, three, four, five, six.

"I read an article that a lot of Ironskins choose to take their own life with Ease."

One, two, three, four, five, six. One, two, three, four, five, six.

The air thinned around me. I took sips of it through a constricting throat, but they just made me dizzy.

"Then why is she still here?"

"Guess she should have smoked two joints. I would have lit the second one for her."

Shut up. Shut up. Shut up.

My fingers went numb, and I let go of the door. My other hand tingled. Breaths kept my lungs busy, and I pressed my hands around my face to hide the flare of the school's lights around my eyes. I teetered forward, almost diving into my locker. A hand grabbed my shoulder. I shook and dropped my hands. My head whipped to face them, my tired mind expecting to see a beautiful demon face come to torture me again. But I stared up into kind blue eyes and a crooked nose. Ace's face had lost his smile. I always seemed to steal it from him. A whole graveyard of stolen smiles fills the back of my mind.

"You okay?"

I blinked at him, swallowing hard. I shook my hands and flashed a smile. "I'm fine." The lie drew my limbs in tight and put a squeak in my voice.

"You're shaking," Ace said, eyebrows knit.

"Just cold." I grabbed one of the six texts, the one I would need for the next exam, or I thought it was. I checked the spine, sighed, and exchanged it for my history text.

As I fumbled with my bag and my book, Ace reached over me and grabbed my jacket from my locker.

"Who were you talking to?" I asked. My voice was alien in my ears. I had only talked to Liam lately.

"Oh, just now? That was Ines," Ace said, holding my jacket open for me.

"Why haven't I met him?"

"He's in B class, so our schedules are opposite."

I turned to him, sweating in my jacket and still shaking, just not as hard with the weight of my backpack holding me down. The bell rang and I jolted, bumping into my locker door. Doors flew open and the last students to finish their exams fled the classrooms. Ace steered me away from my locker and locked it up. With a hand on my shoulder, he led us to the exit.

The gritty Senn air coated my lungs with soot and ice. I pulled my jacket close around me and descended the steps. A siren blared down the road, competing with a chorus of honking cruisers.

"You think you're going to ask him out?" I asked as we weaved our way through the crowded courtyard.

Ace smiled with his eyes on the ground and ran a hand over his blushing face. "No, I don't think so." He shook his head.

"Why not?"

"I don't think I want my first relationship to be long distance. He's off to advanced ed to study law, and I'm off to Guardian training soon. We'd barely have time to start anything."

I held my hand over my nose as we passed a few girls smoking at the gate. "But if you like him, why not just go for it?"

Ace tilted his head to the side, his face still smiling but

softening with thought. "I want a relationship. Someday. With someone special. Something that can grow slow, with honesty and loyalty." His breath made delicate curls up to the grey sky. "What do you want in a relationship?"

My eyes found him through all the fog in my head and froze. I was just talking about it because it gave my mind something to focus on outside of that last shitty week. I shrugged off the question. "You like guys and girls."

Ace chuckled. "Yes."

I licked my lips and the cold stung them. "Like sexually too?"

"Well yeah, I think I would like to be sexually intimate with my partner, wouldn't you?"

Heaviness filled my chest. My throat went dry, and my mind went blank—a dark, empty expanse. When Tōmas kissed me, I wanted it. Anything more than that, though, was just as blank as my mind. I wanted something in the moment his lips touched mine. I wanted the touch, the closeness. Is that what I wanted in a relationship? Closeness? It was so simple, but intangible.

Ace bent a little to look me in the eye and gave me a weak smile. "You don't have to answer that," he said, his soft voice slipping through the expanse in my mind. He answered my questions so graciously and I gave him nothing.

"Ines is cute though," I muttered.

"He is, isn't he?" he said, a bounce in his step.

My laugh was dry and short, but it released pressure in my chest.

We picked up Liam from his school down the road. He filled the lull in conversation with a few anecdotes from the day. As we drew close to the point we usually parted ways, Ace stopped.

"Want to study a little together before I head home? I

could order us some food." He dug his hands in his pockets and shrugged. His mouth twitched as he bit the inside of his cheek and scrunched his shoulders up.

A cruiser slowed and the driver rolled down the window. "Eh, outta the way, cutch."

"Yeah, nice to see you too, Mr. Alver." I held up my pinky finger and scrunched my nose at him. I pulled Liam out of the way.

"I was just thinking it might be good to do some review together since you've been out all week."

"I'm fine. I'm all caught up on the material."

Ace fogged the air with a sigh, his eyes pressed closed. My stomach dropped and my hold on Liam's shoulder tightened.

"It's only been a week, Rin," he said. "I just want to make sure you're okay—"

"I don't need a babysitter, Ace," I said through my teeth. Liam squirmed out of my pincher grip, and I shoved Ace back the way we came to get him out of earshot of Liam.

He held up his hands. "I know you don't."

"And I don't want to talk about that night, ever. Especially not around Liam. Do you understand?"

The lightstone lamp above us flicked on as the sky pitched darker.

Ace pressed his lips and avoided my eyes. "No, not really, but I understand it's what you want."

"Fine," I said, stalking back to Liam. "We can study here under three conditions. We study silently, you order us iidai from the place down the road, and you say nothing about the mess. Got it?" I pointed a finger at Ace.

"The mess?"

"What'd I just say?" I threw a hand in the air and started for my apartment building.

"Right. Right. I'll abide by all terms." He trotted to catch up with us.

As we ascended the stairs, the haze started to form around my head again. My heart pounded as the sting of Ease hit my nose. Sweat coated my skin as my eyes went wide with the effort to keep my steps steady. The toe of my boot clipped one of the steps and I stumbled into Liam. Ace caught me by the waist.

Swallowing my body's desire for the drug, I brushed Ace's hands away. "Stop it," I hissed over my shoulder.

We made it to the apartment and knocked slush off our boots, shuffled in, and piled our coats on the couch. I clicked on my flower lamp and cringed at piles of junk around my bed. I scooped up a bra and a few shirts and dropped them in the laundry basket. I took long breaths of the stale air as I transferred the dirty dishes from my bedside to the stack in the sink.

Steadying myself by wrapping up in my green sweater and a pair of thick socks, I asked, "Liam, what are you going to do until dinner, buddy?"

"I don't know. I got a bunch of books from the library for the break."

"Well, that sounds great. Why don't you start one of those? Ace and I are just going to be sitting here studying for our exams." I set my text on the table where Ace had already settled himself with his notes and coloured pens.

"Are you okay, Rinnaya?" Liam asked. The protective covering of the library book crinkled in his grasp. His face pinched and his skin paled as he looked at me, just not in my eyes. "You seem . . ."

Ace glanced up at me, a pen poised between his lips and his eyes wide.

"Dark," Liam said.

Ice flooded my veins, and I crossed the room to avoid a freeze. I took Liam's face in both my hands and smothered him with kisses. He giggled and pulled away.

"I'm perfectly fine, buddy." I hugged him, giving myself time to repaint my smile for him.

"Okay," Liam said, and crawled onto his bed.

I turned away from him, clutching a hand to my chest, tingles spreading up my arm. I sat with a huff and opened my text. Ace's eyes fixed on me and I glared at him as his mouth opened.

"Rule number one," I muttered.

He nodded and before he turned back to his notes, he leaned over and rummaged around in his bag. Straightening back up, he set a container of home-made cookies between us. He picked one out and set it out in front of me.

As I nibbled on the cookie, Ace got lost in his studies. A crinkle formed between his brows as he sunk deeper into his focus, muttering from time to time to memorize dates. I studied the dishes, the piles of clothes, muddy shoe prints, smudges on my one window. Giving myself one moment to entertain the questions about relationships, I imagined someone to share my space with, maybe once Liam was on his own. With the mess, it seemed impossible, a dream. All the while, I sunk deeper into a different place. I stared at my text and into an all too recent history, one filled with Ease. It pulled at me hard, right into the present.

What I told Ace about catching up on material over the last week was more or less a lie. I was caught up before my short jaunt through the party scene, my handshake with death, and my brief hospital stay. I always read ahead. I read a lot of things. School textbooks, informational texts about beasts and various plants, about tonics and powerstones. It's what kept my mind from getting to that escapade earlier. So, instead of studying the week before exams, I took Liam to school, slept through the day, and went back to pick him up. Every time I passed the third-floor door, where the smell of Ease held permanent residence, I always had the urge to meet the tenants.

Ace left around seven thirty and I had Liam in bed by nine, thankfully with no fuss. I was tense from trying to keep myself from visibly shaking, and I didn't want him to ask about the dark. I reviewed the history material a little more while Liam drifted off to sleep, but mostly I waited. He shifted from side to side as the green starlight filled our little world. I attended to his long breaths, making sure they were the right length to warrant leaving without him noticing. I clenched my jaw, sickened because they were never long enough, yet I still unlocked the door, stepped into the hall, and locked all the bolts.

I took the stairs slowly, planting my feet to each step before moving on to the next, avoiding scraping my boots or touching the railing to make it ring through the stairwell—nothing to wake Liam.

An electropulse beat heralded my arrival at the third floor. The lick of sweetness in the air drew me to the door of the one apartment I never looked at. I stood in front of it, lungs tight, heart pounding, tapping my thumbs to my pointer fingers over and over again.

The fluorescent light above had one bulb burnt-out, one flickered, leaving the third to cast a sick white light above me that merged with the starlight seeping through the hall windows. The grey walls were green in the light. I counted the dents in the door. Maybe if I just focused my mind, the gnawing desire in me would go away. Was it the Ease or the handshake that had a tighter hold on me? My thorny weed had grown two heads.

I raised my hand and knocked on the door.

My feet slid back, I urged myself to follow them. But I stayed put until the door opened.

The sweet smoke hit me like a wave, my stomach churned but I couldn't tell if I was nauseated or giddy. A man stood in the doorway, a joint of Ease in one hand and a book in the other. He had dishevelled, short red hair, pale skin, and wore a loose t-shirt and sweats. The features of his face were plain, his eye sockets sunken, but his eyes were kind.

"Who are you?" he asked, crinkling his brow, and peering into the hall behind me. "Ah wait, I know you. You're the girl from upstairs. What brings you down here?" Folding his arms, he smiled and poised his joint near his mouth.

My mouth went dry. I had no business there—stupidity was what brought me down the steps. It hurt me. How could I go after it again?

"You want Ease?" He raised an eyebrow.

"Why else would I be here?" The tension in me spiked, and I crossed my arms to keep myself together.

"Sorry. But uh"—he shrugged—"I can't sell to you."

"What? Why?"

Head lolling to one side as he leaned against the doorjamb,

he motioned with his Ease filled hand to me. "You're Ironskin. I know what it does to you."

He knew I had no business with him either. *Stupid idiot. Just go upstairs and sleep it off.* But the smoke curled around me like a rope, keeping me grounded on the third floor.

"Look I just need a hit. Don't you have something, I don't know, lighter?" Heat filled my cheeks. "I-I knew it was stupid, dangerous to try it, but now I can't stop thinking about it." My shoulders slumped with the shake in my voice. Pressure built behind my eyes and I sniffed, running a hand over my face.

His body was like a spindly barricade between me and his dark apartment. Looking over his shoulder, he muttered, "Shit," and hung his head. "Yeah, I have something for you. It filters some of the chemical that gives you the high. Shit's expensive though."

I nodded, shifted on my feet, and scrunching the sleeves of my sweater in my fists. "I'll pay."

The guy set his book on a table just inside and set his joint in an ashtray. He left me in his doorway and went to a dresser by the window. "What's your name?" he asked as he opened a drawer.

I shut my eyes to the glow of the tip of his joint. "What does it matter?"

"It matters," he said, his back still turned, but his voice was soft and musical.

"Rin," I muttered.

Coming back, he said, "I'm Donny. When did you take your first hit?"

I furrowed my brow at him. "A week ago."

"All right, here. Just the one, and it's on me." Donny gave

me an intense, wide-eyed stare as he handed me the joint. "Ease gets to the head fast, but it sticks around for a while. For most people, once it leaves the blood, they're good. They don't need another hit; they might want one but won't need it."

I rolled the joint between my fingers. Donny tapped his fist in his open hand.

"For you, it's a lot different. Straight Ease hits your nervous system like a hammer, shocks it. Your cells actually recognize it like it's essence, so they drag it in. You've literally been runnin' on Ease for an entire week. That's why the craving is hitting you hard now. Your cells are finally breaking it down. But if you don't get the Ease again, your body's going to take a different kind of hit. It's going to start breaking down essence too. And that's no good. You'll risk a heart attack without more Ease."

A cold sweat broke over me and a tear trickled down my face. "Fuck," I said, wiping it away.

"Taking a little at a time, and increasing the space between hits, your body's going to get accustomed to working without it again. You smoke this one and then you come back for another in two weeks. No sooner, no later."

"Damn it, why didn't they tell me about this at the hospital?" My voice screeched as it came out of my constricted throat.

"People in this town are all grit, you know? We forget there's a furnace burning the fuel to make that grit." He rubbed his hand over his heart. Dropping his eyes, his voice quieted. "They probably thought you were a goner."

My limbs hung long and heavy. I couldn't bring my eyes to look at him any longer. "Why are you doing this for me?"

"As messed up as it is, it's only right." Donny turned to the table by his door. He took my hand and pressed a lighter into it. "Nice to finally meet you, Rin. Wish it was under better circumstances."

"Thanks," I whispered, clutching the Ease and the lighter. "Donny."

I bolted down the stairs. I thought the biggest mess I had gotten into was over once I left the hospital. But I carried the mess out. I always carried myself with me, so no wonder. Stumbling onto the front step, I drew the joint to my lips and clicked the lighter. The cold, damp air tingled my fingers. I clicked and clicked. The wind blew and the flame hid from me.

My head fell back as I grunted and fogged the air. I dropped to the step and braced my elbows on my knees and tried one more time, shielding the flame with one hand. I breathed in and smoke flooded me. Tears trickled down my face as the smoke warmed my lungs. My mind cooled and I exhaled.

I'd used the Ease to fade from life and now I was using it to crawl back into it.

It was the cold that was the comfort. Cold was easy to control. It didn't spread and burn and catch others on fire. If I was cold, then no one else would hurt. It was an easy way to drown and still stand upright. All I really wanted—want—was to keep my head above water long enough to stand on steady ground so I wouldn't fade. No more ghosts inside. I wanted my face back, a face not hidden from Liam by dark.

Fuck, that wasn't okay. Ace was right to worry. All he knew was my ghost, and he still knew me a lot better than most. I needed him, always have, always will. Illyson was too much for me without him. If this weed that grows inside me, attaches itself to me, becomes me, is going to stick around for a while, then I need a reminder that I'm someone underneath all that. Even weeds grow flowers. Even weeds can't live without water.

32

JOHANNA

Tʜᴇ sʜᴏᴛ ʀɪɴɢs ᴏᴜᴛ and the rifle kicks back into my shoulder. Clicking on the safety, I lower the rifle, noting the lingering sensations through my body, looking for any discomfort that could hinder my next shots.

"Nice work, Johanna," Brand says from behind me. "Move on to five shots."

I nod, tucking a curl behind my ear.

"You've done this before?"

Lining up the shot, my shoulders are weighed down by my dad's reassuring touch. "Long time ago," I say.

I fire five rounds. The repetitive impact, the singe of draining firestones, the glare of the sun, it all builds the hazy image of me and my dad on the Senn firing range a few months before he died. I swallow the lump in my throat.

He said I was almost as good as him. Almost. I asked him why Mom didn't want him to take me to the range. He smiled thinking about her and said that she wanted me to focus on fire manipulation. They didn't use rifles in their Guardian training days, so she didn't trust them. He called her old school. I laughed at that, but he also said that even though she was always a little slow to come on board with new things, I shouldn't let that stop me from doing what I wanted. Eventually she would come around and be my biggest supporter. He told me to never forget that.

I always thought he was my biggest supporter, the one who understood me the best. But maybe the only thing I got right was that he was always right. Turns out, Mom is my biggest support. I just hate that I only see it now when his support isn't an option.

She's the one who told me that it's okay to just find people who fit. I glance at Jeff as he fires a few shots at the target next to mine. I feel like I fit with him. Since the day I met him, he didn't make me want to barf. But we just haven't had that this year since he tried to kiss me.

I draw in a deep breath and clear my throat, so I don't startle him before he shoots.

"So, are you avoiding me, or am I avoiding you?" I ask.

Jeff glances at me. Looking down the sight of his rifle, he says. "As much as I hate myself for it, I've definitely been avoiding you."

"Good. Makes me feel better for avoiding you."

"We're both stupid then?"

I huff and pull the trigger, but my rifle just steams. I pop the burnt-out firestone and get a new one, shaking my head. "But

I'm not really avoiding you, Jeff, just thinking. Stuck. Sometimes I feel like I might be missing something by not . . . reciprocating your feelings." My face flares hot, and I fan my armpits before snapping the new firestone into place.

Jeff smirks and takes his shots. "But that's the thing. Even if you haven't been avoiding me, I still haven't been able to say I'm sorry. It might have hurt, but"—he runs a hand over his locs— "you don't have to reciprocate my feelings. Ever."

I rock from foot to foot, trying to move with my coursing essence so it won't make me sick. "I know that," I say, with a lump crawling up my throat. "When I do feel something for someone, it's strong, but it's just not romantic, and everyone expects romance to be the strongest, the thing everyone wants. What if I'll always be missing something if I can't feel things that everyone else feels?"

My face is a raging inferno. This is not an ideal time to have this conversation, but I'm grateful to have something to do with my hands and with all the shots cracking through the air, no one is paying attention to us.

"So, if I'm understanding you correctly," Jeff says, clicking on the safety and turning to me, "you worry that your strongest emotions will never be reciprocated because everyone else's strongest emotion feels foreign to you?"

"Yes." My heart pounds in my chest. "But if you just said that I don't have to reciprocate your feelings, why should I want someone else to reciprocate mine?"

Jeff shrugs. "Everyone wants to be loved. So, is it safe to say that you're avoiding me because you see me having romantic feelings for you, and you have friendship feelings for me, and they don't align?"

I drop my arms and lean my head back, letting the sun soothe me. "That's exactly it."

"I think they'll even out," Jeff says. Birds twitter from beyond the wall, in a frenzy from all the shots and the stench of metal and firestone. "You'd only be missing something from life if you let other people's expectations get in the way of being yourself."

A smile breaks over me, sending a rush down my back and I laugh. "You're so cheesy."

"But I am right. To be honest, I think I'm going to miss a lot of myself if I stay here. I think that's why I've really been avoiding you."

"What do you mean?"

"I don't know," he says, shaking his head. He runs a hand over his face. "It's just amazing that you can know all this about yourself. All I know about myself is that I don't want to be my dad. I came to the academy because I thought it would be the furthest I could be from him while still providing for my mom and being a good role model for my brothers. But I don't know." He drops his head. "Being a Guardian is dangerous."

My trigger finger freezes. Is he thinking about dropping out? Leaving?

My heart skips a beat or two or three. I try to swallow his words and process them, but they stick in my ears like wraith bells, ringing over and over again. I don't want him to leave. I open my mouth to say something, but Brand calls over to us.

"Kingsman, Warren. Slacking off in my class?"

We set up again and fire off a few more rounds before the end of class.

"All right, everyone. Good work today," Brand says.

With resounding clicks, we put down our rifles and turn to

face Brand.

"Training has been going very well as of late. I'm impressed with you all, and I think you will do an excellent job in the tournament-decision match tomorrow." She gives us all a nod. "Between now and then, make sure to listen to each other so you all know what you're worried about, and where you can support each other."

"Yes, Commander," we say in unison.

"You're dismissed. Ace, Niko, Rin, you're on cleanup."

I glance at Rin, and I stick my tongue out at her. She rolls her eyes, grabbing my rifle and hers. Stretching my arms over my head and giving my shoulder a rub, a light shimmers inside the empty training room. I stop, armpits exposed, as the light shifts into a flowing dress and wispy long hair. The Silver Wander Wraith beckons me over with a frantic shake of her glittering hand.

The wraith reminds me that I'm Soul Tethered to Rin because I had regrets—I couldn't let her go without her knowing how much she really meant to me. I can't do that to Jeff. He needs to know that I care and support him no matter what, no matter where he goes.

"Jeff," I say.

"Yeah?"

"You feel obligated to be here, to be a Guardian because the world puts Guardians on a pedestal right next to the glory of ruling and power." I clench my fists. That's not why I want to be a Guardian. I have my own reasons, my own pursuit of peace, but I don't want either of these pursuits for Jeff. I see it in the way he deflates with this lie of glory surrounding the Guardian system.

"I don't think I want that," Jeff says. His voice is clear in the stale air, soft and full like it always is when he speaks the truth to me. "But I can't just leave. I worked hard to be here. I used up my mom's hard-earned money to go through the junior-training program." His words run together, and he turns away from me. "I have to go through with it."

I march over to him, skirt around his towering frame, and poke him right in the chest. "The only thing you have to do is what makes you feel whole, so your brothers can know they can do the same. Do what makes you fucking happy."

Jeff pockets his hands. Looking down at the ground, he nods and bites his lip. "Are you happy, Jo?"

A wind picks up my curls and shifts them around my face. I didn't think it would happen so soon, but when Rin hugged me the other day, it was the first time I felt at peace.

"Yeah, I am."

"Good. So, you gonna sit with me at lunch today?" he asks.

"Save me a seat." I point with my thumb back to the training room and the wraith shifting like smoke. "I think I left my echo in there."

Jeff saunters off to the academy building. I bolt into the training room. The heavy heat that gets trapped inside during the summer months tangles around me with the wraith's smoky scent.

The wraith's face scrunches together as she wrings her hands. "I only have so much time with you in this world and we need to talk."

I chuckle. "What, do you have a curfew or something?"

The round, endless depths of her eyes narrow. "In a way, yes. It takes me a lot of time to come here from the tunnel."

Pressing my lips together, I shake my head at myself. I used to talk to my stuffed animals when I was younger. Ms. Freckle-Butt had a science lab under the bed where she would perform top-secret experiments and talk in hushed tones to her assistant Floppy-Long-Ears so no one would hear them. Ms. Freckle-Butt had suspicions that Crabby-Face wanted to steal her research and had her placed bugged. Now I have secret conversations with Wander Wraiths. Just a normal day for me.

"So, stop bitching about me making you wait, and let's finish that conversation we started."

The wraith's eyes narrow and her form shudders as she clenches her fists. Drifting close to me, eyes level with mine, she says, "I've come to warn you. Wander Wraiths are not fooled by the energy used to manipulate minds in your world. I see everything as it is and more. I've come to tell you that Alyxia, the Queen of Emberstead during my rule of ancient Sarr, is still in this world. I have sensed her around your campus."

Running my tongue over my teeth, I stare at her with my head tilted to the side. I don't know what I was expecting, but it wasn't that.

I step back from the wraith. "And how does this information help me release you from your Wander Land?"

The wraith presses close again. Clutching the wall, I take a long breath of musty, sweaty air. I plant my feet on the ground. She's not taking me to her Wander Land this time, and I'm not letting her out of my sight without answers.

"Who are you?" I ask, my voice cracking.

"My name is Nolaria, Ironskin queen of Sarr." Her silver energy quivers, sending her hair flipping and swirling around her. A thrum of cold and heat passes through me, as if a blue flame was just as cold as it looked.

"I defeated Alyxia's invasion into my land and worked toward peace between our people," she says. "She has a powerful Mind Fire technique. She can transfer her mind into another person, partially and completely. She transferred her mind into her daughter before she died. She has done this for centuries to acquire more power for the Emberstead Lineage by her own hand. Each generation she seeks out a woman with impeccable Mind Fire abilities and manipulates her to do her will. Manipulation after manipulation, she has harmed countless hédin. She was behind the Death Ritual in the Fourth Great War and is known to some as The Captor."

My jaw drops. I press my back to the cool cement wall as I sweat and slide down the wall into a crouch. The wraith—Nolaria—crouches before me, washing me with licks of energy. Fuck this. Why can't she find someone else to piss over with her confusing messages and unexpected pop ups?

"No more shit, *Nolaria.* Why did you choose to come to me about all this?"

"I have communicated with countless Emberstead women trying to put a stop to Alyxia. Their hearts did not heed my call to peace. How could an Emberstead help an Ironskin? In this world, the spirit and the mind always clash. But when I saw your Soul Tether, I knew you could put an end to Alyxia, you and Rin. But you both need your full power."

"Both?" I clutch my pounding heart.

"Yes."

"But that would mean . . . "

"The tether has to break."

My essence jolts through me and tongues of fire flicker

around my hands. I pound my fist against the floor, extinguishing them, smoke curling between me and the queen. I may want to break the tether now, to give me and Rin freedom to live our own lives, but she's wanted to break our tether all along. What fucking disrespect she has for something that saved Rin's life.

Nolaria stares at me and I shiver in her icy gaze. My mouth fills to the brim with ash and fire, my soul aching as it resists the truth.

I grit my teeth. "One of us has to die. The door has to close."

Nolaria nods. "But not just any one of you."

"Me. Because if she dies, I die. Because the tether is one-sided," I say.

Nolaria nods.

I heave a breath and it sends my head reeling and my stomach spasming. "But th-that defeats the purpose of me being able to defeat Alyxia, you said me and Rin. You're telling me that to get rid of this bitch, I have to die. That's fucked up." My voice bounces off the walls of the training room. I am beyond caring if anyone can hear me. I just want her out of my sight.

"Death is only the beginning of what you will have to endure. You have to trust Rin. And she needs to trust herself. I can't stay any longer." Nolaria stands to her full height, leaving me chilled and my eyes stinging from her light.

"Wait, what does Alyxia want now, why is she here?"

Nolaria mouths something, but there is only static in my mind. Her light flares and she vanishes.

"Fuck, Nolaria!" I rock forward onto my knees, reaching out into the empty room. "Get your ass back here! Those other women were right not to help you—this is insane."

This is too much. I can't get caught up with an ancient

woman's fixation. Wraiths always play with people. Nolaria has played me this whole fucking time. But I can't deny it. I believe her. I really do. Shit. I'm insane. If I don't know what Alyxia wants, don't know what she's planning, then I can't do anything. First, we get Liam back. Yeah, that's the plan. One step at a time. *I can do this. I can. No, no I can't.*

I fumble for my echo that has been in my pocket the whole time, tears shivering down my cheeks from hot eyes. *It's too much.* From my conversation with Jeff, to explaining my Soul Tether to Rin, to talking to wraiths and being asked to die for the sake of the world. It all rakes my skin, peeling it away, exposing the pink flesh underneath—raw, naked, just a glowing form in the dark of the world like the way my mind paints me in the Wander Lands and my own mind.

I link my echo to Mom's and press the lightstone to call. I clasp the echo to my ear.

"Joey?"

Mom's voice rushes through me.

"Mom?"

"I'm here, hon. What's going on?"

I choke back a sob, running a hand down my sweaty legs. "You were right. Helping a Wander Wraith is no joke. I don't know what to do . . . "

Mom's sharp gasp draws out a long silence, letting my pounding heart fill my ears, my long breaths pinch my lungs. "Mom wha—"

"This Wander Wraith. Has she told you who she is yet?"

"She just told me her name. Nolaria." I drop my head to my knees. The name is not new to me. I've heard the story of Nolaria, I've seen Rin read her story over and over again at school, in the back of the class. It's like Nolaria's story gave her strength, but knowing her weakens me. "Mom?"

"She contacted me once. She told me she needed help, but I had you to think about. I couldn't get involved with something that could put me in danger, leaving you alone. I told her I wanted to help her . . . but I couldn't."

"So, what do I do? If you couldn't help her, then who can? You're the strongest person I know."

A breeze makes its way into the hot training room, cooling the sweat on my brow.

"That's not true, hon. You're the strongest person you know."

People always say that, to find strength in yourself. It's always in the worst of times, to prepare yourself for something bad. It takes a different kind of strength to dive into something bad, and I don't know if I have that. I've always fought for something better than what I had.

I sniff. "She said Rin and I would both need our full power . . . I'd have to sever the tether between me and Rin . . . I'd have to die to do that. She wants me to fucking die and to trust Rin."

Death has never been a topic of discussion in our house. It's always surrounded us, infiltrated our home and our friends, but we don't know it. I can't find the questions to ask about it.

My tears fall. Mom is silent until she draws a breath and says, "Do you trust Rin?"

"I trusted her once, but not anymore. I love her, but I don't trust her."

"Maybe you need to trust that she loves you too."

I touch my hand to my chest where Rin's arms wrapped around me.

Can I dive into something terrifying with a friend? Would she really know what to do if I died? What does that even mean? I guess if we can come back from five years of cold shoulders, beat the shit out of each other, and make it through, then maybe peace between Emberstead and Ironskins could really be possible.

Mom lets out a shuddering breath. "Don't do anything that you don't want to do. I want you to be safe, for Zenta's sake, I don't want you to have to die for this world . . . " Her pause winds around my heart. "I love you, Joey."

She could tell me what to do. The woman I wanted to get away from when I was running off to the academy was good at making plans for my life. Her last words are stronger than any control or safeguards she could construct around me.

"I love you too."

RIN

Between the pages of my Beasts and Plants textbook is my memory of the team. Tearful eyes. Loving faces. I run my fingers over each of them, an easy smile taking hold of me. Setting the memory aside, my stomach aches. That was the day I went to go get Liam, and I failed. It's almost been a year and a half since I hugged him. He needs to know I love him and that he was right when he saw my dark, that his sight shouldn't be used against him or hidden. He deserves a real smile from me.

If all goes well tonight, Professor Hans will contact Stephen and tell him that my death affinity is under control. Then hopefully Stephen will take me to the Revival.

I finish the last three paragraphs of my Beasts and Plants reading about drenna weed flowers and their analgesic properties and snap the text shut. As I slip on my shoes, a knock sounds at the door.

I open the door, still tugging my shoe on. Ace waits outside with his arms crossed and a distant look in his eyes. His blue hair is unstyled, and he wears a loose pink t-shirt and shorts. The fading light of the early summer evening glares through the hall window, bathing him in gold light.

"Hey," he says. "Is Eliote here?"

"No. Johanna wanted to go over a few sword techniques with her. They're in the training room."

Ace runs his hand through his hair and sighs. He shifts his bare feet, his face drawn long, cast in gold on one side. This isn't right. I don't like this look on his face, like there's something cutting him inside. I wonder how many times he's seen it on mine. I toe off my shoes.

"Want to come in and wait for her?" I open the door wide for him.

A smile flickers on his face as he steps into the room.

I crawl onto my bed and pull the covers over my legs. Ace sits cross-legged at the end of my bed, propping up his chin with one hand. I keep my eyes on Ace. His mouth twitches as he chews the inside of his cheek.

"You want to talk about it?" I ask.

Ace folds his hands in his lap. He curls his fingers together and then uncurls them. "Something's going on with me and Eliote."

The tightness in Ace's brow tugs at me. "Is it something to do with what happened in training the other day?" I ask, drawing my knees to my chest.

"Sort of, but it's been this whole year."

"Did you, I don't know, did you do something or . . . "

"I don't think I did anything, I think it's just"—he looks over his shoulder to Eliote's tidy side of the room—"me."

"What do you mean?" I lean my chin on my knees.

"It feels like she is mad at me for being me."

Sometimes I think Eliote gets mad at me for being me too. Now my blood heats thinking about her being mad at Ace for being himself—the person who's stuck to me and been kind and supportive ever since I scowled at him and broke his nose. But it cools, remembering that she also experiences death in a profound, visceral way, she lives my dreams with me, and sees how alike me and my brother are.

"I don't think she means to," I mumble into my knees. "She just sees all the darkness that we get to hide from ourselves."

Ace nods. He flops down on his back, raising his arms over his head and letting them hang off the edge of the bed. The sunlight leaves a tinge of red on his dark skin as it dips closer to the sea. I pull my text back onto my lap as Ace's eyes fall closed. The furrow is still there, with pain drawing lines on his face.

"Rin?" Ace says after a while.

"Yeah?" I settle my back against my pillow.

Ace folds his hands over his stomach, staring at the ceiling. "When you were . . . unconscious after doing Ease, red light like the light that comes from your eyes when you use the death affinity, it like . . . appeared above you . . . not from you." He unfolds his hands and runs his fingers down his arms. "It went into you and made patterns along your skin. It centred around your forehead, lungs, heart, and followed the lines of your veins even before they put the antidote mask on you."

A flash of light dances in my mind. Right above me. I don't remember it being red. It was a fluorescent light. Faces floated in and out of that light. Plastic rimmed my face, my lungs ached to expand but only drew in pain.

I don't think that's the light he's talking about. I rub a chill from my arms.

"Why didn't you tell me?" I ask.

"We never talked about that night. What was it? Was it the death affinity?"

"No," I say in a soft voice as I lie down on my back next to him. My feet dangle while his legs curl over the edge and his feet hit the floor. "It was Johanna."

Ace tilts his head to me. "Johanna?"

I nod. "Yeah. We're like linked or something and she . . . saved my life because of it. You both did. If I didn't get the antidote mask on, she might not have been able to give me my energy back. She would have died too."

In the worst moments of my life, Ace and Johanna have been there for me. They take care of me when I don't know how to take care of myself. It has hurt them though. Now they carry these burdens that I don't carry. Ace does it so gracefully.

"I'm sorry I put you through that," I say, eyes fixed above as they fill with tears.

"I don't want you to be sorry." Ace's soft voice fills my ears. His presence beside me is a constant and I am so grateful for it. "It's just what's going on with Eliote," he says, "is making me think about how I don't catch on to things going on around me unless it really interests me. Not that you don't interest me or Eliote doesn't interest me, it's just that I don't see what you don't show me. I trust you and I trust her, so with that thinking, I just rely on whatever you're willing to tell me. I want you to be honest with me when I ask you how you're doing, because

I'm going to believe you. But because of that, I didn't know you weren't okay . . . " His voice chokes and grows thick and I squeeze my eyes shut, sending the tears tumbling down my face. "I mean, I knew something was wrong, I-I just didn't know you were suicidal. And I still don't know why Eliote is struggling. I'm so sorry. I want to be better. I don't want to see you hurt like that."

I press the heels of my hands to my eyes and shake my head. Ace takes a breath that shudders the bed. "You did everything you needed to do for me," I say. "You were always there for me. That's all I need, all I want."

"But I dragged you to that stupid party. I left you and started talking to someone else. And now I've been focusing on stupid essence manipulations I don't need to focus on. I've been selfish."

I wipe my face with the corner of my blanket and push up from the bed, leaning on one hand. "I don't even know what's really selfish anymore. You were just doing something for yourself." A sterile tinge drifts through my memory. Oron told me that taking care of someone doesn't mean never doing anything for myself. Maybe I could have had the freedom of that statement if I hadn't attempted to stop my heart with Ease the night before. "You had fun at a party. You like learning new essence manipulations. Those things aren't against us. And I like to see you happy."

Ace hangs his arm over his face, a silver tear glistening down his cheek.

Head full and heavy, I take a long breath. "You can't see what others are going through all the time. It's not your fault for not seeing something if someone is good at hiding it. I've hidden a lot from you over the years, and I want to stop doing that."

Ace sits up. The motion sends a few books sliding off my bed into a pile of dirty clothes on the floor. For a moment, he's still, head bent, and hands clasped between his knees. I lean forward and wrap my arms around him. "Thank you for being you, for being with me."

He puts a strong, warm hand to my shoulder and whispers, "Always."

A rush fills my chest, like spring wind, cool enough to soothe, warm enough to melt the winter. I can't believe it took me this long to believe him.

Voices break the silence in the hall, and I let Ace go.

Eliote comes in and freezes. She stares at Ace for a moment and her jaw twitches. She glances from him to the golden sunlight streaming through the window and squints, pinching the bridge of her nose.

Patting Ace on the knee, I stand.

"Talk to him," I say, giving Eliote a quick hug before pulling the door closed.

My body is warm as I walk down the hall. Somehow, just like the sessions with Sovya, talking with Ace about things that hurt us soothes the bleeding inside me. Maybe now my death affinity will be content to stay inside.

34

ELIOTE

It's too early. The sun is still up and Ace's crackly void fills the room.

Adjusting my tank top and smoothing my hair, I say, "I told you to come after nine," and move over to my dresser where the grip of the void loosens.

Ace sits on Rin's bed, hunched over his knees. I blink, shifting my sight, just like I do in the night with auras. The staticky, dark void appears like a shadow around him. It's beautiful in a way as it glistens like shiny black onyx, but looking straight at it brings an ache to my chest.

I straighten the glass bottles of perfume and face cream on my dresser, the glass clinking and sunlight streaking through their smooth, geometric planes.

With such gentleness, Ace says, "I know. I'm just worried. I need you to tell me what I'm doing to make you uncomfortable. You can barely look me in the eyes."

Rin's blankets shift as Ace stands and books clatter as he trips over them. Coming closer, the void rakes the back of my neck. I turn to face him, but step back into the corner of the room. Ace's face pales and he stops his advance.

"Sorry," he mutters.

My heartbeat taps in my throat. I swallow, pushing down the spike in adrenaline from the unknown. I don't want to keep the space between us. My hands itch for him, my skin wishes for the cool flow of his aura to come back.

"I don't understand this," I say through gritted teeth with clenched eyes and fists.

"What? What don't you understand? Just tell me, please." He reaches for me, but stays back, his eyes wide and brows furrowed.

"This!" I fling my arm out in front of me into the crawling emptiness surrounding him.

Looking at the space between us, he touches his hand to his head. "Is it your sight? Is something wrong?"

"It's changed."

Ace drops his hand.

"Ever since my home was attacked . . . " I press my hands to my forehead. "I can only see auras and essence at night." My breaths come faster. Ace rounds my bed with tentative steps to sit down. His eyes stay on me as I step into the middle of the room, keeping the distance I want to shatter intact. "And in the day . . . I see intentions, I think."

"Well, can you describe it to me? What you're seeing?" Ace says, facing the window.

I face the mess on Rin's side of the room—blankets twisted, books and clothes everywhere, a bowl and spoon sitting on a precarious stack of texts on her desk.

"Well," I say, closing my eyes to everything, letting in the quiet. "Rin, she"—I sit down on the floor and lean on her bed, eyes still pressed—"has this field of deep red around her. It lashes at her, at other people. It hurts. It's dark. Johanna is the person whose aura I still see all the time. Pink." The sweet blush of her aura brings a smile to my face.

"And mine?" Ace's voice drifts on a soft wave over to me.

"There's nothing there, just shimmering darkness. It's like static, and it clings to me." I pick at my cracking nail polish as he rolls the information in his head.

"Intentions," Ace says as he clicks on the lamp beside him. "Johanna knows herself, and I think she wants to keep knowing herself more."

"You think that's why her intentions look like her aura? They're aligned?"

He shrugs. "Probably." Pressing his lips together, he stifles a chuckle.

"What?"

"You said her aura is pink?"

"Yeah, why?"

"It's just surprising, but also, why wouldn't it be pink? It feels so right."

I smile at him, quietly sitting in the shadow around him. It's like he draws strength from it. "What about Rin?"

As he runs his hands together, his smile fades. "Rin—" His brow crinkles. "She wants the best for others but not for herself. There's a lot going on there that I would never be able to explain."

I take a shaky breath. I push off the ground and slide my feet into his void. The empty rush floods my lungs and snakes over my skin. My insides squirm, but I cross the room and sit next to him. "And you?"

"I don't know. I just feel like this is where I want to be. At the academy. I want to be a Guardian, and I want to be close to Rin and to you."

Heavy tears fill my eyes. "Sometimes I see light in you when you look at Rin."

"She's my best friend, El." Ace turns to me, eyes filled with conviction. "I almost lost her once. I have the strongest intentions toward her because I swore I would never leave her alone."

"Right, right. I know that," I say as a tear streaks down my face before I can catch it.

Ace runs a thumb under my eye, but I pull back, wipe my face with the back of my hand, and turn away from him. Wrapping his hands around my waist from behind me, he leans his head on mine. His lips graze my ear. He inches closer. As he presses his lips to my neck, my eyelids fall closed in response to the soft pressure. Everything quiets. Warm breaths wash over my skin.

Ace pulls my hair to one side and I lean my head to it. Each kiss to my skin is like a blot of ink, spreading and colouring me inside with light and warmth. One hand cradling my jaw, one on my side, Ace turns me to face him. "Why do my intentions scare you, El?"

I draw a shaky breath as I let my eyes open. Ace's sapphire eyes bore into me as he strokes his thumb along my jaw, sending shivers down my neck.

As the sunlight fades and the faint glow of green touches

the sky, the void and Ace's aura overlap. He is a vast ocean of shimmering blue, deeper and wider than I've ever seen. The depths are full of love, and the waters are content to churn and grow and swell in the space they have been given. I am lost in that sea.

Auras and the clarity of the night are realities that I don't share with anyone. But touches we can share.

I slip my hand behind his neck and I lean into him, my skin craving his touch. Guiding his face back to my neck, I set my other hand on his side. Ace kisses me, and with a heavy breath, he says, "You didn't answer my question."

All I want is one moment where I don't experience something entirely different from everyone else. I just want to feel one moment with him. One moment where all we see is each other and all we feel is the other's skin. I tilt his head up and kiss his lips. I press my eyes shut against the world, against his aura, but the waves still crash. They flow through me, pounding against me as if they are the heart inside him. So why are his hands gentle on my waist? Why are his kisses restrained? I want him to throw me on my back and press his body around me so I can feel everything that he feels.

I part my lips and my tongue grazes his. Our lips become wet as I hurry our kisses, hoping for a passionate return. I tuck my hands under his shirt and slide them over his solid core, up to his chest.

His lips fall from mine. My breaths stop. His hands gather my wrists like a bouquet, and he kisses them gently.

"Why are you stopping?" I whisper.

"Do you think . . . that you might project your own feelings onto the intentions you see?"

All the warmth I gathered on the tips of my fingers from his body drains out and gathers in my face. Gritting my teeth, I turn my face away as he continues to cuff my hands so I can't touch him.

"Do you think my intentions feel wrong to you because we don't want the same things?"

"The tournament will tell me if I'm meant to be here, if I'm meant to be a Guardian," I say.

Letting go of my hands, Ace cups my face and turns me back to look into his deep blue eyes and to be washed in his aura. "That's not what I asked."

I take a breath and it shudders out of me. I've had to know so much more than everyone to get here, and I know so much more about everyone than they would care to admit, but right now, I don't know. My stomach has gone sick, and my arms are weak, and all I can do is shake my head.

We sit side by side, facing the window as tears rush from my eyes. Ace curls his fingers around mine.

"I don't know," I say through a sob.

"It's okay. You don't have to know."

Blue washes around me and I squeeze Ace's hand. Clearing his throat, he says, "If you leave, I will do everything I can to support you and to support our relationship. I want this. I love you. It just depends on . . . "

I don't know if I want him to say it or if I want him to keep it inside. It depends on me, if I really want this. I don't want it to end, but there is a part of me that knows exactly what he meant when he suggested I might project my feelings onto his intentions. My feelings and his intentions aren't a pair.

LANCE

My team lines up for essence-pressure tests and vitals outside the infirmary. My Monitor, Officer Merez, has been called in for the event and will be required to attend the tournament if we are selected to compete. Mycul snickers as Merez takes me in to the opposite side of the room to do the pressure test himself.

"Sit," Merez says, gesturing to a wooden stool. He sits across from me, bringing one leg up to rest his clipboard on.

We go through the checklist together to make sure I've been staying clean and taking care of my health. Each check mark takes a strike at my gut—slashing away each mistake, each stupid choice—leaving it a raw, bloody mess inside. At least they're check marks and not exes.

The sterile environment stirs the itch on my skin. I shift in my seat, shrugging my wings as they stiffen. They ache like stakes in my back. I know this stress won't be good for the essence-pressure test. I can't identify the cause though. Training has been good for the most part, but my hands pulse with essence. They flicker in and out of existence. One moment, light-brown flesh, the next, my gaze dips down to the floor. My stomach lurches with the sick pain stabbing through my chest. I keel forward, sticking my head between my knees. I blink and my hands reappear with Khalie in my arms, red blood pouring over them, slick and warm.

The LPs pried her out of my arms. The click of essence-neutralizing cuffs resounded through my skull. Her snow-white wings and long, black hair dripped over the edge of the stretcher. The air was charged, bitter with energy, all because of me. She was taken to the morgue, and I was taken to the Guardian station.

I answered every one of their questions with coursing essence wearing away my patience. Energy crackled under my skin with nowhere to go, blocked by the current of the cuffs. Face streaked with tears, I was unable to wipe them away—the cuffs were too tight. They locked more than just my hands. Sweat poured down the back of my neck and made rings under my armpits that stuck my shirt to my body. The questions took forever because I still had blood on my hands and Ease numbing my mind—I couldn't focus.

The blood is still there even now as my skin hides from me.

Merez lays two heavy hands on my shoulders, bringing me back to the infirmary. I can't lift my head to him. I breathe deep and keep up the search for my hands.

"Our emotion is the energy of our minds. It manipulates the world around us and affects our entire body," Merez says, his voice low, infusing me with a grounding force. He lets go of my shoulders and runs his hands down my arms to find my hands. He grips them and cool green light and vines spill from him, surrounding my translucent skin. The vines and delicate leaves mark out my hands, giving them the illusion of physicality and depth.

"We have emotions that steady us and emotions that unsteady us. We cannot become invisible if we are not steady. Search inside for what grounds you, even when the world cannot see you."

I bring my eyes to meet his. His light-plum skin is hard and weathered, stretched tight over chiselled bone. He frowns deeply and keeps a steady gaze. I nod to him.

Merez wraps the pressure cuff around my arm. "Invisibility is extremely powerful. Have you gone completely invisible yet?"

"Yeah," I say, my voice raspy. "But when that happens, I can't get it to go away."

Nodding and marking down the pressure readings, Merez says, "Scholars always speculated that one lineage might develop an ability such as this. They speculated the Fyrra because they are so connected to the environment they live in, to the soil and the plants and the moon. Becoming one with it seemed to be the next step. But Lavarians have connection to even the charge in the air, the gas particles themselves, the water. When you consider the properties of water and gas in our atmosphere, it becomes clear that invisibility is an extension of water's reflectiveness, gas's intangibility, the impact of slight electrical charges, and kinetic energy. All these properties are steady, but unseen." Merez holds up the perfect blood pressure and essence-pressure readings.

"Thank you, Merez," I say, giving his huge hand a shake. The tips of my fingers are still lost, but his grip reminds me they're there.

"I will be in the stands if anything happens today," he says. "But I believe you will be seeing far less of me from now on."

My gut cinches as I leave the infirmary and head to the arena for the match. Inside me, everything is raw, new. The past that has always been caught on my skin itches. It's not me. The boy with the blood on his hands and Ease in his head and alcohol in his veins—he's not me. My heart breaks for him though. I've lost him, even though he wasn't me. I had to let him go, and I can't look at my skin without seeing him. The problem all along was that I tried to forget him. Maybe with that effort, I really built him up. If I had left him alone, in peace, maybe the wound would have shut, scabbed up, and stayed closed. The wounds wouldn't itch anymore.

I want this tournament to go well. For the first time in a long time, I don't feel like I need to hide a part of myself or have someone acknowledge me to feel like I'm worthwhile. I want my team to succeed today, and they'll need me to step up.

The rest of the team catches up to me as I enter the arena. A bunch of instructors line the railing in the stands with clipboards ready for notes and stern faces. They create a wall of sentinels over us as we put on our protective gear for the match to decide which team will go to the tournament.

"All right, Lancy boy. No screwing shit up," Mycul says. He slaps me on the back and shoves past me, swaggering into the middle of the arena.

The door to the training room opens and the advanced team files through.

"Please line up facing each other for us to begin," Evelyn says into an ampliphone.

As we line up, something about standing on one side with Mycul, Aris, and Litha, and facing the advanced team, where my real friends are, seems cruel, comical even.

Niko drums on my shoulders as he passes. "Let's see you put those gym gains to work, hey Lance?" he says, turning backwards to give me a grin as he moves farther down the line.

With a chuckle, I hang my head, but Jeff grabs my chin and yanks my head back up. With a straight face, he says, "Head up, man. Give it your all." He struts past me, glaring down his nose at Mycul and the rest of my team. Mycul crosses his arms and stares back.

Ace gives me a handshake and Eliote squeezes my shoulder. Passing me with a nod, Johanna takes her place in front of Mycul. She runs her tongue over her teeth and gives it a click, raising a sculpted eyebrow at him. Her lip curls, making the small, white scar stand out from her freckled face.

I clench my fingers as Rin stands in front of me. She wears grey sweats, a black t-shirt, and her hair tied up in a messy bun. Taking a steadying breath, I get a whiff of coffee and something sweet. She smiles at me, her stormy gaze cool and intense under her dark eyebrows. Taking a step forward, she says, "Hi," and finds my fingers with hers.

I squeeze her hand with energy running through my veins and heat crawling up my cheeks. "You feeling okay?" I ask.

She nods.

Mycul scoffs beside me. "This is a fucking joke, isn't it? They're not going to give us much trouble. The Luminee bitch is a dud anyway."

The entire advanced team moves in on him, any light in their eyes blinking out of existence.

"Take it back, man," Ace says.

Niko bounces up and down on his toes, raising his fists, the top of his head only coming up to Mycul's chin. "You're a little dick, aren't ya? Big mouth, little dick, yeah, that's what I see."

"*Sufach te feknah, bachho,*" Rin says.

"What'd she say?" Mycul's face scrunches and his swamp eyes narrow.

"She told you to suck her dick, bitch," Johanna says, getting right up in his face.

Kal, Ira, and Aris push back against them, but their insults don't compare. Litha pulls Mycul's arm to get him away from them. I steer Rin away from Mycul, her silver eyes still carving a direct line to him.

"Everyone, quiet," Evelyn shouts. The stream of vulgarities echoes through the arena. Glaring over the top of her gold spectacles, she crosses her arms with a wide stance. "We don't have to do this," she says. "We can just send one team to the tournament. If you keep conducting yourselves like this, we'll forget the match and just send the fourth-year team. You want that?"

"No, Headmaster," we say in unison, straightening out our lines.

"Mhm, that's what I thought." Evelyn does a half turn on her heels, still giving us a scathing side eye. "In thirty seconds, I will terraform this entire arena into a battleground. If you cross the line into the dead zone, you're out. Your goal is to have as many members of your team still in bounds after ten minutes. The team with the most members in bounds will be selected to represent Akinnera in the tournament. You will not have time to strategize with your team because this drill is about adjusting to your environment together." Evelyn marches off, her high heels clicking, and she boosts herself up to the stands with a pillar of earth. "You have been given only Protector vests as that is what standard Guardian uniforms allow. Your only rule is, no projectile-essence manipulation in close combat, to encourage hand-to-hand. Sustained abilities, armours, and states such as shadow phasing and spirit affinities are fine."

The ground rumbles and dust builds around us as the arena floor splits open with a deafening crack. I stumble back and the rest of my team scatters as a wall of rock rises out of the ground, stone scraping and the musk of earth strangling my lungs. I jump back to get some space between myself and the growing wall and flick my wings to propel myself into the air.

Landing back on my feet beside Aris, he grabs hold of my arm to steady me. "Group up," I say. "We have to stick together and stay in the—" The ground lurches below me and rises fast. I'm thrown to my knees. Dust clouds my eyes and the rumbling chatters my teeth. Once the movement stops, I flap my wings to clear the dust.

"Lance, you okay?" Aris calls.

"Yeah," I say, scanning the arena from the top of the twelve-foot-tall boulder.

Around the left side of the wall that erupted from the belly of the arena, Johanna and Ace stand together building fire and water all around them.

"I see them," Mycul says. With a flash of red, a sword flares in his hand. "Let's go," he yells and bolts toward them.

"Wait, they're going to block us, so we've got to go around," I say, leaping off the boulder and careening down to the ground. "We have to go around."

But Mycul and the others barrel toward Johanna and Ace.

The mass of fire and water collide with a crash and the corridor between the behemoth boulders fills with steam. It floods over my team. I back up, trying to keep their shadows in sight and not be drenched by mist, but the heat douses me, and my breaths become thick with moisture.

"Aris," I say.

"I've got it," he says.

The heat shifts and wind whistles through the stone corridor. I drop into a squat, lowering my centre of gravity against the torrent, and bring my wings in close to my body. The wind sweeps the cloud back over the advanced team. But with a heavy thud, a white armoured bear with red eyes leaps through the mist. Bracing myself, I grit my teeth as the bear—Niko—roars and barrels toward us. He takes a wide path around us, pushing us up against the rock.

"Kal, wall!" Mycul yells.

Together, they bring up a wall of flame blocking off the rest of the advanced team.

I grab Aris' arm. "Johanna can bring that wall down, if we go up now, we might be able to catch them off guard before they see us."

Aris nods.

I sprint toward the wall of flame, leap and thrust my wings, launching myself over the scalding fire with Aris trailing right behind. I land all the way behind the team near another boulder blocking us in. Jeff whirls around to us. Aris is still in the air but with a clench of Jeff's fist, the pull of the Karess clings to both of us and Aris drops to the ground. I bolt toward Jeff, closing the space between us. I need to engage in close combat to limit his earth attacks.

"Jeff, she's there, do it," Ace says as the fire wall vanishes. He sprints in front of Jeff and throws his fist at my face. I dodge right, wind from his strike grazing my cheek. Over his shoulder, through the mist and smoke, bright-red eyes sparkle at the other end of the stone corridor. Rin bolts toward my team and slams her fist into Mycul's gut. Stone builds up behind her, trapping everyone in, and at the same time, Jeff crumbles the wall to the left of us. On the other side is the line of the dead zone, so they've blocked us in and simultaneously found a way to throw us out of the playing field.

Ace lands a kick to my gut. I gasp but slow my breath, combating the spasm. I tighten my core and block his next fist.

Panting and sweating from the effort to manipulate two whole walls of earth, Jeff backs up behind his team. Litha shoots out of the shadows and slams her fist to his face. He stumbles back an inch too close to the dead zone. As soon as he readies up, Litha has faded and reappeared to take her fight to Eliote.

Aris dashes behind me to finish the work Litha had started, exchanging blows with Jeff.

Ira sprints up behind Ace and jabs him in the back. He grunts but stays steady, blocking my strikes and Ira's with quick swipes of his arms.

Rin bolts straight for Ira. She wraps one arm around Ira's waist, lifts her off the ground, spins, and chucks Ira out the opening to the dead zone. Ira screams as she flies through the air and Ace shoots out a stream of ice. Ira hits the ground on her side and skids along the ice out of bounds. Litha sweeps in and out of shadow, dancing herself and Eliote close to the dead zone. Eliote lands a fist to Litha's gut, but with a few more shadow phases, they're only steps away from the dead zone. Litha slinks out of the shadow, she catches Eliote with a foot behind her ankle and Eliote topples out of bounds.

Steam, sweat, and dust cling to my skin. Flames flare everywhere I turn. I take deep breaths, letting my muscles learn the rhythm of Ace's attacks. Quick, precise. I focus on my breath, making my counter moves quicker.

Ace ducks under my arm and sprints away behind me. I turn on my heel, ready to chase after him, but he's five feet away one moment, then I blink and his fist plows toward my gut.

Pain rips through my side, but so does Ace. Through me. Through my gut. My gut that is tangled in pain, and invisible. Ace hits the ground and rolls. Staring blankly in my direction, mouth agape, his eyes don't find me. I grasp at my side. There's a hole. My fingers should grasp my gut, but they plunge straight through. I pat my torso, fingers contacting my physical body, but at my side they still sink through. The control over my breath vanishes and my throat tightens, my vision blurs.

I stare through my body as my side fizzles with pain as if, cell by cell, it's rebuilding itself. Sweat pours down my back and my ears ring.

"Lance?" Ace says, still searching for me from the ground. The rush of essence through my head warps the sound of his voice so it echoes back and forth through my ears.

Ice, fire, earth, bears—it all flashes around me as I fade back. I launch myself into the air and soar over the walls of stone, landing uneasily on my feet as my stomach churns. I collapse in a heap against the rock, shouts and the snap of fists and bone drifting over me.

Tapping my hand to my side, the hole isn't so pronounced.

Pressing my fingers in, pain and static fill the gap until it's fully formed again. I swipe an invisible hand over my drenched face and hold my breath for a few seconds, my heart thudding in my chest.

"Damn it!" a voice shouts like it's a cry from the nine hells. Mycul must be out.

This is ridiculous. I need to get myself together. Literally, my body just fell apart. It doesn't make sense.

I press my eyes shut and replay the last few minutes—the chaos, the smells, the lights—all of it runs through me like a fever dream. Despite my body's reaction, I'm not freaked out. Energized with essence and pain, yet underneath there is light, a space. There's a space in the rush for me. I just don't know why this makes me fade.

To my right, something taps, and the sound of panting jolts me. I open my eyes and jump to my feet to find Litha bent over her knees.

"Lith."

Litha squeals and slaps her hand over her mouth.

"It's Lance, it's Lance, don't freak out."

"What the hell? You ditched us," Litha says, looking straight past me, stray purple hairs sticking out of her ponytail and blood streaming out of her nose. Clenching her fist, she grunts and smears the blood off her face with the back of her hand. "This whole tournament is fucking ridiculous, but you don't get to run away from me, from us, y-you can't do that."

My heart skips a beat, and my breaths hitch as her glassy eyes look straight through me. "I know. You can yell at me later."

Litha tilts her head back and presses a finger under her nose with a wince. "Mycul's pissed."

"I heard. Who's left?"

"Just you, me, and the Emberstead and Ironskin from the other team." Litha huffs as a silver wisp of essence curls around her nose. "I can't take another hit from the Ironskin without a helmet. I can't keep up with her. It's like she knows where I am even in the shadows."

"Damn it, she does. With the death affinity, she can see me too."

"Shit, I hear them coming. How do we play this?"

I run my hand through my sweaty hair. Litha turns to the sound of footsteps and backs up. I set a hand on her shoulder to let her know where I am.

"I'll take Rin. Maybe if I stay off the ground it will be to my advantage. No time to find another way to a dead zone. I've seen these two fight at the Festival of Two Moons, and they're stronger together. We need to separate them."

Closing her hand over mine, she says, "I can maybe shadow phase Johanna as close as possible to the dead zone, but after that, my essence will be shot."

Her hand on mine fills some of the space in me, deep inside where it's calm and empty. I don't stand alone. Litha's always been with me in whatever capacity she could be, even if that was making jokes at my expense. The calm space inside me makes me fade from the world, to stay separate, but the connection grounds me. It's almost like being calm is energizing.

"You can do it," I say as my essence curls through my body in easy waves, my skin reappearing.

Litha glances at me, a furrow between her eyebrows and purple eyes narrowed at me as Rin and Johanna round the corner. She nods and faces forward, shaking out her hands and shifting her feet. Above the towering boulders is the time board. Just a minute now.

"I'll make you a shadow."

"Right, let's finish this shit," she says with an exasperated sigh.

At the other end, Rin holds her hands together. Johanna sticks her foot in them, and Rin launches Johanna in the air. She sails over us and punches at the air, sending a ring of fire down around us.

"Let her land," I say to Litha.

I bend my knees and take long steady breaths, my heart pounding. Johanna plummets to the ground with a wave of scalding heat. She lunges for Litha. With a heavy breath, Litha windmills her arms, keeping space between them. She spins to the side and ducks under Johanna's kick. Behind Johanna, Litha tackles her, cinching her arms around Johanna's waist. "Now, Lance."

I leap into the air, spreading my wings wide, a shadow unfolding below me. The tip of my shadow merges with Johanna's, and both girls vanish. I fly over the nearest stone wall and land on top. On the opposite side, they reappear, engaged in combat, legs and arms flying. Johanna's fist strikes Litha in the face. Litha screeches, but channels her energy back into her body, honing each of her strikes and landing a kick to Johanna's gut, sending her out of bounds.

Howls and cheers erupt as both our teams gather around Johanna.

"Nice work, Litha," Aris calls through cupped hands.

Rin appears behind me on the wall. Her blood-red eyes and the breathy laugh that escapes her sends a chill down my spine.

She sprints toward me, and I ready myself. I swing my leg high, but she ducks and slides right under me. Merging into a roll, she dives off the cliff.

"Shit." I dip my head and run as fast as I can, leap off the ledge with a powerful thrust of my wings and a stream of electricity propelling my feet. I grab Rin, redirecting her path away from Litha. But heat and power envelop me as Rin twists her body, throwing my wings off balance. I let go and in a blink of an eye Rin's foot sinks into my gut and I hit the ground, light from my vest flashing.

Rin lands next to me. In a blur, she crosses to Litha and punches her in the gut, sending her straight out of bounds, Mycul and Aris breaking her fall.

While Rin's back is turned, I launch myself back in the air. Almost to the top of the boulder, a vise clamps around my legs. I grab the ledge, but the rough stone slips out of my grasp. Rin hurls me back at the ground like a doll. I crash to the hard arena floor and tumble out of bounds.

I roll over onto my side, the arena shaking as the stone labyrinth sinks back into the ground around Rin. Particles of rock and dust stream around her, over the rest of us, out of bounds, and into Evelyn's hand, solidifying into a sphere.

My vision spins and I cough as I try to prop myself up on my hands and knees.

"Well done, everyone. Congratulations to the advanced team. I'm looking forward to seeing you compete in the tournament," Evelyn says, turning her back to all of us and heading out the arena doors.

I cough again, my essence fizzling inside me but slowing. A strong hand scoops around my arm, helping me up, and the dark, warm scent of coffee drifts around me.

"I'm sorry," Rin says, gripping my arm, blond hairs sticking out at all angles. She tries to hide her sheepish grin with her hand. "Are you okay?"

"Yeah," I say, smiling at the concern in her glittering silver eyes. I tuck a hair behind her ear.

"Finally decided to show up, huh?" Mycul says.

"You guys better get out of here. Might get ugly," I say to Rin.

She gives my arm another squeeze and leaves with her team.

I turn to Mycul. "Yeah, sorry about that. Just had a little trouble." I shrug and walk past him.

"You just threw the match so your girlfriend's team could win."

"She's not my girlfriend."

"Yeah, but you're trying to get in her pants, aren't you, huh? Let her feel strong and good about herself, so she gets horny for ya. I've seen it a thousand times."

"Don't talk about Rin like that."

"You're not denying it. All you think about is that damn cutch when we've been busting our asses to get to this tournament."

"That's it. You're done," Litha says.

"Shut your mouth. This is between me and him, and his inability to control his fucking essence and his fucking dick."

"No, I said you're done." Litha shoves him off me with both hands. "He has nothing left to say to you, and you're just making shit up, so you're done. And we're done."

"You're breaking up with me over this? This has nothing to do with us, Litha."

"It has everything to do with us." Darkness spills from

Litha's purple eyes. The shadow her body casts over the ground is inky and writhes around her. "I've tried for so many years to be noticed by popular people like you, to be in the inner circle, the drama, to feel like I was part of something. But all you do is whine and complain and make people feel like shit because you're shit. I feel like shit with you, and I didn't do anything about it because I believed I was shit too." Her voice strains out of her. I put a hand on her shoulder, heart pounding, but she jabs her finger at Mycul. "Lance's kindness is contagious and you're just a poison, so piss off!"

Mycul opens his snarling mouth.

"Shut up," Litha snaps.

His chest heaves and his breath fills the entire arena, hot and scathing. Litha shrugs my hand away. Brushing at the blood on her face, a smile sparkles in her eyes.

Aris clears his throat. "So . . . I think we can get forms to request a team change from outside Evelyn's office," he says, running a hand through his thick curls and ignoring Mycul's dark glare.

"Lead the way, Aris." Litha holds up her pinky finger to Mycul and marches out of the arena with Aris.

Slipping my hands into the pockets of my shorts, I follow them. Mycul's hot, sweaty hand grabs my shoulder. "You're pathetic. Letting her fight your battles, hiding in a fight. What kind of third-year can't control his essence like that anyway?"

I stare at him. Like Litha said, I have nothing to say. I have nothing to defend. He's not a threat.

"Don't want to forget your echo," I say, nodding my head toward the bench along the wall where his echo and water bottle sit.

Mycul's face blooms red. Teeth clenched and bared, he takes a step back. "You're weak Lance, weak."

Maybe in a lot of ways I am. Or maybe I have been. But in all the ways he's thinking, all the things he sees as weak—kindness, peace, quietness—I'm the strongest I've ever been. Staring right into the depth of his swamp eyes, it strikes me how sad it is that he doesn't have those things and I say, "Are you sure about that?"

RIN

BRAND SHUTS THE DOOR TO THE TRAINING ROOM, keeping her eyes on Lance and Mycul out in the arena.

"Sounds like a bit of a personal dispute," she says.

"Yeah," I say, also peering at them through the window. My heart hits a heavy beat as Mycul and Lance stare at each other. Lance turns and walks away, but Mycul grabs his water bottle and chucks it at the back of Lance's head. I cringe and Brand chuckles.

To be fair, she's the only reason I'm here right now. Not because she let me come back, but because she taught me in the Vein and she protected me. Even after being arrested last year, having to deal with me and go after Liam, and the Vein burning down to the ground, she's still here next to me.

Brand shakes her head and turns to the team.

"Brand, wait." I turn and almost grab her arm, but snatch my hand back before she sees me reach for her. I catch her eyes for a moment and they strike through me, so I drop my gaze, dusting some of the grime from the fight off my shirt.

"What is it?" she asks.

"The technique you taught me in the Vein, it's been really helpful to control my death affinity."

Her sweet and woody scent drifts over to me. I can't tell her about Professor Hans. That doesn't mean I can't tell her how I've been doing it.

Brand adjusts the collar of her white shirt. Behind her, my team high fives and discusses the match. Clearing her throat, she says, "I'm glad. How have you been able to master it?"

"I've just focused on the emotions that trigger it, you know, but not just how they affect me physically. It's more about how they are me in a way. The way I think, my memories, they inform everything. And then I focus on the emotions one at a time," I say and crack the knuckles of my left fist.

"Hm, compartmentalizing." Brand nods, but her lips press together and her sleepy eyes squint at me.

"Yeah, I guess you could say that."

"You know that an emotion is never invalid, and that they can coexist without cancelling each other out."

My hand twitches. When the Vein was attacked, all I wanted to do was hold her hand, for her to not let go of me, even though I could barely look at her. My body still tenses just having her voice hit my ears.

I roll my shoulders and shake my head, realigning my thoughts with how I've been controlling my death affinity. "I guess so, I just don't know—"

"I want to apologize, really apologize to you."

The lights sway in the breeze like they always do when we have the side door open. They shift over Brand, teasing light and shadow across her face.

"For what?" I ask.

"For not taking every chance I had to be there for you and for everything I put you through in the Vein." Brand takes a step toward me, hands clenching and releasing at her sides. "I just wanted to have you close for once. I wanted to protect you. I made it worse."

A light warmth rises in my chest. Her words have a direct link to my heart, and I almost believe she wants me close. "I don't think you made it worse," I say in a quiet voice, eyes trailing over to my team at the other end of the room. Eliote's face is flushed, and they pat her on the back, consoling her with words and smiles. "I saw all your efforts and they weren't for nothing." The shirt on my back, the sweats, the shoes I'm wearing, I know she's the one who bought them for me. "I'm glad to have you in my life. Thank you for apologizing though."

Brand sighs, following my gaze to the team. She folds her arms and says, "I meant to say all this when we talked the other night—"

"The other night?" My brow tenses and I glance at her out of the corner of my eye.

"Right, when we met in the arena in the evening."

My stomach twists. A door slams inside the arena, jarring my awakening senses. I turn to her. "Brand, I've barely talked to you since I've been back at the academy."

Skin tightens around her jaw and the tendons in her neck strain as she swallows. She blinks once and her eyes lock on the ground.

"Damn it," she whispers. "She's here."

"What?" My shoulders rise and I hold my hands to my chest as the room expands around me, filling with an intangible weight.

"Thea, she's here." Darkness drags her tone. Her lips part with a breath and her eyebrows furrow as she shakes her head.

"What did you say to her?" I ask.

"You, well, she asked specifically about Stephen and where he is." Touching her brow, all the colour drains from her face. As she dips her head, I catch a glint in her eye—the youthfulness of a memory. "I told her that we tracked Stephen to Sarr and that we've told the LPs there to detain him on sight."

"If the attack on the Vein was to get information on the Revival, do you think Thea may want something Stephen has?"

"The utanic Death stone. Maybe. I just know that if she's using illusions against me, then she might be tricking you all."

Running her hands through her curls, her Commander persona shatters. Her eyes press closed. A shuttering sigh slips from her lips, cooling the air around me. "She swore to me that she would never use illusions against me. Never. Until she did, and I lost her . . . or she lost herself."

The way Thea's demeanour changed instantaneously when Brand faced her sparks my mind like the burning in her eyes. Thea said she was trying to stop someone. Could that someone be inside her?

Brand drops her hands. "Or she lost herself," she mutters, moving into the centre of the room. She calls the team to attention, rebuilding the suit of Commander armour. I follow her, still holding my hands tight to my chest.

"Everyone listen up. It's come to my attention that someone has been impersonating Rin here at the academy," Brand says.

The team is quiet. Niko's mouth opens and his face pinches as he begins to say something, but Jeff nudges him, shaking his head.

"Her name is Thea Khole. She can impersonate anyone that you have a personal connection with, if she's seen you and that person. If you've had any situations where someone has asked you a direct question that might give her information about Rin or her brother or me, let me know."

Breath gathers inside me and I can't seem to release it. I have no idea what's going on. As the silence drags and my lungs start to ache, my feet lose their contact with the ground. My body knows it's not supposed to be here before my mind does. I can't let any of this go on. I've controlled my death affinity. It's time to find my brothers and bring them home.

Johanna raises her hand. "No one *living* talked to me but . . . a Wander Wraith told me that she's sensed Alyxia around our campus."

"Alyxia, as in the ancient Emberstead queen?" Brand asks.

Johanna glances around the room, her face growing red. "Uh . . . Yes."

"And who told you this, Johanna? What wraith?"

Dropping her eyes to the floor and fixing the waistband of her shorts, Johanna says, "H-Her name is Nolaria. She wants my help to defeat Alyxia. Mine and Rin's help."

My heart pounds in my throat. I blink, unsure where to look as the team asks questions. Jeff steps over to Johanna and puts the back of his hand to her forehead. Johanna bats his hand away with a snarl.

Her eyes grab me and heat washes over my mind.

SHE JUST TOLD ME HER NAME. I DIDN'T KNOW IT WAS HER UNTIL A FEW DAYS AGO. I KNOW SHE'S IMPORTANT TO YOU.

It's fine, I'm just . . . just surprised.

SHE'S THE ONE WHO TOLD ME ABOUT THE SOUL TETHER.

Eliote shifts her feet. "I felt a strange, powerful energy three nights ago," she says, clutching her lightstone.

"That's the night that I thought I talked to Rin. We're not dealing with just Mind Fire illusions. We're dealing with mind possession." Brand's eyes strike me. "This is The Captor."

"I didn't think that was a recorded Mind Fire ability," Ace says.

"It is unique to Alyxia. Everyone please be on high alert," Brand says. "I'm not sure how these two abilities will interact with spirit sight or if Rin will be able to see through the manipulation with her death affinity, so rely on your better judgement. Call each other's echos if you're concerned you may not be talking to who you think you're talking to. I will have mine on my person at all times."

The frown on her face, the waver in her eyes, the glossy sheen glinting light in her eyes, puts a shudder in my breaths. Her face flushes before she runs a hand over it and straightens it into the blank sheet that her Commander persona requires.

Everyone brings out their echos and Brand reads out her number for them to log. After a string of clicks and flashes from each echo, Brand says, "I need to go relay this information to the headmaster." She marches to the door but then turns back to us. "This is Guardian work. Use all the training you have gained in your time here."

As the team disperses, murmuring to each other and glancing around with wide eyes, I grab Johanna and pull her aside.

"What . . . " My mind stutters over all the information that's come out today and crashes to a halt on Johanna's mention of Nolaria. She's been talking to the woman I clung to for strength all these years, the woman who made me believe I could make it through this life.

"What the fuck?" Johanna says, filling in the silence.

"Yes, what the fuck is going on?"

"Nolaria thinks we're the key to taking Alyxia down. But we have to be at full power."

I am so fucking tired of people thinking my abilities are the key to someone else's personal grievance. "And how are we supposed to do that?"

Johanna runs her hands together and adjusts her shirt without looking me in the eye.

"Johanna?"

"We have to break the tether," she says.

My heart jumps and sinks straight down to the pit of my stomach. "How?" My voice rings in my ears.

"I have to die."

"No." I put up my hands. "No." Johanna tracks me as I pace with my hands on my hips. "No."

"We're not going to do it. At least not until we figure out how you can bring me back. Just calm down."

The training room has cleared out and the voices in the arena have faded. Johanna and I stand alone in the centre of the room. I shake my head, staring at our feet.

"What about a Revival stone? Can't those bring people back

to life?" Johanna asks.

I shake my head. "The only three known Revival stones are held by the Revival. Even if we could get our hands on them, they don't work like you think they would." I pinch my eyes shut. "One stone revives someone for a short time, an hour maybe. Three stones together draw on all vital energy with a direction." My blood will direct them to revive all Ironskins with spirit affinities from the Hold. Shivers run down my back. "There's no way to use them to fully revive just one person. It's not an option."

Johanna runs her tongue over her teeth, hands on her hips. She is so sure of the Soul Tether. I can't see it, I can't feel it, I don't even know anything about it. Johanna is here though. I pushed her away so many times and she's still the one left standing with me. I'm not going to let her fall first.

The disconnect between my body and the academy grounds has not wavered throughout the day. Classes came and went in a blur, and I wolfed down as much food as I could to press the ache away. I clench Lance's sweater to my chest as I stand outside his door—the only place my feet wanted to go.

I raise my fist and knock.

As the door opens, Lance says, "Aris, for the last time, just go talk to her. Oh—"

"Hey," I say, holding up his sweater and going stiff in the knees.

Lance stands in the doorway, one hand on the frame, in low-rise sweats and no shirt. His light-brown skin looks so smooth over his tight abs and toned shoulders. Every curve and angle of his body is pleasant to look at. I can't seem to draw my eyes back to his face. "Uh—"

"I thought you were Aris," Lance says. As I pry my eyes away from his body, he looks down at me with a wide smile, and he bites his lip as he leans forward on the door frame. "He's been here three times tonight to ask about Litha."

"Oh, well, she's beautiful, so no wonder he's interested in her—uh, you want me to come back later? Looks like"—I wave his sweater at his bare chest—"you were in the middle of changing or something."

Lance steps closer, and his dewy forest scent washes over me.

I turn away, heat filling my face. "I'll come back later."

He grabs my hand, drawing me back to him, and I hide my face in his sweater.

"I'm sorry," he says. "Just wait here. I'll put on a shirt if it makes you more comfortable."

He disappears into his room, and I let out all the hot air in my head with a sigh, pressing my eyes tight. Once I hear the click of the wing-securers, I step back in. Only the lamp on his dresser is lit, giving his room a warm glow. The open window lets in the sound of nocturnal birds and the low rush of the waves.

"Sit," Lance says as he sits down cross-legged on his bed.

I join him, picking up the book he's left face down. I turn it over to read the title, but my brain doesn't make sense of the words. My eyes shift to his bed, where we lay together. I was warm the whole night with him wrapped around me. Not the sweaty, itchy warmth that my death affinity brings. It was soothing.

"What brings you by?" he asks, tilting his head to the side.

"Just bringing back your sweater," I say, setting the book back down and rubbing my eyes to clear my head.

"You could have kept it if you wanted to."

I shrug and pull my knees to my chest. Lance watches me, his brown eyes narrow and soft, as he leans back on his hands. "Something else?"

Keeping my eyes on the swaying tree branches outside his window, I say, "I just wanted to see if you were okay. Seemed like your team didn't take the loss well."

Lance chuckles. "No, they didn't. But I'm okay, really okay, actually. Thanks for asking."

The softness and hope in his voice relaxes my shoulders and I tilt my head on my knees just to look at him.

"You and Litha seem close." The words come to my tongue like they've been waiting there, looking for an opportunity to jump from my mind without consent.

"We've been friends for a long time," Lance says, and I lose his eyes.

My heart skips a beat. Why would a friend make him look away like that? "Have you ever been something other than friends?"

I catch his eyes for a second as a breeze tangles between us. They waver and his mouth twitches, and I lose them again.

He shifts, picking at his nails. "Not exactly."

"What do you mean?" The question quiets my voice, like it's losing its grip on the conversation, not wanting to keep up with the replies.

"I guess when you're a teenager and lonely, you grasp whatever comfort you can find. Drugs, easy drunken conversations at parties." He shrugs. "Casual sex with a friend," he mumbles to himself.

"Did you love her?" My gut aches with each unexpected question.

"No, well, I love her because she's my friend. She's not a great friend really, still a good one though. But no, I don't love her, not like that."

Shifting to mirror his cross-legged posture, my mind is like a sieve instead of a deep pit with a trap door locked from the inside, me as the lone resident. All these questions slip off my tongue to his ears, and he responds like they're the most normal musings in the world. And maybe they are normal, or maybe they're the grime sloughing off the walls of my cave where the weeds grow—the light that touches other people's faces and brings genuine smiles is finally breaking in. My lungs are scraped raw, my ribs hollowed out, my stomach churns with a wash of disinfectant. But there are layers to my pit, more traps, more locks.

Lance's hands slide into mine on my lap.

I swallow, and in a barely manageable whisper, I say, "Some teenagers don't have sex when they're lonely. Some of them just . . . decide to stop breathing."

My hands are limp and his are tight. The sheets beneath me are crumpled and my skin prickles with the cool night air.

"When did you decide to stop?" Lance asks, with more of his skin touching more of mine. The threat of a switch turning off the flow of sensation hovers in the air between us.

"Just over two months before we met."

Lance leans forward, tilting his head to look me in the eye. "Two months?" His face with gentle eyes, his hushed words, his hands, all have the same tension—a straight, taut line toward me.

I nod. "Two months."

"Do you still think about, well, I mean the other night you said—"

"I think about it all the time. I just don't want to do it."

"That's a pretty big distinction."

"Really? It feels small most of the time."

His dark hair hangs low over his eyes as he stares at our hands. "What do you feel when you're with me?" he asks.

"What do I feel?"

"Yeah, sometimes you don't want me to touch you and then sometimes you do." He shrugs. "You never put your arms around me, but you'll hold my hand. It's not a criticism, just an observation."

I let my eyes close, but they want to flutter open. My skin holds imprints of greedy hands, my senses spike, waiting for an intrusion. I press my eyelids tighter. My heart is noisy, unsettled in my chest. The tissue of my lungs hopes my heart will steady because it is tired and weak. I open my eyes.

"I like feeling your arms around me," I say. "I like seeing your hand in mine. It's easier to convince myself it's real if I can see it and feel it. It's hard to convince myself that it's worth holding onto someone when there's no guarantee they'll be around for long. Ace and Johanna, it's been really hard to trust them. And Eliote might be leaving. And my family—"

"Slow down, it's okay, I understand."

My heart picks up speed and my armpits sweat, my lungs take sharp sips of air as Lance lets go of one hand and holds my shoulder. Each of my fingers still encased in his is eager to tighten around his.

"I like to see your hands in mine too," he says. "I don't want to make you promises that you're not ready to accept, but I want to be with you. What do you want?"

How? How could he want to be with me? How could he know? My stomach aches with the proposed reality, with the contrast of his tenderness and the grime that coats my heart. There's no guarantee that it could be true. It all weighs on my ability to accept it.

I raise my eyes to his, taking a long, ragged breath as my heart slows with his warm hand stroking my jaw.

"I want you to kiss me," I say in a breath.

His lips are on mine, his hand behind my neck gently drawing me in, all words vanishing with the fulfillment of my request. I can't move. Every muscle is tuned to the heat spreading over me. The rush of blood and breath and thought all quiet at his touch. A slight tug of my hair as his hand tightens its grip sends shivers down my spine. Lance's lips fall away, and his breath slips over my chin and down my neck.

In the quiet, in the stillness between his patient breaths, I move my hand to his side. The other follows. With my hands resting on him, pressing into him, I close the gap, kissing his lower lip.

Our kisses come like air—in and out, sweet with the taste of his skin. His hand falls from my neck down to my waist. Both his hands pull me in, rounding my back, over the tender skin of my weak spot. And they stop. Like a slicing cut of a blade, my nerves sing from the scar up through my body. Lance's fingers curl into my shirt.

"Wait," I say into his lips.

He smooths his fingers over my scar and the nail pricks.

"Rin—"

"You can't." I push away from him with Tōmas' face looming in my mind, arms caging me.

Tōmas' hands would have felt my scar.

In the moment, I never thought of it, but his hands were all over me that night. Does that mean he knows where my weak spot is? Fuck, he could really hurt me, or tell someone who would hurt me. Thea. What if she wants to hurt me?

Ice rushes in my veins and a cold sweat breaks over my body. I throw my legs over the side of the bed and stand, my lungs aching for breath.

"Rin, are you hurting yourself still?" Lance asks, following me across the room to the door.

"No," I say, my vision filling with dark spots.

I put out my hands to brace myself as the room spins. My body becomes weightless, and small, quick breaths burn my lungs. I catch myself on the door and press my face into my hands. Air comes in shallow bursts, fogging the varnish on the door and wetting my hands.

Lance comes up beside me. "Just breathe," he whispers. He presses one hand to my chest and one on my weak spot. The pressure on my chest soothes the heavy beat, letting hot tears stream down my face. The warmth over my weak spot, the support, is like medicine and it stings.

"You're not supposed to know," I say.

"About the scars?"

"My weak spot. You're not supposed to know where it is. No one is. My own parents didn't even know where it was."

Lance leans closer, pressing his lips to the side of my head. "Why shouldn't anyone know?"

"Because people use knowledge of someone's weakness to

hurt them. Johanna did it to me. If the Revival knew where it was, they could take my blood and . . . or Tō—" Strength leaches from my body and I double over, Lance's arms wrapping tight around me.

"Weakness should be tended, not hurt," he says, voice small and wavering. "You don't believe that I don't want to be with Litha, do you? You don't believe I won't hurt you?"

"I want to," I say into his shoulder.

"How about just for tonight? You can stay with me if you want to. But if you don't, then that's okay too."

The pause of pounding heartbeats grows long. Lance's hands hold me. The shape of them on my body is confident but careful. Tears soaking into his shirt, I nod. "I'll stay."

Lance leads me back to his bed by the hand. He gets in first, keeping hold until I settle in beside him. He lies on his side and pulls the blankets over us.

I want to believe that there are no falsehoods in his words, that everything he says he means with all his heart. But feelings change. What if I can't reciprocate them, and he loses all this energy on me? I don't want to hurt him just as much as he says he doesn't want to hurt me. My body doesn't understand the comfort, wrapped in his arms, in his sheets that smell like him. I never thought I would sleep beside a man without expectations of love or touch or sex. All I know is that with the lack of expectation, my breaths slow and fill my body, clearing my mind, and his arm is heavy on me in the best way.

37

E L I O T E

My brother would let me tag along with him and his friends when they went to concerts in Tien Bay. Mostly local bands, heavy rock, electropulse, anything to make the ears ring and the heart pound. The music would shake my chest as the lights flashed around me. Everyone had a collective love for the thrill of the music, hands in the air, jumping, dancing, shouting. I was part of that energy; it was natural and kept me going. Festivals were the same. Throngs of people celebrating common ancestors or community or the new moon.

When I was fifteen, I stood behind my brother at a concert. All the vitality of the music and the collective enjoyment soured with a wash of purple smoke that billowed around him. In that moment, my soul shut off and was compacted under cement bricks. I knew there were secrets hidden in the aura surrounding him, but not what they were. I knew there were expectations, but not how to achieve them. I knew there was pain, and it had to be covered because Luminee were light and dark and not in-between because the in-between is where the imbalance of the soul starts. All of this strangled me. My brother turned, looked at me, and smiled. I smiled back because what else was I supposed to do?

It wasn't long before my parents started fighting and their true auras showed. I worked hard to keep everything right inside me, inside our house, and never spoke out of turn so their auras would stay calm, and I wouldn't have to feel all their rage.

Auras. Intentions. If I could see my brother now, I think I would be able to make sense of the pain he feels. I would see where his intentions draw him—two directions, one for the sake of appearances and one for the sake of himself. The divide, the stretch and strain on the spirit is where the pain comes from.

I stand in the arena, in the line to sign our team in for the tournament. Voices rise to the high ceiling and fall down around me, filling my chest with reverberation as every province's teams file in wearing different coloured uniforms. Families and attending professors fill the stands.

Ace holds my hand as we wait in line. He turns to me with clear eyes. There is weakness in his smile though, the same weakness that keeps my hand tight in his, and my lips sealed tighter. I still crave his kisses and his touch. His aura is still sweet to me. I can't speak to him, though, because the words that have been forming for a while now will rush out, and it will be too soon. I stand on my tiptoes and kiss his cheek instead—long and hard—closing my eyes and my ears so I can just feel him close.

I put aside my approach to this tournament. No more tests.

Today, this tournament is for fun. Nothing else. I want to have fun with my team. It's not good to work so hard without having fun. I forgot that.

Ace returns a light kiss to the top of my head. The line moves, and we shuffle forward.

Lance shoulders his way through the crowd. Niko flags him down, and he pushes his way through the crowd over to us.

"Hey, wanted to wish you all luck," he says.

"Oh please, you came to wish Rin luck," I say and blink a few times, letting his intentions into my vision. A river of liquid silver streams around him. It reaches out, tangling around Rin. A light-blue string stretches from her to him, and another to Ace and Johanna, me, Niko, and Jeff. I blink and strings from every one of us weave together in every colour.

Lance blushes and runs a hand through his hair.

"Why not just admit you guys are a couple? I've seen Rin leave your room in the morning on multiple occasions," Jeff says.

Niko peeks around Jeff. "Wait, you guys are hooking up?"

Rin's eyes widen and her body goes stiff as a board. She opens her mouth, but nothing comes out.

"Just sleeping together," Lance says with a shrug.

I chuckle and give Rin a nudge with my elbow. "You do know that *sleeping together* is a euphemism for sex, right, Bird Brain?"

"Sleeping," Rin blurts, raising her hands and pressing them to her bright-red cheeks. "The key word is sleeping."

"Hey, get your head out of your ass. It's your turn," Johanna says, and pushes Niko up to the sign-in table.

We each sign the waiver stating that we understand the risks of the tournament and we vow to uphold sportsmanlike conduct. We're handed the tokens we'll need for the first trial and our school's uniformed Protector vests. I bend over to write my signature and glance over my shoulder. Lance cups one hand over Rin's jaw, stroking her with his thumb. Rin looks up at him, running her fingers over the hand stroking her face. Lance leans down and kisses her, shifting his wings around them as soon as Niko and Jeff clap and holler at them. Even though my throat goes tight, they bring a smile to my lips.

We head to the locker rooms to change into the uniforms— black pants, a black jacket, and a Protector vest with red and gold accents and the Akinnera crest on the breast. Once we're changed, we form nine even lines in the arena. The buzz of voices hushes as Evelyn takes a podium in front of all of us, her face projected on a screen above her.

Rin stands beside me, fiddling with the straps of her vest and cracking her fingers. The air is unsteady around her. I give her a nudge. "Why are you nervous?"

Her eyes are glazed and she stares off into space. I take her arm and give her a little shake.

"What?" she says, blinking her eyes and shrugging off my hand.

"Why are you so tense?"

"I just talked to Professor Hans. He's going to contact the Revival."

"When?" I shake my head at the sudden rush of blood. "When are they going to reach out to you?"

"I don't know."

"Should you tell Brand?"

She shakes her head. "Not yet. I need to talk to them first."

Static crackles over the amplimonitors. "Welcome, everyone." Evelyn's voice wraps around the arena. "Today we have the privilege of hosting you all for this tournament to foster comradery, showcase your skills, and build community between academies. Thank you all for being here."

Everyone in the stands—professors, parents, students out of classes to watch the tournament—claps and cheers. The competing teams stay quiet, looking around at each other, surveying the competition. A few turn to shake hands with the closest team. Rin stares straight ahead, loose hairs dangling in front of her face.

Leaning over to her, I whisper, "Just have fun with me today, okay?"

The stone in her gaze cracks with a blink and she glances at me, her lips softening into a smile. "Right, thank you."

"The first trial will take place outside the city wall on Moon Hill," Evelyn says.

Gasps and murmurs spiral around us.

"We have Guardians posted around the trial boundaries in case of trouble, but remember that your children are all trained for this. The boundary has been searched and cleared of beasts this morning and is being checked once again as we speak. Now, the trial at hand will take two hours. First the underclassmen will compete and then the upperclassmen. Teams will compete by acquiring tokens from other players and returning them to their base. Students, please hook the three tokens you received to the rings on your vests."

I roll the cool metallic tokens in my hands. They're oblong, gold plates with the Akinnera crest and a clasp to secure them to the rings on my vest. I press the clasp to the ring and the two prongs slide inward, allowing it to hook onto the ring. It stays secure when I give it a tug, but Rin tugs hers and it comes right off. I take hold of my token again and give it another yank. It comes off with a click.

"You will start at your bases, evenly spread out. You will have two hours to gain as many tokens as possible. Each token is worth one point, so each team has a starting score of eighteen points. Losing your token, negative one point, gaining another team's token, positive one point."

As Evelyn explains the rules, I shift my sight, scanning each team. Some intentions are strings like the ones holding our team together. Some intentions are nebulous, wafting back and forth. I can use that to our advantage, hopefully, to know which teams are tight-knit. Once on the field, I might be able to see the direction a team intends to attack and see if a team plans to target us.

"The six teams with the most points will move on to the next trial. Memory tech has been set up in the forest to broadcast your progress to the audience. Now, please meet your instructors at the door, and they will lead you to your base. Strength of the ancestors."

"Strength of the ancestors." The arena swells with the refrain.

The team ahead of us in purple and silver vests—the Valisor team—heads to the door. Half of them are Lavarian, one with sleek white wings, another with huge, fire-red wings that flick behind her, sending a gust of wind over us, and one with scruffy silver wings. Their intentions tangle into a collective storm above them. We follow them, Ace leading the way. I set my hands on Rin's shoulders, giving them a quick rub. Rin checks over her shoulder, a smile spreading a wash of pink to her cheeks.

Marcus meets us at the door in a blue academy uniform. His

scruffy beard has been shaved to a clean strap around his dark, chiselled jaw, and he holds his head high, nodding to each of us. To me, he holds out a *rahanaso*, and presses it into my hands.

"I ran it past Evelyn and the other headmasters. They've all given their permission for you to carry a weapon." He nods to me.

My heart pounds as I wrap my hand around the handle. I pull at the sheathe and a glint of sunlight reflects off the blade. "Thank you, Marcus," I say as strength comes back to my limbs.

"All right, team, let's move out." Marcus starts into a steady jog, his limp only slightly tilting him to the one side with shorter strides.

We head through the city gate and to the right, along the wall. We run a mile and curve left, passing two bases before we come to a pedestal with a gold container and the Akinnera crest on it.

A faint staticky voice sounds through Marcus' communication device. He presses his finger to the switch on the earpiece. "Akinnera in position."

Turning to my team, the forest is calm with a slight breeze, and sunlight sprinkles our faces with gold. Each of my team has a different coloured string. Johanna and her beautiful blush-pink, Jeff's dark-green like the forest, Niko's is a bright, bold orange, Ace's deep blue. I know I'm only focusing on the intentions between each other. I focus my eyes on Rin. The small light-blue strings fade and two wings shimmer around her. They are bright red at the tips and blue at the base. They resemble the wings of the birds that soar through her aura, which means, like Johanna, she's come to integrate her intentions a little more closely with her heart. The wings glow and thunder, shocking my nervous system with an overwhelming calm.

"What is it?" Rin asks, stepping toward me, a twig snapping beneath her foot.

"Nothing," I say. "You're just beautiful."

Her silver eyes sink into me, her features rest, no frown, no smile. "Thank you," she says under her breath, the wings shivering around her.

But even in the wash of rainbow, in the rest I find standing next to Rin, there's another intention here. Not another team, an individual. It is tar—thick, sticky, difficult to move. Is it a student? Just an overwhelming intention that trumps a whole team? Or maybe another instructor leading their team to their base.

"Okay, we've got a count down. Three minutes," Marcus says.

I give my arms a shake and stamp my feet. The afternoon sun beaming down on me starts a sweat on my neck. I focus my sight away from my team, searching for other teams' intentions throughout the forest.

A tranquil, layered, green light shifts through the thick foliage left of our base. It wraps through the trees, moving toward us. "Eeth is to the left of us," I say, and my team gathers round me. "To the right"—a storm rages through the trees but it just rolls over itself, churning in place—"Valisor."

"Who do you think we have a better chance against?" Jeff asks, running the back of his hand over his sweaty forehead.

"It looks like Valisor is going to stay put for a while. Eeth is going to make a move on us though."

"I say we go against the Eeth team," Ace says.

"You want to just face them head on?" Johanna asks.

"Rin can flank them again because she's so fast in her death-affinity state." Niko slaps Rin on the back.

"I don't know. It's a bit different when there's more than one team. What if I get caught by another team?" she says.

"Can you carry one of us with you?" I ask. "I mean, you can carry Niko in his beast form."

"One minute," Marcus says.

"Yeah, that could work. It's a bit weird but if one of you is willing to ride piggyback, I'm okay with it."

"I think it should be Johanna," Jeff says. "You guys always fight the best when you're together."

"But if we get separated for too long, there's no way we can call them back. Johanna and Rin's mental connection is literally like having an echo between them. I think Ace should go with Rin," I say.

Ace and Rin exchange a glance. The blue thread that stretches from Rin to Ace, and the dark-blue stream that flows from Ace to Rin, are both straight and strong. They nod.

"That's it, you're on the clock," Marcus says, clapping his hands. "Go get those tokens."

Ace climbs onto Rin's back as the rest of us sprint up Moon Hill toward the flowing dark-green light. A pulse of red hits us from behind, bathing the forest in ruby red for a split second. I check over my shoulder as Rin and Ace dash off into the forest in a blur.

The green waves stay in sight as we climb, but they're fading. "Johanna, tell Rin they're changing course. They're headed west."

Our feet pound the uneven terrain, leaves and twigs crunching and breaths coming long and hard.

"She says she sees them. They're going to engage," Johanna says between breaths.

Jeff chuckles.

"Shit, she's fast," Niko says.

The ground shakes and red light flashes through the forest, followed by a ray of pure white light and a streak of icy blue. We pick up the pace, my lungs already starting to ache.

My vision clouds, and the hairs on the back of my neck prickle. Black tar coats my skin and a humming sound coaxes my mind to slow, but my feet keep moving, my arms keep pumping. Someone's here, someone's inside me.

YOU'RE NOT GOING TO TELL THEM I'M HERE, SWEETY, a voice hums through me. YOU CAN'T. I'M IN CONTROL.

I want to scream, yell, stop running, some kind of warning to alert my team of the invisible intrusion, but I just keep moving.

My mind squirms. The ache in my lungs heats and then wanes like numbing gel has been spilled all over them. Sensations of my chest expanding with each breath melts away.

All I can do is lock my eyes on Jeff's back, focus all my attention on him, and push my body forward at max speed. My body rips out of the tar, and I smack into Jeff.

"Woah, watch it, Eliote, we'll get there when we get there."

"Sorry." My voice comes out raspy and small, reviving the ache in my chest. The forest is trembling, and the humming voice and the thick, black tar is nowhere in sight. The chill on my skin despite the blaring sun is not a disproportionate reaction though. This intention, wherever it is now, is so heavy, and dynamic. It's pure fann. Mind Fire.

In the clearing ahead, a tree hits the ground with a thundering crash, blocking off the Eeth team. Ace and Rin leap over it, engaging in combat.

"Johanna and Jeff go left. Me and Eliote right," Niko yells.

I open my mouth, wait, no, I don't open my mouth to speak, to warn the team about the presence, the aura. I can't open my mouth. My footsteps never falter. I thrash through the brush, brambles clawing at me, begging me to stop just as my mind tries to grab control. My body joins the fight. Light flares through the tree trunks, flames, ice, it all explodes around me. Even as my legs kick, and I swing my blade, and I weave through the fight with my practiced moves, I can't control them.

Darkness hovers at my back, trailing down my spine in a slow, heavy burn, but absence is left in its wake. Almost cold, almost hot, it scoops the ache of breath from my lungs, leaving them numb.

Sweat streaks down my face like the swipe of a tongue. As my fist pulls back to strike, pain similar to a flame digs in at the base of my neck. Tears spill from my eyes. I urge a scream from my throat, but it is blocked just like the command to my body. My teeth are glued together, spreading a crackle through me from the crown of my head, down my neck, breaking through my limbs and all the way down to my toes. Heat brushes my skin and steals the ache away from me. The fizzle of sparks sings through my veins and heat smothers them too. Breaths come steady through my gritted teeth, but I want to ravage my lungs with a torrent of air because it's not enough. The dance that I've taught my body, every move, every striking pose, keeps going.

My breath is not mine, it's been stolen, just like every cell of my body. It's fading fast. All I know is darkness. All I know is knowing. Tears are out of reach. Pain has washed away. Wind, breath, sweat, nothing grounds me, but I know my body is moving and I can't redirect it. Knowing is not life, not when I can't feel the world on my skin before choosing when to kick, when to scream. In this moment I know more than I should. The dark, sticky intention has fused into my own, it's taking hold of my knowledge. She is conscious—of me, of herself, of me knowing her, of the heat still in my feet.

This other consciousness, the thief, she has access to everything I know. But I haven't explored all of myself. I know there's more, more than I could ever imagine.

Maybe that's been my problem all along. I don't have essence, but there's so much more inside me that I haven't even considered. I've focused on my sight, my strength, and my skill. Is my mind my weakest attribute out of all of them now? Or is it my greatest strength? There are still things I don't know about myself yet. The unknown, that's mine. I'll find it, and I'll grab it before she can.

The pause, the waiting game before ultimate surrender, what a thrill. This naïve girl thinks she can resist me, but I'm in control now. This body she carries held too much stress—a pinch between the eyes, weight in the limbs, the heart so overrun by worry. I knew it would be easy to take over. It was inevitable and I've been merciful to take it from her. Dear Zenta, if I was cursed to be essenceless such as this one, I would have ended my life long ago. If it wasn't for her eyes, I wouldn't bother to possess her.

Shifting through the girl's knowledge of weapons handling, I select a few moves I think will be best for the fight at hand.

The skin shivers against me, shaking off the numbness with slick sweat. a weight drops in her stomach and I dig into it. I search for the bitterness of bile in her throat and the ache in her jaw as I draw her sword. My awareness drifts along the swell of sensation and I cut it off, leaving her nerves barren and numb. Soon I will reach the toes. Soon her senses will fade to none.

Lunging at the first combatant, a Luminee boy, I strike with the blade. It whips the air as the boy jumps back.

As I draw back the blade for another strike, the girl's vision locks on a string of light. It stretches from his right hand to the body's right shoulder. I spin, kicking his hand, interrupting him before he strikes. The body's instinct is to lunge closer. I lean into the instinct and shift my grip on the blade, slamming the pommel to the boy's chin. A crack rings out and the boy cries, bringing a spring breeze of delight to my mind. The girl's body only grimaces and shudders, the blood in her feet still warm.

Poor thing. Can't even enjoy the spoils of her training.

The opening is clear. Trusting the keen instinct of the body, I thrust the blade, link it into the clasps of the boy's tokens, and rip them off his vest.

I suppose giving the team a win would be payment enough for using the girl's body.

Retreating into the forest, not wanting the boy to get a chance to steal the tokens hanging from the girl's vest, I shake out the body's feet. The heat still lingers above her ankles, and halfway down her fingers. They are warm at the tips and cool at the knuckles. Why won't this body let me take her pains?

I don't want you to take it. It's my pain. Get the hells out!

The body's hands tremble like the leaves of the trees. They jerk upward, but I shake them away. Heat jolts from her fingertips to her knuckles, pressing through her palm. Her skin screams with a pulsing ache. How annoying.

Forcing my consciousness through the nervous system, I press her arms down, but her hands flex, the heat inching back through the forearms. I narrow the body's vision onto her glossy black fingernails. Her fingers bend at odd angles. A sharp snap, a pop, and pain splinters through her hands. Blood flushes her skin, swelling in her knuckles. Her wrist snaps backwards as I urge it away. The mangled limbs loom closer, heat bolstering with each break of bone.

Her fingers slap around her throat. The black nails sink into the skin like iron rods and dig for the windpipe. The body gags and doubles over, lilac hair spilling forward, and light exchanging for dark blots of shadow.

The mouth drops open. The crawling, desensitization of my Mind Fire releases from her throat, replaced by harsh, insistent agony of broken flesh.

Out.

The demanding little bitch.

I link one nerve to another, wiping the heat and pain away from her skin, but her fingers keep digging into her flesh, blocking the air to her brain. Every link I make gets extinguished with the lack of air.

The body slumps in on itself. Only a sliver of light makes it through her eyes. Her lungs burn and her limbs shake, still her fingers grip tighter.

I release my focus from her hands and redirect it to her thighs. I throw one leg forward, the body follows, slamming to the ground on its side. The pain in the elbow throbs and I rip it out of her, yielding a rush of cold down the length of her arm.

I loosen the grip of her pincher fingers and slam the hand to the ground. The force throws her forward and her face collides with the earth. A twig lashes through the skin of her cheek and hot blood trickles down her face. I expand the reach of my numbing flame through the entire body, gaining command over her last finger, her last toe, and throw her into motion.

The weightlessness of her body rings like a gong. Its thrill is like nothing else. I steer her back into the battle.

Can't choke yourself on the battlefield, my dear. Don't you want to win?

I slam her fist into an opponent without resistance in her muscles. The pulsation of blood, the tremor of muscle and the effort to control it all, falls out of existence as the body goes silent.

"Eliote, you were so amazing," Rinnaya says as the team waits for their tokens to be tallied back in the arena.

So much like Nolaria, Rinnaya stands without the confidence she should. It sickens me, the softness in her silver eyes, yet the hardness of her mind, so many walls built up, it baffles me.

"What happened to your face?" Rinnaya asks, tapping two fingers to the body's bloody cut.

"Took a nasty right hook. These new Protector vests are rather an unfortunate switch." My words come out raspy and weak from the body's swollen throat.

Rinnaya's eyes squint as they take in the bruises around the body's neck. "What . . . " Her fingers trail down the neck, icier than even the bodies cool surrender to my control.

I snatch her hand away. "I'm going to get a curestone."

"I'll go with you, if you want."

"No, I'm fine. I'll meet you for dinner." I turn away from the iron wretch before she can protest. She'll be more than suspicious if we stay together since my mind is still becoming accustomed to her speech patterns. This body knows that the Revival is coming to meet with Rinnaya. Rinnaya trusts this body, so if I can stay in it long enough, I can get her to tell me where they are. I'll get my hands on the stone with this body's sight to guide me to its energy.

I shoulder through the crowd of students. The ampliphone system crackles, and the students collectively turn to the podium for their headmaster to announce the results.

"With a lead of twenty tokens, Akinnera Academy has taken first place for this trial."

The crowd erupts with applause, and I let a smile grace the body's face. It curls to one side in a half smirk.

Don't be so proud of yourself.

Hot pricks stab through the body's fingers. The toes curl inside her shoes, burning like embers. The heat stirs through the soles, up the calves, striking the knees with a stiffening ache. And yet, even with the pain flooding every system this body contains, it starts to run. The heart pounds, pumping rapid gushes of blood, spiking the breathing rate, and light flares in the mind. My mind wavers as a light suffocates my consciousness.

I try to spread the fire back through her limbs, but they just keep moving, ignoring my offer to numb the pain, moving the body outside. The light swims in my mind. It's like a gentle caress from a mother. No, it's angelic. No, not even that. A mother is too human, and an angel is too high praise. This is clarity, surety as the body moves down the hill into the city of Akinnera. She plants her feet and lets the sweat pour from her, inhaling long rough breaths.

In Luminee homes, you never enter without addressing the host. So, let's talk, Alyxia.

How is she doing this? Her body just keeps pushing through the pain and the tension. The skin is slick and yet chills tumble down the spine. I want to retract myself from it. It's too much, too raw—mortal insignificance. But leaving this body will do me no good.

Every break of skin and bone should be a point of neural activity that I can grab onto, but she resists the analgesic control of Mind Fire, and the body's nerves smart in rapid stabs of teeth-clenching pain, random and intoxicating. I need every part of her body. One finger that feels is one connection to the brain that I don't have access too. She's not mine yet. What is she holding on to in her mind that I can't know?

Alyxia. Eliote. Both names are resounding truths inside me. Truth is never plain. It is never apparent to the eye. Lifetimes are dedicated to it, and mine is just beginning. I've been naïve to run through this life without her, myself, Eliote. I've been so lost. And so has Alyxia, this ancient force, a mind so focused on one intention that it has pushed everything about herself back.

All I know of Alyxia's past is the one event that unquestionably altered her and created her intention. Cold, hard intention to gain all the power she can. In that moment, she was young, sweet, and innocent. Adults swarmed around her, and she watched with wide eyes. Her mother regarded her with a smile, her father lifted her in his arms. One day, the Emberstead kingdom would be hers. He put her down as music played. She danced and another young girl danced with her. But a scream rang through the grand hall that dripped with gold and crystal. Red light engulfed everything. It spilled from a woman, tall and elegant, with flowing blond hair and porcelain skin. The people around Alyxia drop. Her mother, her father, the court, all dead.

Heat strikes through my face, leaving my lips numb as they twitch to speak without a thought to form words.

"My goodness, you are persistent," Alyxia says through my mouth, in my voice. My voice. I've never experienced my voice like this before. It is smooth, dark, like velvet. "I suppose I have time for a conversation. We just need to head back to the academy first."

Flame blisters through my body, jerking me back with a violent whip as Alyxia shrouds her memories, and the skin of my torso goes numb.

Why are you here? I can't control my mouth; all my focus pours down to my feet. My vision blurs and blood pools in my mouth where I've bitten my tongue.

Alyxia's memories are hidden from me now, but my mind is wound around the rock-solid intention that keeps Alyxia going. She wants to hurt Rin. It's an ache, a need, it's red hot like fire, and consuming like the red energy that poured from that woman in her memory. The death affinity. Alyxia hates it.

Alyxia twists my mouth. "I don't want to hurt her. I want her to succeed."

That's a lie.

"Not entirely." Blood swirls through my saliva, seeping through my teeth and spilling over my bottom lip. A lick of heat taps through my tongue. "I want her to stop the Revival."

You want to hurt her, so why haven't you done it yet?

"Because Thea won't let me. That's the trouble with sharing a mind, both your wills get mixed up. You feel it, don't you?"

The hold on my feet breaks and I turn back to the academy.

Thea. She's your host body. Your mind resides fully in her, and you use her body to manipulate essence for Mind Fire?

"Yes." There is a reluctant strain on my voice.

Thea is protecting Rin?

"Thea is infatuated with Daalza, or as you call her, Brand Highcaller. As such, I won't hurt Brand or Rin." My voice hushes as Alyxia coaxes my lips to repeat. "I won't hurt Brand, and I won't hurt Rin."

Why don't you just find a new host?

"I won't let her hurt Brand!" The scream and emotion from my throat shudders through me—alien to Alyxia's poise, alien to my own goals. Vibration stirs in my throat, reforming words that hold composure. "But you could."

You're an idiot if you think I would hurt Rin for you. Why did you choose me?

"You're close to Rin, she trusts you, doesn't she? And you have such pretty eyes." She forces me to chuckle. "Rin's brother has something I want. It seems that Rin will lead me right to him in her pursuit to save her little brother and stop the Revival. All I have to do is get her to tell you where they are. And she will."

What does Stephen have that you want?

The presence that takes up space in my mind and sinks through my body, wanes, releasing my pain back into every infliction on my body. Like knives through my blood, it floods me and I grab hold of it. Turning myself around, I sprint back down the hill.

"Let's just say that a little stone made in your town is just the thing I need to finish the work on my prison."

The utanic Death stone. That's all I comprehend before my vision goes spotty, and I have to redirect my focus back to my breaking body.

"Now, not much of a conversation with you interrogating me, is it? Tell me, how are you so present with me in your mind? You have no Mind Fire abilities, no essence abilities at all."

You and I have a very distinct similarity. You've been in so many minds. There are so many thoughts and emotions and expectations and desires that plague you. But there's one person that is a mystery to you.

"And who might that be?"

You.

Me. I have no idea what I want, what I need, where I should be, what my unknown qualities are.

We have both pushed ourselves so far back that we are still unaware of ourselves. We take up space in our own minds the same way we have this conversation. We know our knowledge, what we have gained through experience, but we use questions and answers to make sense of ourselves. I ask questions and you provide answers. It's why you gave up the information about the stone. The neutralization of a question with an answer is gratifying. Like numbing pain with your flame.

I won't let her hurt Rin, and I won't let her get to her brother. I can stall her.

Each step sends a sensation of breaking glass through my shins. My skin is burning and my throat fills with blood. I just keep taking steps though, farther away from the academy. Sharing a mind with someone is nothing new to me; it's keeping hold of myself that has always been the problem.

38

RIN

"Eliote?" I say, barging into our room.

With a quick scan over the disaster of my side and the tidiness of Eliote's, my stomach lurches. She wasn't in the infirmary and she's not here. Why was she acting so strange? She didn't say anything during the trial today, just kept fighting. I pace the room, stepping over books and clothes, chewing my nail. Where the hell did she go? Maybe she just needed some air. I'll check the courtyards and the grounds around the academy.

On Eliote's dresser sits her echo. The lightstone blips from all the unread messages and unanswered calls from the rest of the team. The dark, bloody prints on her neck cloud over my mind, sending needles through my veins. I snatch her echo, leave our room, and slam the door behind me, shuddering the windows at the end of the hall. Someone hurt her and now she's gone. My heart leaps into my throat as I hurry back downstairs.

Ace and Marcus meet me at the bottom.

"Did you find her?" Ace asks. He wrings his hands and still wears his Protector vest and has smudges of dirt on his face.

"No, just this." I hold up her echo.

"Shit," Ace mutters and runs his hands over his face. "Where is she? She was fine before the trial started, wasn't she?" Shoulders shaking, he paces back and forth. "I . . . I thought she was fine, but during the trial she just . . . I could see she was in pain, but she just kept going."

I stop him in his tracks as his hands fall from his face. Taking him by both arms, I bring him close and hold him, my own heart shaking me, so we shake together. "We're going to find her."

Marcus' echo flashes. He reads the message. "Evelyn checked the memory tech. Eliote left campus by herself. She could be anywhere. We keep looking." His eyes flick to both me and Ace and he gives a solid nod. "Jeff and Johanna are checking the upstairs classrooms." He taps out a message on his echo. "I'm letting Niko know to stay on the ground floor. Ace, you check the outdoor training fields."

"I'll go back to the arena," I say, letting go of Ace.

"Good," Marcus clicks off his echo.

Ace swipes his forehead with the back of his hand. "Rin, the marks on her neck, what happened?"

I draw in a shaky breath. "I don't know, but we'll find her." Swallowing the tension in my throat, I give Ace the most confident smile I can muster and head into the crowded lobby.

Shouldering my way through the bodies, I search for Eliote's light-purple hair.

As I come to the entrance, a cool evening breeze sweeps

over me, and a hand grabs my arm from behind. I turn quick, yanking my arm, and sidestep out of the way for someone to pass by.

Professor Hans stares down at me. His dark eyes shift and he clears his throat into his fist. "You need to come with me."

"I'm a little busy, we can't find Eliote and I'm worried—"

"The Revival sent someone to speak with you," Hans says, stepping closer and lowering his voice. His hand hovers at my shoulder, wavering in a battle of urgency and restraint. The roar of chatter around me muffles to just his voice.

"Stephen?" I ask, throat tightening.

"He sent Adia. She won't wait long. If you want to speak with her, you come to my office now."

Squares of red, gold, and blue play over his face from the stained glass and shadows grow under his eyes. My heart speeds and aches, ripping down the centre. Eliote might need my help, but this might be my one chance to get answers, to finally get to my brother. I swallow hard and nod to Hans, cracking my knuckles on one hand, pushing a stray hair behind my ear with the other. I check behind me and side to side, but no one notices as he leads me to his office.

Hans holds the door for me, and I step into his office with tunnel vision and acid in my throat. But I let my shoulders fall, relaxing the muscles of my face, and set determination in my gaze. It's determination to get Liam out of their grasp, and both of us out alive, but Adia just needs to see determination to help the Revival, to bring back the dead. I can live under that lie. I want to restore our families, but in a different way.

The rays of evening light drift through the open window, giving the room a lens of gold, specks of dust catching the light.

The haze thickens the air and my throat constricts. Adia sits in an armchair by the window. Her long, black hair falls in a silky sheet over one side of her face, concealing the peachy scar on her cheek. The other side of her face is dark, backlit by the sun, and she taps her fingers on the armrests.

"Your professor tells me you've made significant strides with your death affinity," she says, crossing her legs as Professor Hans shuts the door behind us.

"Yes, that's right," I say, my tone easy and flat.

Tilting her head to the side, Adia says, "That's wonderful news. Every time an Ironskin grows into their strengths, it's a beautiful thing, but I can't help but wonder why you have had a change of heart."

I keep my eyes on Adia. Lies have always been easy, but it's the confidence that sells, not a quick answer all the time. I take the seat by the desk, Eliote's echo flashing between my hands, and mirror Adia's crossed legged posture. "I told you I didn't believe you had our best interest in mind, and you proved it by kidnapping my brother—"

"We did not kidnap—"

I hold up a hand to her. Breaking our mirrored position, I lean forward over my knees. "My family is everything to me. Ironskins have always been divided. I need to make a choice to be as close to my family as possible. That means Liam and Stephen. If the Revival means so much to Stephen, then I'll do it." There is too much space around Adia. It should be filled by a tall man with dark hair, dark eyes, and a dark smile. Stephen should be here. I know it would be risky, but he never comes for me. I'll go to him if it gives me even the slightest hope of bringing him home, to stop his hurt from bleeding out and hurting other people. "I've honed the skills you need for the Revival and you're going to take me to my brothers, both of them."

Adia stands and her silver eyes dart to me. "Let's see it then, your control over your death affinity." Blocking the light of the window with her wide frame, she clasps her hands behind her.

I lean back in the chair and with a single breath, heat runs through my body like a hot water tap turning on. My vision bleeds red, my face itches, my back tingles with energy. My veins fill with a ruby-red light.

Adia is all shadow and my light carves out her features. I turn to Professor Hans, painting him in red. He presses his lips together and nods. I blink and the room goes dark.

"And your life affinity?" Adia says, her voice lowered.

My pulse taps through my skin, still revelling in the surge of power. It's been so long since the ghost infested me, but a smile curls my lips. I am the ghost.

I sink my awareness into my body. Into the empty space in my chest, the dark corners where weeds hide and rot grows. I find the corner longing for touch, but not just to be touched but to touch others, to protect, and nurture. It is cool in these places and light spills into my veins. Breaths come easier with the blue glow from my eyes. My arms and legs fill with strength and my back straightens. I put my hands before me, palms up, and glistening light-blue streams sprawl through my wrists and my fingertips.

Adia's scar is crimson—her weak spot—but she is unmoved by the display of light.

"It's not enough," Adia says. Her hips sway as she carves a path to the door.

I stand and block her. "What d'you mean it's not enough?"

"You must integrate your affinities for the Ritual to work," she says.

Chills run over me as I clench my fist. I'm not good enough for them yet. "Then teach me. That's what Geret wanted, to teach me."

"Geret is a kind, trusting man. But if Professor Hans is correct about you being Soul Tethered, it's pointless to even try."

Professor Hans was the one who told them about our Soul Tether. Of course. He must have learned it from Johanna's memories.

"He was right to give us this information. It builds my trust in him, but with you, my trust falters. He's made his choice to side with the Ironskins, but you wish to keep your bond with an Emberstead." Adia's feet fall heavy as she takes a few slow steps back to me.

Professor Hans' office is slowly shrinking around me. I search for breath, but my lungs are stiff. "I've done everything I can," I say in a voice that is nothing close to the power they wish for, the confidence I had just a moment ago. I lean into the quiet desperation and twist it into sincerity, letting it drip into my next words. "I want to help you."

Adia raises her chin. "You don't deny it, this tether to the Emberstead girl?"

"The bond is one-sided. I can't get rid of her." I dig back into the past where all my disdain for her rotted my heart and steel my face. "But she means nothing to me."

My heart pounds with the clock on the wall. I turn to my professor. His eyes are wide, and his brows furrowed. Stepping to me, he puts his hand on my shoulder. "She's done the work, Adia, her cells can be activated by both affinities. What about the transfusion?"

"What transfusion?" I ask.

"I have been working on activating the lifeline code that produces the protein which allows activation of both affinities in Stephen. The procedure is ready, but it will be taxing on his mind and body," Adia says, tilting her head and running her eyes over me. "A transfusion of your blood would provide red blood cells that are accustomed to both affinities. All he would have to do is control them. It would work just as well, without the strain. It would be temporary, but it would work."

Stephen and I have the same blood type. "You have it." The words jump out of me, letting my lungs breathe. I just need to get to Liam. If I can get to the utanic Death stone and destroy it, I'll tell them I'll do anything. This has all gone on too long, and I'm sick of them pissing around.

A smile graces Adia's lips. "I will leave Akinnera to fly to Sarr tonight, where we will meet Stephen and Geret. I will come pick you up in a silver Nexin cruiser. If you do not meet me in four hours at exactly ten p.m., I will leave."

My mouth twitches as I keep it from grimacing. This means so much to them. They really think it's the only way. Such an urgent, life-altering thing, and yet they believe so strongly that it will solve their problems, their pain.

"Just some of your blood. It's a small price to bring our families back together and reclaim what is ours," Adia says.

Professor Hans opens the door for her. The rumble of voices has faded like the sun, and a breeze rushes through the small office.

"I look forward to showing you our homeland. The land of Sarr," Adia says over her shoulder.

"I look forward to seeing it," I say. I wrench my face into a smile, forcing my skin to believe it, to feel it, but all of me is numb. There is no feeling for what this Revival will bring. Does that make me selfish? Or is it really the noble thing to move forward in this world without the baggage of the dead, without the deeds of the past? No, I cannot be without them. They live still—in me. All of that. The greed of my ancestors, the pain they caused, the death that plagues them, plagues me. The memory of the dead is what will make our hearts pursue a better world.

"I'm doing this for the world, too, you know," Adia says. "The same woman behind the Death Ritual is making strides to keep gaining power. We can't let her gain the utanic Death stone. The people we raise will fight against Alyxia."

I wait outside by the side entrance to the school. Staying in the shadows, gravel crunches under my feet. I press my back to the wall and slide into a crouch with my heart thrumming in my chest. Leaning my head on my knees, I take long breaths, letting the stillness of the night press on me, the rustle of leaves smooth over my racing thoughts.

Last year, Adrianne told me something that still haunts me. She said our choices define us. All my choices throughout my life have been based on fear, necessity, and now this. What does choosing to go after one person I love say to the other person I love who's in danger? Eliote is still missing. We've been taking turns looking for her, going out into the city in pairs while some of us stay at the academy in case she comes back. But Adia will be here in fifteen minutes. I'm making a choice.

Heat crawls through my mind. It crackles, becoming the

one thing on my mind. But I grab a handful of dirt and clench it in my fist. I force my body to sink its senses into the gritty texture, the coolness, but Johanna's voice forces its way through.

WHERE ARE YOU?

Shouldn't you know?

I'M GIVING YOU THE CHANCE TO TELL ME YOURSELF THAT YOU'RE DOING SOMETHING STUPID, STUPID.

This is why I don't tell you things.

YOU CANNOT GO OFF BY YOURSELF. ELIOTE IS STILL MISSING.

The door bursts open and Johanna marches out. The green starlight strikes her with a cool glow over her skin and highlights stray curls. She looks left and right, spots me and sighs. With a grunt, she squats down in front of me. "Fuck, Rin, what are you doing?"

I wait for the heat to fill my head. Johanna just stares at me, her eyebrows scrunched and green eyes piercing. I set my jaw. "I'm going to get Liam."

"Not by yourself, you're not," Johanna says.

"Yes, I am." I slow my voice, making sure every word is crystal clear.

Standing, Johanna plants her hands on her hips. She inhales, starts to speak, stops, and throws her head back. "I told you I would help you. I've always had your back. Why can't you just fucking trust me?"

"I have to do this alone."

"No, you don't. Now get off your ass, go inside, and we'll come up with a plan together."

Staring up at her, I shake my head. "No, I can't let you get involved in this. I know you said you would help me, but this has to be discreet. The Revival gets spooked anytime the Guardian system gets involved, any time the Vein gets involved, and you're a fucking Emberstead," I say, gesturing to her.

Johanna puts her hands together and presses them to her lips, letting out a long exhale from her nose. "How can I make this clear to you?" She closes her eyes. "You do not have to save the world by yourself. That is toxic. It's your default, and you have to break it now or else you will be alone forever or die."

I grunt and stand to face her.

"This is my only chance to get to the Revival. They're coming to get me in five minutes. Now get the fuck inside before you screw everything up. They can't know you know about this."

Tears glisten in Johanna's eyes, and my heart drops to my gut. I clench my fists.

"We're better together, and you know that," she says. "Let me go with you."

"They know about our tether. It has to break for me to integrate my affinities and perform the Ritual. They'll kill you without a second thought to break it."

Any one of them wouldn't bat an eye before sticking a blade in her back. Adia, Geret, Stephen, whoever else is with them. They want to build their power against Emberstead and getting rid of them one at a time would keep them right on track. I push off the ground and my stomach cinches. I swallow the urge to vomit and shake the stiffness from my arms.

"We could overpower them, just like we did to defeat the clone—"

"I don't want to overpower anyone," I say. "I'm going to

make a show of my allegiance, destroy the utanic Death stone, and sneak Liam out at night."

"Let me help you." Johanna's voice is low and shaky, thick with emotion as her eyes waver and her mouth grimaces.

Pressure builds behind my eyes. I draw in a breath that suffocates my thoughts and grab hold of Johanna with both hands. She shakes in my grasp, or I shake her, I don't know, I just can't let go.

"You can't come with me because I can't lose you," I say with a crack in my voice and tears spilling down my face.

Johanna's face is wet and so clear without any makeup. Her lips quiver. "What did you just say?" she whispers.

"You mean more to me than anyone. I need you and I can't lose you." My heart bleeds out in these words. I can't take them back and I don't want to. There's nothing truer. "I know what the Revival is willing to do for their cause. They've harmed so many innocent people. There would be no restraint for an Emberstead girl."

Johanna throws her arms around me and holds me tight. It hurts to be held like this, like the world is ending and I'm the thing she can't let go of. Our relationship hasn't been easy. I know it's not easy for her to be tethered to me. It could be easier if I held on to her though. I wrap my arms around her, and for one moment, security is an option, even with all the darkness in and around me.

"As soon as you know where you're going, you tell me. I'll keep the mental connection as long as I can," Johanna says.

"Can you do that?" I ask into her hair.

"I'll try my best." Pushing me back, she swipes her eyes with the back of her hand. "Once you know where you're going,

I'll tell Brand. We will get an airship and come for you. We'll touch down far enough away so that you have an escape. Just the team."

"No, I don't want to put them in danger either."

"If the Revival spooks at anything Vein or Guardian, then we're all you've got. It'll be a rescue mission, not an attack."

"Okay. But what if—"

"It'll work. We'll make it work."

A light flashes through the night and I jump. I push Johanna back into the academy. "She can't see you. Go find the others."

Johanna nods and squeezes my hand. I shut the door and am shrouded in dark, my blood going icy, and my jaw stiff. I swipe away my tears just as the cruiser rounds the corner. Despite the warmth lingering in the air, my body shakes and my hands are numb. But as the cruiser pulls up to me, warmth floods my mind.

I TRUST YOU.

Letting out a breath, I open the cruiser door and slide in next to Adia. Professor Hans is in the back seat; his face is stone, and his eyes follow me as I fasten my security belt. The cab is warm and the lights of the metres on the dash are glaring red like death-affinity eyes. Adia's silence is deathly in its intensity. Glancing at me with her chin raised, she keeps one hand on the wheel, and one rests on her thick thigh. She turns the firestone key and the cruiser rumbles. Driving in silence, she veers onto the motorway headed out of the city where we'll meet the airship to take us to Sarr.

39

JOHANNA

I PACE THE HALLS IN NOTHING BUT MY SPORTS BRA AND SHORTS. Heat swells through my body like the rays of the summer sun. Sweat soaks my back and images from Rin's surroundings flash in my mind—a cruiser, a woman, a dark field outside Akinnera, the inside of a small airship. I run my hand along the wall, steadying myself and focusing on the cool marble under my bare feet as I move from room to room.

I filled the team in on what's going on with Rin. At the moment, Jeff is at the local airbus station checking to see if Eliote was spotted there. Ace is glued to his echo, waiting in the lobby in case she returns. Niko is taking a few minutes to rest before he relieves Ace. Brand was livid when I told her Rin had left, but she's contacting the Guardian station to be on the lookout for Eliote and to secure us an airship to Sarr.

It wasn't too bad keeping the Mind Fire connection for the first two hours, but these last two have been hell. They should be landing in Sarr soon. Dear Zenta, I hope so. The farther away Rin gets, the more essence concentration I have to use.

From time to time, a murmur fills my mind with a cottony shuffle. Rin must be talking to the woman she's with. I focus my eyes on my feet and my mind on the heat connecting us. My mouth is dry, and my eyelids are heavy. I don't have enough energy to keep up the Mind Fire and catch every word. I have to trust that Rin will let me into her thoughts once she gets useful information.

I roll my neck as I fill a cup of water in the dining hall. The coffee pot next to the water cooler is tempting, but I have no idea how chemically altering my conscious state would go over. I can't mess with my mind at this moment, just need to stay awake. Downing the water, the dry ashy taste on my tongue washes away just as my mind ignites with a crackle, sending a prickle of heat over my scalp.

WE'VE LANDED. NEAR THE SHRINE OF KEENA, SOUTH OF LAKE NAII. BUT WE'RE GETTING INTO ANOTHER CRUISER. I DON'T KNOW WHERE WE'RE GOING YET. I'LL LET YOU KNOW.

I shudder as images hit me. The emerald sky reflects off a glassy lake. Mist rises through tall grass and reeds where core-energy boulders hide. My body takes in the information from Rin's mind and translates it into the sensation. My lungs tighten against the humid air, my feet sink into moist, fertile ground, the low-hanging branches shroud my sight in darkness.

Got it. Stay safe.

Legs giving way, I slump against the wall, letting the Mind Fire burn out for just a second. Tension sinks into my mind and my heart thumps hard. It echoes back to me through my mind and body as Rin's heart shudders in her own chest.

I'M SCARED.

I know. Brand's getting a ship. We'll come to you as soon as we can.

Pushing off the wall, I let the movement stir my essence again to keep the connection. I pour myself another cup of water and down it, swiping sweat from my brow. Leaving the dining hall, my jaw drops as Eliote steps out of the shadows. She takes a shaky step forward, still in her tournament gear.

"Eliote," I say, then lunge for her as her knees buckle. She collapses into my arms, her *rahanaso* clattering on the marble floor.

Every inch of her is trembling, taut muscle, and her skin is burning up. I tilt her head to look at me, but her eyes won't focus. Blood is crusted over her chin, her black makeup is smudged and streaked under her eyes. The cut on her face is an angry red, never touched by a curestone. With one hand, I tap my shaking fingers to the inky bruises on her neck, breathing in the last signatures of her sweet perfume, sweat, and something smoky.

"What the hells—"

"Alyxia," Eliote rasps. "I'm sorry, I'm sorry, I'm sorry," Eliote mumbles. "She got to me. It took everything in me to fight her off. Sh-she wants to hurt Rin. Where's Rin?" Eliote's brown eyes become dark and steady as they find me, tears welling at the corners.

"Sarr, she went to get Liam back."

"Damn it. Alyxia just sent Thea to Sarr. She knows the Revival is there, just not their exact location. Rin's going right to her." Eliote jerks in my grasp and a trickle of dark-red blood spills over her lip. She clenches her teeth and nausea fills my stomach as ice spears my heart.

I push back the stringy purple hairs caressing her face and draw her close, letting her put her full weight on me and wrapping my arms tight around her. "It's okay, I've got you, you're going to be okay, and we're going to get Rin home safely," I say. The stench of burning rubber lingers around her.

All the heat from my Mind Fire has dissipated from me, and I'm left with trails of shivers along my jaw, down my side, and trembling, icy fingers. Alyxia really is a threat to us.

A heavy tread sounds down the hall to the lobby. It quickens, and I lift my head, even though it's heavy. Brand drops to her knees beside us. She wears jeans and a grey, hooded sweater, her hair is scrunched up high and her reading glasses are stuck in the curls on the top of her head.

"Thank Carnity." She pulls out a curestone from her pocket and presses it to Eliote's neck while simultaneously checking her pulse. "What happened?" She looks at me.

"Alyxia got to her," I say, taking the curestone from Brand and holding it for Eliote, the bruises fading to a yellow green.

"Damn it," Brand says, shaking her head. "Did she get information out of you?"

"Alyxia," Eliote mutters, trying to sit herself up straight. "She wants to kill Rin. We can't let her get to Rin."

Brand stares into Eliote's eyes and puts a hand to her shoulder. "Eliote, I am so proud of you for holding her back this long. You did so well." Eliote's shoulder's hunch and she buries her face in her hands that are swollen and covered in scrapes. "We are going to get Rin back to safety before Alyxia can get her and before the Revival forces her into the Ritual. You do not have to come. You've fought hard enough."

"No, I'm coming. That stone was built from the fear of my people, and I want to help Rin." Eliote's voice is stripped of its sweet air. It is clean and clear, blunt sentences with full stops and no questions. "You can't make me stay here." She turns back to me and looks me straight in the eye. "I'm bringing my fight to them."

Pushing out of my arms, she stands and a drop of blood hits the floor where she was sitting. There's a shake and a darkness in her eyes. I get up quick and put my arm back around her waist to steady her.

"I'm good. I can walk," she says.

"Would you just let me fucking hold you? You're shaking like a leaf."

Brand yanks her glasses from her head, pulling out stray hairs from her bun, and turns on her echo. Thumbing through the messages, she says, "Let's get the guys together. We've got a ship. Johanna, has Rin given you anymore information?"

"They're on the south side of Lake Naii, near the shrine of Keena. But they're moving."

"Good, I know where they're going." She clicks off the echo and leads the way back to the lobby.

Ace bolts out of his chair as soon as we round the corner. He throws his arms around Eliote and cradles her head.

"Where's Jeff?" I ask.

"I'm here, I'm here," Jeff says, bounding through the front door. "Thank Thesta, you're okay, Eliote." He gives her a quick side hug.

As I sprint up the stairs to the guys' dormitory, I follow the train of ice Rin's mind has left across the province and let the churning heat in my body rebuild the connection.

We found Eliote. She's okay. But not okay. You are not safe. Alyxia wants to kill you.

SHIT.

I pound on Niko's door, my heart pounding even harder.

"Niko, up." I open the door and cross the room, yank Niko out of bed and push him into the hall.

"I'm up, I'm up. Is Eliote okay?" he asks.

"Eliote's back. Time to go get Rin from Sarr."

As I drag Niko into the sitting room to meet the team, Lance opens his door.

"Hey, is everything okay?" he asks.

"You." I shove Niko into the sitting room and he stumbles into Jeff. Grabbing Lance by the shirt, I say, "You're coming too. Your girlfriend likes to do risky shit on her own, and now we have to make sure she gets out alive. Get used to it."

"Johanna, slow down. Where did she go?" He grabs my shoulder and turns me to face him. Hair tousled and eyes searing into me, his wings pull in tight behind him.

"Rin went to get her brother, and we need to make sure she gets back safely. We'll fill you in on the way. Are you in or out?" I say, hands on my hips.

If I didn't know I could only read Rin's mind, I'd be fooled by the volume of his unspoken words. Lips parting, his eyebrows stitch together. His hand finds his heart and his fingers clench into his shirt. "Of course I'm in," he says. "But what about the tournament?"

"They forfeited the tournament the moment Rin left," Brand says, coming up the stairs. "Now listen up. We get Rin, the utanic Death stone, and the Revival stones. The stones are volatile, so don't let any energy interact with them. We have no idea how they would react, especially the utanic Death stone. We will not engage in combat unless absolutely necessary."

"Isn't this the sort of thing a highly trained Protector team would do?" Jeff asks, helping Niko over to the couch across from Eliote and Ace as he rubs his eyes.

We all go quiet. Ace's face is drawn as he holds the curestone to Eliote's neck as she rests her head on his shoulder. Lance folds his arms over his chest, sitting on the arm of the couch beside them. I don't have anything to say to that. I know Rin wanted it to be a secret, but with Alyxia out there, it complicates things.

Standing in the middle of the stoic group, Jeff puts his face in his hands. "Thesta help me," he mutters.

I hurry over to him. "Jeff?"

"I don't know if I can do this, Jo." He shakes his head, taking long breaths, and puts his hands to his hips with his eyes closed.

I swallow hard and lean my head on his chest. "I know, I'm so sorry."

"My family. I can't get hurt. Training is one thing, but getting out there . . . they can't lose me."

My stomach drops. I turn my gaze to Ace, heart aching as his mouth twitches while he also takes a moment to calculate the risks—for all of us, for himself, his beautiful family.

"He's got a point," he says. "I'm going. There's really nothing that would stop me from making sure Rin and her brother get home safe, but we don't know what we're up against. With Alyxia involved, it complicates things."

"Who's Alyxia?" Lance asks, dragging his hands through his hair.

Ace gestures to him with the curestone. "Exactly."

"I've seen Rin's reaction to how the Vein and the Revival have split," Brand says. "I know she decided to go by herself because she wants to avoid conflict. You're right, this is spur of the moment, but you all have exceptional skill, and you work better together than many high-level Protector squads." Crossing her arms, she dips her head and sighs. "But you don't have to come with us. It's your choice."

Niko shakes his head. A deep frown cuts his face, and he throws up his hands. "You're going to have to convince me. I care about Rin, and a year ago no one would believe those words, but they're true. I just"—he wrings his hands—"I feel like she's highjacked everything, you know? All the drama last year, and now we forfeit the tournament. I don't know."

Silence falls over us like a heavy blanket. Eliote's eyes are unfocused and red rimmed. Ace slips off his glasses, leans over his knees, and holds his face in his hands.

"This Revival effects us all, Niko. And they're not going to stop until they get it," I say in a hushed tone, and wrap my arms around my bare stomach.

Niko presses his lips together, nodding, but his eyes are weak, tired, and disbelieving. Of course they are. Emberstead and Ironskins have made Illyson their playground, taking what they please and never giving in return. We've ruined this place for everyone. I have to go. None of them have to get involved with this.

Lance pushes away from the arm of the couch. A draft wraps around him fluffing his wings as he paces, letting his eyes drift up to the ceiling.

I turn and walk toward the stairs. "I'll go by myself."

Eliote catches my arm before I can get to the steps and yanks me back. Turning me to face her, she squeezes her eyes shut and says, "You're not losing Rin, and you're not here alone." Her voice crawls from her throat like it had to push past dirt and cobwebs just to be heard.

Her eyes are as dark as night. The smell of burning tar is still strong. My mouth is dry, my throat aches. She's said those exact words to me before Rin left last year to console me. I don't want to lose Rin, of course I don't, and I know I shouldn't doubt my team, but this time her words aren't meant for consolation.

Jeff ties his locs back. "My mom tells me that the energy we consume and expel on the Karess leaves an imprint—*Ha'ken* she calls it. If we leave behind positive energy, it heals and creates areas of lush vegetation for other hédin to enjoy lifetimes in the future. She says both positive and negative energy will always be present. I can do what I can to prevent negative *Ha'ken* wherever I am." His words are measured, sure. "I'm here right now. I'm in." He claps his hands together.

"You're not obligated to do this," I say.

"But if I'm going to leave this place and waste the money she spent on the junior-training program, then I'm going to do what she would do. She would help."

Lance steps forward. "We have more control over the world

we live in than we realize. I'm in too." His wings twitch behind him.

"Me too," Ace says and turns to Niko. I turn to him, too, my heart pounding in my throat.

Niko sighs and stands. "Can I at least get dressed first?"

Brand chuckles. "Yes. Get dressed. Johanna, put a shirt on. Eliote, get some electrolytes into your system. We leave in ten."

Eliote's hand finds mine. It is burning and slick with sweat. Her other hand twitches around her *rahanaso*, and with her eyes on the ground, she says. "I bring my fight to them."

If there is anyone I trust to give me encouraging, inspirational words, it's Eliote. These words aren't a pep talk though. They're warnings. We're not alone, and she's bringing her fight to them.

40

R I N

WE DROVE AROUND LAKE NAII, but which side we're on now, I don't know. Each turn leaves my brain reeling and I lost track of single turns until they twisted together in a knot. I open the cruiser door and the air, thick with moisture, pours around me. It is perfumed by the light-blue rillia blossoms on the bushes lining the gravel path. It's a spicy smell but sweet, too, like the mixture of cinnospice and dried plums Mother would put out during the Festival of the Heart. Moon beetles glitter through the dark, a few touching down on my arm as I get out of the cruiser. The unkempt path has slivers of core energy glowing through cracks in the earth, sending a subtle vibration through my feet.

My breaths are short, straining against the moisture in the air, trapping the nighttime heat. I use Adia as a model—how to breathe the air, how to walk. She knows why she's here, and I need them to believe I'm here for the same purpose. She steadies her gaze on the path before us, so I let my eyes relax, and clear the feeling from my face one muscle at a time. The posture is not difficult. My mother taught it to me.

"This way, Rin," Adia says. She moves down the path, gravel crunching underfoot without turning to look at me. Adia's long, dark hair swishes behind her, reflecting a sheen of green starlight.

Professor Hans comes up behind me. As he urges me forward with a steady hand, the moon beetles flicker off my arm and fly through the dark to touch back down on Adia. She moves a finger to one of them and lets it crawl onto her hand.

The path curves through the thick trees at a slight incline. A bird calls and another responds. A low growl in the distance pricks my ears. All through the forest are small ponds. Some ponds connect to each other with stone paths and bridges, lanterns set about them to illuminate the forest. A ring of heat sweeps from one side of my forehead to the other and the thump of my heart lessens, knowing Johanna is with me. I can only imagine how the connection strains her.

We come to a clearing and the path becomes a wide courtyard ringed by lattice fencing and crawling vines. A mansion stands at the other end. Its face is all windows, spaced by dark wood pillars with white stone bases. The roof is peaked like the roofs in the Ironskin sector of Senn, and a lantern is lit at the base of each.

Crossing the courtyard, I clench my fingers as shadows move inside the mansion. I step onto the smooth tile at the threshold and slow my pace, letting Professor Hans pass me. Through the tile, red and blue and purple make swirling patterns through the stone. The thickness in the air can't weigh down the shiver that passes through me.

The threshold opens into a long hall, a rectangular pool of water stretching the length of it, lined with the same hard wood pillars. As we remove our shoes and make our way down the left side to a doorway, the smell of incense fills my nose.

Adia checks over her shoulder. The moon beetles twitch their wings, flashing green and purple light across her face.

Geret waits for us at the edge of the pool, his face dark, and arms at his sides, trembling. He wears a dark suit like the last time I saw him, his hair styled to perfection. A few more wrinkles line his face as he smiles at me.

"This is the home of Keena, our great ancestor. Rebuilt after the Fourth Great War and maintained for her people," Geret says. His voice is soft, like the trickle of the water in the pool. "The high volume of surface core energy in the area will allow us all to be at full strength for the Ritual. Some of our people have gathered here already. Some will join us tomorrow when we will celebrate our reunion with a banquet." He motions for us to follow him.

As he takes a few unsteady steps, Adia comes up beside him and takes him by the arm.

Pressure builds in my chest and cuts off my words. All this history, all this beauty, and it's where they want to perform the Ritual that will disrupt the meagre beginnings of a world without war.

"The deposits of core energy also repel beasts that might be attracted to the Death stone," Geret says, but my ears catch on the sound of feet running through the hall beyond the door. My heart skips a beat. I know those feet.

I pick up my pace, passing Adia and Geret, heart pounding in my throat, longing pulling the tension in my body tighter.

The doors fling open, and I can't keep moving. My mind is hot, my heart thrashing, and my knees weak. Liam runs through the door, his face already pinching and his eyes glistening with tears. I fall to my knees as tears gush down my face, catching Liam in my arms. He sinks into me.

The time away has left him thin. He trembles when he should hold still. His arms are limp and his face curls into my neck as he whispers, "You can't be here. This is all wrong."

My arms tighten and I grit my teeth, barricading a scream. I breathe long breaths, bringing my heart back to the quiet, reverent tempo. I bring my mother's face to mind and pull it over me like a mask—the farce of a woman who can carry everything for everyone. Screaming will be for later.

"This is all for the best," I say so everyone can hear me. Lowering my voice and my lips to his ears, I whisper, "Trust me." I disguise the words with a kiss.

I stroke his head as he lets out a breath. My ears ache with the small sound. It's hollow, tired. In the story of Nolaria, she had Renya and the others with spirit sight keep the Death and Revival stones. They protected people from misusing the stones and their rituals. Liam, with his spirit sight, is the keeper of the stones now, but he hasn't been given command over them. He's saying no, his whole being is fighting with a resounding battle cry of no, and they just won't listen.

Gently pushing him off my shoulder, his head lolls without the support. "Why aren't you asleep, buddy?" I ask, running a thumb along the dark circles under his bloodshot eyes.

Liam locks his fingers around my wrist and my pulse taps through my skin under his touch. "I felt your spirit."

My heart swells inside me and I smile through my tears.

"Really?"

Liam nods. From my knees, I used to be level with his eyes, but now I look up. His face is taking on the slightest angle as it evolves from the young boy I knew. But his body jerks and his smile drops as Stephen appears in the doorway behind him. Without the glare of death about him, his face is long and pale, his dark eyes sunken, and his hair hangs long around his face.

Adia walks over to him and encircles him with her arms. Stephen embraces her, leaning his head on hers, his eyes squeezed closed. As they open, they land on me. Expression vanishes from his features and light struggles to touch his eyes. I struggle, too, but I push through. I see a boy who sat beside me on the stairs while our parents fought. We joked until the light left him when our father refused to stay and help him, to stay and build us up.

My mouth parts as I search for words to greet him, but all the weight I've carried between the two of us crashes down on me and I shut it. I want him to see me and greet me like we were back then.

"I believe rest is in order for all of us," Geret says, taking steps around me and Liam as Adia and Stephen part. "Stephen, please show Rinnaya to her room."

Nodding, Stephen sets a firm hand on Geret's shoulder. The shift in his face as he looks at his mentor builds with all the emotion that I've never seen in a look toward me.

"Hans, I would like to have a word," Geret says as he turns left down the hall, his voice reverberating off high ceilings and stone.

Taking one last look at me, Professor Hans follows, nodding to Stephen.

"This way," Stephen says.

 456

Water trickles in the pool as footsteps fade down the hall. The quiet is spiked with tension and the light shift of my clothes as I stand is as forceful as a windstorm. Liam squeezes my hand, and we follow Stephen into the corridor beyond the door.

The stone walls are buffed smooth, mitigating the summer heat. Dark wood doors with intricate carvings are spaced evenly throughout the hall. Images of flowers, beetles, people—they tell stories that might be real, but their beauty is mysterious, just myths.

Heat taps a beat through my head.

WE'RE IN THE AIR. SHOULD BE IN SARR BY MORNING.

Liam tightens his grip. His eyes are wide and glittering with lantern light. His lips twitch, but I shake my head at him and squeeze his hand back. Johanna's presence can't be known.

Stephen looks over his shoulder, eyes catching mine, black beads, precise and calculating. "You came."

My mouth is dry, my tongue thick and stiff, but I roll my shoulders and lean into the comfort Liam's tight grip gives me. "I did."

"Adia told you about the transfusion?" he asks.

I nod.

"And you'll do it?"

"Yes, I will."

"Why?" The question is quick, probably because he can't see my younger self, he just sees me—and I'm not someone he trusts. His shoulders tense and his footsteps slow as he faces forward again.

I won't lie this time.

"Because I love you." The words break free. Chained for so long, my body is weak without them. Like rigid stakes, they held me up. The stakes did more harm than good, creating callouses and deep wounds that bleed freely now. But there is more space inside me.

Will he ever believe it? When this is all over? Or will this one truth be tainted once I use it to stop him from getting what he wants?

Stephen stops, turned to one of the overly beautified doors. "You can stay here." His tone is soft and low.

I take a step to the door, keeping my eyes on him. In a momentary glance, it's there. The pain in his eyes that labels him as hédin, that hides him from the clutches of his demons, that keeps him fighting. I smile at him. It's firm but it hurts, and Stephen turns away from it, making his way back down the hall.

"Can I stay with you tonight?" Liam asks.

"I wouldn't want to be away from you any longer." I open the door and pull him close to my side as we enter.

The room is long, simple, and spacious. At the far end is a floor-to-ceiling window overlooking the front courtyard. There's a bathroom separated from the rest of the room by a folding screen. Incense burns on the table by the bed, the only decoration. The floor changes from smooth tile to wooden slats. For a moment, my feet are home. In all of this, my body picks up familiar sensations in this unfamiliar place. My heart can't be tricked though.

"Someone's with you," Liam whispers.

I lead him over to the bed and have him sit down beside me.

"Johanna," I say with the same hush. "She's keeping a Mind Fire connection to me until I can tell her exactly where we are.

My team is coming to get us."

"So, you're not going to do the Ritual?"

"No." I brush his hair out of his eyes. "But we need the Revival to trust that I'm here to cooperate. I need you to tell me everything you know, about where we are and about the stones."

Liam rubs his eyes and leans on his knees. "I-I don't know much. We just got to this place a few hours before you did. We move around a lot and split up. Sometimes I've been with Stephen, sometimes Adia, sometime other Revivalists. We're in Sarr, I just don't know where. The stones though"—he goes rigid, his eyes fixing on the floor—"they're locked up with a star crystal lock. We'll need the key. I feel them all the time and I feel everything everyone else feels."

I rub his back as sweat dampens his shirt. "And what do they feel?"

"No one wants this Revival for the same reason. No one sees themselves clearly."

"No one wants it for the right reason?"

"I don't think there's a right and a wrong here. It's just not good, not clear. Some want war, some want their families back. But . . . " He finally looks back at me.

"But what?"

"You. You see yourself clearer than any of them."

I fold my hands into my lap. Rolling my neck, I let out a long sigh. "That can't be—"

"You see through your own eyes and the gate is open."

The gate, the one surrounding the flower garden of my soul, where the birds and the moths live, what he drew for me last year. Pressure builds inside me and my eyes prickle with tears. "I'm just learning."

"They don't want to learn," Liam says.

I swing my legs up onto the bed and curl onto my side as Liam scrambles over to the other side. We lie facing each other in the green starlight shining through the window.

Liam reaches for my hand. "When will we leave?"

Tracing his fingers with mine I say, "I think . . . I think we'll have to stay one day."

"But what if they want to do the Ritual tomorrow?"

"They want to have a banquet. I hope we can just be here tomorrow and then leave in the middle of the night. My team is coming to meet us." I swallow hard. "They haven't taken any blood from you for the Ritual, have they?"

"No. They say it needs to be fresh." Liam buries his head in the pillow, and I draw him near me as my body goes ice cold. Leaning into the heat that still crowns my head, I make my thoughts as clear as possible.

Take a rest, Johanna.

I'LL CONTACT YOU IN THE MORNING.

Closing my eyes, I focus on Liam's breathing beside me, holding him tighter once they lengthen instead of leaving and closing the door to him. Even after learning about myself and how much I'm like my family, I am not my mother. I don't wear a mask anymore.

I sit in the small bathroom of my room on a stool in front of the mirror. Adia says the banquet will be traditional dress and has come to do my hair. She said that Ironskin hairstyles take time and precision. It's a process, one that I can use to my advantage. Adia has answers. I know she knows the inner workings of this Ritual. If she can deduce a scientific process to activate both affinities in Stephen, then she has to know every detail about the Ritual and the Hold. Father wants to break the hold to release the captives into the Beyond. Adia wants to break them into our world. Two heads of the same beast.

Adia wheels a cart with cosmetics and hair-styling tools beside me and selects a brush. Her reflection in the mirror is different from the strength she projects. Her eyes are tired, not alert like they usually are. Her hands shake as she lays the brush back down to tie her own hair up. Standing right behind me, she looks into the mirror—her scar on full display without the long veil of dark hair. Her lips quirk in a quick smile and then she brings the brush to my head.

"Why does the Ritual need both spirit affinities?" I ask, as she glides the brush down my scalp, over my neck and shoulders to the ends of my hair at the middle of my back. I shiver as the prongs touch the crown of my head again and Adia tugs it through the tangles. Adia glances up at the mirror to catch my eyes. She raises an eyebrow.

"I've been taught to control them," I say, taking hold of the chunk of silky hair she's sectioned and tossed over my shoulder. "I haven't been taught how they link me to the dead."

She hums a low note as she lowers the brush. She holds her hand up and examines it with soft eyes. "The affinities link us to the Higher Plane, the holding place for spirits. Ironskins with spirit affinities can create paths directly to the Higher Plane. Someone with the life affinity uses their own spirit to create a path. By placing their palm on a dead person, they create a path to wherever their vital energies lie, even if they are split through the Lesser Worlds or gone to be with the ancestors in the Beyond."

"Don't people who use Angel Palm die?" I ask.

Twisting a tiny chunk of hair into a long, thin braid, Adia glances up at my reflection. "Yes, most who use Angel Palm don't make it back to the Karess because it takes such a toll on the spirit to find the vital energies and guide them back. Their mental energy and essence go to strengthen their spirit. But by that time, it's too late."

I drop my eyes to my hands, running my fingers along my veins, my veins that glow blue and red. "Most? Who's made it back?"

"There has only been one report of an Ironskin returning along with the person they revived, and they had both spirit affinities," Adia says softly. She takes my chin and tilts my head back up for her to continue layering braids and leaving loose hair in between. "No one knows how they did it because they isolated themselves and refused to speak of it."

My stomach growls and my fingers are icy as Adia finishes another long, thin braid and pinches a silver ring on it.

I quiet with this information. The stress in my body thrums in my ears without conversation to mask it. Somehow, having both affinities is protective against the side effects of Angel Palm. It has its own toll though. There is no way to play with death and come out clean, except Demon Palm.

Adia finishes the layers of free hair, twists, and braids, with the shiny silver rings and sections the top layer of my hair into three parts and begins to braid it all together.

"And Demon Palm? How does that work?" I ask as Adia moves over to the cart to search for something, holding my hair tight.

I glance at the window. In the courtyard, people are gathering. They wear silk dresses and suits and go barefoot over the packed gravel. A woman lifts her long, silver skirt as she walks, and a polished gold bangle catches the sunlight. I always dream about my mother in traditional dress, even though she never really wore it.

"Demon Palm draws another hédin's vital energies into the Ironskin's body. They can then use the spirit they have absorbed to create a path into the Higher Plane, sending the mental energy and essence along with it. It's not as taxing as Angel Palm so the Ironskin who uses the ability survives." Coming around to face me again, she presses an eye-lining tool to my eyelid. I try to keep my breaths calm, but there is no calm inside me.

"So wouldn't integrating both affinities just cancel them out?" I ask.

"No, it becomes restorative. In the Hold, spirit, mind, and essence are separated. Each of the three Revival stones used in the Ritual calls to one vital energy, bringing it back from the Hold. Unenhanced blood becomes the organic material to restore physical bodies. The integrated dual affinities restore the person's consciousness of the past and present by uniting vital energy."

This Ritual will restore full awareness, then, not like the cloning process that they did before where only memory was intact. The people trapped in the Hold will have their own agenda, their own grievances against the world. The majority of them will be those who died from the Death Ritual. They'll have their minds focused on finishing the war.

"What about the utanic energy? What does it do?"

"It creates a bridge between the Hold and our world."

Adia dips a small, round brush into a red mixture and presses it under my eye, making a big dot right under my iris and a series of smaller ones out to the side, mimicking the winged eyeliner. She takes another brush with a blue mixture, I close my eyes, layering worlds behind my eyelids as she puts layers of makeup on my eyes. "Will the Hold break for good if we do the Ritual?"

"No. We're not changing the Hold's energy, only making a bridge. The Hold will remain."

Utanic energy changes passive energy to utanic and active energy can use utanic energy to change another type of energy to a desired outcome. If the Ritual will create a path between worlds, then are we manipulating the active energy of reality?

"What kind of energy is the Hold?" I open my eyes. The woman is still outside, hair in intricate twists just like mine, and I can't look away.

"I believe the Hold was made from a pool of jint energy in the Higher Plane." Adia sprays my hair with something that stings my nose.

"How do you know all this?"

"Because I've been to the Hold. Spirit affinities are linked to the higher void through the jint pool. We can pass through the plain temporarily. Or we should be able to. Before the war we were able to. My life affinity only draws me to the Hold. The walls of the Hold repel me, like they refuse to be close to my vital energy."

Adia's essence is jint, but the life affinity draws on the unama side of jint energy. The inner wall must be the fann side. If someone with the life affinity were to manipulate the outside of the Hold and someone with the death affinity were to manipulate the inside, then maybe it would break. But in the Hold, vital energies are split. How do two people stand in the Lesser Worlds to break the Hold without dying? That's impossible.

Losing patience but gaining confidence in my understanding, I say, "Tell me about Alyxia."

Breath raises Adia's chest and she lifts her chin. Her eyes cloud with a dark veil as they shift past my head. "She took over Thea as her host nine years ago. She possesses Thea's mind fully but can also expand her consciousness into other people, controlling them remotely. Alyxia has been in many different minds over many centuries." She swallows. "Even my mind." Her words are steady and plain as she taps a finger to her scar. "She's slowly gaining control of many followers, and she wants to take over Illyson. While she manipulated me, we shared one mind, and that's how I know she created the Hold. She manipulated an Ironskin with dual affinities to perform the Death Ritual, which killed everyone with the affinities at the time and trapped them in the Hold." She stops with her back to me. "Other than that, I have no memory of what she made me do."

"I know what it feels like to be manipulated by her," I say softly.

My heart beats heavy. It's overwhelming as her pain and mine collide. Adia stiffens and doesn't respond. She shared her pain, but it is not for me to comfort, it's fuel. Just like Stephen's pain.

"And the utanic Death stone," I say. "You want to use it for the Revival before Alyxia can use it to change the energy of the Hold, change it to a mental hold, so only Mind Fire can be used to send someone into it."

"Exactly." Standing, Adia reorganizes the hair and makeup items on the cart and pushes it back along the wall. The murmur of voices drift into the room, echoing the murmur of blood through my body. A breath of heat sweeps down my neck.

My reflection catches me. My eyes are bold, shining silver outlined in black and adorned with my affinity colours. My hair is gently pulled back, small strands left to frame my face.

"You don't want to break the Hold even if you knew how," I say before I can stop myself. "Once all the Ironskins with the death affinity return to the Karess, they can send any Emberstead they come across into the Hold."

"You and your little brother are so naïve." Adia lets out a breathy laugh that grates on my nerves, and she shakes her head.

My mask is cracking. I let my intentions show, my feelings. And now hers are showing—dark, twisted cracks through her protective wall.

"The Emberstead are not innocent people. They are complicit with Alyxia's desire. She doesn't just manipulate people, she knows what they want. Power, and she can give it to them."

"And we're not innocent people either, right? If someone's not complicit with Alyxia, she controls them. The Revival kills those who oppose their goal. Isn't that what Geret did to my father?"

Adia leans close to me, right by my ear, hand on my shoulder, silver eyes like moons fading behind a lens of blue light. She whispers, "I will not hesitate to do the same to you." A sharp point presses into my weak spot, like a hairpin. "I believe you were given your abilities for a reason. I will not hesitate to take the blood from your weak spot." The point releases from my back. "I won't let you and your brother go home until your blood is on my hands."

Warmth bleeds from my face, my expression cools, I become the iron of my skin.

A threat. She thinks she can beat me, break me, win me over. The obsession with bringing back their power spills over, poisoning everything around her. All of them. Geret's exhausted. Stephen can barely look at me. And Adia? The hair-braiding comradery was just a show. They all are a threat. But threats pump my blood. I've faced death too many times to be afraid of it anymore.

41

RIN

I STAND IN THE MIDDLE OF THE CROWD OF IRONSKINS in their silver and black silks, but I am the only one in purple. A few, like Stephen and Geret, wear red suits, and Adia is dressed in a light-blue silk dress that flows over her curves. Her hair hangs long as always but with a lattice of tiny braids and silver rings laying over the free hairs like a net.

My face is hot as I smooth the skirt of my two-piece ensemble. The purple skirt is silky and layered with different material making it wide and flowing. The top is tight to my body with long sleeves that hook around my middle fingers to keep them in place. Delicate silk buttons trail up my chest to a tight silver collar. A sliver of my skin is exposed between the top and the skirt, but the humidity sticks the top to my body. I'm thankful to be barefoot with dangling silver anklets cooling the tops of my feet.

With all the silks, the glittering, elegant jewellery, the colours of my affinities branded all over my face and body, the expectations of me are heavy. I can carry them for one night. For one night I will smile, wear the clothes, and show my strength. The mask is easy to put on, but uncomfortable on my face. Once this night is over, I need my hands on that star crystal key to get the utanic Death stone, I just have to figure out where it is. If not, I'll grab the utanic Death stone on the day of the Ritual, then Liam and I will run.

Liam is next to me, clutching my hand as we follow the crowd of Ironskins into the grand hall. He wears a black suit with silver stitching, a rillia blossom embroidered on the front pocket, and an open silver circle painted on his forehead.

We come into a wide hall, mosaic tiles spreading throughout the room and around a triangular pool of water. A wooden walkway rings the hall to a rounded outstretch of glass overlooking ponds and marshland, steaming with core energy and muggy heat. The hall is filled with golden light, and in our glimmering clothes, we are planets revolving around the triangular pool. The pool absorbs the sun, rippling like fiery molten rock.

"Do you know who has the star crystal key, Liam?" I ask, moving us to the side of the crowd, my voice mixing with others.

"No, I can't sense powerstones anymore, just the utanic Death stone. I can't explain it." Liam shakes his head and touches his finger to the paint on his forehead. "But I know either Geret, Stephen, or Adia will have it. No one else."

I scan the crowd for Professor Hans. Maybe he can use his Mind Fire ability to figure out who has it. I put my hand on

Liam's back and we shuffle into the centre of the crowd, where Professor Hans stands with a glass of pinichu berry cider.

A server passes us and I take two glasses. Handing one to Liam, I say, "Professor Hans, can you use your Mind Fire to see who has the key?"

"I could," he says, but points to the ceiling. "But there are powerstones throughout the room, even powerstone dust in the paint." I nod to him and tilt my head to the ceiling, trying to make my face look awed by the silver and gold stencilling. "Once I am able to leave this room, the key may have changed hands too recently for me to get a read on a memory. I may only be able to read who had the key this morning."

My stomach drops. I'll have to find another way. I can't break through a star crystal lock. I can break a lot of things, but not that.

Adia ushers us to the central table at the tip of the triangle pointing at the windows, sun to our backs. Scooting his chair closer to me, Liam keeps hold of my hand. He watches everyone take their seats and from time to time he flinches, his eyes crinkle, and he runs his hand over his face.

Chatter and laughter roll through the room, but as Stephen joins us at our table, Liam's fingers sweat in my grasp and his eyes go wide. There must be energy trailing Stephen that I can't see that shakes Liam to his core.

Once everyone has been seated, Geret comes down the centre of the room with the hush. His ruby-red velvet suit has rillia, beetles, and moons embroidered over the silk collar. He walks on his own, with sure steps, and his hand tucked into his lapel to hide the tremor that never seems to still. He stops at our table and turns to address the room.

Geret is still. He holds his shoulders back, his blond hair is swept off his face. One day here, with the higher presence of core energy, seems to have given him new life. He's a different man, stronger, a threat.

"Keena has blessed us all with her presence as we join together to celebrate," Geret says. His voice washes through me like a stream, bristling the hairs on the back of my neck with shocking cold, and pumping my heart with the rush. "Today we gather to celebrate our reunion with one daughter. Rinnaya, we are pleased to have you with us."

Everyone touches two fingers to their foreheads and then to their hearts. My lips part, but I'm not sure if words are required. I sit straight in my seat, crushing Liam's hand, and scan the faces of the crowd. Crisp grey eyes, blood-red lips, some with smiles, others with stone-cold expressions and raised chins. Adia tilts her head, hiding her scar but not the sharpness of her eyes, like a point to my back.

I turn to Stephen. All the adrenaline coursing through my veins dissipates, evaporating through my skin, leaving me numb. My sweat is cold. He holds his eyes on me as if he cannot see me. He crosses his legs and turns his attention back to Geret.

"We still have time before we perform the Revival Ritual to reform our nation, but not as long as you may think. Today, we make history as one of our own has altered his very own lifeline code so that he can now activate both life and death affinities."

Murmurs roll through the room, tying the air into a tense knot in my chest. My heart thrashes against it. Liam looks at me with wide eyes. Adia raises her chin to me, stone in her eyes, her lips a straight line. Geret has waited for me. Stephen and Adia don't have that patience, though, they aren't as trusting. Or maybe none of them trust me, but Geret has enough confidence in their plan. If anything goes wrong, he can redirect, start over, just as he's done all these years. Adia said this lifeline-code alteration would be dangerous. She didn't want to use it unless she was sure I wasn't going to help them. The hair pin to my back was the moment she made her decision.

Geret takes a seat at our table as Stephen rises. He steps up onto the wooden walkway, his shoes tapping and echoing over the hush. I turn in my seat, keeping him in my view, as a pain sinks through my stomach. Stephen stands with his arms spread out and his back to the sun, eyes closed tight.

"Rinnaya," Liam whispers. "Rinnaya, it's not right. Something's wrong."

Stephen's eyes fly open, red light lashing out of him, filling the room with heat. I squeeze Liam's hand as he squirms in his chair.

"He's going to hurt someone. He's not ready," Liam says. "Rinnaya, do something."

The red light cools to the ethereal blue of the life affinity. It flashes as Stephen blinks and a smile crests his lips. He rolls back his head, drinking in the world through his new eyes.

Energy strikes through the air. I scan the room. Three rows of tables, eleven in total. I'm in the centre, so I might be able to cover them all.

Glimmering and shifting, the light darkens to violet. I grab Liam in my arms as the air thickens. A pulse of energy hits just as my life affinity rips out of me like needles shredding my skin. My wings expand across the room. The integrated energy slams into them. The hall vibrates, glass clinks, and shrieks split the air. I gasp for breath as the light recedes and the golden rays of the sun warm my back again.

I snap my wings and they vanish. Whirling around, the ghost light lingers in my vision. Stephen braces himself on one knee. His body heaves for breath, but he rises again to his full height. As he straightens his lapels and runs a hand through his dishevelled hair, my face twists, and I don't care if he sees it. If that had hit Liam, he would have been knocked out. He might have died without essence in his skin to block it.

Applause clatters around me and I drop back to my seat, Liam shaking beside me. Will a burst like that be enough for the Ritual or does it need to be sustained?

A hand rests on my shoulder. I jolt. Professor Hans stares at me and says, "Are you all right?"

I nod. I smooth my dress and smooth a smile on my face. My breaths are shallow and aching. A flicker of heat hits my mind but vanishes in an instant, as if chased away by the scent of spice and meat that flows through the hall with the arrival of servers carrying silver dishes. Liam drops his head to his hands, and mutters, "Power, all they see is power."

I pull my spine straight. Tonight, I might not be able to get my hands on the star crystal key, but maybe I don't have to.

I breathe. In and out, I breathe and perform motions of eating, and shaking hands, and speaking with the other guests all through the night with invisible strings controlling me. I wait until Adia has gone to mingle, and Stephen has left the room, and Geret is surrounded by his guests. Leaning into Professor Hans, I say, "The technique we've been working on. It can drain energy from more than just trees, right?"

Professor Hans' eyebrows quirk.

"People, powerstones?" I ask.

"Yes, if one so desires."

I can't break a star crystal with brute force, but I can drain the stone's energy with my death affinity. "We leave with the stones at midnight."

The mansion creaks with the night winds. The halls have quieted since everyone left the grounds. Liam and I lie still in the dark, without sleep, the cadence of Liam's breaths quick and tense. Every creak sends adrenaline through my veins.

For one minute, I shut my eyes. Breathing in through my nose, I hold it for five counts, and let it out through my mouth for five, counting over and over.

The door opens as the hour approaches, and Professor Hans slips into the room without a sound. I sit up, taking Liam's hand and tugging him off the bed.

Professor Hans' dark eyes glint with the starlight.

"Are you ready, Liam?" I ask, my mouth dry.

"Yes," Liam says. There's urgency in his voice. I put a hand on his shoulder. His neck is clammy with sweat. "I just want to get this over with."

"We will. We're going home," I say.

Liam steps in front of us into the dark hall. Wind haunts the mansion with howling whistles, and the dark wood doors lose their detailed carvings to the hold of inky black shadow. Liam leads us left into a corridor that wraps around the right side of the building. I check over my shoulder, clenching my teeth and tuning my ears to any sounds.

Running shaking hands through his shaggy blond hair, Liam stops outside a plain door at the end of the hall. He points at it and steps back, hands running down his face and feet shuffling. He squeezes his eyes shut.

The star crystal glimmers, illuminating the lock with a white-yellow glow. I fill and empty my lungs one last time and let the heat of my death affinity crawl through my bloodstream. My vessels burn like embers. I hover my fingers over the lock and a low thrum sounds as the air around my hand wavers. I press my fingers closer and they tingle with static. The yellow fades and new energy fills me, lively and bright.

The lock clicks.

Holding my hands out to steady myself, I pause. My senses are stimulated by the rush of blood inside me, the faint hush of Liam's breaths, and the spike of heat at my temples. I take the handle and open the door.

Inside, the room is dusty and smells of mildew. In the centre sits an iron chest.

Kneeling in front of it, I push open the lid. Liam lets out a shaky breath. On a black velvet cushion sits three clear, diamond-shaped crystals, glimmering with a pink sheen. At the centre sits the utanic Death stone.

I found the stones. We'll be coming to you soon.

My spine heats with Johanna's recognition, but my hands go cold as I stick the Revival stones in my pockets.

As I take the utanic Death stone, Professor Hans gasps behind me. I spin around.

Stephen's hand is clamped around Professor Hans' throat. My brother's eyes bleed red, lines of blistering blood vessels clawing away from them. He lifts Professor Hans off his feet and shoves him against the wall. Hans chokes, and flames flicker around his hands as he grasps at Stephen, but they never gain a hold.

I lunge forward. Before I can get to him, Stephen's palm burns red. Professor Hans' pale skin blackens under Stephen's touch and a pulse of energy thrusts me and Liam back. Liam screams, crumbling to the floor. His cry breaks into sobs and he slams his fist on the ground.

Tears blur my vision as I try to grab him, dropping the utanic Death stone, but Liam shoves me away.

"Why would you do that?" Liam's voice crashes through the room as Professor Hans' body hits the floor, his dark eyes still searching for his flame. Liam yells, "He loved you!" Heaving a breath, saliva drips from his mouth and tears spill down his face.

All I can do is let the horror of my little brother completely broken on the floor happen, my own body trembling, unable to breathe. He puts his hand out to Professor Hans, caressing the air around him, but there can't be an aura, nothing to grab—it's all been sent to the Hold. His fingers close around air and he's left, head bent, with nothing.

Stephen bends down in front of Liam.

Liam shrugs away from him, hyperventilating. "W-why? Why would y-you do that? You're sick."

Stephen's head tilts to the side, dark, dead eyes returning from beneath his burning-red sight. "I guess we'll have to bring him back from the Hold then," he whispers.

Liam reels back and grabs the utanic Death stone from the floor. "Fine, do it then," he screams. "I don't care anymore." His small hand clenches the serrated stone and jabs it to his arm. With gritted teeth and a wash of tears, he yanks it. A streak of blood slashes across his skin and pours over the Death stone.

Like a shock of electricity, I lunge and scoop Liam into my arms, pressing my hand to the flow of bright-red blood.

Come now! I need help. Everything's gone wrong.
WE'RE ALREADY ON OUR WAY.

I press my lips to Liam's forehead that still holds the circular mark as warmth gushes over my hand, slick. Holding back a gag and memories of my own skin breaking with my distress, my body shudders. I came too late. Both my brothers are broken by a Ritual that hasn't even been performed.

"What are you going to do now, Rin?" Stephen says.

Letting go of Liam, his blood dripping from my fingertips, I push him behind me. Heat billows inside me—from the Mind Fire, my blood, and my spirit. Red light swarms my vision and my blood vessels burst to life, carving red lines all along my skin. "Just stay back, Liam."

Horns burn on my head just as a blood-red tail whips out behind Stephen.

42

E L I O T E

I *won't hurt Brand. I take my fight to them. I'll get the stone. Close their prison.*

My body. It moves. Flashes of trees through blackness. Intangible. Not yet. I have to wait.

Each of my thoughts takes on a different quality, but all merging into one desperate tangle of desire and intention.

I take my fight to them.

That one's mine. The velvet one. Just wait.

Prison. Brand. I take my fight to them. I take my fight to them.

A tree trunk turns to ash, leaves flicker and burn out, a branch crackles and breaks away, leaving only darkness and my voice. Alyxia forgot her voice so long ago, but I refuse to forget mine.

I take my fight to them.

A prick on my finger. *My fight.*

Heat on my tongue. *My fight.*

I take my fight to them. I take my fight to Thea.

My voice sings one last time as the sense of body and pain fades.

I push the body as fast as it can go, trailing behind this team that will lead me right to the stone and to the Angel's Demon.

I won't hurt her.

If this body was familiar with an eye roll, her eyes would be at the back of her skull.

The world rushes by this body. The path we follow will soon merge with Thea's. I gather every tree Thea sees, every pond and marshy puddle, and construct her location, layering it with the information this body gives me. Our paths will cross in just a few minutes.

In the darkness of night, the stars shine bright and the body's eyes awaken. Each of these hédin children becomes mystical, not just flesh and essence. They are wrapped in colour, and my mind is taken by a strange energy. My thoughts run on paths that lead to memories. I've bound those memories with chains. I banish the energy with a shake of the head and focus on the path as we approach the mansion.

Thea's presence sinks into me, spreading the crackle of power through my mind. It is like an inferno, an undying flame.

I take my fight to them. I take my fight to them. I take my fight to them.

The thought screams at me and a pain shoots up the body's right shin.

Thea appears in the clearing ahead of us at the gate to the mansion. She is a scalding flame of Mind Fire as she disguises herself as Rin. Brand and all these children have such strong feelings for this girl, and she'll bring them all down.

I take my fight to them. I take my fight to Thea. I take my fight to them.

A suffocating ache pulses in this throat.

The thought is a mountain of force, pushing against me.

The team shouts out to Rin and they push themselves faster. The essenceless body's eyes finally catch on green energy billowing from the mansion. The utanic energy. A thrill sings through my mind. I push this body's feet faster to the door. The energy calls with a lilting melody, rousing my desire, fortifying my pursuit.

I won't hurt Brand. I take my fight to Thea. I take my fight to Thea.

The melody crashes like a wave in the ocean, extinguished by a cutting pain through the body's shins.

Thea. Thea. Thea.

The rushing thought wraps around me, around the body.

I take my fight to Thea.

The body is in line with Thea. The team surrounds her, their Rin. They console her, ask her questions, but I can't find their voices.

The sting of pain catches in both of the body's legs. It circulates in the blood. It ravishes the nerves leading up the torso. Her arm catches the flame of pain and her hand latches onto the *rahanaso* at her side. I grab at the ache, try to control it, and rein it in to bring it back to the numb nothingness. Banish this essenceless girl's mind.

The ring of metal against metal scrapes the air. A glint of starlight licks the blade. The body bashes into the Nytrue, throwing him to the side. The Emberstead girl wraps her team in a sheath of Mind Fire, pulling them back and clearing a path to Thea.

"Now, Eliote," the Emberstead girl yells.

With a straight line to Thea, the body bites her tongue and swallows her own blood.

Auras rake over me and the blood pools in my throat, cutting off the flow of air to my lungs and denying my brain the oxygen needed for Mind Fire to spread. Alyxia's cruel vice on my mind loosens. I let the pain in my body consume me. My muscles shake. Splintering pain claws in my shins. Stress fractures. Somewhere along the way, while I ran through Akinnera, my bones began to crack. I had to give in and wait. Now it's mine again.

My pain. No one will ever take it from me again. No one will use it against me. *You are the cause of my pain, and I'll be the last pain you ever feel, Alyxia.*

The unknown truth of my spirit begs for my acknowledgement through my blade, the spilling of blood, the release of a cruel life. I greet the truth with a pounding heart and the chorus of pain from every broken bone in my body. I blind my light with the power of darkness that Alyxia couldn't see in such a frail, naïve body, that I could never see.

I gag and spit my blood on the ground. "Get out of my head!" I scream—a strip of velvet torn down the middle—and thrust my blade at the illusion of Rin.

The blade plunges into her gut. My skin crawls and my heart

pounds as Rin's face vanishes replaced by a woman with pale skin, jet-black hair, and black eyes. Alyxia's hot vise dissipates from my mind. A billowing cloud of thick, black tar churns around Thea, clawing at her. Anguished faces appear in the cloud with yawning mouths and vacant eyes—silent screams into the dark.

Blood pours from Thea's stomach. I yank my blade from her flesh. Essence billows out of the gash. Powerful Emberstead essence with an unmatched affinity for Mind Fire—the one thing that marks Thea as Alyxia's most viable host. I'll drain it all from her so Alyxia has no more essence to manipulate, no more energy to dig her talons into other vulnerable minds.

I pull back and aim for the bitch's neck to cut off the head that Alyxia resides in.

Brand's firestone pistol cracks and the bullet slams into my blade, knocking it out of my hands. Her fist collides with my face. I hit the ground hard.

"You can't kill her!" Brand screams at me. Her eyes are like blades, rimmed in red, and her teeth are bared. A light-peach aura wraps around her, wispy and gauzy, dragging around her and swarming over Thea. Tears stream from Brand's eyes as she pins me down. "Killing Thea will just release Alyxia to find another host. Thea doesn't deserve to die like this."

My ears ring, blood courses through me, flushing my cheeks. I drag breath through my butchered throat. Johanna. She would try to take Johanna, and there's no knowing if Johanna could resist Alyxia. I glare at Brand's eyes as they sting through me and jerk my head in a nod.

Thea clutches her bleeding wound, blood pouring over her hand and onto the gravel path. An explosion of heat like a solar flare bursts out of Thea. Brand and the team are thrown back.

I tumble over the ground, smacking my cheek on the gravel, but the star crystal in my vest takes most of the impact for once today.

Thea sprints to the door of the mansion, but like a shock of lightning, Brand closes the gap in a second. She aims her pistol at Thea's ear. She squeezes the trigger. Thea deflects with Mind Fire before the bullet leaves the chamber and Brand's arm is thrust backward. Brand sprints around Thea and throws her fist at her. With Mind Fire, Thea hurls rocks at Brand's head, but Brand dodges all her attacks with deft speed. Jeff backs her, manipulating gravity around Thea, pulling her feet one way and her body in another. Still, Thea's mind corrects her course. Niko, in beast form, takes any chance he can to thrash his claws at her.

My feet are like lead and my blood is boiling acid as I stare at Thea—Alyxia controlling Thea like she controlled me. Breath expels from my lungs, and I heave another, my vision clouding and narrowing in on her.

Ace grabs my arm.

Johanna is already sprinting into the mansion. "We need to get you and Liam out of here," she screams. Lance leaps in the air and soars over the fight after her.

"Come on, Eliote. We have to move." Ace's face replaces my focus.

His eyes are wide and his mouth grimaces as he clutches my face with shaking hands. My tears match his, but my body is in so much pain I can't do anything about it.

"El," Ace sobs. His ocean crashes over me. "El, we'll find Liam and get you both out of here."

I push a breath into my lungs. All of this has to stop—the Revival, Alyxia's control. She tampers with innocent lives, all for power. That's all the flow of essence is for, and I don't need it. I take Ace's hand and stumble with him into the mansion.

A crash from deep in the mansion shakes the walls and cracks split the tiles beneath my feet. We keep running, following the tremors. At the end of a long, dark hall, Rin stands over Stephen, the scarlet glow of death spilling from both of them. The doorway behind Rin is demolished and rubble is scattered around them. Rin bends and grabs Stephen by the collar. The muscles in her arms strain her skin, her veins bleed bright red. She lifts him off the ground and flings him like a doll into the far wall. He bursts through the wood and stone, and the entire building shudders.

Rin whirls around. Her bright eyes flick from me and the others back into the room with the destroyed wall. She stretches out her arms and a boy rushes into them. Liam.

Teal haze drifts around him. It flows through the destruction and tangles around me—an ocean breeze, briny air. Through it, silver lights make my heart shake. In his eyes is gleaming essence. It's steadfast, cellular essence, the essence that fills Rin to the very core, but this is just in his eyes.

I rush over to him, swallowing the cry of anguish with a fresh taste of blood in my mouth as pain strikes through my shins. Grabbing his shoulder, I turn him out of Rin's arms and stare into the brilliant essence in his eyes. I fall to my knees with shaking hands hovering over his eyes while tears spill from my own.

Gasping, Liam's eyes fill with tears too.

"It-it's in your eyes," I whisper.

A smile flickers over Liam's face as he touches two fingers to my forehead. Even as my heartbeats shake me, I am paralyzed, transfixed by the sweetest aura I've ever seen.

Liam stares into my eyes and says, "Yours is green, like starlight."

A sob and a laugh bubble out of me, but it turns sour as black edges around my eyes. My body teeters and my breaths are slowing. Muscles giving way, my hands drop from Liam.

"Eliote," Rin says and catches me. "El, you're going to be okay. We're going to get you out of here."

Her icy fingers brush my face, and her demon eyes sparkle above me. I brought my fight with Alyxia to Thea, and I won. But I can't fight anymore.

43

LANCE

I CAN'T FIND THE SOURCE SHAKING MY CORE. The light in the hall is multi-coloured, green and red and blue and silver from the crackle of electricity around my hands. Every part of me is frozen; I just stare at Eliote passed out in Rin's arms.

Cradling her, Rin shakes Eliote. "Stay with me, okay?" She pats her face and Eliote's eyes flutter open.

"I'm still here, chicky," she mutters.

Red light disperses through the settling dust around the hole at the other end of the hall. Rubble crunches and Stephen's dark form appears through the hole.

"Rin, I'm not against a fight, but you could have asked nicely," Stephen says, his voice sardonic and lilting. "Look, you've put another hole in a wall, in our revered ancestor's home." He tsks.

I duck as a fireball flies past my head at Stephen. Ace follows Johanna's fire with shards of ice that whistle as they cut through the air.

Rin holds both Eliote and Liam close to her chest as the mansion trembles again, pieces of plaster crashing down around them. Rin looks frantically around her, eyes like a beacon in the night. I find my breath.

The most vulnerable people in this situation are in her arms right now. This is why I chose the Guardian path—to right my wrongs, to protect people, not hurt them. My unchecked essence killed a girl I loved and now two hédin without enhancements are in front of me in the midst of a battle for power. They are my priority.

I drop to my knees and reach for Eliote.

"No." Rin's voice is a shock, amplified by her death affinity. She holds Eliote tighter.

"Rin, I can get them out safely," I say.

Lower lip trembling, Rin turns to Liam and runs her hand down his face. She looks back at Eliote and shakes her awake. "I got them into this mess." Tears well in her eyes and dissipate into vapour between us. "I did this," she whispers. "I came back to the academy."

I take her face in my hands, forcing her sorrow-blossom eyes to look at me. "Then finish this. Take care of Stephen, and I'll take care of them." Rin's lips part but I shake my head. "You have to trust me. I can get them out of here without anyone seeing me."

A sob breaks from Rin's throat. She plants a kiss and her tears on Eliote and Liam and then loosens her grip on both. I pull Eliote onto my back. "You've got to hold on, Eliote. That's all you have to do. Hold on tight."

Her thin arms cinch around my neck. Heavy heartbeats hit my back.

"You can trust him, Liam," Rin says. She meets my eyes. "I trust him." Her heavy breaths hit me and then her lips. I lean into her, my heart swelling and my throat constricting because her passion strangles me. Her power weighs on me and the taste of her is sweet.

Rin pulls away as Stephen bolts into the hall, a haze of energy around him, and sprints toward us. His eyes are trained on a jagged, jet-black stone on the ground with blood dripping off of it. He snatches the stone and grabs Rin by the neck, smashing her into the wall.

I pull Liam into my arms. A cry rips out of me and I flex my hand. Electricity strikes at Stephen, but the energy leaps back to my hand without any effect.

"Go!" Rin screams, pushing herself out of the new hole in the wall. She pulls back her leg and whips it at Stephen. A brilliant-blue wing bursts to life, blocking her foot. Stephen's chuckle electrifies the air.

Clutching Liam to my chest, I turn and sprint. I take air into my lungs, acknowledging the space it creates, the strength it gives my muscles, the way it mimics the rush of my essence. The more I focus on my breath and the static inside me, the more space I create—infinite and free.

My hands disappear, and my clothes, and Eliote's legs dangling around me. My space, the space that I take up in this world, has expanded around Liam and Eliote as the atoms and charges making their bodies become linked to mine. Eliote gasps, peeking over my shoulder at an invisible Liam.

"Whatever happens, and I mean *whatever* happens, do not let go," I say.

Breathing long, even breaths, I let the flow of my essence be the cadence of my feet.

"Wait," Eliote rasps behind me. "Someone else is out there."

"Geret," Liam says. "He'll see us even if we're invisible."

I keep running. "Just trust me."

Focus, Lance. You can do this.

During the trial match, Ace tried to hit me, but his hand went right through me. If I can keep my invisibility wrapped around all of us, then anything anyone can throw at us will go right through.

Focus. Stay calm. I can do this.

I quicken my pace through the central hall and turn into the foyer, running straight past two Ironskins coming toward us.

In the open doorway to the mansion stands a man in a red suit. Hot air gusts through the long room, rippling the water in the shallow pool. He stands with his back to us, hands clasped behind him, watching as our friends battle against Thea. The small portion of the front courtyard is warped by gravity and firelight flowing around his shadowed form.

I take a step, breaths loud and shaky, Eliote's arms are like vises crushing my chest. But I keep moving. Geret turns. Facing us, red light spills from his eyes, adding to the distortion of the physical world around him. My heart pounds in my chest, but its temper is distant. I keep moving. I expand the reach of calm inside me until it connects with the tiles beneath my feet, the stone walls, the wooden rafters. The difference between the solid states and the water—even the air around me—increases, exciting my essence.

Geret's face twists in a frown and he takes a step forward. "You cannot hide from me," he says, his voice like a ghost song.

"I'm not trying to."

With a flash of red light, Geret sprints toward us. He pulls back his arm, his palm glowing red, and thrusts it at me. The contact radiates through me, but static ripples through all of us, and Geret's hand passes straight through our bodies. Eliote gasps. I sprint as fast as I can to the open door. Spreading my wings wide, pounding my feet, I leap into the air, thrusting my wings as hard as I possibly can.

I stagger through the air in the manipulated gravitational field, straining my wings again and again to gain height. Pain shoots through the tendons and muscles connecting my wings to my back and I let out a cry, still moving them through the repetitive motion.

Levelling out, I release the space around me, and with it, the invisibility. The wind beats my face and the heat envelops me.

The rush of my essence is waning and my vision blurs in and out. Eliote shrieks as we plummet to the tops of the trees. Twigs scrape at my exposed arms, and I gasp for breath, straining my wings one more time, getting high enough to see the ship. I angle down again, fanning out my wings to slow our momentum, but not enough and I hit the ground hard. My legs give way and I tumble over, grasping Liam's head to keep it from hitting the ground. The muscles in my back pulse with dull, aching pain.

"I–Is everyone okay?" I ask as Liam scrambles out from under me.

"Yeah," he says through a breath.

Eliote rolls over and pushes herself off the ground and nods, her hair quivering around her face, and hands digging into the ground for support.

"Good." I let my head rest on the damp ground, one wing twitching behind me and my chest heaving with each breath.

A tremor shakes the ground, and I cringe. I really hope this was all worth it, that this was the right thing to do instead of staying to fight alongside the others, because now I can't fight. My wings can barely move, and my essence is depleted, running in choppy streams of static up and down my arms. With a spasm through my wing and a jolt of essence, thunder rolls overhead and rain sprinkles down on us, cooling my skin.

JOHANNA

MY FLAME CLIMBS THE GLACIER OF RIN'S MIND. Fire and ice vanish, leaving only steam in my head, a haze, a lens. It alerts all my senses and awakens my limbs. My heart pounds in unison with Rin's as thick clouds roll overhead, blacking out the stars. Energy spikes through the slick, humid air. Ace, Rin, and I face Stephen, our backs to the demolished mansion. Beyond the mansion, Alyxia is right on our asses.

Mom said it was my choice.

With everything that I thought was impossible or ridiculous, that made me feel like I was going crazy—wraiths, Soul Tethers, just wanting to have my friend back—I was right about it all. I had to believe what I was seeing and know it was true.

Rin turns to the mansion, tears streaking her face, taking in the relic of her people with anguish in her eyes. I knew she was my Soul Tether before I ever doomed our fate. It's like a tune that's been playing in my spirit for a long time, and it has finally met my ears so my mind can memorize it. Spirits already know what they are. Our spirits and minds will always be tethered but our bodies, our essence, can't stay that way. Right now, I'm here with her. I will protect her at all costs. When it comes time to break the tether, I'll let go. I have to. Alyxia has ravaged the Karess for far too long. She's hurt our friends, our families, our lineages. The Revival will do the same.

Stephen stands a few metres away from us, the utanic Death stone clenched in his hand. "Rin, give me the Revival stones, take your little friends, and leave." He shrugs, tossing the bloody stone in the air and catches it. "Or else someone's going to get hurt."

Thunder claps, sending a tremor through the ground. Something crashes into the smouldering flame behind me, sending sparks into the air. I clench my fists. They're gritty with dried, salty sweat. I take a step forward.

"I'd like to see you try," I yell to Stephen over the wind, raising my chin with a taunting smile on my lips.

Rin snaps her head to me and yanks my arm. "What are you doing?"

Blood rushes hot inside me. "I'm not leaving you."

Her face is inches from mine, blotchy red and wet. "Take this and get the hell out of here," she says through gritted teeth, slipping a Revival stone into my hand.

"You can't get rid of us, Rin," Ace says.

Stephen's burning eyes flash silver-blue. "Shouldn't be too hard," he says, his casualty sickening.

"Holy . . . I thought Stephen only had the death affinity,"

Ace says. He shakes out his hands and bounces on the balls of his feet.

"He changed his lifeline code," Rin says.

She grunts and releases her nails from my skin. Swiping the tears from her face and taking a long breath, she presses another Revival stone into Ace's hand. "I don't want to fight you, Stephen," Rin says.

"Ah, right, you want to become a Guardian." He takes a few sauntering steps forward, rolling the utanic Death stone in his hands, letting the blood blot his skin. "Just let the world keep doing what it's doing, not making real change. That's what you want."

"There's another way. We can free everyone imprisoned in the Hold by breaking the barrier and letting them move into the Beyond," Rin says.

"And what changes here on the Karess? Nothing. Alyxia will always be out there if we don't stop her."

"You're doing exactly the same thing she's doing, trying to control people into fighting for you."

Stephen stops. The mocking look that he uses to look down on his sister, falls. The tendons in his neck strain and the blue life affinity flickers in his eyes. "I'm nothing like Alyxia."

With a pulse of energy, a blinding light floods the mansion grounds. I throw up my hand to block my eyes. When I lower it, Stephen has doubled—one flesh body that now bleeds death-affinity red through the eyes, one pure-blue energy that mirrors every one of Stephen's movements like a shadow.

Breaths become heavy in my chest. There's something off about the spirit double. I've never seen a projection like this, never even seen Rin project her own life affinity wings, but Rin is an entirely new entity when she uses her life affinity. She is pure force. This double of Stephen is a fragile imitation of Rin's power.

"The utanic Death stone. Get it," Rin says and locks her eyes on Stephen. "I know how to take him down. I just need you to buy me time until I can activate my life affinity and get close enough to him."

"I'll get the stone," Ace says. "Why can't you just activate the life affinity now?"

"Because I'm too fucking pissed off."

My essence surges as a pulse of energy hits the air around Rin, bringing forth a glowing tendril of red energy. Ace and I step back as the tendril writhes and takes shape, encircling Rin. Sharp spikes protrude from it, a leaf of blood-red sprouts from it. A flower blooms out of the energy, then another, and another. The glow of demon horns crowning her head fades as the spiny tendrils of rillia spin all around her.

"Sometimes I wonder how we could ever be related," Rin says. "But I finally get it. You're Father's son. You thought you were like Mother, that she understood you. But you and Father are both too obsessed with your missions, making huge changes, that you neglect the people around you. You're Father's son and I'm Mother's daughter."

"This is for all of us, Rin. I'm not going to let you stand in our way any longer," Stephen says. A three-pronged tail flings out behind him in unison with ethereal wings from his double. The red glow in his eyes eats away at his pale flesh with streaks of red blood vessels expanding from his eyes, inky black filling in the whites. But Rin's eyes fill to full capacity with red energy and every blood vessel in her body burns red. Heat spills around her and my skin becomes alive. Drinking it in, I flex my fingers and let my essence flow in a heady rush. It's violent inside me, bolstered by Rin's energy wrapping around me.

Drawing a deep breath, I let my head fall back. Plates of fire armour shift over my body, clinking into place. Flexing my fingers, five blades burst into existence above my head, illuminating the dark night, and reflecting off the pond.

Ace is unmoving, eyes focused on Stephen. His hands twitch at his sides, ice frosting over his skin.

"Ace—"

"I'll get the stone." The ice on his hand travels down his leg, making a shimmering line through the damp grass, over the pond to Stephen. Above the line of ice, the world is frozen. Water in the air freezes, the grass is still, and the pond has no ripples. Fuck. While we all whipped out our energy dicks preparing for this fight, Ace made something productive—a time void line. It's like the one he created last year when we did the pillar challenge, except this one is smaller, and so much more controlled. He turns his head to me and a smile flashes on his face. He disappears for a second and reappears with the utanic Death stone in his hand.

"Run, Ace," Rin says as Stephen dashes forward.

Ace bolts just as Rin and Stephen's energies crash together, sending a shockwave through the clearing.

I send forth flames to engulf two boulders. They tear out of the earth, and I hurl them at Stephen and his double. They're obliterated by Stephen's demon tail even as he engages in combat with Rin. His eyes flare and their bones clash. Rin's vine spins like a sun at her back. It stretches and lashes out at Stephen just as his tail protects him.

I gather the pieces of rock with my mind. Focusing, pressing through the structure, the pieces explode into sharp shards. My mind burns and syncs with Rin's. The connection is deep, unwavering in its strength.

Without even transferring a thought, Rin jumps back and shifts the ring of thorns and blossoms in front of her. I fling the boulder's shards in a torrent to trap Stephen and his angel. They deflect the shards, flinging them in all directions, but Rin's death-affinity projection blocks them as they're flung back at us. I sweep my hands in front of me and the great swords take aim.

Someone crashes into me from behind just as I send the blades toward Stephen. I jolt forward, smack the ground, and tumble over myself. In a series of earth quaking blows, my blades decimate the ground, all missing their mark. I roll over, metal at the back of my throat and mud sticking my hairs to my face. Ace lies crumpled on his side a few feet away. I scramble over to him.

"Are you okay?" I yell at him.

He grimaces as blood spills out the side of his mouth. He clutches the Death stone to his chest, and yells, "Watch out!" Whipping his arm out, he sends the pond water in a wave over us.

A woman bursts through the wave, brilliant, electric-blue light spilling from her eyes. She lands between us and slams her fist to the ground. The damp earth squelches and rips open. I tumble into the crater but let my momentum roll me back onto my feet, and I slam my ember-plated fist to her face. Her head whips to the side and Ace clobbers her with a mallet of ice.

An explosion of red and blue light paints the sky with a deafening crash. Rin screams and hits the ground hard, just a few metres away. I jolt toward her, but the woman leaps out of the hole. I send fire to my feet, grab Ace, and propel us out of the hole after her. We drop to the ground, but the woman with life affinity eyes isn't alone anymore. Next to her is a man, eyes burning with the death affinity and his body wrapped in projected energy. It twists and darkens into armour with a horned helmet and hooved boots.

Piecing together images and names I picked up through the Mind Fire connection with Rin, my heart quivers inside me. Geret and Adia. I grit my teeth as my body thrums with heat, my armour singeing the drenched grass. Steam billows around me.

Adia's light flares and drains out of her eyes, revealing silver irises as a full spirit double dashes forward.

I throw my fist at Adia's spirit double. It collides with a pulse of energy. I block her fist, avoiding a fatal blow. As I stagger under her force, cracks creep down my armour. I can't waste my essence to seal them, because Geret is moving in on Ace. Ace kneels on the ground, gripping his ribs.

Rin, we can't beat them, but you can. The real you. The full you.

NO, NO WAY. NOT NOW. I DON'T KNOW HOW TO BRING YOU BACK. AND IT WILL UNLOCK THE DUAL AFFINITY STATE. THAT'S WHAT THEY WANT.

You'll know what to do!

HOW DO YOU KNOW?

In one motion, I clamp one hand around Adia's double, and thrust my other hand toward the real Adia. I throw the double back and pull Adia forward, my mind lining them up with a blaze of heat through my head. Adia and her spirit double crash together and reintegrate. I hurl her into Geret. He catches Adia like she's a fly and rights her on her feet.

I gasp for breath. Adia's spirit double moved on its own, Stephen's doesn't, it copies him. It's as if Adia projects her life affinity with her spirit energy, making a sentient double, while Stephen's spirit remains inside him with his death affinity. A spirit affinity must make a person's spirit viable when separated from body and mind. Rin is aligned with both life and death spirit affinities. They'll be able to merge if I die, and then the Revival will happen. But maybe if she projects one, separating the two aspects of her spirit, they won't integrate. She said she needs her life affinity to defeat Stephen. It has to be her death affinity then.

Release your death affinity in a projection like Adia.

All I get in return is a gale of ice through my mind.

Ace is on his feet and the air takes a frigid bite that sizzles over my armour. Ice shards fill the air, rising out of the pond, solidifying from the moisture in the grass, and even descending from the clouds, unveiling the stars. Ace's body shakes as he directs every shard's deadly point at the demonic man and the angelic woman. They speed toward them, slicing the air in a symphony of sharp whistles.

The ice bombards Geret and Adia, and Ace drops back to his knees, planting his hands on the ground. Ice froths around him, and crawls over Adia and Geret. They thrash their arms, and the ice cracks and shards fall off them. But Ace dips his head and strains his arms forward, regrowing the ice all around them.

I sprint for Adia. The ice turns to slush below my feet and sprays in all directions. I leap and smash my fist to the peach scar on her face, demolishing the ice. Adia sails back and crashes into the mansion.

You have to release your death affinity.
I DON'T KNOW HOW!

A gust of wind lashes at my face. Geret's arm slams into my side. The force shatters my armour and the shards curl into wisps of smoke as I slam into the ground.

The horns of his helmet loom over me, black except for a dull red glow around the edges. The stars twinkle around my vision. I push into the ground and slide back, my clothes dragging through the mud. My muscles pinch and my hair catches underneath me. Ace charges at Geret and slashes an ice sword at him, but Geret whips his arm behind him, smashing Ace back.

Rin.

My mind is cold, my essence trickles through me, no more than a thread. I can't call her.

"Release it now!" I scream as Geret raises his arm, a spear growing from his armour, and ice clawing at his back. The ice splinters and shards rain down on my face. I thrust my palm out with a blaze of fire. It flickers around Geret. He raises his spear and thrusts it down at me. "Now!"

I throw myself away from it, but the blade rips through my shirt and slices through my side. I shriek, slap at the spear, throw flames all around me, as hot tears stream down my face and blood spills from me. I thrust my hands in front of me, making a plate of fire. Geret pulls back again. The tip of the spear collides with the projection. A splinter skitters through the plane. Death burns in Geret's eyes. He grits his teeth. My arms tremble, but I push against him, screaming, my throat becoming raw, and my vision blurring.

A roar bursts from Geret and the tip of the spear splits my projection and plunges into my rib cage. It rips through skin, lacerating my muscles and nerves. Bone snaps and my body convulses around it, bringing more flesh around the blade to be shredded. Light bursts behind my eyes. Pain grows into every cell, like it's all I've ever known. I slap my hands around the spear, but my arms can't move it. I groan, forcing every muscle to move, but nothing responds.

Geret snarls above me as my essence tangles around his spear like smoke.

"No!" The scream is distorted, wavering and pitched low, but Rin's voice echoes all around it, rough and bitter. She collides with Geret in a blur of red. She pulls her fist back and slams it into his armour. She slams her fist into him again and again. With each hit, my vision fades. I keep my eyes trained on Rin, fighting the dark.

Rin is the only light in my eyes as I lose touch with every sensation, with everything my body has known. I can't access my memory—all I know is Rin. She cracks Geret's armour. She pulls back her fist, but he strikes her face. She lurches back into Stephen. Thrashing against his grasp as Geret pushes off the ground, she tangles her rillia projection around Stephen and kicks Geret back down.

I blink.

Strikes ring out and Rin screams. Hit after hit, the fight vibrates the ground beneath my aching body.

My eyelids flutter open and Geret is beside me, still, his chest still rising with breath, but unconscious. Did she hit his weak spot?

Rin's freezing hand caresses my face. Is it cold, or am I cold?

Slick blood pools over my tongue and tears stream down Rin's face.

"You can't leave me, you can't, please." Her voice cracks and she collapses over me.

"Don't . . . " My lips are stiff. Words gurgle through the blood. My throat spasms. "Don't do something fucking stupid. Finish this. Trust . . . "

Her hands are cold. That's what she's always been to me. Bitter cold, but calm to my flame. She grips my shoulders.

Dark taps her hands away.

"You . . . don't need the girl who . . . says you're not enough."

Dark takes my voice.

"Johanna!" Rin screams. "I–I need you. I don't know what to do. Please don't . . . "

Dark breaks through the light.

The break digs deep, searching for the last bit of essence to sever, the last bit of neural activity.

"Jo—"

The dark takes her voice from me.

I'll find it again.

45

R I N

MY HANDS TANGLE IN HER BLOOD, in her curls. The break in my heart claws down my core; it burns through my flesh, bleeds hot, cauterizes, and fills. Something is filling inside me with energy. It rushes and builds. The break tears Johanna away from me, further and further away. I grab her. Her heat still lashes out at me, but the break is still breaking, and I keep filling.

My heart beats in lagging strokes that sting my veins. My skin and bone and muscle pulse. The break pulls a cry from my lungs. Energy wracks me from the inside. Violet light spills with my tears.

The sense of my body is useless to me, and the sense of time is even more of a hopeless burden. The ache in my stomach, the plummeting sensation, grows long through the years of my life, connecting death after death, and loss after loss in violet ribbon.

My essence crackles. My body is quiet, but my mind is terror and heat.

Johanna's eyes follow me in death, watching me as my whole being rests in the chaos.

"Rin," Ace screams from behind me.

My body jolts, but I can't turn. A wash of tears falls hot down my face.

Pain slices through my weak spot. My jaw drops, and breaths sputter through me. Trickles of blood soak through my clothes. The sticky hot smears over my senses and the pain cranks through me. I turn, my body tilting and jerking as I right myself.

Stephen's demon tail hovers in front of him, the middle tip pointed down, dripping my blood onto the utanic Death stone. Liam's blood stains his hands, the crimson glow stains his eyes.

The Revival stone in my pocket vibrates, sending pulses through me until it rips through the fabric and hovers above the utanic Death stone. The Revival stone I gave Johanna flies through the air. Ace holds the stone I gave him in both hands. Silver light fans around it as he attempts to manipulate the time around it, but the stone shudders, breaks through his fingers and collides with the other two and the Death stone. They spin, clacking together, wind stirring my hair.

Voices ring out all around me as the stones spin faster, cutting out a dark void. A tear in reality, connecting this world to the Hold. The ground shakes as the voices whisper and cry, rising to the sky and down deep inside me. Pain explodes through me. Light rains down over the mansion, dyeing the sky an otherworldly, inky violet, and paints the clouds lavender.

An image flashes in my mind of a battlefield. Sensations grip my consciousness—the fever after a death-affinity strike, the sting of a blade, the tremulous ache for power, the darkest, most ultimate despair. It all crashes through the void like a tsunami, and I am only a small barrier between it and the rest of the world.

You don't need the girl who says you're not enough.

I claw at my head, doubling over as the power expels from me and the cries fill my mind. This power in me is all-consuming. It is not a stealthy ghost syphoning my energy, or a hungry beast lashing out. It is both of those things. It wants and it knows and it reaches for everything. It knows every hurt life can bring and every sweet lie of death. A balance of self-preservation and self-sacrifice that cancels out, leaving only self. I don't know this energy though; it's made its peace when I have yet to find mine.

As purple light ripples off me, it takes a flowing path up over my head, down through my heart, wrapping behind me, under my feet and back up to my heart. As it rushes through my body, I sink into it. I search for the energy that first made me feel alive, the energy I unlocked to save my brother from rifle fire in a grocery store, that grew as I rekindled my relationship with Johanna. I take it back. All the power my pain can give me, all the energy I put into loathing, I give that up. Johanna already did it for me—for all of us.

Red light rips out of me. The world thunders and the Revival stones and the utanic Death stone stop spinning. They streak past my head. The black void snaps shut with an explosion of force and in its wake stands my death-affinity spirit double holding the stones. She glistens. She is power and might and anger and I love her.

The filling from the Soul Tether finally stops. My body teems with energy. The skin on my arms crackles, midnight-blue energy spilling over them. It sparks and thrums, and as I move my arms, a noise fills the air around me like the echoes of a thousand voices. My entire body has transformed into energy, not a projection, not an embodied glow that spills through the slits of my eyes. It is as full and opaque as the energy of my death-affinity double. It is true to me and knits my weak spot back together.

"I can still do it," Stephen says. His voice grates on my nerves like brittle shards of glass. It pulls on my heart and I turn to him. "I can still integrate the affinities and open the path myself." Violet light flickers in his eyes. He heaves a breath, face twisting as he clenches his teeth. "I can . . . " A drop of blood trickles from his nose.

I hold out my hands to him. "Stephen, please, we can break the Hold another way. We can stop fighting, please, you can't take this strain."

Taking an unsteady step, the light flickering out of him in jagged purple streaks, he says, "I've given up my life for this." His steps stop. My heart beats heavily, sending ripples through the energy of my body. My breaths freeze. "And now my life is going to end." The serrated edge in his voice dulls, leaving behind a dead monotone. All the light vanishes from his eyes.

My flesh body and my essence have melded so closely that as shivers shake me, the earth quakes. "Stephen?" I say. "What—"

Ace stands behind him. "You really think you're going to win today, Rinnaya?"

Rinnaya? Ace has never called me by my full name. He knows I don't like it. Alyxia. She's caught them both.

Adia's face appears in the rubble of the mansion, her eyes silver as she climbs over a fallen beam. "You really do keep learning in this life," she says. "I thought it would be easier to control the essenceless Luminee girl, but it turns out strong essence and a weak mind is actually the key to manipulating people."

Emerging from the shadows around the mansion, Brand, Niko, and Jeff approach like sleepwalkers, their faces drained of colour and their eyes trained on me. My death spirit steps to me and takes my hand. The shake in my knees echoes in the pulsing grip between our hands.

Thea skirts around Brand. Her dark hair flows in the hot wind. Scarlet blood drenches her clothes, and essence escapes a wound on her stomach in tufts of silver. She looks into Brand's eyes with her head cocked to the side and a cruel smile stretching her face.

Snapping her eyes toward me, Thea says, "Our meeting was so short in the Vein. It's wonderful to see that you've grown a little since you cowered in the dark." Her eyelashes flutter as she folds her hands gracefully.

My team and my brother stand in a line behind her, flames flickering from the mansion and the ice and slush under their feet. I can't move. I try to keep my thoughts quiet, or loud, I don't know how to keep her out of my own head. There's no indication that she's trying, but I can't let her get the chance.

"I would love to kill you right now. It would pose such a rewarding challenge. But our dear Thea won't allow it." Her voice is too sweet and too twisted, like a bad wine. "I will just take the stone."

She thrusts her hand out, and a flare of orange sparks around the utanic Death stone. Thea pulls it toward her and takes a step. As her foot touches down on the damp grass, the ring of light surrounding me wraps around it. The Death stone drops to the ground with a thud and Thea drops her hand. Her body sways in my aura of red and blue. A breath seeps from her lips, like it's been stuck in her lungs for so long that it's had to fight through debris to be released. Her eyes relax, spilling tears down her face.

I breathe. Bringing my awareness to my feet, all four of them, and all four hands, I take steps to Thea. The grass wrinkles underfoot. "Thea?" I say, my voice doubled, but quiet.

She touches trembling fingers to her tears. "You . . . you'll never beat her on the Karess."

My team still stands like sentinels behind her, unmoving and unblinking. Except for Stephen. His lips twitch and a croak escapes with a breath. "Rin," is the only word that comes out.

Both my spirits kneel by Thea as she sinks to the ground. Embers flicker in her eyes, but a sweet air battles that cruel smile from finding her lips. "Alyxia's spirit and essence are in the Lesser Worlds. That"—she shudders—"that's where you fight her."

"Can you get her out of my friends?" I ask.

Thea licks the tears from her lips and turns her head. Eyes falling on Brand, she clutches her chest. "I think so. But please . . ." Her shoulders hunch around her bloody hands cradled over her heart. Squeezing her eyes closed, she whispers, "Please tell Daalza I never stopped loving her. That I'm sorry."

"She never stopped either," I whisper back.

A moan mixed with a cry bursts out of Thea. She pushes off the ground, bashing me out of the way and sprints to the trees. A surge of heat is left in her wake and my team falls to the ground. Ace catches himself on one knee, panting and clutching his side.

Red death affinity energy smoulders through Stephen's body, shaking him and blazing in his eyes. Staggering forward with one shoulder slumping, and drawing hissing breaths through his teeth, he lunges for the utanic Death stone.

His tail lashes out at me. I spring back just before it demolishes the ground I was standing on. He grabs at the stone in my death spirit's hands. She cradles it and backsteps with sorrow on her face. She just keeps moving away from him, her footsteps light, and her nature bleeding gentleness into the air.

I shoot toward him, faster than ever, and grab his arm. I yank it and fling him behind me. He sails through the air, and I sprint to catch up. I jump, sending a shock wave out around me and cratering the earth, and slam my foot into Stephen's flailing body. He crashes through the trees, and I dash after him. Grabbing him by the shirt, I pull him out of the splintered wood.

Through the trees, and across the marsh, Ace stands in front of the dilapidated mansion. He nods his head to me, a field of ice surrounding him.

I fling Stephen as hard as I can back to Ace. Sprinting across the marshy land, I reach Stephen just as Ace encases Stephen's body in solid ice. I lunge forward and wrap my hand behind Stephen's neck.

"W-what are you doing?" Stephen's voice is hushed and broken. Tears glisten in his eyes and turn to mist as the heat of his death affinity burns them away.

"She knew we couldn't all be together again. That's just the way it has to be."

My fingers prickle and are drawn to the skin outlining the smooth patch of his weak spot on the back of his neck. Stephen's death affinity calls to the blue spirit energy in my veins. I grip his neck and violet light spills around us. The red drains from Stephen's eyes and tears slip down his cheeks. Head falling to the side, his breaths become long and easy as he is forced into sleep.

The young man I once knew appears in his relaxed face. I can almost hear the electropulse pounding through invisible echobuds as he sleeps. My fingers trail down his neck and fall limp at my side. The light of my life spirit drains away from my skin. I draw in breath as my bones quiver inside me without the strength of my spirit.

Ace comes up beside me, bent and clutching his side. The ringing silence gives space for his footfalls on the damp grass to catch in my ears.

"Rin," he whispers. "Are you . . . " He shakes his head, abandoning words and taking me into his arms as tears stream from my eyes.

I gasp for breath into his shoulder, locking my eyelids tight against Stephen, against Johanna, and our unconscious team. Another breath comes, pushing the first out. They come fast and bitter. I suck them in and cough them out as my body shakes, and my blood stings inside me. A wave of heat passes over my neck and my stomach lurches. Ace gathers my hair as I bend over and barf into the grass at Stephen's icy feet.

Ace presses his head to mine and rubs my back.

A moan escapes from my strangled throat. I pound my fist on the ground. My body hasn't left behind the rushing sensation of my energy coming back to me from the Soul Tether. Even though I've split myself in two, it's still too much. It's restless. Digging my fingers into my knees, I sit in a haze of vibrating skin and worn-out senses, my vision speckled with dark spots.

Ace shakes my shoulder. "Look," he says.

Across the singed and trampled grass, fields of ice, puddles and craters of exposed earth, is my death-affinity spirit. She is brilliant red energy confined to my female body shape. Her hair is like fire flickering around her as her wide eyes examine her glowing hand. She trails her fingers down her arm with a gentle smile. She stares up at the mansion as the sun rising behind it bathes it in a golden sheen, and red and pink streaks fill the sky. A flare-wing moth flutters around her. It flits about her head and down her body and up her arm.

My stomach sinks as my death spirit's brilliant eyes trail the moth to Johanna. She rushes over to her. On her knees, she lifts Johanna's head onto her lap, the moth resting on Johanna's chest. Tears drip off my chin and my death spirit picks stray curls out of Johanna's face and splays them over her knees. Her light warms Johanna's face as she runs her fingers over her freckled cheeks and bends over, pressing her lips to Johana's forehead.

My eyes flare with blue light for just a second, and my death spirit's eyes find me. The force of her stare draws me forward. Death and life are two sides of one existence, one being, and two sides of one jint prison. The Hold. It repelled Adia, her life spirit energy. It won't repel death. I shuffle on hands and knees.

"I can save her," I say, pushing up to stand.

"What? Rin, no you can't." Ace grabs my arm, but I pull away, drawn to my spirit and all the pain and love possessed in the gleaming form. "Angel Palm will kill you, Rin." His voice cracks and he bolts in front of me. "I won't let you sacrifice yourself for her."

I stop, hands heavy at my sides, breaths finding their way into my lungs at an easy pace, clearing my eyes. "Don't worry. I don't need to sacrifice all of me."

I sit down beside Johanna, and in front of myself.

My death spirit tilts her head, and I draw a breath—her crimson chest rises in unison with mine. Stretching my hands to her, she wraps her red fingers around my wrists and pulls me in. My arms hold tight to the energy that has been trapped in my body for almost nineteen years. She is warm, bright, full, and free. Tears trail down my cheeks and down her back. My heart pounds and reverberates through her, sending my pulse back through me.

I let go and Ace drops to his knees beside me as I hold my death spirit's hand and place my free hand on Johanna's chest. A breeze blows my hair across my face, and I project my life spirit into my whole hand. A pale glow brushes against Johanna's skin. The energy in my hand pulses. With each pulse, heat spreads over my hand in my death spirit's grasp.

"Holy Carnity," Ace says.

The brilliant woman of blood-red beside me fades into a transparent wisp. With thunder in my chest, and a silent scream parting my lips, she's gone. The flare-wing moth flutters in her absence.

46

JOHANNA

Tʜᴇ ᴅᴀʀᴋ ɪs sɪʟᴋʏ ᴀs ɪᴛ ᴡʀᴀᴘs ᴍᴇ ɪɴ ɪᴛs ᴅᴇᴘᴛʜ. My body sinks in it, my breaths swim in it, and as the dark washes back and forth over me, both dissipate. Their labours cease.

The dark is infinite, but not like in the Wander Lands. The dark here takes shape—solid ground, sky, a line of ebony mountains, and stars. How can starlight be dark? They are darker than the night, and brighter than the day.

My feet are blush again, my body rosy, but the energy that it's made of is different. It knows its own form; it is fuller than my mental energy. My essence courses through me in cyclical waves. Bright light spills from my core, shimmering through my pink body. My form is different too—it's not a female body, it moves and curves in its own way. My spirit. It knows its true form. It clings to womanhood but not so tightly, as if femininity was a suggestion, an essence itself, not an absolute.

I take a step and the ground rumbles. The inky dark cracks open and spiny shards rise out of it. They grow and plate together into a tree trunk stretching to the stars. My pink form quivers as the boughs bend to the ground, sweeping it with their firelight leaves. I drink in its beauty because I can't drink anything else, and I revel in the sensation of lack of breath, lack of desire for breath.

The trunk splits, opening wide, letting light spill from the other side. I stare at the light, waiting for it to disappear, but it stays, even as my memory counts seconds that don't exist here.

The light warms my soul.

Soul.

A concept has never been so real. It's a whole. I am whole. In this form, I know truths about myself. It's my spirit that brings the clarity. If Rin can gain this clarity through her spirit affinities, then I know she'll know what to do. And that's why I'll wait for her to bring me back. I don't know how long she'll be, or how she'll make her way here. Nolaria gave us a mission to carry out. I can't go through that door until I complete it. Rin will know how.

The tree reaches a branch to me. The glowing leaves embrace me. The light and a song ring around me, they harmonize with the song my spirit taught my mind. Energy pulses in my being. I move toward the light. The song builds and it layers calm over me.

But the light wraps around me like a rope and pulls me. It leans into the knowledge that Rin will know how to fix the mess left in the Beginning while I stare into the Beyond. Tugging me with its offer of peace and fullness, the light envelops my mind, fills me, and moves me closer. But as I move with the light, I lose the chorus. The depth of the song is gone. The tune from my soul is distorted with the loss of melody. The melody is not in the Beyond. I have to find her.

I turn away from the light and face the jagged line of black mountains and a glassy lake. With a tremor through my body, the lake takes a more distinct shape. Purple seeps into it. The rounded shores straighten into long edges and come together in corners. It rises into the darkness above—a dark-violet prison.

I run as fast as my body can take me through the endless expanse. Cries ring through the abyss, and I fall to my knees before it.

Like a storm, it hits me with striking clarity. This is where she'll meet me. I step right up to the Hold, my feet hovering over the inky pool below. I hold out a hand to the violet barrier, and it roars inside me with countless howls, pushing me back. Inside, there are forms that look hédin, like Wander Wraiths. They weep, trying to grasp glowing erratic energy—their essence— and their spirit light. Through the muddied chaos, she's there.

Pure, brilliant, red energy. A luminous red star. The spirit I chose to link myself to. My Soul Tether. She takes graceful steps to the barrier and lays her hands on it as she takes me in. Her head tilts to the side, a gentle smile shimmers through her lively energy as she takes in my full being for the first time.

I long to cry for her, to hold her, because she is trapped, torn in half, while I am free. My essence just pulses, aching to break the barrier and run to her. As her melody reaches into me, I reach for her, but I am thrust back by the barrier between us. I stumble, and my glowing pink form is swept into an energetic embrace. Her spirit has taken my place in the Lesser Worlds, just to make a path for me to go home.

Air bites my lungs. Essence beats against my flesh, and my blood runs ragged. My mouth is dry, and the stench of iron and earth fills my nose.

Light breaks through my eyelids, sharp pain stabs my eyes. My hand twitches to my side. I heave a breath and the air rips at my throat. The seconds are long and hot and I move and pain slaps me back down. "Fuck," I scream.

Above me, blond hair sways in the hot wind. Cool hands brush my face. A winter gale lashes through my head.

YOU'RE HERE.

Tears drip from Rin's face, landing on my cheeks. She yanks me up and my side screams in pain. "Shit, Rin," I say into her as her arms crush me. Blood seeps in an itchy trail down my body, but the wounds on my stomach are stitching themselves back together.

I ignore it all because something is different. Inside me, my essence is thin, wandering, and seeking. It meanders through my essence channels like a lost child. A sensation hits my mind like a cold wave, drenching my mind in an unfamiliar voice.

IT ACTUALLY WORKED.

I lean into Rin, wrapping my arms around her and hiding my face. People shuffle around me. More shifting and footfalls and rushing breaths come at my senses. I hold Rin tighter, breathing every smell of sweat and dirt and fire around her, trying to push away the voices that don't touch my ears.

THEY LOOK LIKE SHIT.

JOHANNA'S OKAY.

THE STONES—ALYXIA'S GONE—SO—OUT OF HERE.

I'M NOT CUT OUT FOR THIS.

WHAT THE HELL HAPPENED TO—

DID SHE SPLIT HER SPIRIT?

I grit my teeth until my jaw aches. I gasp, letting off the pressure. The voices ring louder and blend together.

"It's so loud," I whisper, and tears burn my eyes.

Rin strokes her hand down my head. "It's okay," she says into my hair. "It's okay." Her arm tightens around me. "I've got you."

Everything burns, and I don't know how to control it anymore, but she holds me.

ELIOTE

Once the High Commander of the Sarr LP department arrived on the scene to detain Stephen, Geret, and Adia, we piled into the airship and arrived back at the academy yesterday evening. We endured a long, well-deserved reprimand from the headmaster, and Brand's position at the academy is hanging by a thread. Everyone insisted I spend the night in the infirmary like Johanna and Ace, but I refused. I couldn't sleep there, not for my last night at the academy. I didn't tell them that. I just let Rin take me to our room in silence. We lay next to each other on my bed, staring at the ceiling until we both fell asleep.

This morning, she isn't here, and the sun is already streaming through the windows. My head throbs and my body shakes as I attempt to hobble over to my dresser on my broken leg. I grasp the doorknob with a pincher grip of stiff white dressings. I can only bend my fingers slightly and can't get a hold of it without pins and needles shooting through them. My heart skips a beat as a pressure clamps around my throat. I strangled myself with my own hands and suffocated myself with my blood. Nausea swirls in my gut as my head becomes hot and my breaths come too fast. Putting my broken leg down to steady myself, I wobble, unable to keep standing to find an outfit for the day, and I brace myself on the dresser.

Alyxia dug a thieving claw into me. She stole my body and my mind. She manipulated me. Still, in the darkness of my mind, where there was only thought and understanding, I found liberation from following, from supporting, and an invitation to myself. I wish I had found that invitation on my own terms. That claw dug up a vengeful truth in my spirit.

My trembling shakes tears from my eyes just as the door opens, and my head is so light with the fast exchange of air. I slump forward, gritting my teeth, sinking in the pain that swarms my body. I jerk as an arm comes around me like the hot, dark grasp of Alyxia. I yelp and try to move away but lose my balance. Rin scoops her arms behind my legs and lifts me before I fall. She carries me back to my bed as sharp gasps rip through my lungs and the tears drench my face.

Rin draws me close. I can't urge my body to stop shaking, but Rin's arms are so strong that there's no way my muscles can resist. I trust her grip. I trust the bright, pure shimmer of her soul. But there's so much I don't trust, that I want to trust but can't. I want to be able to trust all of them again, my team, Ace, the headmaster, and Brand. All of this happened under their noses though. There were apologies for how everything went down, thank-yous for the work we did as a team. It was labelled as excellent Guardian work once the reprimands for leaving the academy during the tournament had stopped. *Guardian work.* The words run through me like poison, and I dip my face into Rin's shoulder as the spasms take over my body.

"I'm sorry," Rin whispers. Her fingers trail through my tangled hair. "I don't know why I couldn't see it. I thought I would be able to with my death affinity, but I can never see Alyxia's manipulation coming." She sniffs and her voice becomes softer with each word. "I should have gone with you to get that curestone."

I shake my head, trying to lift it and form words in my mouth, but Rin shushes me.

"You don't need to say anything," she says.

She lets go of me and makes sure I'm upright and steady with both hands on my shoulders to right my slouching torso. Standing, she goes to the closet.

The air shimmers around her as light-blue wings drape from her back. There is no longer a red glow to fill them out. They are limp and they twitch to the sides like they're reaching for something they lost. I turn my eyes away as a twist of anguish rings through me.

My eyes land on a wheelchair in the middle of the room.

"Don't look at it yet, okay?" Rin says, turning my wet face back to her. Her cheeks glisten with tears too. She doesn't touch them, and she doesn't touch mine, she just holds out a pair of shorts and a purple t-shirt to me. "Is this good?"

I nod, fumbling for the hem of my night shirt with my stiff fingers.

She reveals a bra and underwear. "How much lace does one person need?"

A laugh bursts out of me with heat in my cheeks and more tears.

It takes me a few tries to get a hold of my shirt again. As I pull it off, the fabric slips out of my grasp. I swallow the lump in my throat and try again. The sun gleams at the corner of my vision and I blink it away, losing my grip again and ending up with the shirt pulled over one shoulder and my arms tangled in the rest, my fingers buzzing with pain. Rin holds out her hands to me, gentle silver eyes looking right at mine. Her cold fingers slip the shirt off my shoulder. She pulls it over my head and works on getting my other arm out. She helps me into the clean underwear without making me feel more embarrassed, and chills crawl over my back as her cold fingers do up the clasp of my bra.

"Where's Liam?" I ask, without emotion to charm my voice into the sweet, agreeable tone it's gotten used to.

"Eating breakfast with the guys," she says, pulling my shirt over my head. Steadying me with one arm and pulling up my shorts with the other, her eyebrows are tight as she works. "You and Liam," she says. "You have essence in your eyes."

I shrug. "That's what it looks like, at least. It must be in the sclera or something, so there's no blood picking up energy to produce a reading on the Registration metres."

Rin wraps her arm around me, and we cross the room to the wheelchair. "Ace told me about how your sight is changing." She moves around the chair to the handles. "That you can see better at night. Like . . . the Ōneera."

The chair is still. Instead of grabbing the handlebars, her cold hands rest on my shoulders. I lay a bandaged hand on one of them, wishing I could squeeze it. "The essence in my eyes is aligned with utanic energy now." *Corrupted.* A new wave of tears spills down my face. The words are bitter as they leave my tongue. I have an undetectable amount of energy, and that energy is only found in beasts on this planet. That energy is not for hédin. "And Liam's might be too. S-so keep an eye on him."

"I'll keep a closer eye on both of you," she says. "But . . . "

The air in the room is a little too thin, the light a little too bright, and somehow she keeps crossing spaces between us. The gaps in the knowledge I've given her, about my sight, and wanting to leave, she keeps filling them in.

"I'm going to leave," I finally say. Her hands get tighter.

I can't tell my mom that my sight is utanic and that I don't want this path that put our family through so much stress. I can't tell my mom that I don't know what I want to do with my life. At least not alone.

"Will you sit with me when I call my mom?"

"Yeah," she says, the word wrapped in sincerity and a disguised sob. "I will be right there with you. But let's eat something first."

I take a long breath to steady myself as Rin opens the door. I let the air out slowly and with it, some tension from my body. My limbs ache, and my soul is heavy, but Rin wheels me into the hall without any effort. I know it's the essence inside her that moves us both, but it's her soul that carries us. I blame her for all this, and I think I should. When I leave this place, I can trust her to pick up her shit. She's done it over and over again and she's stronger for it, kinder, more powerful. I trust her to do Guardian work.

In the middle of the hall, Johanna throws her door open. She waddles out wrapped in a blanket, wearing echophones over her ears and sunglasses.

"New look?" Rin asks.

Johanna scowls and blows a stray hair out of her face. "You're lucky you just turn blue with your full strength." She plops herself down on my lap and swings her legs over the armrest, gathering her fuzzy blanket up into her lap.

"Oof, does mindreading make you gain a few pounds too?" Rin says, feigning a struggle to get us rolling.

"It's eight in the morning, and I've already had enough of your shit," Johanna says.

My lips curl in a smile and I giggle, wrapping my arms around Johanna and leaning my head on her shoulder. Patting her stomach, I say, "I think it's just abs. You got eight in there yet?"

"Everyone just shut up and stop thinking for one fucking minute, okay?"

"Whatever you say." Rin snatches Johanna's sunglasses and puts them on.

"Hey!" Johanna winces and rubs her temple.

"Poor baby," I say, giving her a kiss on the cheek. Johanna shakes her head as her cheeks flush and she shields her eyes from the light.

Rin wheels us to the elevator, then to the dining hall. We gather up some coffee and pastries to take to the back of the school where we can sit in the shade, away from wispy intentions and brains full of thoughts.

The sun is already hot, but Johanna lies on the cement in the light, wrapped in her blanket.

"I'm confused. Do you want the sun or not?" Rin asks, squatting at Johanna's head to resituate the sunglasses on her face.

"Ow, you put it in my ear."

Rin chuckles, "Sorry," she says and leaves the glasses sitting skewed on her face.

"The sun gives me energy, but the light aggravates my headache."

It's funny how a fann star and a utanic star can have such different effects on us. I sit with my back to the sun, and even though its warmth is a comfort to my body, my eyes find it too bright too. Rin takes a piece of pastry and stuffs it into Johanna's mouth. Johanna chews and coughs while Rin chuckles and sips her coffee, watching her struggle.

I stare at my wrapped fingers of both hands, bracing my own pastry between them. Rin and Johanna will always have each other. I've only been in their lives for a year and a half. I love them both dearly, but when I leave, will that even matter? Such a short time, and what will they remember of me? That I could barely carry a dummy full of sand a few metres? That I was manipulated by an evil queen because I was an easy target? That I quit?

Johanna bolts upright. Gathering her blanket around her, she shuffles over to me. Her face is flushed and sweat has dampened her hairline. Gripping my knees, she says, "We'll remember that you landed a hit when none of us could. You fought her."

Rin's brow furrows, chewing slowly. A light sparks between her and Johanna. She drops her pastry and scoots in close to me too. "We'll remember that you saw every part of us and still love us," she says.

"We don't care that you're quitting, because it takes way more guts to find your own path."

Both girls sit on the ground in front of me, hands on my knees.

"These years at the academy have been the hardest years of my life," I say. "Maybe I wasn't meant to be here in the first place." I wipe my eyes with my bandage.

Rin shakes her head. "You made a choice, and it wasn't a wrong choice to come here. Whatever is right for you is still out there."

The wind blows my hair over my face, sticking strands to my wet cheeks. I sniff and clutch my lightstone. The stone was a gift. My grandmother knew I could never light it, but she gave it to me anyway. It's like she knew I would need it, to remember that nothing is wasted on me. My time here was not a waste. It was tragic, hard, and something that I need to step away from now, but experience isn't a waste, friendships aren't a waste, and maybe I would always follow and be used for the rest of my life if I hadn't come here and seen just how strong I am.

I called my mom and told her everything, every bloody detail and hard truth. It's my dad who shows up with the cruiser. The sun glints off the glossy black finish as he pulls into the front courtyard. My stomach flips. He steps out and buttons up his blue blazer as night-wing moths flutter around him. Nodding to my teammates gathered around me, he says, "Eliote, are you prepared to leave?" He folds his hands in front of him, keeping a few feet of cobblestones between him and the group.

"I'm ready." I turn to my team instead of saying it to him.

Ace is behind me, hands gripped around the handles of the wheelchair, creating more energy and static around me with the tension. It clings to me, making my stomach churn and my throat tighten. Johanna sits on the front steps, hugging her knees with a deep scowl and tears glistening in her eyes. Shuffling from foot to foot and cracking her knuckles, Rin's face twists and she presses her lips together.

"Come here," I say, beckoning her to me with broken hands.

She leans in and wraps her arms around me as I take a long breath of the coffee and cinnospice lingering around her. Each of my team members hugs me one after the other, but as all their distinct smells and their intentions circle me, Ace doesn't let go of the handles of my chair.

Jeff runs a hand over his face. A green wisp spirals behind him. I want to call it back into this circle, but it's not my place to decide where others' intentions lie.

Johanna nudges him. "You've got to tell them sometime."

The team turns to Jeff. His throat bobs and all that fills the silence is the clang of swords from the training grounds. Letting out a breath, his eyes stay on Johanna. "After this year, I won't be returning either."

Niko's head snaps up. He grabs Jeff by the arms and shakes him. "What? You can't. Our team's all falling apart."

My dad clears his throat. I can't pull my eyes off my team yet. They are my team, always will be, and no matter how far apart we are, I know we'll always fight for each other.

Ace squeezes my shoulders. "You ready?" he asks, his voice soft and warm in my ear.

I take in the glimmering white stone of the academy, all the stained glass images of Protectors and Warriors, their powerful essence abilities displayed for the whole of Akinnera to marvel at. I am ready.

Ace wheels me to Dad's cruiser. The scent of lightstones and incense prickle my nose as Dad opens the door for me. My fingers sting, and a pain spikes through my leg as Ace helps me into the cruiser. He squats beside me, cradling my hand instead of shutting me in. I run my free hand over his cheek, my unbound fingers drinking in his smooth skin. His broken ribs are already healed. Curestones aren't very good at healing bone, unless there is essence present. His bones have healed and mine will require daily curestone treatments for the next week or two. That doesn't bother me though. It's my pain.

"I'll call you once you're home," he says, keeping his eyes on our hands in my lap. "And we can vision call too, as many times a week as we need. I want to support you, even though we're apart." His chest heaves with a breath, but mine aches.

I push my hand through his hair. I trace his face and his lips even though my fingers twinge. "Please don't call me," I whisper as a tear trickles down my cheek.

Ace winces, his eyes pressing closed, but I tilt his face, bringing his sapphire eyes to me. His intentions shade the space around us in sparkling black shadow.

I take a long breath and hold up my lightstone to him.

"I've been treating myself like a companion light," I say. "It glows in response to a Luminee's touch."

Ace tilts his head to the side, chest rising with a preparatory breath.

"But I want to see myself glow all the time."

"You do, El, you glow all the time." He takes hold of my wrist as my hand falls from his face. But I can't let him hold me anymore, so I slip out of his grasp, still leaving our hands together in my lap.

"But I don't know what makes me glow, just for me, what makes me happy."

"Are you . . . " His jaw twitches, the glittering sparkle in his eyes fading. "Come on, El." The break in his voice creates a sharp edge that pricks something inside me. It bursts, pushing out the tears before I can catch them. He says, "We can make it work."

"This hurts so much, Ace. But I can't take the love you freely give me anymore. Not when someone else could have it. You have helped me realize so much about myself, but I don't think the comfort you give me is what I need right now. Stepping away from what I know here, where I'm still trying to catch people's eyes with a light I don't have, they're unknown, unstable steps. But what I've always known is hurting me. I want to shake that."

Tears stream down Ace's face and his chest has stopped moving, building a dam against a sob. He raises my hand to his lips, pressing warmth to my skin and tears into the bandages.

"You were wonderful to me," I say with thick words that I trust and need to say. "Please be just as wonderful to someone who can give you the same wonder."

"I'm sorry I'm holding you back," Ace whispers.

"No, you held me up."

I wrap my arm around him, and he leans in. His lips graze my ear as they find my cheek, lingering, maybe longing to go lower, but he leaves the kiss there and steps back. Eyes on our hands, he lets go. The air around my fingers in his wake is bitter but energizing, cleansing to my tired body.

I wave through the windshield to my team and Ace's back. For a moment I sit alone with my broken body in my dad's cruiser in limbo between two worlds that have not been good to me because of my lack of essence. The dream of the Flight Academy was just that, a dream of acceptance and recognition from others. But it would be the same as forcing myself to stay here, instead of finding what I need. I smile through my tears, my body rests, and I know two things for sure. Eliote Nohar does not want to fool Ace Dalaan and rob him of love that could be appreciated so much more by someone else, and Eliote Nohar does not want to be a Guardian.

48

R I N

THE FOUNTAIN IN THE CENTRAL COURTYARD of the academy keeps me company with its gentle rush at my back as I take long breaths of the fresh night air. The water cools the air and the breeze raises the hair on my arms. The sea salt makes the air coarse, not like the wet air that weighed down on me in Sarr. I run my hands over my arms. I cringe as the ridges of my fingers scuff over scaly skin. My pulse pounds underneath it, awakened by how vital it is that the touch is so real.

The tether breaking released my energy into its full form, leaving my life affinity just a blink out of reach, the light sparkling behind my eyelids. It's expectant, ready. But its anxious need to give leaves my body aching for sleep because I really have nothing to give. Sleep won't come though. It won't come for a while, not restful sleep anyway. Not without Eliote filling the space on the other side of our room, and maybe not until I'm reunited with my death spirit.

Without my death spirit, I am different, still me, but I was only starting to see all of myself and let my death spirit show. She is opinionated, angry, loving, and gentle. She ached, and now I ache even more with her gone. I only got a taste of what I might be if I were whole. In losing her, I hope I can round some of the sharpness out before she comes home. My life spirit is sharp edges, walls, relentless strength. Maybe I'll see the true me behind the mask of bright-blue eyes and welcome my death spirit back with the kindness she deserves, the way I would have when I was younger.

Leaning on the bench, I let my head fall back. My body is grounded by the hard wood beneath me, the coolness of the night, the brightness and pure-green colour of the stars. The stars reach for my eyes. They're the same stars as in Senn, the ones I stared at from my bed at night in my parents' old house, or outside my apartment with Liam inside, and always closer than they should be—a comfort, too close for their own good, like Eliote.

It's strange having Liam here, but he'll be going home as soon as Oron can come get him. It makes my mouth dry just thinking about letting his hands go tomorrow. He could stay awhile, maybe. I need to show him that he can stay with me, even after everything. He didn't deserve any of this. I know it's going to take him a long time to process. I hope I can help him do that, but I can barely help myself.

The door to the courtyard squeaks and two flare-wing moths fluttering around the fountain change course in a hurry to investigate. Johanna comes through the door and bats the moths out of her face. They settle on her shoulder as she crosses the path to sit with me.

She sits about a foot away, her green eyes bright, and she smells like curl cream and clean clothes. But there are bags under her eyes and her shoulders hunch forward as she sits with her hands between her knees. She lets out a long sigh, running her tongue over her teeth. The crease between her brow gets deeper.

"Thoughts get really weird at night," she says.

Taking one hand from between her thighs, she runs it over her eyes. Her fingers shake and her knees bounce.

I take her hand and cup it in mine. It burns against my cool skin. As I stroke my thumb over the back of her hand, the need to do something, be somewhere, and protect everything I love, fades. Johanna's knees calm and the heat in her fingers diffuses evenly between our hands.

"Shit," Johanna mutters. "That Soul Tether must have been doing some heavy lifting."

A shiver jerks my body as the tiny legs of a moon beetle tickle the back of my leg. Its wings flick as it settles, casting a pale glow behind my knee.

Johanna leaves her hand in mine and leans her elbow on the armrest. A cricket chirps over the trickle of the fountain and the flowers rustle in the breeze. All I can do is blink and breathe. Images of the last few days crash behind my eyelids, and the tether's break still rips inside me even though the void has filled. It's like energy pressing at new stitches. The weak flesh holds but with a pinch and burn. Johanna felt the tether's effects while it was still intact, and I kept running from it. She kept it strong while I didn't even know it existed.

"It's always the same way with us." I push the words through the growing thickness in my throat. I search for the right words to fill in my meaning. Johanna chuckles beside me, filling my mind with heat.

I still feel like I have to explain myself to you, even if you can hear my thoughts.

Johanna shifts, crossing her legs and raising her eyebrow at me.

Sorry, know my thoughts.

She nods with a smirk. The starlight highlights the scar on her lip and the scar on my knuckles.

You're always a level ahead of me. What do you think it would be like if I had known about the tether?

YOU THINK A LOT ABOUT THE PAST. IT HELPS YOU UNDERSTAND. BUT I DON'T THINK THE SOUL TETHER IS SOMETHING YOU'LL UNDERSTAND BY LOOKING BACK. YOU DIDN'T KNOW ABOUT IT. WE JUST HAVE TO ACCEPT THAT.

I just don't understand how I didn't know.

I DON'T THINK YOU WERE READY TO BE KNOWN BY ME LIKE THAT.

A breeze blows Johanna's curls over her face as her cheeks flush red. Her eyes take a wandering path away from me into the dark shadows of the night, and her hand wanders away too. My fingers follow after her and I turn to face her. She presses her eyes closed against the tears.

"Nolaria told me that we can defeat Alyxia, you and me. But I don't think I'm ready." She taps the fingers of her free hand to her temple. "My power isn't the same since the tether broke. I–I can't move anything with Mind Fire. I can't make armour very well. I think I'm going to have to relearn how to do it. All the strength I got from you made it easy. I can read anyone's mind now, but I can't control that either. Compared to Alyxia, I'm under-levelled, Rin. But if we wait too long, then she'll find a way to get what she wants."

I draw in a long breath of dry air and sweet jaden lily. My full power, the dual affinity state, it was too much for me and yet the rest I felt with it was intoxicating. The way my life affinity and Stephen's death affinity drew together and left him sleeping soundly. My unama-jint essence and Johanna's fann essence, it creates a calm between us. The only way we got through all this was with the rest that came with the balance between extremes.

"The Revivalists were too eager to take her down with a war, a war she wants to keep perpetuating." I swallow hard. "We've been rushing. Half my spirit is locked in the Hold, and we still don't know how to get to it. Alyxia's out there, but we don't know how to stop her. We'll split even more if we keep running after her."

Johanna nods.

"I–I think we need to just rest," I say. "Finish the year. We'll be stronger then."

Johanna pushes her curls out of her face and wipes at her tears, keeping her gaze on the ground. "Do you think we're still tethered? I mean, maybe when I died . . . " The crease between her brows releases. Her eyes become unfocused and her throat bobs as she swallows. "When I died, maybe just our essence connection was broken. I was still drawn to your spirit in the Hold. Do you think . . . no." Johanna's eyes latch onto me, clearing and glinting with starlight. "The Soul Tether isn't what makes our relationship special. I–I don't need a spiritual, mental, or physical bond to tell me what I feel. I don't need a Seer or a wraith to tell me . . . "

"You're enough," I say. The words are sweet and light on my tongue, true. As I squeeze Johanna's hand, my heart pounds in sure heavy beats and my blood awakens every part of me.

My fingers are stiff as I pull another piece of tape. I stick it along the sterile gauze pad on Liam's arm.

"You need to keep this on for just a few days," I say. "The curestone healed the cut, but your skin is going to be a little tender."

"The skin is all itchy," Liam says. He keeps his eyes on the patch as my fingers fumble over it. His shoulders are bent forward, his straggly hair hiding his sweet face from me.

"This will keep you from scratching and aggravating it more."

The gauze has a stuffy, mothball smell with a sterile tinge. Taking a final piece of tape, I pinch it too hard, folding it over on itself, sticking it together. "Shit," I mutter.

Liam shifts on the bed.

"Did you get enough to eat for breakfast?" I ask.

He nods, finding me with his eyes. They squint and my stomach takes a leap as he catches on to what I'm doing, what I've always done. Keep him comfortable because everything is going to shit.

I clear my throat. "Oron got a rental cruiser to come pick you up so you can have a quiet trip back home."

Tilting his head to the side, he sighs. "What do you have to tell me, Rinnaya?"

I smooth my thumb over the tape. There's no easy way around it and he deserves the truth. "What do you remember about our father?"

Sunlight streaks across his face as he turns to the window. "I just remember Mom really loved him. So much that she wanted to be with the ancestors alongside him."

Those are the words I gave him years ago. I thought they would be comforting, but they set the air on fire, and they burn as I breathe them in.

"That's right," I say, sitting back on the floor in front of him. "But the thing is, Father never made it to the ancestors."

"What do you mean?" His eyebrows furrow. "I guess I don't really know what happens after death. They might be with Ashnaho and Neuoa, or just blobs in empty space, maybe just gone from existence."

"I'm not talking about the logistics of death, Liam. I'm saying he's still here. He came back from the dead."

There's cold in his eyes that shouldn't be there. I'm supposed to keep the cold away from him, so that he doesn't have to hurt, so he doesn't have to cause himself pain when his world is crashing down on him. But I failed to keep him safe, and maybe that's the problem. Maybe he needs to see it all.

"What?" he says. "Did someone use Angel Palm on him?"

"No. He found his own way back."

"Come on, Rinnaya, stop. I might prefer to look on the

bright side of things, but this isn't bright." Tears glisten in his eyes and my eyes prickle. I wouldn't stop them even if I could, because it hurts, and I want him to know it hurts and not think that it shouldn't.

"You're right, Liam. It isn't bright."

Our tears fall, no sobs. They line my face with heat, they drip off my chin, they soak into Liam's shirt. His lower lip twitches and his face pinches. I lean forward and hold on to his ankles hanging off the bed.

"I opened the door because it was Stephen," he whispers. "I felt Stephen's spirit outside the door, so I opened the locks. I felt other spirits with him but didn't care. I just knew Stephen was out there and I was so happy. I thought he was finally coming home." He runs his hand over the gauze. "But I guess they never really come home."

I swallow hard and press my hands to my face. Father told me he would always come home. He told me to keep kindness close when people hurt me. I was six when he told me that and I believed it, and twelve when he let it go. The first part I've left behind too. I think my father didn't know what he was talking about. He may have been older and wiser, but he didn't know what kind of impact a promise like that could make, and how easy it would be to break. The second part, maybe we're both still grasping for it.

"I didn't do a good job, Liam." My voice is all air.

"But you did. You kept us safe and fed, and Oron was there when you weren't."

I shake my head and he quiets. His eyes shift over me. A small breath expels from his nose as he settles into the quiet without any more empty justifications for how I kept us alive.

"You saw the darkness in me," I say. "I dismissed it. I always kept up my guard with you."

"You always hid the truth," he says. His mouth quirks into a sad smile.

"That's right."

Swinging his legs a little, he sets his gaze past my ear. "Before you left for the academy, I would see your essence fade for a while, then when you would come back smelling like Ease, it would be steadier so . . . I didn't say anything because it was helping you."

A sweaty chill rakes down my back.

"But when you were Eased, I'd still worry because your spirit looked like it was ready to jump out of your body."

He knew everything. It must have been so confusing, so stressful, terrifying even. I run my hand over my pounding heart. "We need your sight, okay? Don't hide it anymore. We need to nurture it, and not let anyone use it against you."

The door opens and a wave of peach and weckler wood wafts over me. Brand stands in the doorway with her hand on her firestone pistol at her side. It's her security, her power. If she's holding on to it, then something's wrong. I brush away my tears as she beckons me into the hall.

"Peter's here," she says, taking the pistol out of its holster.

"You've got to be fucking kidding me." I run my hands through my hair and pull.

"He says he has to tell you something." Brand twirls the pistol. Shaking her head, the glasses on the top of her head slip down. She holsters her pistol and rips the glasses off her head in a huff. "He knows Liam's here too. He wants to see him. I told him in the most commanderly way possible to go fuck himself, but he insists on seeing you."

"Well, I do appreciate that, but I'll talk to him. Would you like to introduce yourself to Liam while I go talk to my father?"

Brand nods. A rare smile curls her lips. She tilts her chin up as she would to look up at someone, but her eyes are level with mine. "Of course."

She turns to the door. I catch her arm. "Thea," I say.

Her arm tenses in my grasp. Lowering her eyes to the ground, they fill with shadow and her cheeks fill with blush. "I heard her," she says, her voice low and raspy. She presses her lips together. "Thank you for what you said, for reassuring her when I couldn't."

Meeting my eyes, Brand puts her hand over mine. She has such a familiar face now, but it doesn't give me that recognizable cold that sinks into my bones anymore. Her eyes bring me comfort and warmth as they harden with hot defiance.

Tears spill down her cheeks. "Thea never let me see her the week before the start of her monthly cycle. She said that as her hormones dropped off"—her voice wavers—"and her body took a natural rest, she would have trouble controlling her illusions. She never wanted to expose me to that. I think the moments when Alyxia has used Thea's illusions against us were the days before her cycle."

My stomach churns as I fill in the words she hasn't said. Brand lost Thea in the moments Thea chose to rest and protect others from herself. In these very halls, Alyxia stole the autonomy of a woman who put others before herself.

"But Alyxia chose the wrong host, because Thea is still strong." The brilliant, loving, bone-headed Commander nods to me, wiping her eyes, and enters my room.

I leave her with Liam, and I flex my fingers as I take the stairs, air building inside me. Father stands with his back to me in the middle of the lobby, hands in his pockets, shoulders broad like boulders. I take another breath at the far edge and hold it to have more time before memories get stirred by his scent. The memories will contradict everything. They'll shake me.

He turns to me and his face brightens. "Rinny, I figured it out, how to destroy the Hold," he says. He steps forward and I step back. He takes a breath, his eyes wavering around me—too much adrenaline, too much eagerness. I keep my mouth shut. "The rifts I've been through have taken me to higher levels of the Lesser Worlds, the Silent Realm, the Higher Plane. In the Higher Plane, I immediately get pushed out, but in the Silent Realm I'm able to move through it. I found a bridge but I can't cross it. I think if we start by going through a rift to the Lower Void, we acclimatize and then are able to pass into the next realm."

His words are static in my brain, disconnected from meaning and disconnected from my heart.

"You solved the puzzle. Death affinity on the inside life affinity on the outside. If we can get through the three realms of the Lesser Worlds, we can break it. You did it."

"Did you find it?" I ask, my voice drawn low and stiff from the effort it took to break through my throat.

"Find what?"

"A rift to the Lower Void."

Running his hand through his salt and pepper hair, his lips tense and a long breath raises his chest. This man makes me want to stab a sharp crystal into my flesh too, because the pain from that would make more sense than what my father stirs in me.

"Then I can't help you. Now is that it?" I shrug my shoulders and let my arms fall heavy at my sides. "Just needed my help, right? Just stickin' the fate of other people on me. Just like Stephen. You know your oldest son is going to prison for what you started?"

"Rin, I'm sorry. You know I'm sorry. I'm trying to make all of this right."

"Mm." I nod, pacing in a small circle around him. "I can travel through the three levels of the Lesser Worlds with you on my back and break the Hold without a sweat. You can spend years searching for rifts between whole fucking worlds. But can you console your youngest child? Can you tell him why his father died, how he's still alive, why his older brother used him for a sadistic Ritual? Can you do that?" I step right up to him. I take a breath full of him, and I know that he can't. He was never home, never with us in the first place, always on a mission. "No," I say. "I'm going to be the one to do it. So go. Go find your rift."

The walls of the lobby aren't so tall anymore, the dome roof not so far away. My father looks small against them. This is where I've grown. This is where I have found and lost myself over and over again. I turn on my heel, headed back into the belly of this monster.

"Wait," Father says.

I whirl back around. Cold passes over my neck and down my back as bright-blue light fills my vision. "You have to let me be mad at you." My voice rings with power through the wide room. "The only version of myself I know is the one that didn't have you."

The young girl who loves him, who's already forgiven him, she stands with me. She clings to me. She is vulnerable even though she is strong. She needs protection. She is small, young, pure. One day, she might grow into me, but I hope I might grow back into her. Maybe her laugh and her joy will come out of me again. We have to build a safe place for her though.

"From now on, Liam and I will see you on our terms," I say. "I need that. I need time to figure you into my life. Liam doesn't know you, you are a stranger. So when we invite you into our space, please come, but respect our home, and respect our ways."

In all my memories, I can't see his tears—I'm not sure if he ever showed them to me. But they're here now, all over his face, revealing the broken parts of him.

Behind him, Oron walks through the doors. He takes his hands out of his pockets, eyes trained on my father's back. His silence is a battle cry. It hits me like a wave and Father turns to him. Oron greets him with another douse of silence. He comes to me and wraps me in his strong arms, pressing his lips to the top of my head.

"I'm so glad you're all right." His whispered words stick a bandage over my breaking heart.

He holds me for a long time, his minty scent cleansing my lungs. Footsteps sound behind us. I turn as Father says, "Liam."

I grab his arm. "No," I say, eyes on Liam. He trails a few steps behind Brand, eyes wide, taking in the sight of a man he doesn't know. "It's going to take time." I look deep into Father's sunken, grey eyes as he shudders. "It's going to take time. You owe us that."

I thought I could make it through the party. Liam deserved it. It was his tenth birthday, an important one, and only a few weeks before I would leave him for the academy. I had to be there, present. But I had already put off that last dose of Ease, and with the noise in the small apartment, the heat, the glares of Liam's friends' parents, my vision kept swimming and the nausea burned up my throat. I tried to hide the shake of my hands by balling them up in my sleeves. But then the pins and needles hit my chest, and I knew I wasn't making it through the night without it.

I tucked the joint up my sleeve. Kissing Liam on the head as he played with his friends on the floor with his new gifts, I said, "Be right back, buddy."

On my way to the door, I grabbed a garbage bag and stuffed paper plates and cups and my half-eaten piece of cake into it for a ruse to fool the other parents. Proactive party clean up. Not withdrawal. The door opened and Oron filled the doorway. My heart raced and the other half of that cake readied itself for its reappearance.

"Where are you going?" Oron asked.

"Just takin' out the trash. Be right back."

His eyes narrowed on me and he stepped to the side, letting me skirt around him, holding my breath in his shadow, and I bolted down the stairs. I ran through to the dumpsters in the alley and threw the bag in, not bothering to tie it. I slumped against the metal with its stench at my back and flicked the lighter. The flame warmed my face, and I drew it into my lungs through the Ease.

The shake in my body stilled. The contents of my stomach rested with another breath. Clouds of Ease settled around me and the cooling sensation drifted from my tongue to my mind. I sank into a crouch. My face went slack, and my eyes stared at the dirty wall with a lazy gaze.

With my previous doses, I liked to entertain the idea of using this low potency Ease for a while. But this one had to be my last. Using any longer and Donny said I would be really hooked. Once I was done that one, it had to be my last or else my rest would always be artificial.

The crunch of snow under heavy feet pricked my ears. I kept the joint at my lips, taking a long drag with my eyes closed, blocking Oron out for just a few more seconds of bliss.

"Should we count this one as an all-time low?" His deep voice rumbled through me, and his bulky frame blocked out the streetlights. "Or just stop counting?"

The Ease kept me silent. The high kept me crouched low. But Oron crossed his arms and scoffed, staying on his high horse.

"Right under his nose," he said. "You're choosing this over being at his party? Rin, you've got to pull yourself together. You're about to go to the Guardian Academy, and Liam's last memories with you are going to be of you high out of your mind."

"Save your breath, Oron."

"Save my breath." He laughed, and it was weighty on my ears, dark in my eyes, and bitter on my tongue. "The one thing I need to be saving right now is Liam. From you."

The itch crackled behind my eyes. Good Keena, he should have been scared. The high was probably the only thing keeping my death affinity at bay right then. I thought it was just the smoke burning my eyes. I rubbed at it and finished the joint.

"Nothing to say, huh? Can't even—"

"Funny, isn't it?" I flicked the joint to the snow at his boots. I stood. Slow. Taking a long breath of freezing air, the first breath not attached to Ease. It sunk heavy in my chest as I straightened up, head falling to the side, the muscles in my neck lax. Shadows grew through the lines of Oron's face and his lips pressed tight. "The one thing that almost killed me, that should have killed me, is keeping me alive right now. Small doses of it are keeping my body from destroying itself."

The harsh line of Oron's mouth twitched. A cruiser passed behind him, electropulse pounding through the windows.

"Yeah, nobody told me either, had to find out from my drug dealer." I shrugged. "He's a good guy," I muttered, shifting my gaze off to the shadows.

"That doesn't excuse your behaviour. You did not have to do this right now. Take some responsibility."

"Fuck, Oron." I took a step forward. He stepped back, and I followed, pushing my face through the cloud of his breath so he could see my bloodshot eyes. "Everything I do is for that kid. I think about how every one of my decisions affects him. I know how bad this looks, but if I didn't go down slowly, I'd have a heart attack. I know it's fucked to go back up there and lie to Liam when he asks why I smell like Ease." I shoved him away from me. "But I'm the one who has to do it, and I'll be the one judged by those parents, so mind your own fucking business and let me handle it."

I turned away from him and slammed my fist into the corner of the dumpster. It caved in and the metal screech echoed through the alley. The cold crowded my skin, and I shook. Oron stared at me, half turned as he steadied himself.

"At least I'm here." My voice cracked. I took a wheezing breath, and my next raspy words stung the air with all the bitterness that Senn taught me. "At least I'm alive, and I have someone to celebrate."

I rested my arms on my head. The stars peeked at me through my arms as my breaths rose up to them. Oron shuffled forward. I thought tears might fall as he touched his hand to my shoulder, but my eyes were dry and stinging, my heart numb.

"You were twelve," he said.

A snowflake fell between us. I dropped my arms.

His voice hushed. "Twelve, Rinnaya. A child. You shouldn't have had to make all those decisions. You should have been able to find yourself before being Liam's everything."

His other hand took my shoulder. I leaned forward and his solid chest caught me. A tear dripped from my eye. It took in the cold and trickled down my cheek, but my skin could barely register it aside from the wet.

"I'm sorry for getting angry," he said. "I know I always do that. Get angry before asking questions. I guess it's because I'm angry at myself for not doing better."

Oron pushed me back and took my chin, turning my face to him, but my eyes stayed in the shadows. "I'm sorry I can't bring them back to you." He dried my face with his handkerchief and steered me back into the apartment building and up the stairs.

Liam had only invited two friends over and both sets of parents came with them to the party. They had never trusted me before, and I lost the bit of trust they were gaining in me as I entered my apartment. My lungs itched, and I coughed. It was like my body wanted them to know, so that at least they could gossip about the truth. Mrs. Raya crinkled her nose as I passed her and she ducked it into her cup.

Liam jumped up, leaving his gifts behind. He trotted over to me and wrapped me in his arms. I ran my fingers through his hair, leaning my chin on his head.

"Rinnaya," he said, looking up at me, still holding tight. "You have flowers inside you."

A smile cracked the ice in my skin. My head swam in a haze, and my senses burned with the eyes tracking me. "Really?"

"So many."

I forgot how many times he's told me that in my life. First when he was six. It was just a normal day. I picked him up from school and as we walked in silence, he let me in on the way he saw me. He waved his hand in front of me like he was running it through a patch of grass—grass and wildflowers. Awestruck, he said it to me softly. "There are flowers inside you."

He keeps reminding me. There's beauty inside that I haven't been able to see because I would rather settle with the weeds and the thorns. But I guess some weeds have flowers. And even rillia has thorns.

49

LANCE

I knock on Rin's door and take a step back into the hall. Shaking out my hands, I turn in a circle, fanning myself with my shirt to air out my pits. The seconds tick by with no answer, sending my heart into my stomach. Releasing a breath, I shake my head at myself and relax my wings.

I hold out my hand and let the jitters steady. Clearing my mind, I sink into the quiet of the evening. Sending a little surge of essence through my body, my hand disappears with a crackle of electricity. Flipping it from front to back, the only indication that it's there is the skitter of static. It brings a smile to my face as calm spreads over me. But as I bring my thoughts to my team—to Aris and Litha specifically—my hand reappears. Knowing when I need to be calm and unseen, for the sake of myself and others, allows me to become invisible. Recognizing where I am needed to be present, to comfort and encourage and even be comforted, brings me back. The people who respond well to me are the ones who need me to stick around. In a way, I'm glad I stayed on my assigned team as long as I did. Aris, Litha, and I all needed it. Now, I need to move toward the people who make me feel supported too.

Raising my hand to knock again, just to make sure, she just might not have heard it, a door slams down the hall. I jump and almost trip over my wings.

"Lance," Johanna yells at me.

"What?" I say, hand over my pounding heart.

"You don't think it's too soon to tell her?"

"Tell who what?" Heat builds in my face as I run my hand over my neck and avoid her glaring green eyes. "I wasn't . . . I wasn't even thinking . . . "

"You were thinking it." Her hair is gathered in a knot and her stray curls bounce as she marches down the hall, pointing her finger at me. "Before you came up here, you were thinking all your mushy, gushy thoughts and don't you come back pouting when she doesn't reciprocate them." Johanna crosses her arms and raises her chin so she can get the semblance of a glare down her nose.

I open my mouth and a croak comes out. I clear my throat. Letting out a heavy sigh and hoping it will settle my heart, it still pounds away like a prisoner in a cage. Shaking my head, I say, "I don't think it's ever too early to be honest."

Still glaring at me, and heating the hall like a bonfire, she purses her lips. "Hm. I guess so." With a hand to her heart, her body goes slack as she pretends to swoon, catching herself on the doorway.

Heat swells over my neck, and I roll my eyes at her, my face spreading into a smile.

"She's coming." Johanna slaps my shoulder and points down the hall as Rin turns the corner. My stomach churns. I adjust my shirt and flick my hair out of my face. Setting my hand back on my stomach, I'm not sure if I'm going to be sick or actually faint in her doorway.

"Stop fidgeting, Lance," Johanna says through her teeth.

"Shut up, Johanna," I mutter.

Rin comes up to us, her head cocked to the side and a sweet smile on her lips. "What's going on?" She crosses her arms and sniffs—her eyes are red and puffy, her cheeks flushed.

"I uh . . . I wanted to show you something." The tension in my shoulders is fading with Rin's presence. "Won't take long. Come with me?" I hold out my hand to her.

Rin unfolds her arms. Glancing between me and Johanna, she squints.

I hold my breath. *Dear Seena, please don't let Johanna embarrass me before I get a chance to do it myself.*

Rin slips her hand into mine. Her skin is cool and smooth. I draw her close to me, breathing in the smell of dark coffee and the cool, evening air that clings to her.

I lead her up the stairs to the roof, keeping quiet, knowing that the red in her eyes is not the death affinity but grief over so many things. At the top, I open the door for her, and the wind blows the hairs that have slipped out of her low bun across her face. She tucks them back and steps through, her shoulder brushing my chest.

Nodding to the blankets and pillows I set on the ground with a few candles, I put my hand to the small of her back. She flinches and her breath hitches, but she moves with me to sit on the blanket. Sitting cross-legged with her back straight, she cracks her knuckles one by one. I unfold my wings behind us and wrap one arm around her. I press my lips to her forehead, and she leans into them, eyelids falling closed and a breath parting her lips.

"What did you want to show me?" she asks, still relaxing into my touch.

"Watch." I point over the railing, out over the water, to Sii.

The lights of the floating city glitter against the growing dark. I check my echo for the time. Almost nine thirty. I place the echo face down to remove the harsh glare from the glow of candlelight and the emerald of the stars.

As she waits, face forward to watch Sii and the sky, I keep my eyes on her. I don't want to miss it.

Rin's lips quirk as golden light sweeps through the night and warms her face. Her smile brightens and her eyes sparkle, blond hairs whipping over her cheeks. I let my fingers gravitate to them and tuck them back.

"The watchtower," she says. "They rebuilt it."

The watchtower on the far edge of the island stretches into the sky with lightstones crawling up its face and spinning mirrors to shine the light in a roundabout motion.

"Thank you for showing me." She turns to me. Her silver eyes search me with hesitation, with deep sadness behind them, with worlds of hurt, and a soft acceptance. Tilting her head slightly, she shuffles a little closer, a little tighter under my wing. "Is there something else?"

Her body warms my side against the breeze, still she is the one who is cool. Icy breath, and cold water. Rich coffee, and cream to cool it. She waits, breathing into our shared space—chest rising and falling with mine.

"I talked to Evelyn about my request to change teams." I lower my eyes. "I know I can't replace Eliote in any way, but with your team losing members, there's a place for me."

Rin shifts one of the candles next to her, spinning it so squares of light twinkle over her skin through the votive. "I'm happy to hear that." Taking a breath through her nose, she looks back up at me. "Something else though."

"Yes," I say, dipping my head. Her hand has found its way back into mine and they lie limp between us.

The smile on her lips recedes to a neutral position as she waits for me to find my words. My heart beats heavy in my chest, stretching out to the person who always waits for me, who wants to hear me.

"I'm just learning who I am," I say, keeping my voice quiet. "I'm learning that I have a lot more space in my heart than I used to. For things that are real and meaningful."

Rin's fingers curl in mine and her neck tenses as she swallows. She nods.

"Rin, I . . . I have so much space in my heart for you. I just want you to know that I love you."

Rin takes a sharp breath, and it nudges my pulse into a frenzy. Holding tight to my hand, she turns her eyes back to the tower. Light kisses her skin and retracts, kisses her again, and retracts. Closing my eyes, I wait for her response, for as long as she needs—the best part of being heard by her is her response.

Her thumb traces down the back of my hand. Her nail scrapes my skin and I shiver.

"Lance," she says, the rasp in her voice fading into the

whisper. "Is it okay if I don't know?" The chill of her eyes draws me back. Their silver sheen hides behind a watery barrier. "Is it okay if I don't know if I . . . "

Her lips stop. I brush her cheek and her eyes fall closed as I cup her jaw.

"Yes," I say. "It's okay if you don't know. It doesn't change how I feel."

Laying her hand over mine, her eyes squeeze tighter. A tear wets our hands. She leans forward, resting her head on my shoulder and my hand slips away from her face, down her back to her waist.

Her breath runs over my neck and past the collar of my shirt. "All I know is that it's easiest to breathe with you. It's easiest to be held by you. And I want to be with you."

I draw her closer so we can't share air, we can only share space. Her body presses against me and her arms wrap around to my back. Her fingers dig into my shirt as my chest expands with air, trapping me in her iron grip.

50

R I N

I WAS BROUGHT IN AS A WITNESS TO THE TRIAL against Stephen, Geret, and Adia. My father received no sentence because he'd withdrawn his involvement from the Revival, but Stephen will serve the rest of his life in prison to atone for his crimes. Today will be the first time Liam has seen his brother in six months. Six months since he saw Stephen kill a man. Six months since he witnessed his siblings unleash violence on each other.

The guard's black shoes squeak. The constant jangle of his keys rings through my ears and they clink in the back of my mind. The air is dry and the lights are too white. My hands sweat in the sleeves of my sweater but everything else is cold. Liam plays with his visitor pass, eyes on the floor behind the guard. His breaths are short, rising to my ears like alarm bells over the jingling keys.

Stopping at a door, the guard unlocks it. Holding it open, he motions for us to go through. Liam takes a step forward, but I clamp my hand down on his shoulder.

"You don't have to do this," I say, keeping my voice low.

Liam's eyes are shifty. He brushes his hair out of his face and pulls at the neck of his sweater. "I want to," he says.

Steadying my breath, I crouch in front of him and say, "I'm really scared."

His eyes steady on me and he nods. "Me too. But he's our brother."

My heart trembles inside me.

Liam's fingers press sweaty prints into his pass. "My brother's a murderer," he says. "A kidnapper. He conspired to start a war. But I don't know that man. I don't even know who he was before that. He did wrong things. But is it wrong to know someone who has done bad things? He's still my brother, and that's all I know."

I smile at him, but he frowns back at me, sending a pin through my heart because he knows when my smile's fake. I shake my face free of it. Taking his hand, I lead him into the visiting area, and we take our seats in front of the glass. My knee bounces and I crack my fingers, counting my breaths. I close my eyes, drawing in the musty scent of stained cushions, the tinge of metal chains, the stench of body odour.

The door beyond the glass clicks. I open my eyes and Stephen sits before us. His dark hair is long, hiding his eyes as he bends over his hands, bound by essence-neutralizing cuffs.

"Hi, Stephen," Liam says. He sits at the edge of his seat, the pass in his hands has a rip in it now.

I grip the arms of my chair. Stephen lifts his head. His throat bobs as he swallows. The chains connect the cuffs on his wrists to the cuffs on his ankles, and they clunk against the table. "Hi, Liam." His voice is muffled by the ampliphone and weakened by the tiredness in his eyes.

"Uh . . . we brought you some things," Liam says. "Just some books. The guards are checking through them now. I hope you like some of them." He talks too fast, using up one breath, and he sucks in another.

Stephen blinks. My skin crawls. After a few moments of silence and Liam's ragged breaths, Stephen says, "Thank you."

"I've read some of them, so maybe we can talk about them the next time I come."

The tension in Stephen's jaw makes the hairs at the back of my neck stand on end. His dark eyes flick to meet mine. It's a shock to my system. A ringing sound sings through my ears, and my breaths are choked in my lungs.

"Yeah," Stephen says. "Maybe."

"Um—" Liam stuffs his hands in his pockets. His eyebrows turn down and he shivers, his shoes scuffing together. "I, uh . . . "

I run my hand down his back. "Why don't you wait outside."

"'Kay," he says through an exhaled breath. "Love you, Stephen."

Liam stops fidgeting and waits. The silence settles in the darkest parts of me. My blood longs for the burning heat of my death affinity. Stephen stares at Liam. His eyebrows are rounded and heavy. His lips part and his breath huffs through the ampliphone. "I . . . " he says, but silence falls.

Liam's eyes fill with tears. He slides off his chair and rubs at them as the guard lets him out.

Pulling my seat up close to the window, my stomach aches

and weight packs it down and puts pressure on my lungs. I clench my fists over the splintered wood ledge. Stephen covers his face with his hands.

"Look at me." The words shake out of me. The only indication that I actually made any sound with them is Stephen's long face appearing behind the glass. I stab my finger at it. "You're going to read every single one of those fucking books. You are going to talk to your brother about them. I will not bring Liam to see someone who does not care about him. Do you want to see him?"

Stephen's lips quiver. Blood flushes his pale face.

I slam my hand on the glass. "I said, do you want to see him?" Blue light shocks the room.

"Step away from the window, miss." The guard's voice booms behind me.

Teeth clenched, Stephen nods, and a tear tumbles down his cheek.

"If there is ever a day when Liam does not want to see you, I will not bring him. I will always protect him first. That doesn't mean I won't come. I want to be here, to look you in the eyes and remind you of what you've done. You killed someone who loved you, and you traumatized our brother. Even with all of that, the worst thing was that you left us. I don't want to leave you alone."

His hands slip from the ledge into his lap, shoulders caving forward. His hair shakes around his head.

"Do you understand?"

He flinches, rubbing his face with his shoulder.

"I said, do you understand?" I yell, as tears break free.

"Yes, I understand," he shouts back. The glass rattles and spit catches on it.

"I can't believe it took me this long to understand, but when Mom told me to be strong, she didn't mean stronger than I had to be or strong when I didn't feel like I was. She knew I was strong. It's who I am. She wanted me to be myself." I sink back into my chair as a sob shakes my body. "I've been trying so hard to find that strength. Now I have to find myself all over again because I lost part of my spirit to save my best friend who died because of you."

"I'm sorry," Stephen sobs. "I lost myself too."

The ache inside me stretches through to the other side. I never thought that I would be able to break with him. He has left me broken over and over again, but maybe this is where it stops—where we stop hurting each other and start healing. But why this place?

I press my sleeves to my face. Curling into myself, I take in hot, stuffy air through the fabric.

"Miss." The guard's voice breaks through the static in my brain. Stephen's sobs are stifled by the ampliphone, but I still catch the sniffs. "Time's up."

The shackles click. I can't peel my hands away from my face. Stephen's presence is always stifling. It's a shadow and a light, and I always know it's there. Its absence leaves a burn.

With a loud sniff, I wipe my nose on my sleeve and mop up my tears. I smooth my hair and straighten my sweater. Running shaking hands down my legs, I nod to the guard, and he opens the door for me.

Liam rushes into my arms, his face pink and eyes red. He presses his face into my shoulder, his hyperventilating breaths shaking through me.

"It's okay, I'm here. I've got you." I sway him back and forth, making myself dizzy as the light streaks through my blurry vision.

"Stephen has thorns inside him," Liam says.

Flowers in me and thorns in Stephen. We've always been linked like that—opposites but part of a whole. Somewhere in him there are flowers, and I've never been able to ignore my thorns.

Liam tightens his arms. "They're hurting him."

Stephen has always held his pain so close. I wish he wouldn't have pushed me away. I wish he didn't believe that he had to stop the bleeding before he came to me, that he had to become something or do something great to reunite our family. Our pain is the same. The least we can do is sop up the blood together when our thorns rip through us.

Liam and I walk out of the prison, just the two of us, without Stephen. When we left the funeral hall without our father, our mother held our hands, but even then, it was me and Liam who held each other up. Or at least I thought so. That was too much weight for both of us. My mother tried to be everything for her family, my father tried to be everything for the world. Neither felt like they could lean on the people around them. I know the strains of Guardian work, but the work calls to me. I can't be everything for Liam without failing. He needs a family. Brand, Oron, the Dalaans, the Kingsmans, we're all here for him.

Johanna believes what Nolaria said is true. I have no right to distrust Johanna. To defeat Alyxia, we'll need each other, and we'll need to fight her in the Lesser Worlds. I don't know what that will look like, but my spirit is already there. I'll find her, I'll free her, and I'll finally breathe again.

GLOSSARY

SLYVIC PHRASES

BEASTS

Noltwyn Alzuke – Black-winged Alzuke
Nodaha downfōst – Horned death beast
Ōneera

ENERGY

Fann – Take
Fau – Primitive
Jint – Sustian
Unama – Give
Utanic – Chaos

MARTIAL ARTS

Dawnranfet – Death brawl
Dawntimdato – Deadly Discipline (the Emberstead discipline)
Feeltens – Wind Palm (the Lifeblood discipline)
Fōsttimdato – Beastly Discipline (the Beastblood discipline)
Masstimdato – Military Discipline (the Lavarian discipline)
Noladakatz – Flowing Hits (the Nytrue discipline)
Oalande – All Leg (the Earthkin discipline)
Selhet – Calm Hand (the Fyrra discipline)
Shodahet – Shadow Hand (the Luminee discipline)
Telando – Eight Limbs (the Ironskin discipline)

Sei fassoa – Stance
Seya le kaset lon Illyson – Way of the Illyson long sword

<u>MISCELLANEOUS WORDS AND PHRASES</u>
Caatslaka adasa – a heartfelt hello (can also be used as "welcome")
Caatslaka adasa de seya le retnolada hold eekala – Welcome to the way of the frozen mind
Deshna ownoloda tens – Demon Palm
Deshna ownolada tens dentreyna ee – Demon Palm steals life.
Dawnranfet – Death Brawl
Ee comtuyo en down comtuyo – Life affinity and death affinity
Eeshna ownolada tens – Angel Palm
Eeshna ownolada tens treyda ee tor pam keh odadown – Angel Palm sacrifices life for a person who is dead.
Eenwa seya ha - The path of life has brought you here (a phrase of honour and welcome)
Heerenada – My gratitude (thank you)
Hédin – humans of the enhanced nine races
Otan sho com tuyo com slyv, otan kin tuyonne, otan caat tuyonne tiho – Our skin as strong as iron, our blood stronger, our hearts stronger still
Sufach te feknah, bachho – Suck my dick, bitch

LAVEESE PHRASES

Hosashu – Celebratory
Tama hantoro – Soul painting
Tama ni orohan – The caring soul—one who is kind, helpful, and forgiving.

FIRTŌN PHRASES

Fenlach calaikah – Iron Wretch
Nimia – Grandmother
Nipan – Grandfather

LUMINEE PHRASES

Belhalia Mavesh na'Vin – Blessings of Ancestor Vin
Ka'haletna – Priestess
Ka'onahalet – Assistant
Mavesh na'Vin visashaya to norshaya ke rishat visa – Ancestor Vin, illuminate the darkness with healing light

OTHER

Vishal – A marking specifying a Beastblood's beast form

ANCESTRY

THE NINE HÉDIN LINEAGES OF ILLYSON, THEIR ESSENCE AFFINITIES, AND FIRST KNOWN ANCESTOR

Ironskin: Body: Keena
Emberstead: Fire: Zenta
Nytrue: Water: Reel
Lifeblood: Air: Afa
Luminee: Light: Vin
Earthkin: Earth: Thesta
Lavarian: Weather: Seena
Fyrra: Vegetation: Holia
Beastblood: Animal: Fōsten

ACKNOWLEDGMENTS

Writing Soul Tether and publishing it just over a year after Moon Beetles release was an exceptional challenge. I never thought I could do it. I really couldn't have done it if it wasn't for the people who encouraged me, supported me, and who were just willing to read these words.

My beta reading team worked with me through many delays as I battled depression and anxiety. They patiently waited for the next instalment of Rin's journey and helped me make it so much better with kind words and gentle suggestions, providing me with a much clearer view of what kind of impact this story made in its early stages. I am so humbled and grateful for you all.

Thank you so much Sorche for always being willing to come on board with my early drafts. You are one of my biggest encouragers and inspirations. Amanda Sloothack, thank you for your unceasing support. You are a gentle spirit, and I am so blessed to have your feedback and friendship. S.C. Jensen, I am so thankful that you take time to answer questions for me and fit me into your busy writing schedule. Having another indie author who understands the struggle and how things work for

Canadian authors is so valuable. Dani Abernathy, thank you for working with me in the early plotting stages. You were so gracious to get on a call and sit with me while I fumbled for the words to describe my desires for this book. Thanks for helping me keep Johanna alive.

Elle Fort, you are so patient. I am so thankful for your ability to take a string of concerns break them down and then help me figure out where the problem lies. I am constantly learning from you, encouraged, and motivated to write better stories for myself and for others who need them.

Franziska, you have such a huge role in how Soul Tether is presented to the world. Thank you for working with me to create a beautiful, magical cover that provokes emotion and wonder. Your work is amazing, I hope you know how thankful I am that you are willing to keep working with me even though I can be difficult and picky.

Finally, I want to thank my family, my mom, dad, and brother, for their constant love and support. Thank you for listening when I just needed to let all my ideas fly out my head, for being patient with me, and reassuring me that I'm not wasting my life writing fantasy novels. You all motivate me to use my creativity to the best of my ability. Thank you for showing me how to apologize and forgive, how to learn and grow, and how to love and be loved.

ABOUT THE AUTHOR

B. Joyce moved around a lot growing up. The movement made it into her blood, and she has never lived in the same house for more than four years. For now, she lives in the woods, by a lake, with her parents, her brother, and their cats. B has taken her time to get to know her path in life, first with a quick jaunt through the scientific realm of psychology and biology, but  went quickly back to artistic endeavours. Alongside her writing, she takes care of her mom, who suffers from a rare autoimmune disorder. Between writing and caretaking, she can be found playing videogames, drawing, and taking long walks.